JUSTIN NEWLAND was born in Essex, Engla
of 1953.

Justin writes secret histories in which real eve
are guided and motivated by numinous and sublir
a touch of the supernatural to history and deal w
religion, evolution and the human's place in the universe.

His debut novel, *The Genes of Isis* (Matador, 2018), is a tale of love, destruction, and ephemeral power set under the skies of Ancient Egypt, and which tells the secret history of the origins of the human race.

His second is *The Old Dragon's Head* (Matador, 2018), a historical fantasy and supernatural thriller set during the Ming Dynasty and played out in the shadows the Great Wall of China. It explores the secret history of the influences that shaped the beginnings of modern times.

The Coronation is his third novel.

Justin does book signings and gives author talks in libraries and historical associations. He has appeared at many literary festivals and regularly gives interviews on local radio stations.

He lives with his partner in plain sight of the Mendip Hills in Somerset, England.

THE

CORONATION

JUSTIN NEWLAND

Matador
9 Priory Business Park,
Wistow Road, Kibworth Beauchamp,
Leicestershire. LE8 0RX
Tel: 0116 279 2299
Email: books@troubador.co.uk
Web: www.troubador.co.uk/matador
Twitter: @matadorbooks

ISBN 978 1838591 885

British Library Cataloguing in Publication Data.
A catalogue record for this book is available from the British Library.

Printed and bound in Great Britain by 4edge Limited

Matador is an imprint of Troubador Publishing Ltd

To my parents.
Life. Will. Love.

Sapere Aude! Dare to be wise!
Have the courage to use your own understanding
– that is the motto of the Enlightenment.

IMMANUEL KANT

Who can tell,
When heads will swell?
Or what'll be felt,
When skulls do melt?

OLD SAXON RHYME

CHAPTER 1

The Harvest Bride

Schloss (Castle) Ludwigshain, Ostpreussen (East Prussia).
The Feast of the Assumption, 15th August, 1761.

As the morning service finished, Marion Gräfin von Adler knelt at the first pew, waiting for people to leave. In front of the Countess, Pastor Leopold stood before the altar. With trembling hands, he was trying to place the silver paten on top of the silver chalice. For a moment, she feared he'd misplace it but eventually he guided it safely home.

Behind her, the congregation filed slowly out of the door. As Marion got up to join them, she adjusted her head scarf over her light brown, wavy hair and accidentally prodded her scalp. A stab of pain shot through it. Oh, too much sun again! She scrunched up her green eyes, hoping it would pass. Her fair complexion paled even more from the stabs of pain shooting through her head.

Her hands sought the amber crucifix around her neck. Touching it conjured feelings of the sanctity of her childhood growing up in Fischhausen, exploring the tunnels of her family's amber mine. It worked, because she felt wrapped in a cocoon of warm memories and the pain ebbed away.

The last to leave, she followed Hans and Sisi, her son and daughter, out of the chapel and into the forecourt where Ursula, her chambermaid, stood waiting for them. The forecourt was swathed in shadows cast by the walls of the castle and enlivened by a cascade of birdsong. The dawn's summer rays glistened on the surface of the lake, yielding a sense that the air was charged with the stuff of life.

Sisi was trembling with excitement and for good reason.

"This is your first time as harvest queen," Marion said, clasping her daughter's hand. "Go with Ursula and she'll help you change into the bridal robe."

While Sisi was dressing, Marion mingled with the sixty or so workers, farmers, small-holders and their children gathered around the chapel entrance. She pressed the hands of one woman, sympathised with another and greeted a third. Bloodshot eyes peered out from gaunt, sunburnt faces. Fatigue had a way of planting its claws into people, but their spirits were as high as the haystacks that dotted the fields of the estate. She was pleased for them; they deserved this reward for their hard work gathering in the harvest.

Christoph, her estate manager, pulled on his long earlobe and pointed his walking stick to where he wanted the people to assemble, even though everyone knew their places, having performed the same festival for years. He was assisted by the local Bürgermeisters, although Marion had to chuckle to herself, because everyone could see they were hindering more than helping, jostling the men and cajoling the women. A knot of screaming children raced around the forecourt, ignoring their parents' pleas to behave. Egor was the worst. Shoeless and clueless, the six-year-old had stuffed his face with berries and resembled a clown with cherry lips.

When Pastor Leopold's large frame emerged from the chapel, the people shuffled to their places ready for the coronation. Everyone assembled in a wide crescent in front of her with the huge rococo facade of Schloss Ludwigshain behind them. Even the ducks and geese alighted from the quiet waters of the lake and flew overhead to see what the fuss was about.

Wearing his usual doleful eyes and sagging cheeks, the old pastor said, "The harvest tradition dates back to our country's founding fathers. Then, we were a small people in a great land. Now, we are a great people in a great land. That's why we'll emerge victorious against our Austrian and Russian foes."

There followed a loud cheer, "For God! For Frederick! For Ostpreussen!"

Leopold continued, "Today is the Assumption of the Mother of the God of the Herbs. Let us give thanks for the riches of the land. And let us pray for those close to us who fight for our freedom on the battlefields."

The congregation bowed their heads. Even her dogs were quiet. Marion mouthed a silent prayer for her husband. *Dear Lord, fill the void in my heart and send my Gottfried back to me, safe and sound.*

Sisi returned wearing the traditional yew-green velvet dress embroidered with gold wheat sheaves and light green herbs, perfectly offsetting her smooth complexion. Her daughter was growing up and starting to look like her, with that slightly square chin, deep-set eyes, strong brow and high cheekbones. Seated on the harvest throne, Sisi was beaming from head to toe as the parlour maids decorated her with posies of flowers and strands of straw.

Ursula snapped at them, "That's enough. Don't make her into a haystack."

Sisi coyly covered her giggles with her hands. Marion glanced ruefully at the absence of a ring on Sisi's finger. At sixteen, her daughter should have been married or at least betrothed. With many eligible young men away, that was unlikely until the war ended. This one had already lasted five years. In the last century, one had lasted thirty. *May the Lord save us!*

Leopold was looking for something with those hangdog eyes. "I've come to crown the harvest queen. Ah! If only I had the wreath. Who has it now?" That was the job of Konstantin, the junior sexton, who'd missed the earlier Mass. That wasn't unusual, because the man had a predilection for vodka, which he worshipped almost as fervently as the Lord. Wreath in hand, he emerged through the crowd and lurched towards the pastor – drunk again. Momentarily blinded by the sunlight, the big man tripped on his loose leggings and fell over, spilling the harvest wreath. Everyone guffawed and pointed at him, spread-eagled on the dust.

Marion wasn't having that. Despite his weakness for drink, Konstantin maintained the church and its grounds and – occasionally – served at Mass. He even taught in the school: in Ostpreussen, everyone had to learn to read the Bible. As she helped him to his feet, she turned to the crowd and said gently but firmly, "No one is perfect. Only angels."

The taunting stopped dead.

"Thank ye, Your Ex-cellency," he stammered, brushing himself down.

Egor picked up the wreath and gazed at it, not knowing what to do with it.

"Be a good boy. Give it the pastor," Konstantin said.

For once, the little boy obeyed his father. Enhanced by an array of herbs, coloured ribbons and braided straws, the wreath was made of spikes of grain, each one taken from a harvested field.

The pastor blessed the wreath. "The harvest crown holds the prospect of wealth and the power of new life vested in the grain gathered during the summer. Today is the last day of harvest. When the sun goes down, we'll take the strands of grain from the wreath and use them as the first batch to be threshed and set aside for next year's sowing. Thus the great cycle of life continues."

He placed it on Sisi's head as reverentially as if it were the bejewelled crown of the Kingdom of Prussia. The crowd threw their hats and bonnets high in the air, prompting the children to rush to pick them up and return them to their owners.

When Sisi adjusted her blonde locks and turned to face the gathering, Marion smiled from ear to ear. The harvest coronation had released some enlightened maturity in her daughter. All of a sudden, her little girl looked all grown up, when only yesterday it seemed like she was a gawky, reckless child.

With his hunched back, Christoph shuffled in front of them. Waving his gnarled walking stick in different directions, he despatched people in groups to the fields around the estate. Soon, only a few remained. Otto was one. The night porter was fond of his tattered Prussian blue uniform, which must have been as old as he was. And just as smelly.

"Otto, you stay here," Christoph said. "Guard the Schloss, oh, and Sasha of course."

Otto adjusted his scuffed navy blue cloth hat. Sasha was heavily pregnant and he replied, "Me? You serious?"

"Yes, why?" Christoph replied.

"I'm the night porter, not the midwife."

Christoph adopted a more diplomatic tone and explained, "Don't you worry about that. The physician attends her."

"Glad to hear it!" Otto growled and spat on the ground for good measure.

"And I'll be here – I'm her husband or have you forgotten?" That was Konstantin again. He and Sasha were Lutherans who'd escaped Catholic persecution in their Russian homeland. Marion had taken in the émigrés. She was like that.

They were about to set off on the annual end-of-harvest tour of the estate borders. It had been a tradition since her husband's family had acquired Ludwigshain nearly a century before. The ceremony was akin to an eagle flying the boundaries of its territory, except that Marion marked hers with grace and by sprinkling a handful of wheat at regular intervals.

She and Sisi sat in the little pony trap next to Grenda, the coachman, who wore a feather in his peaked cap. Alongside her, Hans and Christoph rode their mares, whose tails casually flicked away marauding summer flies. Grenda tapped lightly on the reins and steered them along the eastern lake shore, where butterflies danced on the water's glassy surface. They headed along the sand ridge overlooking the quiet course of the River Pregel in the valley. Below them, the green water meadows and golden yellow fields basked in the ebullient rays of the summer sun. The panoramic view, the sultry day, the bright light and the trundle of the cart had a timeless quality.

Christoph rode up to the trap. He had something on his mind. "How is the Graf, Your Excellency?"

"From his last correspondence," she replied, "he is in good health."

"Praise the Lord. Did he say if we are winning the war?"

"He did, and yes, of course we are," she replied with a forced smile.

Two years previously the Russian Army had occupied Königsberg – the capital of Ostpreussen – barely four hours' ride away. Since then, the tide of the war had turned against King Frederick. She needed to keep up their morale, so she wasn't going to tell that to her estate workers. Nor that the King's army was smaller than both the individual armies of their Austrian and Russian enemies.

"It's only a question of time," she added with deliberate ambiguity.

"That's good," Christoph said.

He rode in silence, distractedly flicking his mare's whip. He kept glancing towards her, as if he wanted to say something else and turned away at the last moment.

"What's the matter? Is it the harvest?" she asked.

"No, Your Excellency," he replied. "We'll bring it in. And it's a good one, no doubt about it. No, it's the maintenance – mending broken fences, clearing the streams, pollarding the trees. It's a huge job and we're short-handed. I wish more men would return."

Her dogs ran alongside her until they spotted a squirrel and chased it across the meadow, before returning to the fold with tongues hanging out of their mouths.

Soon they could hear the plaintive cries of the peafowls in the nearby pheasantry.

By the time they'd reached Löwenhagen, the next village, the sun had climbed high in the sky. Sisi took off her wreath and waved her fan to cool her face. In this heat, even a small breeze was a welcome reprieve. They trundled passed the Municipal House, where a life-size statue of King Frederick I, the present king's father, seated on his stallion, dominated the village square. In every house, the doors and windows were flung open. Other than a few dogs and a stray pheasant or two, the village was deserted. Everyone was in the fields. At the other end of the village, they came across the church and the fishing lake.

Along the bumpy path to the next hamlet with its Lutheran chapel, they passed by the fields, where the workers waved cheery greetings. They veered off the main track towards Barthen from where they could see the two strands of the River Pregel – the Neuer and the Alter – sluggish in the summer heat.

Passing by the rickety barn, the old cattle shed with a gaping hole in the roof and the water meadows, they encountered a large herd of cows. Squatting in the shade of a tree like a Chinese sage and wielding a shepherd's crook was…

"Caspar!" Sisi blurted out. "I'm so pleased to see you."

The young man dithered, frozen by the sudden attention. Marion was frightened by what she saw in him, or rather what was absent in him. Caspar had been conscripted at the raw age of sixteen. That was two years ago. Now his face looked as dry and crumpled as a discarded cleaning rag. He wore leggings and a simple peasant's smock that was too big for him.

Sisi jumped down from the trap and went to greet him.

Caspar hobbled towards her, leaning on his crook, saying, "Boris, heel." And a large, boisterous, black and tan dog bounded after him.

"What are you doing here?" Marion asked Caspar. "I thought you were at the front."

"He was shot in the leg," Sisi explained. "He received an honourable discharge."

Friends since childhood, Caspar and Sisi had played, ridden, and made mischief together with the other rapscallions on the estate. Caspar's family was far from the aristocratic rank of the von Adlers, meaning anything more than cordial friendship was socially unacceptable.

"How long…?" Marion asked.

"I-I come back to Barthen two day ago." He spoke like he had a potato in each cheek.

"Why didn't you tell me?" she asked her daughter.

"Oh, Mother," Sisi replied, waving her hands in the air, "you've been so busy with the harvest, I've barely seen you."

"I still need to know who is on my estate," Marion said firmly.

Sisi ignored her, turned to Caspar and in a voice as soft as rose petals, asked, "How are you? How is your leg?"

"I been better," he mumbled, tapping his leg with his crook. "And Papa is poorly."

"I'm sorry to hear that," Sisi answered.

Caspar switched his balance from leg to leg. Uncomfortable in the full glare of the von Adler family, the boy had left his confidence on the battlefield and wasn't going to get it back soon. At least Boris showed him plenty of affection, jumping up at him and licking his hand.

Caspar plucked a strand of grass and began chewing on one end of it. He stared up at the cloudless sky, a look in his brown eyes as empty as that of his cows. Out of the blue, the dog barked at a rabbit and Caspar jumped out of his skin. In a flash, his voice and demeanour changed, as if a cloud had passed across the face of the sun.

"Line up and do your duty!" he snarled, his strident voice reminiscent of a drill sergeant. "The Russians must not pass. We're gonna defeat them."

The poor boy was transported to the battlefield and was shouting commands to imaginary comrades.

"Caspar, there's no danger here. We're friends," Sisi comforted him.

"Ah," he replied and plucked another straw.

"Caspar's got his family," Hans said, apparently trying to offer her some reassurance.

"Oh, yes, his mother's dead and that leaves him and his father," Sisi observed pointedly.

"I don't care, it's an honour to serve your country," Hans said. "I'm ready and willing. I'd wear the Prussian blue any day."

"Be careful what you wish for, little brother," Sisi replied. "Besides, you're too young. You have to be sixteen to wear the uniform."

"Children, don't squabble. Besides, there's nothing we can do," Marion said.

"But there is, Mother," Sisi insisted. Marion raised an eyebrow – her daughter rarely answered her back. "We've more rooms in the Schloss than acorns on an oak tree. Caspar and his father can move in there with the staff. We can feed him and get them both well again."

Marion asked, "Is that what Caspar wants?"

Caspar looked at the ground for what seemed like an age and then shook his head. "No, Ex-cellency. Papa's ill. He don't wanna move. Caspar stay in Barthen with Papa."

"That's settled then," Marion said. Now Caspar was back, she would have to keep a wary eye on him and Sisi, in case their relationship became inappropriate.

Sisi got back in the trap and they moved on. With each field they passed, the workers serenaded the harvest queen with cheers and hurrahs.

Grenda encouraged the mares down the slope and along the wide river bed, mostly dried out by the summer's heat. Their spirits were lifted by the river's cool, refreshing waters and Grenda's whistling of his favourite tune. They followed the flow of the river until they reached a small inlet and anchorage for rowing boats to cross the river. From there, they headed up the valley slope towards the village of Steinbeck. Hans reached the top of the ridge first, where he brought his mare to a halt. Bathed in bright sunlight, the boy shared his father's blue eyes, high forehead and fiery looks. He pointed at a cloud of dust in the distance.

A column of horses was galloping towards them along the ridge road, in pairs, flags flying in the breeze.

"They ours?" Sisi asked, more in hope than expectation.

"Nah!" Hans snarled. "See the blue and white stripes? They're Russians!"

Marion swallowed hard. He was right; Imperial Russian cavalry – on the road from Königsberg.

"What are they doing here?" Hans asked.

"I don't know." Her voice was hoarse.

The lead rider was wielding his sword above his head. Grenda seemed dumbstruck by the riders. The trap had ground to a halt in the middle of the path – their path. Their commander led the charge and had no intention of halting the column.

Marion shouted, "Grenda, they're not going to stop. Move us. Quick!"

At the last moment, he hauled on the reins and the trap slid out of the way onto the verge. The column raced by like a whirlwind, stirring up dust in their faces, the horses' hooves pounding the dry earth and thundering in their ears.

"Hussars. Imperial Hussars," Hans declared. "Fifty of them, I'd say."

She didn't know about that, but she did know they were arrogant and they'd left an acerbic taste in her mouth.

"Christoph, let me have your ride," she said, then coughed, her throat hoarse from the dust cloud.

"Yes, Your Excellency," Christoph replied.

"Hans, come with me," she said and mounted the mare astride.

"Where are they going?" Hans asked anxiously as they set off.

"That's what I want to find out," she said. Deep down, she feared she knew exactly where they were headed – and why.

CHAPTER 2

Fear of Famine

He has filled the hungry with good things,
But has sent the rich away empty.
THE GOSPEL OF LUKE 1:53

When Marion's horse galloped into the forecourt at Schloss Ludwigshain, Konstantin's heavy brow was frowning at a young Russian officer on the steps of the main entrance. Ursula was haranguing one of the adjutants while Otto was flapping his arms like a bird with a broken wing.

"Your Excellency, s-so glad you're here," Otto stammered. "'Fraid I couldn't stop them."

"You did your best," she replied. "Leave this to me."

Hans took the reins of her mare and she dismounted.

The Russian cavalry carried on ransacking the stables. Working in small teams, they rounded up as many horses as they could find and hitched them to anything with a wheel. They led wagons and carts into the storage barns and filled them with barrels of seed and corn. Yelping with joy, a knot of cavalry pushed its way past Konstantin carrying slabs of meat, loaves of bread, racks of eggs and baskets of vegetables.

Dear Jesus, they're raiding the kitchens.

She found the officer in charge, a middle-aged, thickset man, with hair sprouting from his eyebrows and his hands. "What are they doing?" she demanded. "Where are you going with all that food?"

Smart in his uniform, as well as his attitude, the officer replied, "The Russian Army needs transport and supplies. They are mine to requisition."

"Not again," she complained. "Two years ago, the Imperial Russian Army barracked an entire regiment on my estate and we've barely recovered."

"I know nothing about that," the officer said.

"You can tell your men to stop."

"I will not," the officer said flatly.

She tried a personal approach and asked, "Who do I have the honour of addressing?"

"Captain Stepan Gurieli of the Guzinskiy Hussars at your service," he said, clicking the heels of his boots.

As she watched the Georgian soldiers load sacks of potatoes, wheat, corn and carrots onto the carts, Marion had an awful, sinking feeling. This was terrible. Without food, both her people and her estate would crumble into dust. She tried again.

"This is the last day of the harvest. If you take everything, my people won't survive the winter."

"This is for the victorious Russian Army," Gurieli said with a snarl.

"Famine gnaws at the soul," she pleaded with him. "At least leave us something!"

"These are my orders," the captain snapped back. "If you don't like them, take up the matter with the Governor General of Königsberg, or better still, Elizabeth Petrovna, Empress of all Russia."

She kept her own counsel on that one.

A younger officer – a lieutenant – joined them. He was the one Konstantin had been berating. He had a slight build and rounded shoulders. Marion particularly noticed his gleaming emerald-green eyes and, protruding from beneath his cap, strands of curly red hair.

"Your report, Lieutenant Fermor," the captain said.

"The men have gathered everything they can," the lieutenant replied.

"Good, then prepare the column to leave," Gurieli said. He bestowed on Marion a smug grin and strode towards his dapple-grey horse.

The monster was going to steal her people's harvest. There was so little time to save her people. She had to stop him. She darted in front of him, arms outstretched, blocking his way.

Mouth agape, the captain stepped back, evidently as surprised as she was by her impetuous action.

"Get out of my way – or suffer the consequences."

Breathing hard, her heart pumping, she glared at him. "Please. Don't steal our harvest!"

The captain leaned forward and barked, "Don't prevent me from following my orders!"

She chose her next words carefully. "This is cruel, vindictive and contrary to the teachings of Our Lord!"

"Bah!" he scoffed. "I don't care. The Lutheran Church is full of heretics anyway."

Silence gripped her round the throat. Fear bared its claws.

"What about the little ones?" she pleaded. "Don't you have children, Captain Gurieli? Leave something for them, I beg you."

"Blame it on that odious King Frederick of yours," the captain replied, tapping his riding whip against his thigh. "Because of his hubris, my countrymen – and yours – die horribly on the battlefield. I've seen hundreds lose their limbs. A whole generation is amputated. So many fatherless families. Don't preach to me about children. Be thankful I'm leaving you your lives!"

"I will not let you leave my people to starve!" Every word was like a peal of thunder.

"Get out of my way, you whore!" the captain hissed.

Hans rushed forward, shouting, "How dare you address my mother like that!"

"Who is this suckling babe?" Gurieli laid on the scorn.

"I'm not a child, I'm a man," Hans snapped.

What happened next seemed to do so in slow motion.

The glint of a blade in the sunlight. Hans' overhead thrust parried by Gurieli. The dagger falling from her son's hand spiralling through the air. Gurieli knocking the boy to the ground and plunging his foot on his chest, then lifting his riding whip above his head.

She flung herself into the trajectory of the whip.

It ripped her cheek and stung her with a shooting pain the like of which she had never experienced. Her knees trembled. By sheer force of will, she urged herself not to move, nor wipe away the blood trickling down her cheek.

Otto and the young lieutenant rushed towards the captain.

"Stop right there!" One fiery glance endorsed her command.

Defiant like a granite mountain before a storm, she stared into the captain's eyes.

"Move out of my way, or I'll have to…" Gurieli said.

The captain raised his whip hand and she winced, expecting another strike. A moment passed. Nothing happened. She opened her eyes. The captain and the young lieutenant were grappling and grunting like a couple of great bears. Hans got up from the ground and she flung a protective arm around him. The lieutenant twisted Gurieli's hand, forcing him to drop the whip.

Gurieli pulled away, shouting, "What on earth do you think you're doing?"

"You struck a lady! Call yourself an Imperial Russian officer? You've dishonoured the regiment!" the lieutenant replied.

"This is the foreigner's true colour!" the captain stoked the flames. "White – like the flag of surrender! You'd have our great mother country bow the knee to Prussians!"

The lieutenant unsheathed his sabre and slashed it against the side of the captain's head, severing his left ear in one swift, clean blow. The ear landed in the summer dust. Blood oozed down the captain's neck, turning his crisp white uniform a sanguine shade of scarlet. The captain stroked the wound, examined the blood on his finger and licked it. His face transformed into one of unadulterated fury.

"You've done it now, little Lieutenant," Gurieli snarled. "You are *under my command*. Your precious uncle isn't here to cosset you."

The cut on her cheek seared right through her. Waves of pain beat against her legs. She felt dizzy and leaned against Hans.

The lieutenant took a step back and bowed his head. He seemed to have realised the gravity of his action. In a grovelling tone, he said, "I-I'm sorry, Captain."

"You will be. Here, bite on this!" The captain pulled out his sabre and drove at the lieutenant, who tried to parry the thrust, but Gurieli ran the lieutenant through the side. She cringed at the squishing sound of the sword piercing his flesh. Gurieli withdrew the sabre and blood spurted in an arc, colouring the sandy ground in a hot crimson stream.

The lieutenant slumped to his knees, clutching his side, blood squelching through his fingers. The captain walked round him, planted a boot on the lieutenant's back and kicked him to the ground, face down.

No one moved. Everyone was in shock.

The lieutenant lay in a pool of blood oozing into the yellow sand, as flies descended on the banquet. Nearby, the captain's horse, feeling the ambient tension, deposited a large volume of stinking excrement onto the forecourt.

"There, Gräfin." The captain's voice ascended the heights of mockery. "There's food for your people. From the horse's arse!"

Marion clung onto Hans' arm, to prevent him from going back into the fray and stop herself falling over in a heap.

The adjutant stumbled over to where the lieutenant lay stricken on the ground, his life oozing out onto the gravel.

The captain barked at him, "Leave him!"

"He'll die, Captain Gurieli," the adjutant replied.

"He struck a superior officer, an offence that bears a grave punishment. Do you want to suffer the same fate?"

The adjutant frowned and shook his head.

"Then pick that up!" Gurieli pointed to his bloody ear.

"Yes, Captain," the adjutant murmured.

"And that." Gurieli pointed to his whip. "Now let's leave this accursed place."

Gurieli led the column off – taking with them most of their horses, carts and wagons carrying the bulk of the estate's winter food supplies. They left behind fear of famine, a pile of steaming horse shit and a mortally wounded Russian officer.

Once she made sure Hans was unhurt, Marion acted quickly. "Find the doctor. This wound needs cauterising. Bring the lieutenant inside."

Otto picked him up by the armpits while Konstantin grabbed the boy's feet. They hauled him as far as the entrance of the Schloss, where a barrel of a man, with a face pitted like the full moon, stood on the steps. Few survived the smallpox, but he had. Arms folded, he blocked their way.

"Alexander," she said to him, "let them pass."

The huntsman ignored her and lanced the boil of his opinion. Pointing to the stricken lieutenant, he snarled, "Him, he's Russian scum. They raped our women and our land. They left him here to die. If it were me, I'd do the same."

"We're trying to save his life," she replied.

"What life? He's not worth it. His soldiers stole our food and our peace of mind. What we gonna feed him on? Berries? Grass? Nah. I see real life in the woods. The beasts of the forest knows the way of things. They'd leave him to die. Not thee, though, Your Excellency. You wanna feed our enemy with food we ain't even got!"

She glared at him like a Prussian Medusa, willing him to turn to stone under her gaze. "Listen to me! That man doesn't even know who I am, yet was prepared to lay down his life for me and my son. What more can you ask of a friend, so how can he be an enemy? Now move!"

While the huntsman beat a calculated retreat, she knew it was a temporary respite. The fear of famine crawled into people's lives like vermin and was as equally hard to remove.

CHAPTER 3

The Sound of Bagpipes

The Lord is my shepherd; I shall not want.
He maketh me to lie down in green pastures:
He leadeth me beside the still waters.
THE BOOK OF PSALMS 23

He felt his life blood ooze out of his side, like a leaking bucket. He blacked out and re-awoke to greet his nemesis – an ocean of pain. Light from a lantern splashed across the room like waves, catching his fading attention. Someone was groaning, crying out in agony… He heard footsteps, someone crossing the room.

"You in pain? Doctor von Ottenhagen gave you our last supplies of laudanum. Oh, you were moaning." A woman spoke in a voice as gentle as a dove.

"Moaning? Not me," he replied. He seemed to be listening to his own voice, as if another person was speaking.

"I heard you with my own ears, I did," the woman said, holding up the lantern. He caught a glimpse of her face and, beyond her, long, solemn tapestries hanging on the walls.

"Who are you?" he murmured. By the Lord, all his strength had been sucked from his marrow. He could barely lift his eyelids.

"Me? I'm Amelia. Looking after you, I am. And you're that lieutenant fellow." With a ruddy complexion, she had fire in her green eyes and wore a bonnet with a tie under her chin, showing a pair of tiny, rounded ears. She reminded him of his first love back in Scotland.

"I'm Ian, urgh… Ian Fermor." The pain pulsed through his body in waves, buffeting his soul. He felt stretched on the rack, being pulled apart.

"You Irish?"

"Scots," he mumbled.

"With all that red hair, had to be one or the other," she said.

"Where am I?"

"In Schloss Ludwigshain, the bestest castle in all of Ostpreussen," she replied. He envied her keen sense of belonging. Memories of his own upbringing in a croft flashed before him; the kindness of his mother, the gruff indolence of his father. The bedclothes rustled as she pulled them up to examine his side. It hurt like blazes.

"Now you're awake, you'd better drink this. I'll get into trouble if you don't." Amelia lifted his head and he took a sip. Oh, it tasted as fresh as the waters of Loch Lomond. Once he had swum there, at dusk, on a moonlit night, naked, with his lover, after which they had made languid, passionate love in the long grasses. He could smell the earth odour of the heather mingling with the scent of her body. Unforgettable. Joyous. Sublime.

Amelia was saying, "… I'll be back right soon."

Amelia, where are you going? Come back. Make love with me.

He blacked out.

He was next aware that the pain had lessened and his body was no longer weighed down by the slough of despond. With his eyes closed, the darkness swathed him in its silent embrace. With it came an explosion of relief. He felt free. The lightness of the moonbeams eased through the gap in the curtains and enveloped him in their silver effervescence.

He eased out of and hovered above his body. How was that even possible? He glided upwards and found himself floating near the ceiling. He was peering down at his own body, lying on the bed. That wasn't normal. He must be dying, or already dead.

He moved *through* the ceiling. Wait, it was solid. This wasn't his carnal body, it couldn't be. He was frightened. A voice spoke to him. Somehow he knew it was his soul. It said:

Follow and be not afraid.

Reassured, he rose higher. Something guided, pulled him upwards. In a vortex, he spun through the cluttered attic and emerged through the roof, standing next to a chimney stack.

Coming towards him like a distant scudding cloud, he saw a spot on the horizon. It was a bird. As it approached, he saw it was the King of the birds, a great eagle, with a wing-span as broad as the Schloss itself.

The bird had two heads. Then he knew he was dreaming.

It glided serenely through the fine mists of the ethereal. A seraphic light shone from every feather and claw of this strange and wonderful being. He felt no fear, but instead felt the force of destiny move fluently through the hidden corridors of his own life. With spectral feathers, an airy body and subtle wings, the eagle swept over him with elegant power.

Then he was riding on its back!

Above the lake they rose until he was so high he could peer down on the twin flows of the River Pregel until they merged in the ruby heart of Ostpreussen, the city of Königsberg. Schloss Ludwigshain was no more than a dot on a huge tapestry of land and sea.

Into the air, light as a cloud, they scaled the heights above Ostpreussen, with the languid Masurian Lakes to the south, the Rivers Niemen to the north and Vistula to the west. Truly, he was flying with an eagle. From his Mercator maps, he recognised the outline of the blue waters of the Baltic.

This was a fantastical journey.

"Who are you?" he asked.

The eagle replied, "I am Adler, the eagle of Northern Europe."

Incredible. Eagles could speak. And he could hear – in the resonance of his soul.

Breaching the Earth's rarefied vapours, a spectacular panorama unfolded below. The Adler showed him its territory, shaped in a huge crescent or arc, stretching from Ostpreussen in the east, through the German Kingdoms and Marks, all the way to the United Kingdom in the west. Its northern End-mark, the country given its name by a rearrangement of those letters, was Den-mark.

"Why have you appeared to *me*?"

"By your cry, you summoned me and freely elected to serve me. There are others like you. Find them. Work with them."

He asked, "What do you want?"

"I have two heads and thus I bring two gifts: the grace of Reason and the grant of Reformation. In truth, humans have great substance but little power. I have great power but little substance. Humanity is ready to advance, to develop. I bring the seeds of that progression. Already it stirs in the lands I have shown you."

"Where? How?" he asked.

"It is the movement you call the Enlightenment."

That is what it was about – the Age of Reason or the Enlightenment, the zeitgeist, the spirit of the times. And he, Ian Fermor, was going to assist its unfolding. He was privileged, exalted.

There was a large jolt. The eagle disappeared into the ether. He was back in the Schloss, locked in his carnal body. The pain returned, bursting over him like a dark, glowering wave. The first rush pressed against his chest like a haystack. He gasped for air.

There were voices in the room. "He's very weak," a woman said.

"Can you hear me?" a man asked.

He groaned. He was trying to recall what the double-headed eagle had said, but the pain in his side bored into him.

"Your Excellency," the man said. "Call the pastor. Don't delay."

Pastor. Call the pastor. The words echoed in his befuddled head.

What do they want with me? To say Mass? Or say prayers? Is my salvation…? My salvation! By the Lord, they think I'm dying. I'm dying.

He blacked out.

He awoke. Brilliant lights illuminated his mind. He kept his eyes closed to see them pulsing in circles of evanescence. Exhausted from fighting the agony, he dreamt of the eagle. If only… the eagle, the mysterious Adler with two heads, would return. He had flown with it over the royal lands of Northern Europe and seen the land of the End-mark. He remembered that much.

More voices in the room… an old man.

"Amelia, did you say his name was Fermor?"

"Yes, Pastor," Amelia replied.

"The name sounds familiar," the old man mumbled. He leant forward and said, "Ian Fermor, I am Pastor Leopold. Can you hear me?"

He groaned an exhausted, "Yes."

Ian Fermor blinked. The two women and two men around the bed were shaded by the lantern and the moonlight beaming through the gap in the curtains. The texture of the light reminded him of how, at twilight, when dusk fell on the glens at home, he would run through the heather field, across the gurgling stream, past the gnarled oak, and burst through the cottage door, to find a welcoming fire and a warm embrace from his ma and a scolding from his pa for his tardiness.

Another memory impinged on the fragile membrane of his mind. During a few moments of euphoric clarity, before the deep veils of pain were once again drawn across his life, he recalled the great times he had shared with his friend James Watt. With a long journey ahead of him, to a bourn from which no traveller returned, he wished he could share a wee dram or two with Master Watt, and rekindle those many fascinating conversations on engineering and instrumentation. That seemed as far away as the gun-metal waters of the Clyde and Glasgow's cramped housing.

Back in the room, the pastor was saying, "Herr Fermor, you are near the end of your sojourn on Earth. Stay with us a little longer while I read you the Commendation."

"He may not know what that is, Pastor Leopold," another woman said.

The pastor cleared his throat and said, "The Commendation is also known as the last rites. Do you understand?"

The last rites – that had a ring of finality about it. The words resonated inside him, like a distant echo. Squeezed between mind-numbing waves of pain, he moaned, "I do. But I can't die. I have… to serve the Adler. I must live."

"It's natural," the pastor replied. "But you have been called to meet your Maker."

"No," he murmured. He was drowning in an ocean of pain and blanked out.

When he came round, the pastor was saying, "Into your hands, dear Lord, I commend the spirit of this man. Ian Fermor, do you want to say anything? Do you seek absolution?"

There followed what seemed like a long silence. Were they talking to him? He couldn't hear, see or feel anything. After a while, he heard a man whisper, "He's gone."

That seemed to jerk him out of the deep somnambulant state into which he'd sunk and he murmured, "Absolution?"

"Wait, he's still with us," a woman said.

The word 'absolution' echoed in his mind. Words rose from the depths of his being, like a buoy, long trapped on the seabed, which, when released, shot up to and bobbed on the surface. With unexpected clarity, he said, "Ach, I miss my home. I came to the Baltic to seek my fortune. I'm leaving it in penury and infamy. I fought in a war that wasn't mine. I killed and I murdered men I'd never met."

He wanted to cry, but no tears came.

"May the Lord forgive you your sins and welcome you into his arms," the pastor said.

The light, the pain, the noise emptied. Everything was hollow, eviscerated. In the room, the people were reciting a prayer:

"*Yea, though I walk through the valley of the shadow of death, I fear no evil…*"

As the mists appeared before his eyes and everything went black, he was sure he could hear the haunting sound of the bagpipes beckoning him to come home.

CHAPTER 4

The Horn of Plenty

Therefore I say unto you,
What things whatsoever ye desire, when ye pray,
Believe that ye receive them and ye shall have them.
THE GOSPEL OF MARK 11:24

As Marion heaved herself up from the chair, the sun had risen and sent beams of light across the room. The aromatic smell of lavender was pungent – Amelia had placed several bouquets from the herb garden by Fermor's bedside and around the room. It served to overcome the stench of death that enshrouded him. His end was thought so inevitable that even the physician had left him to attend to another sick person.

After Pastor Leopold limped off to prepare for service, Marion said to Amelia, "I must go back to my chambers. Can you stay with him?"

"That I can, Your Excellency. He's so cold, he is." Amelia rubbed the man's hand in hers. "Poor lad, he's not long for this world."

"I'll return as soon as I can." She hated leaving him like this. It was likely to be his last day. The young man had defended her honour and her son's life in the face of that Georgian brute Gurieli. But Fermor couldn't defend her people. She had to do that.

Many depended on her: her close family, Sisi and Hans, and her brother Dieter von Bernstein. There was Christoph. When her estate manager stared at her with his trusting, bovine eyes, her heart melted. Then there was Konstantin and his pregnant wife, Sasha, and their brood of four children. They relied on her to provide a roof over their heads and food in their stomachs. As did the rest of the estate: the candlestick makers, the carpenters, skinners, blacksmiths, millers, ploughmen, bakers and farm workers. Famine had stalked the land before.

She was a simple woman in a privileged position, née von Bernstein, now von Adler. At times of crisis like this, she wished her husband was by her side even more than usual, but Gottfried was fighting for the King and for Ostpreussen. Alone, she had to stay strong for her people. There was a way. She had to believe she would find it.

One question burned in her mind – how was she going to guide her people to next spring? It was a gargantuan task, akin to Moses parting the Red Sea for the Israelites. During Ostpreussen winters, the ground was frozen for months, the snowfalls were deep and bitter east winds howled in from Russia. With barely any food, the harvest stolen, they would slowly starve to death. And the children? Oh, the children. She could imagine their gaunt little faces, and their eyes empty of sparkle, pleading for food which didn't exist. Famine was a cruel, insatiable demon that would just as soon devour a grown man as a six-month-old child. They must have gravely offended God.

Her wound was throbbing, sending pulses of pain from her cheek. The top of her scalp was still tender. She was weary from the tumult of the day and the awful events of the night. At least Hans had recovered from his ordeal with Gurieli, and was riding and making mischief with Konstantin's sons and the other boys on the estate.

She closed the door to her chambers and lay on her bed – only for a moment, she promised herself. Swathed in a cocoon of gentle shadows, she fell asleep.

In her dream, she heard seraphic voices. The singing caressed and soothed her troubled mind. The chorus was a sublime ensemble, a celebration of the light. In the hidden depths of her mind, she heard a woman's voice. "Your Excellency, wake up."

"Uh," she murmured.

"You're dreaming."

"Ursula?" she asked. She sat up and rubbed her eyes, disappointed that the dream had ended so abruptly.

"Yes, Your Excellency, it's me. They're outside."

"Who? The Russians?" *Oh my God, they've come back. What do they want this time?* She panicked.

"No, it's not them." Ursula pulled the curtains. Sunlight streamed through the window. Sounds of sweet voices lifted her spirits and blew away the clouds of doubt and fear. "It's a serenade. It's waiting for you."

The singing was as glorious as she'd heard in her dream. "A serenade?" she asked. "What are you talking about?"

"See for yourself," Ursula said.

The southern facade of the Schloss faced the lake. The northern one faced the broad swathes of the Pregel valley. That was where the singing was coming from. It was like the voices of mermaids rising from the river to greet the dawn. As she approached the main door, the singing was closer, surrounding her, lifting her soul, the notes dancing on the motes of early morning sunlight.

She hesitated in the vestibule. Fearing to tread another step, she remembered their terrible plight. Remembered? How could she forget it? It would be in the sullen look of despair, like the masque that death would see in the mirror. She had let them down, abandoned them. The land had given them the food and she'd let the Russians steal it.

She heard words, a chorus…

"*Give us…*"

It was singing.

She knew that, deep down, they were terrified of the dreadful scars of famine; the old folk who aged ten years in one; the children who shrivelled up and wrinkled with age; the new-borns who died in their mother's arms. It was tragic.

"*Give us this…*"

The singing was subtle, like the feeling of being part of a greater chorus. Each voice different, but together, the same.

"*Give us this day…*"

They want the day. They sang for the day, each one a new gift.

"*Give us this day our…*"

This singing was closer, louder and immanent.

"*Give us this day our daily…*"

It could only be…

"*Give us this day our daily bread.*"

She walked through the vestibule. Kadow the butler stood smart and erect by the open door, a broad smile on his face. The choir were three abreast in a crescent, with their backs to the castle, facing the broad green meadows overlooking the valley. Their singing had a subtle quality that arose from their inner beings. It was as if… yes, of course, they sang not to her but to the land and to the land's keeper, their Lord. The host listened to their poignant cry, a cry that came from the soul of every person and that spoke to the soul of the land, ushering a presence that cupped each person in a gentle hand and led them into quiet green pastures.

"*Give us this day our daily bread,*" they sang. No one acknowledged her presence, though they parted to let her stand in their midst. She was part of the singing and the singing was part of her. She was the light and the light was in her.

The singing reached a brilliant crescendo, as the sun rose above the forest trees and bathed them and the castle in its glorious rays. Even the Lord of Hosts seemed to bend an interested ear to the divine chorus, curious as to what disturbed its peace that balmy August Sunday morn.

A light, warm breeze rustled the trees. A fox scurried through the undergrowth, chased by Marion's dogs, closely pursued by Caspar's Boris. His owner must be close by. When the singing stopped, everything else did too. She clasped her hands together in prayer, seeking the silver chalice of inspiration. There had to be a way to preserve the moment, the profound sense of hope: something that prevented them falling back into the slough of despond. Yes! She had it! She called Hans and whispered in his ear.

"You know where to find it," she said. The boy stared back at her with those blue eyes bright with the bloom of youth. "And while you're there, be a good boy and inquire of Amelia about the health of our patient."

Hans raced off like a rabbit. While she waited for his return, she ran her eyes along the faces in the choir. Most of them wore a rugged air of grit and determination. Sisi was talking animatedly to someone. Oh, Caspar. Who else?

Hans came scampering back carrying a small cloth bag.

"What did Amelia say?"

"That Fermor's a fighter."

"Glad to hear it. Thank you, Hans. Can I have…?"

"Yes, here it is, Mother," the boy said, pulling out a curved horn from the bag.

"The Horn of Plenty," Christoph cried. "A wonderful idea!"

The crescent horn was reputed to originate from a fertile bull back in the thirteenth century, when the Teutonic Knights invaded and converted the land of Ostpreussen to Christianity. The von Adler family had acquired the horn and, over the years, it had become a cherished symbol of hope whose subtle notes, spurred by prayer and piety, spread fecundity across the land.

It had worked before. It had to work now.

Christoph took the horn. Over the years, her estate manager elicited a wonderful sound from the magical instrument.

For once, Konstantin was a picture of sobriety. He butted in with his usual brand of gruff Russian delicacy. "Give it to young Caspar over there. Let him blow the horn."

"Me? No, I can't do that." Caspar hung his head.

"Yes you can, that's a wonderful idea," Sisi agreed with a winsome smile.

"Caspar returned from the front line. In itself, that's a miracle, that's religious…" it always was religious with Konstantin, "… because that gunshot to his leg saved him from the fires of hell. Instead, he's come home to tell the tale. If anyone can bring the spirit of salvation and renewal to our land, he can!"

The sentiment was met with unanimous approval, while Sisi stared at her Caspar with those sleepy eyes of hers. Eventually, with multiple encouragements, but mainly because of Sisi, he accepted the honour.

Everyone listened. With the horn pressed to his lips, he puffed out his cheeks and blew. The note of plenty spiralled out of the instrument and swirled above them like a strange, invisible presence. Gradually, it filled everyone with a beneficent hope that, in the end, they would have enough food to endure the winter. Would the land give of herself for another year? No, she couldn't, because she had nothing left to give until next year, apart from broken wheat chaffs and piles of discarded potato skins.

As the angelic sound dispersed, it induced in them a solemn belief that the food would miraculously appear from somewhere, somehow. The deed was done. The horn had been blown. They had made their petition. All they had to do was wait.

It had to work. The alternative – death by famine – was unimaginable. Death by creeping malnutrition – the older folk had stared into the bleak, empty eyes of famine, an experience never forgotten.

Quietness fell on them, as natural as the pall of dusk. They tarried. They knew why. They tarried for words, her words. She had to say something. Words were cold comfort to the mother of a child with a swollen belly, protruding ribs and sunken, sallow eyes. She stepped out in front of them, facing the Schloss, facing her future.

The birds in the trees stopped singing. The ducks and geese stopped cawing. The ravens stopped cackling. They too wanted to hear what she had to say. She had to find words, not just any words, but *the* words.

She peered into their souls. At first she saw the hope rekindled that, yes, they could survive. Behind it lurked a terrible menace, a consuming fear of a long, enduring death. A struggle with a lynx or a bear was a noble death. Slaughter at the hands of the Russian foe was an honourable one. But death by famine was to be pitied, feared, abhorred.

The ruthless killer was the third of the Four Horsemen. Riding the Black Horse, it left hunger in its wake.

The testament came to her. "My name is Marion Gräfin von Adler. Although titled, I am one of you. Never doubt that. I love, I cry and I bleed and I hunger, just like you. There's no difference between us. I weep, like you. I have days of sorrow, like you. Never forget we are the same, we are one."

Ursula was as bullish as ever, what with her heavyset brow, stern face and brown eyes. Today, she was the voice of the estate. "We see you, Your Excellency," Ursula replied. "Every day, you eat the same as us. We respect that and we respect you."

"Thank you." As she spoke, she got the feeling she was addressing her charges, from the youngest to the oldest, the blacksmith to the innkeeper, the cook to the miller. There was an accord, a light that shone and glowed between them, protecting them from harm. She went on, "Schloss Ludwigshain is my home, as much as it is yours. I am staying here. You are my people; you are like members of my family. My life is here. My love is here, with you and because of you."

Those words dispelled the angst. Just as the bright rays of the sun dispersed the black clouds of doom, so their claustrophobic fear lifted from them, easing their burden. It was replaced by the deep sense of belonging to the Schloss, its fields, meadows and woods. Ensconced within that settlement, their eyes changed. Something else looked out – a trust in the beneficence of the Lord.

Ursula's voice was pleading. "What are we going to do, Your Excellency?"

"Pray for guidance from the Lord."

"Beggin' your pardon, Your Excellency," Ursula said, clutching her hands together in prayer. "How will that feed our little ones through the winter?"

"Prayer and piety, Ursula – have faith and the Lord will provide for us," she replied. "Until then, we must be frugal. Let's gather the stubs and stems and the loose sheaths in the fields. There we'll find a second harvest. Waste nothing!"

The choir gave a hearty, uplifting cheer, gathered their baskets and set off into the fields.

CHAPTER 5

Adler, Eagle

Bless the Lord, O my soul, and forget not all his benefits:
Who forgiveth all thine iniquities;
Who healeth all thy diseases.
THE BOOK OF PSALMS 103

Like a shaft of brilliance, sunlight blazed through the slit in the curtains. Ian Fermor struggled to move a muscle. Everything ached, bones, limbs, muscles, but he was determined not to succumb to the pain.

His side hurt. No, it was more than that, it was excruciating. He had this impulsion to stand, to walk. He put his weight down on his leg. His side hurt so badly the pain struck him like a bolt of lightning.

The door creaked. A woman padded across the wooden floorboards.

"Dear Lord," she said. "Where do you think you're going, jumping round the room?"

"I have to walk…" he said. Nearly falling over, he grabbed the side of the bed.

"Hold it there, young'un. This ain't no time for chasin' foxes. Get back in that bed, this minute!" The woman's voice sounded vaguely familiar.

"Who are you? Where am I? Where's my unit?"

"Good questions," the woman replied. "The Lord might know where your unit is, I surely don't. And me, I'm Amelia. We were introduced and you've forgotten my name already! Tut-tut."

"I'm sorry. What happened to me?" he asked.

"Run through by your capt'n, you were."

"I was? Oh, yes, it's coming back to me. He struck a lady. It was shameful," he said, gripping his fists.

Amelia put a beaker of water to his lips. Mmm, that tasted good. So thirsty, he could drink a lake.

He looked down at his nightclothes and asked, "Where's my uniform?"

"In the soak. There was more blood on it than from an ox. Anyways, you'll not be needing it for a while. The physician, he said for you to rest. And rest you will, you hear?" Amelia said, heading for the window.

"How long have I been here?"

"Four days. Today be Wednesday, all day," she said, opening the curtains. The light bathed the room with motes of brilliance.

"And remind me where we are?"

"Schloss Ludwigshain, the von Adler family estate."

"Adler… Adler. That sounds familiar," he said, scratching his head.

"Well, it should do. They're as big a family in Ostpreussen as you can get," Amelia replied, chirpy as the rays of sunlight on her face.

"I see," he murmured.

"Hope you do," Amelia muttered between gritted teeth. "Heaven only knows how you still breathe the Lord's air. You rest while I fetch Her Excellency."

He closed his eyes and kept seeing a gigantic two-headed eagle ease across his field of vision. It couldn't be real, could it? He opened his eyes and it was gone. He was saddened, because at least it was a distraction from the scorching flames of pain that wracked his body.

Another woman glided into the room, her long skirt rustling on the floor.

"Who are you?" he mumbled.

"Marion Gräfin von Adler," she replied.

"Adler, eagle. Eagle, Adler."

"Yes, that's what Adler means," she replied.

She had a nasty cut across her cheek. "My captain," he mumbled. "He struck you."

"Yes, he did," she replied. "And you paid a heavy price for your gallantry."

"It… it was worth it," he said.

"It was…?"

"Why? Don't you think a man should defend a woman's honour?"

"Yes, of course, but it very nearly cost you your life."

"I should be dead?"

"Such things are the Lord's grace, especially after…" she said and paused.

"After what…" he prompted.

"You… you don't remember?"

"No, I don't," he said.

"You lay in death's arms so we called the pastor. He absolved you and made the Commendation – the last rites. The miracle is that you are still here to converse with me. Young man, you have been given the precious gift of life not once but twice, you are doubly exalted. Grab it with both hands and never let go."

"I will, thank you," he said.

"I have to fetch the physician when he comes by with Amelia. I won't be long. Do you think you can stay in bed until then?"

He murmured a deliberately incoherent reply and she left the room.

By the Lord, he had come back from the land of the dead. He had to give thanks. He heaved his leg over the side of the bed. Ignoring the spasms of pain, he slid his tired, battered torso over the bed and lowered himself to the floor. An explosion of pain shot through him. Gradually, it subsided and the mist cleared from in front of his eyes. For a sublime moment, he could think clearly.

Kneeling by the bedside, he clasped his hands in prayer and said, "I've seen surgeons cut the limbs from soldiers who've been awake, heard their screams howl down the night and seen grown men succumb to the terror of their own shadows. Never have I seen them return from the shadow lands of death. This is a turning point. My Lord has kept me alive for a reason. I pledge to find out what that is and prosecute it to the best of my ability. I must abandon my past life. Because I had the Adler vision here, in this place, this is where I must seek out the threads of that new life."

He heard footsteps and a woman's voice in the corridor. He couldn't move, so he stayed put, caught in a moment of grace and power. Pains cramped his body. The mists returned before his eyes.

"Catch him," a woman said.

He awoke in bed. Amelia was fussing over him like a mother hen. She smelled of fresh bread. She must have been baking.

It was left to the Gräfin to reprimand him. "You're not to get out of bed!"

"I agree!" the physician said, entering the room. He was old, tall and quite distinguished-looking in his old, black, tatty morning suit. His feet shuffled across the floorboards like he was walking on ice.

"Ah! There you are, von Ottenhagen. Where have you been?" the Gräfin asked.

"I've both good and bad news," the doctor said. His voice was weary.

"Tell me the bad first," she said. Then the good always sounded that much sweeter.

"I've been in Barthen. I'm afraid Caspar's father has gone to meet his Maker," he admitted.

"Such a loss, Franz was a fine man," she said. *I know what my daughter will be asking of me now.* She paused before asking, "And the good news?"

"Sasha's had a lovely baby boy," von Ottenhagen said. "I'm relieved that both mother and child are well. Tell me – how is our miracle patient?"

"I'm well, Doctor," he murmured. His eyes drooped and he fell asleep.

CHAPTER 6

St. Bartholomew's Day

Though in the midst of life we be,
The snares of death surround us.
FROM A GREGORIAN CHANT

Marion sat in the front pew of the little chapel, listening to the embers of Pastor Leopold's sermon.

"This is St. Bartholomew's Day," he intoned. "On this very day, nearly two hundred years ago, a French Catholic mob massacred innocent Protestants on the streets and in their houses."

The pastor seemed to carry the fury and indignation of the entire Protestant world, because he thumped the pulpit and shouted, "Never forget what those martyrs suffered in our cause!"

It sent shivers snaking up and down her spine.

The service over, Marion strolled into the forecourt in the shadow of the tall oaks, swaying in the warm breeze. The staff waited for her at the main entrance. She had asked the cook, Margaretha, to provide Konstantin and Sasha with a simple christening feast. The big man took a swig of vodka and called Egor to him. He knelt down and clasped his son in the gentlest bear hug.

"Go catch us some fish!" he urged him.

"Yeah!" Egor cried. The little boy's face lit up with mischief aplenty. He raced across the forecourt to the lake and, with unabashed glee, plunged his hands into the still waters. As Konstantin stood up, he wobbled on his feet and nearly fell, just managing to steady himself on a tree trunk. Undeterred, he let out a huge guffaw, his laugh filling the bright morning.

As Egor played fisherman, Konstantin turned to the staff. With a huge grin on his face, the Russian counted one to five on his fingers and announced, "Five! I am the proud father of five children."

"And so you should be," Marion said, watching a butterfly drift dreamily by.

Sasha emerged through the great entrance doors, her jet black locks in stark contrast to her pale complexion. She was nursing a newly-baptised Joachim.

Konstantin roused them all with the opening phrases of the traditional christening song until they all joined in, Hans and Sisi too. The castle walls resonated with its delightful melody, lifting the spirits and celebrating that most precious of gifts, a newborn. Marion reflected its joyous tunes sometimes later turned to grief, because many a christened child never survived the week of its birth.

Konstantin led his guests towards two long tables, on which was laid out the christening feast, a sadly inappropriate misnomer if ever there was one. What with the estate's meagre food supplies, the best the kitchen could muster were wind-blown, worm-infested fruit, some nuts, lettuce leaves, and a few plates of potato skins. The rest of the table was filled, conspicuously, not with food but with green-leafed boughs and a few decorative sheaths of wheat.

Even as he turned to look at it, he glanced away, ashamed, and hunched his shoulders like he was carrying the weight of the world. She felt a pang of sorrow for him, but she had to put the estate first. The winter, as everyone knew, could be brutal. She couldn't release any morsel that would jeopardise their survival. Spring was a long way away.

Despite her misgivings, it was sad to see the river of the man's pride dwindle into a trickle. No one took a piece of the food, so Marion relented and asked Christoph to bring up two flagons of mead from the cellar.

When he came back, she said quietly to him, "At least they have something."

"Yes, Your Excellency, sweet and always a bulwark against famine," Christoph said quietly.

Konstantin jinked his beaker against hers and shouted a toast, "To Joachim! A long life!" His jubilant voice echoed around the great forecourt.

"To Joachim!" everyone repeated.

A single 'Hurrah!' extended into a longer cheer, which slowly got louder until it reached a thumping crescendo. Further down the lake, flocks of birds and ducks flew off in disgust, their peace interrupted by a distant intruder. The interloper's identity soon became clear – another cavalry troupe, this one led by a highly-decorated man astride a white stallion, kicking up a pall of dust.

Christoph yelled that fearsome word…

"Russians!"

Damn! This time it really was. They were back for more. Well, they wouldn't find a crumb. She'd spirited it all away.

The solitary word echoed around the castle walls, unleashing an unruly presence amidst the gathering, dispelling what little goodwill and bonhomie remained. Everyone scattered. People ran inside the many outbuildings, some back to their cottages, while many of the staff shot back inside the castle.

Chasing a red squirrel, little Egor dashed out in front of the horsemen.

"Egor," his father yelled. "Wait!"

Everything seemed to grind to a halt – the birds ceased their chatter, even the dragonflies stopped flitting across the placid lake. Egor froze – right in the path of the onrushing column. The lead rider pulled hard on his reins. His horse reared up in the air, neighing wildly, its hooves skidding and twisting in the dry dust.

Egor gaped. Holding up his hands, he toppled backwards, the horse's hooves rising high above the little boy, who slipped and fell beneath the wild horse.

As the rider hauled on the reins to alter the angle of the horse's descent, a man rushed out from behind an oak tree and snatched Egor in his arms and out of harm's way.

She, Hans and Sisi ran over to the man, Konstantin stumbling after them. The man lay flat on the ground protecting the boy and with his back to them. The lead rider leapt from his horse. They reached the stricken boy at the same time.

The man cradling Egor turned to face them. More in surprise than anything else, Marion blurted out, "Caspar! You, you saved Egor."

Caspar got up and bowed his head, as timid as a wren.

Konstantin grabbed his son. "Egor. You foolish boy. Don't ever run off like that again!"

"Father, I was chasing a squirrel! The red one!" Egor frowned hard. For him, as for her, red squirrels meant bad memories. When Sasha arrived, the little boy's fortitude broke into a wail of tears as his mother pressed him to her breast. Konstantin hugged them both and wept tears of joy.

Sisi was full of praise. "Caspar, you were so brave."

Poor Caspar blushed from ear to ear, which seemed to embolden Sisi, whose every word dripped with admiration. "You risked your life for Egor."

Sisi touched him affectionately on the hand and he twirled away, embarrassed by the close attention.

Behind them, the cavalry unit had lined up alongside their horses. Their sabres were drawn and pointing to the ground. Some of the men handled muskets.

"What's this, another massacre?" Leopold blurted out, shaking a provocative fist at the lead rider.

"Pastor, that's quite enough," Marion said. Her heart was thumping as much as her mind was racing. What were the cavalry doing here again? Had she really hidden the remaining food as best she could? Doubts gnawed at her soul.

Russians were Catholics, albeit of the Orthodox variety. Her people were Lutheran, of the Protestant variety. The Russian cavalry were armed with sabres and a killer instinct. Her people were armed with nothing more than prayer and piety. On the anniversary of St. Bartholomew's Day, was history about to repeat itself?

She swallowed hard when she saw streaks of crimson on the Russians' sabres. The men were Cossacks, universally feared as the most callous of men.

Konstantin waved his fist at the cavalry leader. "Herr, you were reckless."

"Do you know whom you are addressing?" the man replied.

"I don't give a damn, you nearly killed my boy!"

Comments like that were hardly going to calm the growing storm.

"He ran out in front of my horse," the man complained. "You should control your children!"

Marion noticed the man's round shoulders, square chin and soft, seductive brown eyes, enough to make a woman weep. When her eyes alighted on his regalia – golden epaulettes and medals dripping from his chest – she asked, "Are you… a senior officer?" The question seemed to dispel some of the growing tension.

The general's equerry replied, "Allow me to introduce the Governor General of Königsberg himself, Wilhelm von Fermor."

"Fermor? So, you're General von Fermor," she replied. "An honour to meet you." The general was renowned for reversing his predecessor's harsh treatment of Ostpreussen citizens.

"I am he," the general replied. "And you must be Marion Gräfin von Adler."

"Yes and I'm pleased to meet you," she replied. "I'm sure you're as relieved as I that no harm came to the little boy."

"Quite so, Gräfin," the general said, a remark that poured balm on troubled waters.

Involuntarily, she touched her cheek, a gesture remarked upon by the general. "That wound, Your Excellency, is the reason I am here in person." Turning to his equerry, he pointed to the end of the cavalry column where a hooded man sat forlorn in the back of an open cart. "Bring him here," the general said.

The man was dragged across the dusty forecourt and hauled before the general on his knees.

"Who's this?" she asked.

The equerry pulled off the man's hood.

"Captain… Gurieli!" she stammered.

Gurieli had black bruises on his face, while cherry-red cuts jostled with a stream of dried, coagulated blood below his missing ear.

"Clearly you recognise this… man, though I hesitate to apply the honorific term to this… renegade." The general's voice was edged with disdain.

"He's the one who struck me and attacked my son."

"That's what I wanted to confirm. Equerry, you have your orders. In the meantime, Gräfin, is my nephew still here?"

"Your nephew? Oh, yes, he's recovering, quite miraculously I might add."

"I would speak with him."

"Before you see your nephew, promise me this…"

"What!" The general spat the word out like it was poisonous. "Don't hold me to ransom on this!"

"I fear neither your threats nor your muskets. I only want food for my people."

"A commendable sentiment," the general said with a sneer. "But I command an occupying force of thousands of men and horse and they all need feeding to conquer the despot that is your king."

"My king is no despot," she countered. "He's an enlightened sovereign, a rarity in these dark, tenebrous times. And I condemn your theft of my food as cruel and contrary to Christian teachings."

"I've listened to your sermon," the general conceded. "Now take me to him."

"Very well, if you insist," she hissed.

Ursula lifted her chin and led the way.

From his bed, Ian Fermor pulled off a passable salute to his uncle. Compared to the wraith of nine days before, he resembled a half-decent human being.

"Lieutenant Fermor," the general said, standing at the end of his bed. "I know what you did to rescue the Gräfin's honour and I know how the culprit Gurieli responded. He's about to meet a fitting end for a man who disgraced the uniform."

"A fitting end?" Marion asked.

The morning calm was severed by the blast of musket shot from the forecourt. She rushed to the window, where a firing squad had completed its ugly business. Gurieli, ex-Captain Gurieli, lay on the ground in a crumpled heap, not far from the very spot where he had assaulted her.

"You murdered him!" she blurted out.

"No, not murder," the general said. "Under military law, it's an execution. Gurieli has paid for his transgression – against you and your son. He shamed the honour of the 5th Hussars."

This was terrible – more violence in the castle grounds. A peaceful soul, she prayed for the bloodshed to end. Though it was a heavy cost to pay – a man's life was never something to be taken lightly – she had stood up for what she believed in, namely her people and the benevolence of the land.

The general spoke to his nephew, "You are to return to your unit. I've brought a doctor to help you. You'll be transferred to Löbenicht Hospital in Königsberg. Now, get out of that bed."

"No, I can't, General," Ian Fermor insisted. "There's no easy way to say this. I want an honourable discharge."

"What?" the general guffawed. He was genuinely surprised. So was Marion. She had not seen this coming. "What greater honour is there than to fight for Empress Elizabeth? You're befuddled with this wound. I urge you to reconsider. Come back home to the barracks with me."

"I am home. This is my home now," the lieutenant said. "This is no idle decision."

"I disagree vehemently." The general leaned forward, his hands grasping the frame at the end of the bed. "You're a man who knows how to make quadrants, rulers, telescopes and barometers. If you leave for the Church, you'll abandon all that training. You told me that, in London, you befriended a fledgling genius named James Watt. I so wanted you to emulate him. Four years ago, Captain Lester brought you to me in St. Petersburg and I made you a sapper in the Imperial Russian Army. I won't see that accumulated knowledge go to waste. And my younger brother in Glasgow will want to know what happened to his son. What would you have me say to him?"

"Tell him the truth," Ian Fermor said, his voice quiet but firm. "This is my family. These people, the Gräfin, Amelia and the physician, have cared for me and healed me. I nearly died. Pastor Leopold read me the

Commendation. It's a miracle that I still breathe God's air. I have to stay. God saved me and I owe him my life."

"You'll come to regret this change of heart," the general replied. "I've seen men follow this path before. This kind of false epiphany soon gets evaporated by the fires of doubt and regret. I'll not leave you here alone with these – strangers."

"I'm not alone and I'm not with strangers. I'm with God. He has a divine purpose for me, one I must pursue with all my vigour."

"Despite your protests," the general said with an air of resignation, "I can't grant you an honourable discharge."

"Why not?"

"Because your first duty is to the oath you took to the army and your unit," the general said. "Since you refuse to return to it, I have no alternative but to give you a dishonourable discharge. This is the last conversation I will ever have with you and you will never see me again. Now, hand over your sword and uniform and may your god go with you on your chosen path."

With that, General Wilhelm von Fermor turned and marched through the door.

For Fermor, another door opened in his life.

CHAPTER 7

The Nativity of Our Lady

Bless the Lord, O my soul, and forget not all his benefits:
Who satisfieth thy mouth with good things;
So that thy youth is renewed like an eagle's.
THE BOOK OF PSALMS 103

Fifteen days after the visit from General von Fermor, Marion was walking along the tree-lined boulevard between Schloss Ludwigshain and the village of Löwenhagen. She was going to the church there to celebrate the Nativity of Our Lady, a feast day she particularly enjoyed, not least because she shared the same name as the Mother of Our Lord. She was arm in arm with Sisi, who was as ebullient as the rays of the sun on this warm mid-September day. Ursula was with them. Hans opened the creaky old wooden gate to let them pass.

"Thank you," Marion said. As she stepped into the churchyard, a pain crashed through her head. Feeling dizzy, she slumped against the wall of the porch.

"Mama, what's the matter?" Sisi asked.

"Oh, it's another attack of the vapours." Ursula's voice was even more anxious than usual.

"You never told me," Sisi grumbled.

"It's nothing of the kind, it's just the glare of the sun and the stifling heat," Marion protested, waving them away. Hans helped to steady her.

Christoph arrived with his walking stick, his hunchback more prominent than ever. "Your Excellency, go home to rest," he suggested.

Sisi had a better one. "Hans, run and find von Ottenhagen."

"No! That won't be necessary. The doctor is a very busy man; I don't want to waste his time on unimportant matters." She shook her head and thankfully the waves of pain receded. "Give me a moment to recuperate. You worry needlessly about me, all of you."

"For good reason, Mama." Sisi was adamant. "You never stop working. You're awake before the birds are tweeting and don't sleep until the owls are hooting. It's too much. You're overwrought."

"I've recovered now," she said, taking a tentative step. "Please calm down. We're here to celebrate the birth of Our Lady. Let's do that as a family."

Brushing away their demands to return home, she stumbled into the church. It was packed, everyone in their allotted places according to the seven Heerschilde. These were the Shields of Knighthood, the divinely-given ordering of society. In practice, it meant that she, as a free lord or lady, sat at the front, her vassals sat behind her, their vassals behind them, and so on, until at the back were people like Manfred, the local skinner. As an unclean member of society, he was Unehrliche Leute or a dishonourable person.

Konstantin wafted the incense censer up and down the aisle, lingering for a long while around the pews at the back, presumably to disguise the stagnant odours emanating from them and mask his own breath.

An air of anticipation swelled in the church. Three rings on the bell and Pastor Leopold emerged from the sacristy dressed in vestments of pale blue, as befitted a service in honour of Our Lady.

Marion's heart was beating like a hussar's drum, because she was about to play a part in the ceremony that had intrigued and excited her for many years. Its centrepiece was a statue in its own chapel in the south transept, concealed behind a pale blue curtain edged in silver.

As he emerged from the vestibule, the pastor was studying a letter. He stood by the eagle lectern and looked at them with withering disdain. With forehead deeply furrowed, he growled, "This morning, I received this letter from the bishop. It seems that in their foolish desperation, people are summoning demons to help them conjure food from the air itself. I'm ashamed to say that these acts were not committed by Unehrliche Leute, but by members of the Heerschilde proper, respectable people who should know better than to dabble with evil spirits. These demons appear with angels' wings, but behind their benign facade, they are treacherous. I warn you all. Beware of false prophets!"

Everyone bowed their heads. This was serious: her own people selling their souls to the Devil.

The pastor tucked the letter into his vestments and tried to break into what passed for a smile, saying, "Now, to the office of the day: it is my honour to invite the Gräfin von Adler to reveal to us, for today only, the mysterious statue of Our Lady von Adler."

Marion bowed to the altar and edged towards the curtain where Konstantin stood waiting for her. Standing next to him was like balancing on a dinghy in a rough sea, because he was swaying this way and that, guided at each turn by the vapours of intoxication. He eventually managed to hand her the pull-cord for the curtain, which she grasped in hands moist with nervous energy.

She recalled the first time she had performed this ceremony. It was soon after her marriage, some seventeen years ago. Then, when unveiling the statue, she nearly fainted with the shock of seeing it. Over the years since, the aura of mystery surrounding the statue had never diminished. An enthralled silence descended on the church.

Pulling the cord revealed the strange and incongruous statue of Our Lady von Adler.

The congregation let out a collective gasp. They always did. Every year.

There was the statue in all its glory – a traditional interpretation of Our Lady dressed in a pale blue upper garment and white surplice, palms flat on her thighs, staring through the walls and out into the depths of the universe. With her other-worldly gaze, she was stealing a furtive glance into the sacred, tremulous core of life itself.

While from the neck down the rendering of the statue was entirely conventional, what was perched on her head was anything but.

There, with its talons buried in Our Lady's head, was an adler – an eagle, a double-headed golden eagle. The sculptor had captured the moment when the King of the birds was about to take off, its huge wings spread wide, its beak open. Its claws were buried deep in her scalp.

With a life-size eagle perched unceremoniously on her head, the marriage of bird and human was both an incongruous enigma and an abiding mystery.

Her own head was aching again. She couldn't move.

She closed her eyes, opened and then quickly closed them. In that moment, she got a vivid impression. The Virgin Mary's head was an egg. An egg! And the eagle was going to rip it off Our Lady's neck and fly off with it.

Then she realised. The eagle was taking it off to its nest.

It was going to keep it by its brood patch to incubate.

The head of the Virgin Mary was an egg, a womb!

When she opened her eyes, the impression had vanished – and was replaced by a tidal wave of pain gushing through her own head.

CHAPTER 8

Recovery

Deliver me from the sword!
Save my life from the claws of the wild dogs!
THE BOOK OF PSALMS 22:20

In the days that followed, she dwelled much about her unsettling vision. She watched the flocks of migrating geese fly overhead, strung out like so many white pearls across the azure blue sky. As the nights drew in, she returned to the church at Löwenhagen. Thank goodness the chapel of Our Lady von Adler was curtained off; she feared that if she saw the statue again, her head would explode. Touching her amber crucifix settled some of her jangling nerves.

That morning, three weeks after the Nativity of Our Lady, the pastor had plenty to say from the eagle lectern – at least it wasn't about false prophets with angels' wings. His hands were shaking but that didn't stop his tongue from wagging. "Friends, we must help ourselves by helping each other. It's simple Christian charity. It's not the first time we've suffered adversity, so we must stay strong."

Outside the church, a couple of dogs were barking loudly, drowning out his sermon.

She glanced at the end pew where Manfred sat alone. Well, no one sat close to a man who stank to high heaven. He was the skinner; he disposed of rotten carcasses and kept the estate free of wild dogs. Besides, he was never seen in the public baths. By always smelling like a melange of rotten eggs and pig swill, he seemed to have raised schadenfreude to the level of an art form.

Manfred slunk out of the church to deal with the dogs, whose violent barks sounded decidedly rabid, a frightening disease for which there was no cure. From outside came hue and cry, followed by a muffled whimper.

One dog was still snarling and barking, so Marion guessed Manfred had killed the other one.

The pastor continued, "When I was a lad, times were bad. For two years, we were ravaged by plague and famine. The shadow of the angel of death strode amongst us. Old and young, men and women, animals, all were taken. Our families were scythed in two and it was God's will. We had offended Him and He was punishing us. If we look into our souls and cut the cords of the wicked, the land will provide our daily bread."

Daily bread: those two little words set her worrying about the parlous food situation. It wasn't as if they could depend on manna from heaven. To survive the winter, they needed grain, seed, and meal. That morning, Christoph had presented her with an inventory of their food supplies. It was the end of September and, based on the experience of previous years, it should have been nearer to Christ Mass. He had even suggested that they sell one of their cattle herds in the forthcoming Martinstag market and use the proceeds to buy grain. They had never done that before and she didn't see the reason to change that.

Back in the church, the congregation marked the end of the service by turning and greeting the person next to them. Behind her, Marion heard the sound of the church door opening and closing. It wasn't Manfred – he must still have been outside, because the wild dog was howling like a wolf.

Someone else had entered the church. By the sound of his boots clopping on the flagstones, it was a man. She glanced back to see his red hair flung on his head like seaweed strewn along a beach.

It was Ian Fermor.

His arrival was met by soft whispers, like a breeze through a field of wheat.

Marion had last seen him just before the Nativity of Our Lady. Since then, Amelia had attended to him, saying he'd been recovering well. Marion was surprised that he was not only fit to stand, but had walked all the way to Löwenhagen.

His face was perspiring but glowing with light, like an angel of the Lord had blessed him. He stood in front of the pastor.

"Yes, my son. What is it?" Leopold asked.

"With your permission, I would like to address the community," Fermor said, his voice weak and barely audible.

There was another bout of raucous barking from outside, followed by some choice expletives from Manfred. When it went quiet again, the pastor said, "Please, go ahead."

Fermor faced the congregation. "People of Schloss Ludwigshain, I thank you for caring for me. Near to death, I was cradled in the arms of Christ. Yet He granted me a second chance at life. I was saved for a purpose. I want to remain here to be in service to that purpose. I ask you: may I make this my home?"

"Nah. Told you once already. Don't want you here. Go home." Alexander's craggy voice burst from beneath the nave.

She wasn't having that. "The man stood for me and my family. That was loyalty, freely given. I respect that."

Alexander wasn't finished either. "Him, he's eating our grub and drinking our water. Me wife's nursed him, good and proper. We got sick bairns, whose mothers ain't got enough food to make milk."

There were more than a few rumbles of agreement in the congregation.

"Anyone else want to have their say?" she asked.

"I do, Excellency." Otto shuffled into the aisle, clutching his blue cloth hat. "This Fermor here may have nice words, but I say he's the enemy. He's Russian."

"Konstantin's Russian and he's our sexton," she pointed out.

"True enough," Otto grunted. "But Konstantin's been 'ere for years and he brought his family here cos the Russians persecuted him."

"Listen to me," she said. "You heard the subtle notes of the Horn of Plenty ring out across the land. That helped everyone believe we can survive. And I give you my word. We can survive. There is enough food for all of us including Herr Fermor."

"If there be enough, how come me gut's grumbling?" Alexander asked, rubbing the offending article. When he was angry, like now, the smallpox domes on his face seemed to glow red-raw.

"We'll have to eat less," she suggested.

The pastor butted in. "Quite so, Gräfin. We must pray for forgiveness."

"Herr Fermor, you defended my honour. You rescued my son. I am grateful to you and I say that you are welcome to stay," she said emphatically. Fermor nodded to her and she acknowledged his respect with a thin smile.

"Thank you, Your Excellency," Ian Fermor said. Turning to Pastor Leopold, he said, "I have a request to make of you. Because of my miraculous recovery, I wish to dedicate my life to God and join the Lutheran clergy. Please make room for me here, I can do anything."

"There's plenty to do in the parish," the pastor replied, scratching his chin. "Konstantin's the junior sexton and now I'm getting old and my hands are shaking, I daresay he could do with some help."

"Most certainly, Pastor," Konstantin agreed. "In God's work, there's a lot of digging, masonry, heaving and lumping of things. You fit enough for that?"

Fermor nodded and asked, "When do I begin?"

"You'll have to learn to read and write in German," the pastor said. "Konstantin will teach you. You can attend his school."

"I have many skills," Fermor said. "Years ago, I trained in instrumentation in London, England. I learned about the Newcomen atmospheric engine."

"We've no use for engines and the like here," the pastor replied. "Even so, we have acquired a new servant from an unexpected quarter."

Fermor sunk to his knees and made a vow, "I will prove myself to you all, including Alexander and Otto."

Fermor must imagine he's been saved for some great purpose, because it's turned his life upside down.

Walking stick in hand, Leopold limped to the entrance while, inside the church, the congregation lined up to receive his blessing. Marion, Hans and Sisi were the first to do so and then retired to the church gate talking to each other. Behind them were the physician, von Ottenhagen, and his wife, Katharina.

There were loud shouts from the far side of the graveyard. A raging dog emerged from behind a line of trees. A man wielding a club was charging after it. The two of them were running towards the church entrance.

It was Manfred. She'd recognise his gangly, awkward gait anywhere.

Von Ottenhagen didn't notice the dog until it was too late. The hound leapt into the air and knocked him to the ground. Von Ottenhagen tried to hold the wild creature at bay with his forearm, which the dog grabbed in its mouth and gnawed at like a bone. While the physician grappled for his life, the skinner arrived and frantically clubbed the animal. The dog lay panting on its side, its mouth flecked with saliva. Even in its death throes, its eyes wore this demonic look. They were bad signs.

Marion watched in horror as the doctor writhed on the ground, clutching the wound to his forearm. Blood oozed through his fingers, staining the entrance cobblestones in specks of crimson.

The pastor had von Ottenhagen's trap brought up and Katharina helped her husband onto the seat. Von Ottenhagen seemed dazed and confused.

"Best take him home," the pastor said, his voice tinged with sadness.

Katharina sat next to her husband and burst into tears. As the trap left the church, an aura of silent fear gripped the little congregation.

The skinner hauled the dead dog onto his own rickety cart, on which there was already another carcass.

As they watched the doctor being driven away, Marion gritted her teeth and murmured, "I pray the doctor recovers."

Alexander had the last word. "That Fermor's already brought us ill fortune."

CHAPTER 9

Reformation Day

For by grace are ye saved through faith and that is not of yourselves.
It is the gift of God.
Not of works, lest any man should boast.
THE BOOK OF EPHESIANS 2:8-9

Reformation Day, 31st October, was the anniversary of the day Martin Luther nailed his Ninety-Five Theses to the door of the church at Schloss Wittenberg.

It was supposed to be a day of celebration. Instead, for Marion, it was a day of mourning.

Marion walked side by side with Katharina von Ottenhagen into the chapel next to Schloss Ludwigshain. She adjusted her black veil and waited while Frau Katharina lit a candle to her husband's memory. At first, the flame struggled for life and then faded away all too suddenly, rather like Carl von Ottenhagen.

Life was strange, Marion reflected. During Candlemas earlier in the year, Pastor Leopold had blessed those same candles, so they were ready to be used as a mark for the births and deaths of the year to come. That one of the candles had the physician's name on it was ironic.

Nor did she think that she would ever agree to sell some of their livestock at the Martinstag market, but she had. Earlier that morning, Christoph had set off to the cattle market in Königsberg to negotiate with the traders. Marion prayed that the sale would enable them to buy enough seed for the winter, which she'd purchase through Moshe Levin Silberstein, a prominent merchant and friend of the family.

The candle mark complete, they filed into the graveyard. Marion pulled in her lapels and tightened her shoulders against a scything east wind. The freezing cold cut the mourners to the quick as the pastor repeated, "I believe in God, the Father Almighty, creator of heaven and Earth." When Leopold finished the Apostle's Creed, he invited them to share the family's grief. Katharina picked up a clod of earth and lethargically threw it onto the coffin lid. Her husband's death had sucked the life from her marrow.

Marion trudged up to the grave edge, picked up a sod and dropped it on the coffin lid. In that moment, it was as if time was no longer relevant… there was just the clunk of earth on wood, bitter tears and cold comfort. The wind howled like an errant spirit around the graveyard, whipping up whirlpools of leaves. Briefly, it evoked happier times, when small whirlwinds ran along the sand dunes of the Amber Coast near where she was brought up as a child in Fischhausen.

Once everyone had paid their respects, she tried to comfort Katharina.

"I don't know what I am going to do without him." The widow dried her eyes with a 'kerchief.

Marion felt her pain. Katharina was a little over fifty years old and the grief etched on her face gave her the appearance of a feeble, old woman. Dressed in a black mourning robe and black veil, she would almost certainly remain a widow. The eligible men were fighting in the killing fields of Silesia and Brandenburg. Conscription had not snared everyone: Gustav, Kadow's brother, had sailed to England, while Heinrich, Christoph's brother, had crossed the Atlantic to America in search of new horizons. Disgruntled by religious wars, they weren't the first émigrés and nor would they be the last.

With her chin trembling with emotion, Katharina murmured, "I-I'm so ashamed, Your Excellency. I'm grieving for my Carl, but I have to confess, I'm also so relieved, no, I'm glad that he's passed on."

"I understand," Marion said, surprised by the candour of her admission.

"No, you don't, Your Excellency," she sniffed. "You don't know what it's been like watching him slowly descend into the madness of hydrophobia. His face contorted, his desiccated body gouged by evil spirits. It was like he was possessed by demons. It was awful."

"I didn't know," Marion said. She'd never witnessed the latter stages of the incurable disease, though she had heard of its terrors. She pressed the woman's hand in hers as they watched the new junior sexton shovel spades of earth into the grave. After a few moments, Katharina pulled away, unable to bear it any longer.

"Don't worry, I'll care for you," Marion replied, her voice a balm of reassurance.

"I believe you, Your Excellency," Katharina said, wiping away a tear. "To me, to Carl, to all of us, you are the goodliest person. You are firm yet kind, strong yet compassionate. We're all afraid of the future, yet you carry our fears without complaint. To us, you are a true saint."

Marion swallowed hard. She wasn't a saint, but she did know that she would fight the mental fight for her people.

Arm in arm, they trudged back to the castle in muted silence.

The Schloss was an imposing bulwark against the east winds and a lifeline of hope for the community. Marion believed they would face pestilence, war and famine and defeat all three, or at least keep them at bay. They would survive. She was determined to not let her people down. She was equally convinced that the Lord would not abandon her in her hour of need.

As she was about to enter the castle, Egor came rushing across the forecourt, frantically waving his hands above his head.

"What is it now?" she asked.

"Horses! Horses!" he cried, pointing back to the lake.

Her heart sank. *The Russians – again!*

A tight knot of horses was racing down the lakeside path. Fearing the worst, she called for Kadow, "Come, help. It's the…" she stopped mid-sentence. It wasn't the Russians.

"By the grace of God," she cried. "I don't believe it!"

Two horsemen raced into the forecourt. Helped by his equerry, a middle-aged man dismounted and strode up to her, chest puffed out like a true Prussian soldier.

"Gottfried," she murmured.

He looked at her with those steel blue eyes of his and she felt her knees tremble. He was a fine man, Prussian through and through, full of deep reserves of honour and integrity. He was neither tall nor short, of medium build, with a firm chin and a glint of mischief in the eye that she found endearing to a fault. He had won her over on their very first encounter, all those years ago.

"Let me see you," she cried, casting her gaze on the gentleman standing to attention before her. "How handsome you are in your uniform! Major Gottfried Graf von Adler."

Her breast heaving with pride, she took a step back and held out her hand to him. As she did, she glanced to one side to see Katharina, her head bowed low in sadness, disappear into the Schloss. But before she could offer her comfort, Hans and Sisi were by her side and they were a united family, a rarity in these war-torn times.

"How long?" she asked.

Gottfried replied, "My leave is for the tridium of Allhallowtide."

"The King has you for three years or more," she replied, with a tinge of regret, "while I get you for three days or less."

"I'm afraid so, my dear," he replied. "Though it's compensated by some great news."

"Do tell, what is it?" she exclaimed. She felt like an excited little girl.

"Tomorrow, you and I are invited to Königsberg Cathedral. Come, I'll tell you more inside."

The staff gathered by the imposing entrance doors and applauded loudly, cheering and throwing their black hats and pink bonnets in the air, as the returning hero made his way up the steps in triumph. To one side, his equerry led their exhausted horses to the stables.

"A lot has happened since you've been away!" Marion said. She touched his army uniform on the sleeve to make sure he was really there and that he wasn't some dreamy apparition.

After dinner, she had him to herself in the State Room. Gottfried wore dark circles under his sunken eyes, testimony to severe fatigue. He sat upright in the high-backed chair reserved for important occasions. More a throne than a chair, on the headrest it had lifelike carvings of the great battles of the Northern Crusade fought by the Teutonic Knights.

She wasn't about to ease his burden, saying, "I'm worried that we've insufficient food for the winter. I sent Christoph to the meat market to sell some of our livestock."

"Times are hard all over Ostpreussen. You must do what is necessary," he agreed.

"We're already on frugal rations."

"As are we," the Graf replied. "Bread and water are often the order of the day."

That was why he was so thin.

He winced and clasped his shoulder, which seemed to be causing him considerable pain.

"What happened?"

"I was thrown from my horse during an assault on an Austrian redoubt," he complained. "I'll ask von Ottenhagen to take a look at it. How is the old blighter?"

"Oh, my dear, you wouldn't know. He was bitten by a dog and contracted the incurable disease. Alas, we buried him this morning."

"I'm so sorry," he said.

"He was a good man," she said. "I fear losing the services of a physician for too long. The people carry their superstitions like precious gifts. They unwrap their old wives' cures – while some may work, many of them simply make things worse. I am already looking for a replacement for him."

"I know someone who can help with that," he said, jumping up and strolling purposefully around the room.

"Who's that?"

"Gerard van Swieten."

"Who is he?"

"He runs the Viennese Medical Academy," Gottfried said. "And before you ask, yes I know Vienna is the capital city of our enemy. But the Age of Reason is unchaining old allegiances and reforging new ones, especially in the fields of science and medicine. I'm sure he'll recommend a physician. Leave it with me."

"I will," she said.

As the heat of the fire cooled, Kadow did what all good butlers do and entered just at the right time. As the fire rekindled, she caught a glimpse of her husband's face in the glow. He appeared quite ghastly, like he'd seen a Prussian ghost rising from the depths of the Baltic.

"Why so sad, Husband?" she asked. "Aren't you pleased to be home, to see your wife, son and daughter, your dogs and your wonderful estate?"

He frowned and put a finger to his lips. In that craggy voice of his, he said, "It's not that, my dear. Of course, I am overjoyed to be home."

"What troubles you then?" She was not going to let it pass.

Once Kadow had finished stoking the fire, Gottfried gestured for him to leave.

As soon as they were alone, Gottfried frowned and said, "It's the war."

"I thought as much," she replied.

"First, let me speak of the King," he said. "What a shining example of a man of the Enlightenment. He follows his own dictum that the King is the first servant of the state. As an example, to the men, the King stays every night in one of the gun batteries, with a bale of straw as his throne. It is a great honour to serve him!"

The accolade hung in the air, until he went on. "This war is five years old." His voice seemed to growl like a howitzer. The bad tidings were coming. "And it's a dire situation. Our brave army is exhausted. What with deaths, desertions and injuries, it's shrunk to one-third the size of our opponents'. We've no money and the vultures are circling. Yet there are two blessings. The first is the King's superb defensive tactics which have kept the Austro-Russian alliance at bay."

"And the second?" she asked.

"Our enemies' rivalry and incompetence," Gottfried went on. "Both Austria and Russia want the glory of delivering the decisive killer blow, yet neither will concede it to the other. Often, we lie awake after a heavy defeat, limbs shattered and morale punctured, dreading the final assault from the alliance – but it never comes. Finck von Finckenstein, the King's chief minister, believes they are incompatible partners."

"Isn't that to the benefit of Prussia?"

When he shrugged his shoulders, she sensed a caveat on the way. "Yes, but it can't continue like that forever. Without a miracle, come the first buds of spring, the enemy will inevitably defeat us."

"You sound like it's already happened."

"They will be hard to stop and we will die trying." His face was fierce, defiant, uncompromising. She imagined that was the mask a man wore when marching into battle.

It inspired her to pronounce her own war cry, a song of old Prussia. "The Prussian people know the Adler family as the beating heart of this great land. If our faith should waver, we will lose. With God on our side, we are unbeatable. We will win this war. I know it."

"I pray that you are right," he said.

"And we're invited to the cathedral tomorrow?" she said, changing the subject.

"For All Saints' Day," he replied, "at which members of the Order of the Black Eagle will be present."

The Black Eagle was Prussia's foremost chivalric order, with recipients from the royal house supplemented by knights drawn from the aristocracy.

"Then it is a great honour for our family," she said, excited to hear the news.

"It's as much a reflection of your unstinting work on the estate, as mine on the battlefield," he said magnanimously. He offered her his hand. "Let's go to bed. For months, I've slept in barns and trenches and tents and I'm relishing the luxury of a bed with dry, clean sheets. I've missed you and I've missed your body next to mine."

She took his hand, warm and strong and climbed the stairs.

For once, she was not going to sleep alone.

CHAPTER 10

The Order of the Black Eagle

Suum Cuique (May all receive his due).
MOTTO OF THE PRUSSIAN ORDER OF THE BLACK EAGLE

For the cathedral, Marion wore a blue sapphire necklace edged in diamonds and a black velvet dress, matching bolero and a heavy overcoat to keep out the coming Ostpreussen winter. It was more than a year since she'd dressed for such a prestigious occasion and she was determined to make an impression.

Alongside husband, Junker, soldier, and friend, she discovered that Gottfried was also a magician, because somewhere, from the Masurian Lakes, or the snows of the Carpathians, she didn't quite know where, Gottfried conjured a plush carriage to take them to Königsberg. As they were about to set off, several wheel spokes snapped, delaying their departure. Gottfried despatched Grenda to look for Herman the blacksmith.

While they waited for him, the new junior sexton wandered over from his new quarters next to the chapel and offered to fix them. It turned out Ian Fermor was a man for machines, having completed a course in instrumentation in far-away London.

After a lot of heavy lifting and rudimentary carpentry and metalwork, the spokes were replaced. Grenda was soon guiding the horses, liveried in their Prussian blue coats, down the great tree-lined avenue, their breath steaming in the chill morning air.

To make up lost time, they raced along the ice-bound road into Steinbeck. My, it was a bumpy ride. From behind the net curtains, she caught a glance of a thatched roof, groaning under a thick wedge of snow. A knot of children raced alongside the coach, waving furiously and shouting greetings, trying to peep inside, curious to see who rode through their village.

The carriage wheels rumbled across the cobblestones on the outskirts of the city. The going was made easier because some civil-minded citizens had piled the snow into neat mounds by the kerb. A long terrace of stone-built houses lined the way. People came and went, conducting their business, chatting amongst themselves, servants carrying provisions for their masters, while carriages passed them by on the other side.

With his peaked cap and long, thin nose, Grenda led them across the Innereienbrücke onto the Island of Kneiphof. To her right, the main square was bathed in the shadows of the tall spire of Königsberg Cathedral. To her left, on the other side of the river, were the busy Lastadie docks and the warehouse district.

The presence of the Junkers drew a healthy crowd of onlookers, cheapjacks and hawkers, as well as a contingent of homesick Russian soldiers. A hoard of carriages was parked in the lee of the brick-built cathedral, jointly dedicated to the Virgin Mary and Saint Adalbent of Prague.

Despite the delays, Grenda deposited them at the entrance on time. She thanked him for his trouble and they made their way through a bustling crowd of well-wishers outside the cathedral. In the large vestibule was another formidable crowd, as people chatted and welcomed old friends. The sweet, pungent smell of incense was quite overpowering.

She could sense the vibrant enthusiasm oozing out from within the inner sanctum where the members and knights of the Order were gathering. She felt like a little girl, feeling the thrill of attending her first Communion.

The interior of the vaunted Gothic cathedral was daubed in Ostpreussen glory. Every buttress, icon and statue was covered in blue flags, standards and colours, like waves from a Prussian blue sea. Boughs of ivy and holly decorated every window and white and blue-flowered autumnal heathers decked the plinths and altars.

Up ahead in the choir was the statue of Albert of Prussia, the Grand Master of the Teutonic Knights, who, after converting to Lutheranism, became the first ruler of the secularised Duchy of Prussia.

Arm in arm with her husband, she savoured each moment. He looked every bit his noble self in his major's uniform, combed and tailored to perfection, and his glittering array of medals and awards. Within touching distance of her birthright, her spiritual heritage, she felt as tall as the tip of the cathedral spire. She was taking her rightful place amongst the high aristocracy. It would be such an honour, for both the von Adlers and the von Bernsteins, if one day he would be invited to join the Order.

As she dreamed of future glories, the usher showed them to their seats, some ten rows from the front, where the members of the Order of the Black Eagle sat. The seating was arranged according to their rank in society and was based on the seven Heerschilde or Shields of Knighthood set out in the Medieval Law Book, the Sachsenspiegel or Saxon Mirror. The best ordering was in the image of God's universe and as long as everyone in it remained true to their rank, His grace would flow into the world.

As the service began, the great organ bellowed out its call to arms. A thousand voices sang the Prussian anthem, the hymn to concerted action:

"Grant that I do my duty as I see it,
As Thou for me, in my estate, decree it.
Grant that I do what must be done, with speed,
And when I do it that it may succeed."

The bishop stood before a golden eagle lectern. With stirring words, he spoke of the Order's motto, Suum Cuique, which meant 'to each according to his merits.'

"Are we not judged by Our Lord according to our merits?" the bishop said. "Are we not given our rewards according to our achievements? Are we not granted absolution according to our piety?"

To end the service, the bishop made the sign of the cross and blessed the gathering, saying, "May the Lord bestow a righteous victory on our armies!"

Everyone repeated the phrase and waited for the members and knights of the Order to withdraw. As they passed her by down the central aisle, they seemed to walk on air, like angels dressed in red velvet capes with blue lining, an embroidered blue Maltese star of the Order on the left shoulder.

She and Gottfried made their way into the vestibule and were soon deep in conversation with a Colonel von Marwitz, an officer friend of her husband. With his arm in a sling, the colonel told her his story. "I was thrown from my horse in battle and broke my right arm, my sword arm!" he said through gritted teeth. "As soon as it heals, I'll be on the front line leading the battle charge."

"And in the meantime?" Gottfried asked.

"Conscription duties," the colonel said.

"Well, the army always needs replenishing with fresh blood," Gottfried observed ruefully.

"I am content to serve King and country," the colonel replied.

Marion admired the man's service and dedication. By this time, she had another headache and felt dizzy. Gottfried, gentleman to the end, found an usher, who showed them to an empty anteroom off the vestibule. She was recovering her composure when an adjutant, a boy not much older than her Hans, poked his nose round the door and asked, "Are you Major Gottfried?"

"Why yes, I am he. Who wants to know?"

The adjutant opened the door wider and in walked a tall, distinguished, middle-aged gentleman wearing a monocle. "Do you mind if I disturb you, dear lady?" the man asked. "I would converse with your husband – in private."

"I wouldn't mind at all, sir," she said and got up to leave.

"No, please stay," he replied, as the adjutant closed the door. "I wanted somewhere out of general earshot. This is ideal," he assured her and she sat down again.

"My dear," Gottfried said. "May I introduce Heinrich Graf von Lehndorff, Kammerherr to the King?"

"Honoured to meet the King's chamberlain," she said.

"Time is short, Major Gottfried, so I'll be brief," he said, adjusting his monocle. "Alas, this war is turning out to be much longer than the King anticipated. The Russian Empress Elizabeth allied with the Habsburgs with one aim – to destroy the rising power of Prussia. Old and sick, she lies on her deathbed in the Winter Palace. I have it on good authority from my spies that St. Petersburg is in a state of frenzied upheaval. Peter is her successor and is greatly enamoured of our King Frederick. He calls him 'The Great' and kisses his portrait, which hangs proudly in his salon."

"If she was to die and Peter succeeds, what will happen?" Gottfried asked.

"Good question," von Lehndorff said. "We hope Peter will reverse Elizabeth's foreign policy. We think that the uncertainty surrounding the succession has seeded doubts in the minds of the Russian generals and weakened their resolve to press home any advantage their Austrian allies might eke out on the Silesian battlefields."

That was very interesting. Hope was dawning on the horizon.

Two other gentlemen joined the discussion. Her husband introduced them. "This is cavalry officer Lieutenant-Colonel Friedrich von Seydlitz. And this is Graf Karl-Wilhelm Finck von Finckenstein, the King's chief minister."

She replied, "The honour is mine, gentlemen."

Von Finckenstein was in no mood for civilities. Speaking in an abrupt tone, he said, "On the day I left Silesia to come here, the King received a letter from London. William Pitt, the British Foreign Secretary, was a staunch supporter of our cause. We rely on British silver guineas to keep our armies in the field. Well, the letter, from our ambassador there, stated that Pitt has resigned. If whoever takes his place maintains British foreign policy, we may keep our subsidy."

That sounded like a big 'if'.

When the chief minister indicated that he wanted to speak to the Kammerherr in private, she and Gottfried bowed out of the cauldron.

On the way home in the carriage, she didn't know what to think. First good news, then bad news, or was it ambivalent? Either way, the overall picture was confusing. She could only do her best and pray for God's help.

At least that night, she could snuggle up again against Gottfried's warm body.

CHAPTER 11

The Columbine Inn

In the Altstadt, the power.
In the Kneiphof, the splendour.
In Löbenicht, the fields.
On the Sackheim, the rascals.
POPULAR KÖNIGSBERG VERSE

She missed Gottfried. She missed his power and authority, his forthright manner, and the air of confidence he brought to her life and all those on the estate. After eight days had passed, Marion didn't know if and when she'd see him again.

She pulled her winter coat around her body. It was like a huge horsehair blanket that kept her warm against the bitter winds blowing in from the east. Everything came from there – the dawn, the Russians and especially the howling blizzards. After so many winters there, she was used to it, as much as that was possible. Today, a hoarfrost covered the earth in an array of diamonds, glistening and dancing in the pallid November sunbeams.

She pressed her palms into her temples.

Ursula must have noticed, because she asked, "How are the headaches, Your Excellency?"

"Tolerable enough." That wasn't strictly true. On occasion, she had been unable to sleep because her head felt like it was splitting in two.

"A shame I can't come with you." Ursula was full of wistful intent. Marion knew her wiles well enough.

"I can manage one night without you. Königsberg isn't like Berlin or Warschau. I can go and come back in the same day if I want." But she didn't want. She had a rendezvous with her brother, Dieter von Bernstein. She hadn't seen him or her aunt in a long time and she couldn't wait to tell them about her visit to the cathedral.

Ursula frowned. She did that when she didn't get her way. "Will you be back for Martinstag Mass tomorrow?"

"No, I have a lot to do in the city. I'll celebrate Mass in the cathedral."

Ursula pursed her lips.

"I'm ready to leave," Marion announced and strode out of the room. A flurry of activity and baggage followed her onto the forecourt. "A wagon – is that all there is?" she asked.

"The carriage the Graf provided had to be returned," Grenda said, doffing his cap.

"Shame," was all she said.

Hans and Sisi came to say farewell. Cecilia, Sisi's governess, loitered behind them.

"Keep warm," Marion said, rubbing her daughter's hands.

"I will," Sisi replied, a moist sparkle in her eye.

My, how proud she was of her daughter.

"Cecilia," Marion said, "during my absence, don't be overly strict on my daughter. While I want you to instil in her the Prussian virtues of honour and discipline, this is in order to develop her into a refined young woman, not a candidate for the Berlin Officers Corps."

"Je comprends, Votre Excellence," Cecilia replied with Gallic indifference.

"Then I will say au revoir."

Grenda helped her onto the seat. It was hard and uncomfortable. Christoph, his back hunched more than ever, squeezed between her and Grenda. It was slow going and the wind whipped the fine top layer of the snow into small whirlpools that danced and spun around the bare trees.

She asked Christoph about his negotiations with the cattle traders. "What price did the herd fetch? Fattened stock must be in short supply."

"I'm afraid that, with little feed, we've been unable to fatten the stock, Your Excellency," Christoph said, with a tired sigh, "meaning the herd we sold was below our usual quality."

"I see," she murmured. There wasn't much she could do about that.

"And our usual buyers – the von Rautters and the von Helldorffs and the other Ostpreussen families – were nowhere to be seen."

"What happened to them?" she said. This sounded alarming.

"The Russians decimated their estates," Christoph said with a dismissive gesture. "Much the same as happened to us. The Imperial Army garrisoned troops in their castles, stole their harvests and requisitioned their transport."

She swallowed hard. "I'm sorry to hear that. I shall pray for them. Then who bought our herd?"

"Russian privateers," he replied. "The trouble is they're supported by their troops, who strut around the city like mating peacocks. I had to accept one hundred thaler."

"What! One hundred thaler, that's a pittance!" She let out a long, slow hiss. "What's this buyer's name?"

"Vladimir Kharkov, Your Excellency."

"Damn him. Not one iota of Christian charity. I'll have words with Herr Kharkov." She had long suspected the Russians' intolerance for all things Ostpreussen originated with their Empress Elizabeth. As a good Orthodox Catholic, the woman detested the Lutheran faith and had surely instructed her occupying force to ruin the land by any means possible.

"You won't get a better price. I tried my hardest, Your Excellency," Christoph said.

"I won't accept it! No sniffling little Russian is going to get away with paying us a trifle for our cattle," she said. "And what of our Martinstag beef – for the estate?"

"After we sent the herd to market, Heinrich and his boys butchered the remaining livestock and stored the cured meat in the cold room – ready for the Christ Mass."

"Then is there enough meat for the winter?"

"There… should be." The old man sounded uncertain. Their situation was dire: neither enough meat nor enough funds to buy cereal and flour. All roads led to Herr Kharkov.

Soon the banks of the Alter Pregel, the old course of the river, and beyond that, the Neuer Pregel, came into view. A knot of Russian soldiers marched by as they crossed the bridge onto the Island of Kneiphof.

The cathedral square was heaving with market traders selling textiles and other luxury goods from the new English factories, from where they would be despatched to Polish nobleman in Gdansk and Warschau. Jewish merchants hurried along in their tall black hats, Hasidic gowns and practised scowls. She imagined they were sharing Moses Mendelssohn's philosophical ideas or reciting verses from the Pentateuch or the Talmud on their way to the synagogue.

By Honigbrücke, the most eastern bridge off the island, men wearing coloured costumes and hats with bells were scrambling around a large tented structure while others were erecting stalls and temporary seating.

"Grenda," she said, standing up to get a better view, "are they who I think they are?"

He nodded and for a moment stopped whistling. "Yes, Your Excellency, I do believe they are the Potsdam Players."

"I thought so," she said and fell to musing on the antics of these renowned, or rather infamous, troubadours, gleemen and performers. If she had time, she resolved to come back and enjoy their performances, even though they were frowned upon by the Lutheran clergy.

On arrival in Königsberg, she had intended to call at Dieter's house and go to the cattle market with her brother. But this deal with Kharkov had irritated her.

"Take us directly to the cattle market," she said to Grenda.

"It's no place for a lady alone," Grenda pointed out to her.

"Christoph will accompany me," she replied. "Leave us at the cattle market and then go and fetch my brother."

"Yes, Your Excellency," Grenda said, cracking the whip.

At the cattle market, the air was shot with the fresh smell of cattle and the mildly cacophonous sound of collective lowing. Scores of livestock were tightly corralled in fenced areas. Asking after Herr Kharkov, she was told to try the nearby Columbine Inn.

Outside the inn, a gleeman was playing a virtuoso performance on the violin. The tune was one of simple elegance. At the crescendo, she swelled with emotion but kept her tears in check. When the player finished, she nodded to Christoph to reward him with a pfennig or two.

"Thank ye, ma'am," the gleeman said, his right eye twitching involuntarily.

"Is that your composition?"

"Wish it was, ma'am," he replied. "No, I was standin' outside a grand buildin' in far-off Vi-enna and this music started up inside. Them notes must have squeezed through the cracks in the walls. I's played it like I heard it, honest. By some boy musician, me thinks."

"What was his name?"

"Dunno. But I's like his music."

"What, pray, do we call you?"

"Gleeman Kunz at your service, ma'am."

"Thank you, Herr Kunz," she said and entered the inn.

The inn stank of vodka, mead, sweat and other unmentionable body fluids. Russian soldiers sang nostalgic songs of home. In a room to one side, a party was in full throe where a man dressed in a tartan kilt was finishing a tune on the bagpipes. What a haunting sound they made. These Scots were an enterprising lot. From Ian Fermor, she knew that many ran schooners between Port Glasgow and the Baltic.

The racket in the main part of the inn reached a crescendo where a Cossack was dancing full pelt on a table. He was energetically encouraged by a coterie of drunken, shouting soldiers until he fell off, scattering limbs and beakers, which in turn sparked the mob into a fist fight.

The owner of the Columbine Inn, a Frenchman named Andre, was having none of that!

"Fermez vos bouches, ou allez-vous-en!" he yelled at them. If they didn't understand French, they quickly understood his meaning from the acerbic tone.

Christoph called out, "Over here, Your Excellency."

Herr Kharkov and his secretary were tucked away in an anteroom behind a desk, on which was sat row upon row of silver thaler, arranged in neat, even piles. Kharkov boasted a droopy left eye beneath which was a deep diagonal scar.

Before she could introduce herself, Kharkov rocked back in his chair and with a knowing, malevolent smile said, "You must be Marion Gräfin von Adler."

"Why yes. How did you know?" she asked.

"You – like me – have a scar on the left cheek. Everyone in Königsberg knows how you got it."

Caught unawares by the remark, she soon regained her composure. "I've come for my thaler, all one hundred and fifty of them."

"No, I agreed a hundred with the crouchback," Kharkov said, pointing at Christoph.

"Yes, Herr Kharkov. You heard me. That's a fair price for my cattle. Now hand over my thaler."

Kharkov turned to his secretary and whispered in his ear. The secretary burst out laughing and pointed at her.

"How dare you mock me!" she said. In one movement, she swept her forearm across the money table, spilling silver thaler into the air and tumbling onto the ground.

"You're mad!" the secretary snarled at her as he grovelled on the floor to collect the coins. Behind her, a truce seemed to have broken out amidst the fighters and she felt the eyes of the whole inn burrowing into her back.

The secretary handed a bag of coins to Christoph.

Kharkov explained, "That's the one hundred t's. That's what was agreed."

"No, that's the down payment," she countered. "I want fifty more. And I won't move until I get them!"

"That's all you're getting!" Kharkov said with a smirk.

"Give me *my* fifty thaler! You thieving rascal!"

Kharkov reached down to the side of the table for something – a weapon? She smelled trouble. At that moment, a tall man with a thin neck pushed passed her and pressed his foot down on Kharkov's hand.

"Dieter!" she cried. What a time for her brother to enter the fray!

"What's going on here?" Dieter asked as he retrieved a pistol from under Kharkov's hand and added, "Now, let's not do anything stupid here."

Marion hastily explained to Dieter what had happened.

"Do as the lady asks," he insisted in that calm, authoritative way of his. "Give us our fifty thaler and we'll go."

"No," Kharkov said, shaking his bruised hand and dowsing the pain with a slug of vodka. "That's all you're getting. You leave or I'll make you."

Drunk soldiers shouted at them, "Go now!" A glass shattered on the ground behind her. Someone stamped on the floor. Another picked up on the tempo of his beat, stamping in time. Soon, all the soldiers joined in… thump, thump, thump.

The noise was deafening, the danger, palpable. The walls seemed to be vibrating.

"Go home, Lutherans!" another soldier yelled, waving a dagger at them.

Dieter's face paled. "Sis', it's not safe. There are too many of them!"

She turned to go and paused. An image flashed into her head – of the statue with an eagle with its claws buried in the head of the Virgin Mary. The divine image of the Adler filled her with courage.

She turned back to Kharkov, who taunted her, "Want a scar on your other cheek, Fräulein?"

Behind her, she heard metal rasp against metal – a soldier drew his sabre. They were outnumbered. The smell of vodka was intoxicating, the smell of fear more so.

"Come on, please." Dieter pulled her sleeve.

She felt the Adler's numinous power pulse through her veins.

She planted her palms flat on the table, leaned over and with her face right next to Kharkov's, said, "No! Damn you! I will have my extra fifty thaler!"

Kharkov stood up abruptly, the chair behind him crashing to the floor. "Take them!"

She braced herself. She had done what she could.

Suddenly, a loud retort shook the room. Her ears were ringing. Her eyes stung and began to water.

Dieter had fired the pistol. Into the ground.

The silence that followed was shot with tension.

As the gun smoke cleared, he wielded the pistol in the air and yelled, "Stop this! Now!"

Kharkov's left cheek was burning bright and his left eye was twitching uncontrollably. Still he didn't budge, not one iota.

"Will you deny the lady a meagre fifty thaler?" Dieter tried again. "Or are you just crooked?"

That seemed to alter the mood in the room, because someone in the crowd hissed, "Come on, Vlad. Be fair to the lady. Give her the t's!"

There followed a brief, but pregnant silence. Then with an air of resignation, Kharkov said, "I'll tell you what, you greedy money-grabbers."

What on earth was he going to propose? She waited; proud, firm and her heart thumping like a bass drum.

"See the fine relief work on the barrel of my pistol," Kharkov said. "It's the best, it's Russian and it's made at the famous Tula Arms Factory. It's worth much more than a meagre fifty thaler. So, you keep my flintlock holster pistol," he added with haughty disdain.

The crowd broke out in raucous cheers. Agitated and defiant, she could barely stand, let alone talk. But she refused to bow to anyone.

"Satisfied?" Dieter asked her.

She managed a weary nod.

"Hah! Now run away, little Prussian people!" Kharkov added.

She ignored the man and instead glanced up at her brother in awe and appreciation.

"Shall we leave?" Dieter asked, holding out his arm for her, which she gratefully accepted.

As they stepped into the freezing Königsberg air, Dieter helped her into his carriage and said, "By heavens! I'd forgotten what an extraordinary lady my sister is!"

CHAPTER 12

The King's Proposal

Argue as much as you will, and about what you will, but obey!
KING FREDERICK THE GREAT

Grenda was whistling a merry tune as he guided the wagon across the bridge and into Friedrichstrasse. Soon they trundled into Junkerstrasse and pulled up outside Dieter's town house. The pale setting sun cast long shadows over the cobblestones.

Philip, Dieter's butler, welcomed them. Exhausted by the ordeal at the Columbine Inn, Marion needed Dieter's help to get down from the wagon. Her younger brother led her into the house and she noticed his limp. Oh, that limp. Yes, it had protected him from conscription, yet the memory of its genesis tormented her. A wave of shame washed over her, even though he'd never blamed her.

He was seven, she fourteen. All day long, Dieter had worn a look as black as the clouds outside. Her parents had told her to look after her little brother. As soon as it stopped raining, he rushed outside. Splashing through puddles, he dashed into the drive and spotted a red squirrel. It was fair game on a wet afternoon. Turning to chase it along the drive, he didn't notice an approaching wagon. The dray was wearing blinders, and so, it seemed, was the driver. In a flash, Marion foresaw what was going to happen, but she froze, and her tongue did too.

She'd comforted her little brother, crying hot tears of grief. His leg was broken and so was her heart. It had healed, but left him with a limp, just as her heart had healed, and left its emotional scar.

"What's the matter?" he asked.

"Nothing," she said.

"You're safe at home with me now," he said reassuringly. "Here, come and greet Aunt Charlotte. She's dying to see you."

There she was, standing in the shadows. In her maternal aunt's rounded visage, and radiant blue eyes, Marion recognised the mirrored reflection of Anna, her and Dieter's mother. Oh, how she missed her – and her father, Lothar. After Lothar had died six years ago, Anna had never been the same. It was as if when he passed, he took the best part of her with him, wrenched it out of her. Soon after, she joined him in the arms of Our Lord; Anna and Lothar, together again.

"Dear Aunt Charlotte, I'm so pleased to see you," she said, heaving with emotion. Her aunt was a blithe spirit. Despite her advanced years, she retained that enigmatic je ne sais quoi that called men to attention when she entered the room. She was dressed in a blue and silver dress, with a frilly shawl and shoulder-length curly wig.

After they'd recounted the events at the Columbine Inn, Christoph counted out the one hundred silver thaler and murmured, "These will buy us the winter grain we need from Herr Silberstein."

"And don't forget this!" Dieter said, wielding the Tula pistol in the air. "Silberstein will give us a good price for it. I warrant he'll give us the other fifty you wanted."

"Yes, I'm sure he will!" Marion chimed. "We'll arrange this with him tomorrow."

"In the meantime," Charlotte said in that squeaky voice of hers, "wipe away that tear. We meet so rarely. When we do, let's be a happy family."

"Of course," she replied.

Eleonore, the young maid, served them tea.

"How are you? How is Gottfried? Hans? Sisi? Tell us everything," Charlotte replied, leaning forward, her ice-blue eyes sparkling like aquamarines.

"They are all well," she said. "Thank the Lord, I saw Gottfried over Allhallowtide. And listen to this – we were invited to a chapter meeting of the Order of the Black Eagle in the cathedral."

"Well, you are mixing with real Ostpreussen aristocrats, my dear," Aunt Charlotte said, retrieving her 'kerchief from her cuff and waving it in the air as if to weave a spell.

There was a knock at the front door, followed by a flurry of activity at the entrance.

Philip announced to a room full of excited anticipation, "Heinrich Graf von Lehndorff."

Marion asked, "The King's chamberlain is *here*?"

"Apparently," Aunt Charlotte said, as if it was a common occurrence to be visited by a close confidant of the Prussian royal family. "Show him in."

Von Lehndorff had a high, wide brow and prominent chin. A tall man with a strong, personal presence, he gave a well-practised bow and greeted them. "Ah, the lovely Marion Gräfin von Adler. We meet again, so soon after the cathedral. I am fortunate indeed," he added, kissing the back of her hand with charm aplenty.

She blushed appropriately.

"Kammerherr, to what do we owe this honour?" Dieter asked.

"Herr von Bernstein," he said. "I believe you are the owner of the Anna Amber Mine."

"Yes, I am," Dieter replied with a note of pride.

"Good, because yesterday I received this correspondence from the King," von Lehndorff replied, fingering an envelope with his white silken gloves. "He wishes me to inquire about a large supply of amber."

Dieter's eyes lit up. "In what regard?"

"I will explain," von Lehndorff said. "You will be aware that, at the opening of the century, the King's father, Frederick I, built an Amber Room and donated it to Emperor Peter the Great of Russia."

"It's well known throughout Europe," Dieter agreed. "Lothar, my father, supplied the amber for it from the Anna Mine and helped with its construction."

"The King wishes to design and build a new Amber Room, one that is both more elaborate and greater in artistic pedigree than the original."

"This is wonderful news," Marion exclaimed.

Von Lehndorff stuck his chin in the air and said, "The King wishes to know whether you can supply the quantities required to build such an Amber Room?"

"I could, without doubt," Dieter said. "Though there are several problems. Since the beginning of the war, my experienced miners have been conscripted, the shafts have caved in, the tunnels are flooded, and the Newcomen engines that pump them out have broken down."

"Mere trifles," von Lehndorff replied, flicking his 'kerchief dismissively. "Like every son, the King wishes to leave a greater legacy than his father's. And he refuses to be outdone by the Russians! Miners we can find. What about the repair to the Newcoming pump?"

"Newcomen pump, Kammerherr," Dieter corrected him. "Alas, since amber is my primary business, my funds are low. I would require some assistance from the King to pay for the spare parts and an experienced engineer to install them."

"An engineer can be found," von Lehndorff said confidently, as if he knew what he was talking about. "What about the spare parts?"

"I can source them from Scotland," Dieter replied. "My father bought two Newcomen engines – they're the pumps – for the mine. Last time they needed repairs was about five years ago. At that time, I ordered spare parts from my Glasgow contact, Donald Lester. By coincidence, I saw him earlier in the Columbine Inn. If we can agree, I can catch him before he sails. But I would need the funds."

"That is a knotty question," von Lehndorff said. "The King's budget is, how shall I say, somewhat restricted. Despite that, he will respect any financial arrangements you make with this Captain Lester."

"As long as there's the promise of the funds, that's quite sufficient," Dieter replied.

"Then I will correspond with the King, who's currently occupied on the battlefields of Silesia. In the meantime, I bid you farewell." With that, von Lehndorff got up and left.

"Well," Dieter said, rolling his eyes. "On the one hand, the King wants to spend thousands of thaler on a new Amber Room, and on the other, he wants me to do it on his behalf."

"Very true," Marion said. "Von Lehndorff will let us know what the King says."

"You should know, my dears," Charlotte said, "that what the King wants, the King gets."

Their conversation was interrupted by the clanging of a bell and a man shouting outside.

"What's that?" Marion asked. Outside, a man dressed in costume on horseback was passing by, led by a second man ringing the bell.

"Oh, it's Martinstag eve. There's St. Martin dressed like a Roman soldier on his horse," Aunt Charlotte pointed excitedly, "and there's the procession of children dressed in their Martinmas uniforms, carrying their lanterns like they were the most precious crowns."

The children's voices were like seraphs, incense rising up to the Lord. They watched the procession move down the street until Philip called the family into the traditional Martinmas meal of roasted meat, red cabbage and dumplings.

Dieter apologised for the lack of a goose, which were in short supply, and swore that the fattened pig was a satisfactory alternative.

That didn't matter, because the meal had a celebratory tone to it and no wonder!

In one visit, the fortunes of the von Bernstein family were about to flower.

CHAPTER 13

The Cords of the Wicked

The Lord is righteous.
He has cut asunder the cords of the wicked.
THE BOOK OF PSALMS 129:4

The next morning, through a fine drizzle, Marion accompanied her brother and Christoph to Königsberg Cathedral to hear the traditional St. Martin's Day Mass. Grenda dropped them by the huge entrance doors and they joined what seemed like the entire population of the city in the old church. The pews were full to overflowing; people were standing in the choir and the gallery. At the back stood the skinners and the gleeman and the other Unehrliche Leute in the city, including the Potsdam Players, a rag, tag and bobtail of performers from the many and various Dukedoms and Electors of Germany. After some robust and joyous singing, the service ended and the congregation filtered out into a cold, clear day.

Marion went across Schmeidebrücke to the grain market, where she sought out Herr Moshe Silberstein, a trader with fingers in every Baltic trade, including timber, grain, and amber, at least before the war. She often felt a pang of sorrow for the shameful persecution her Christian flock had wrought upon his people. Recently, she had petitioned the mayor to accept a group of Jewish refugees from Kaunas in Lithuania, who had been expelled from the city in the latest pogrom.

She admired Silberstein's views on the enlightened spirit of their times and often enjoyed philosophical debates with him on theology and ethics. Today, though, the matter at hand was business, in which Silberstein bartered hard but fair. She wanted the best deal she could obtain for her hundred thaler. Dieter too wanted at least fifty for the Tula pistol.

Silberstein was wearing a traditional black Hasidic dress and top hat. He had a small, lithe, mobile face, out of which peeped these cut-diamond eyes, which seemed to look right through you into the next world.

At first, Silberstein offered her a black deal and when she refused, he called her back and proffered an improved deal, which she again refused. The Jews liked doing things in threes, so it was no surprise when he made a third offer, which she accepted. To seal the deal, she agreed to barter the Tula pistol. Overall, it would provide precious seed, flour and wheat for her people to survive the rest of the winter.

She asked, "When will you deliver the goods?"

"Your Excellency, the grain is stored upstream in the Sonne warehouse. I will personally bring it to Schloss Ludwigshain tomorrow." His words emerged out of the depths of his ragged salt and pepper beard.

"Good. Until tomorrow," she said.

On the way to Dieter's house, her brother spotted the crowds around the fair and chirped, "Sister, let's go and see the Potsdam Players. They always put on an entertaining show."

"Let's." She was easily persuaded. She was in a buoyant mood after the successful completion of the grain transaction. Besides, it would remind her of better days when their parents took them to the circus to feast their senses on the wild animals of the world.

The three of them headed for the large tented area by Honigbrücke: Honey Bridge for a honeyed experience – that was good enough for her.

They first encountered two professional fighters, strapping young men built like oxen, knocking large chunks of flesh out of each other. Bare knuckle boxing was the worst kind of fighting. The crowd of off-duty soldiers and scabrous citizens were raucous in their enjoyment of this most brutal of sports. Betting was rife too, contrary to pious Lutheran practices. One of the boxers landed a hefty blow, sending his opponent flying in the air to land ignominiously on his backside. Marion winced and glanced away. She hated any kind of violence. Besides, she had had her fill the day before in the Columbine Inn.

Pushing their way through the Martinstag crowds, she, Dieter and Christoph were next assailed by two men taunting a bear on a short tether tied to a thick wooden staff sunk deep into the earth. One gleeman was playing a jaunty tune on his flute. The other danced just out of the bear's reach, while dangling a piece of raw meat in front of the ravenous creature, an act which was driving it to frenzied distraction.

They quickly passed on to the next performance, where a heaving crowd was guffawing at a man riding a pony around a ring, guided by a second man dressed as a clown. That was even more amusing when she noticed that the rider was sat facing the opposite way to his pony. While it jogged round the ring at a steady pace, the rider identified himself by holding a mirror in one hand with a stuffed owl perched on his shoulder. These were the emblems of none other than Til Eulenspiegel, owl-glass man, a jester figure renowned across Saxon lands. As absurd as his name was his dress – chequered black and white squares adorning a tatty troubadour's costume. Little bells stitched onto the ends of his hat and coat tinkled to his every move.

Til was talking to the clown. "You know – I'm Russian," he claimed.

"How's that?" the clown asked.

"Because my pony wants to go one way and I want to go the other."

"Why does that make you Russian, Til?"

"My pony wants to stay here. I just want to go home to Russia!"

Amidst gales of hilarity, he adroitly turned his little pony so it was trotting the other way around the circle.

"This way," Til cried to great acclaim. "My pony wants to leave, I want to stay. Tell me, who would want to go back to the arms of Mother Empress Elizabeth?"

The crowd bent over double with laughter, tears streaming down their cheeks.

Til wasn't finished. He held the mirror up to the crowd so they could see it, held it in front of his own face and yelled, "How handsome!"

Still facing the wrong way on the pony, he leant forward, lifted the pony's tail, smelled the horse's backside, and pulled a horrible face at a pungent odour to the accompaniment of more gales of laughter.

Even Marion smirked. But Dieter was no longer by her side.

"Where did he go?" she asked.

"Over there, Your Excellency," Christoph replied, pointing him out.

Dieter was engrossed in another performance. Scores of people surrounded a circus ring in the midst of which were four players acting out a bizarre tableau. One of the actors had an upturned funnel on his head. Marion thought he must be a doctor – or barber surgeon – of some kind, because he stood over another man, presumably a patient, who was seated rather uncomfortably on a chair. Beside them, a monk and a nun stood in silent witness by a round table. If the doctor's headgear was peculiar, the nun's was even stranger – a book balanced precariously on her head.

The doctor she recognised from the Columbine Inn – it was Kunz the gleeman.

The patient's name, written in large letters on an identity tag hung around his neck, was Lubbert Das. Lubbert was massaging the top of his bald and shiny head. He was also one notch from petrifaction. His full moon face was creased in an alarming frown, revealing what was left of blackened teeth. An amber-coloured liquid seeped down his trouser leg and dribbled onto the ground. How revolting!

"Doctor, doctor, it's me pate," Lubbert complained, rubbing the offending article.

"What's wrong with it?" Kunz asked, a malevolent look in his eye.

"It's on his neck," a joker called out from the crowd, to the rich amusement of all.

"It 'urts," Lubbert said. "Me head feels like there's a smithy inside it and he's wielding his hammer against it, bangin' and bangin' he is."

While the crowd were sent into hysterics, Marion felt shivers up her spine. She couldn't believe it. Joking aside, Lubbert was describing the same symptoms she suffered. The only saving grace was that Ursula wasn't with her. By now, her chambermaid would be demanding answers to awkward questions about her constant head pains.

When the crowd stopped laughing, Kunz asked, "What do you want me to do?"

"Master, cut the stone," Lubbert cried out.

To cheers of approval, Doctor – now Barber Surgeon – Kunz pulled out his trepanning equipment, a crude modified drill supported by its own housing. Once he had secured the housing with clasps to either side of Lubbert's scalp, he proceeded to twist the drill bit down into the crown of Lubbert's head.

Ouch!

Kunz played to the crowd, pausing after each turn of the screw, whipping up their emotions. When the drill bit finally pierced the skin and drew blood, a trickle oozed out of the wound and dribbled over Lubbert's eye and down his cheek. The crowd yelped with malicious enthusiasm, which served to draw in more people, until there were hundreds baying for Lubbert's blood.

"Turn the screw!" they bayed.

Her own headache was splitting; it was as if the drill piercing Lubbert's crown was piercing hers. With his limbs quivering uncontrollably, Lubbert fainted and his head lolled to one side. The monk held Lubbert's head upright between his hands, so that Barber Surgeon Kunz could continue the operation, in which he extracted a square segment from the crown of Lubbert's head.

He waved this flabby piece of flesh above his head like a trophy, crying, "Behold!"

The crowd were like demons, shouting and yelling, their faces drawn in wild bloodlust. The men waved their hands in the air and the women wriggled their hips provocatively.

The trickle of blood running down Lubbert's face developed tributaries.

The monk inserted a square piece of wood into the trepan on Lubbert's crown and coated it in a watery salve. Dieter, more familiar with trepanning than she, explained that the piece of wood was to prevent the brain matter from leaking out!

Argh! She swallowed bile at the thought of it.

Barber Surgeon Kunz called for quiet. Everyone bowed their heads.

Next it was the nun's turn. Perfectly still until then, she gently lifted the book from her head, opened it, and recited the words:

"The Lord is righteous: he hath cut asunder the cords of the wicked."

"Amen," the crowd responded.

No! she thought. *Is that what's inside my head – the cords of the wicked?*

CHAPTER 14

An Act of God

And to the woman were given two wings of a great eagle,
That she might fly into the wilderness, into her place,
Where she is nourished for a time, and times, and half a time,
From the face of the serpent.
THE BOOK OF REVELATIONS 12:14

Marion pulled back the curtains and peered out of the window. The first cracks of dawn hung indolently in the mid-November skies. The day was clear, except for a thin tranche of velvet mist that sat on the waters. The lake was still, its surface full of leaves. The first pieces of ice floated on its crystalline surface and the birds had deserted its shores. For once, she could even hear Otto checking the gates and doors around the Schloss.

On her return the previous night, she'd lain awake, her head pounding, terrified about how she could cut the cords of the wicked without enduring the brutality of trepanning. That circus operation had scared her. She felt a creeping inevitability that, sooner or later, she'd be forced to undergo trepanning. She'd never survive it.

Her mind drifted across to the scene by the lake, where a light early morning breeze had blown up. The mists drifted away until only pockets remained, etching the scene with an ancient, primordial air. The sacred dance between mists and lake had been played out since time immemorial, the difference being that it was witnessed by human eyes, which elevated its significance beyond the mere mingling of elements and into the heightened realms of witness and communion.

A brisk knock at the door roused her from her reverie. It was an Ursula knock.

"Come," she said.

Her chambermaid carried in her breakfast, a thin crust of bread and some warm milk.

"Your Excellency," she said with a bow, as she put down the tray, picked up a duster and wiped the surfaces in her room.

"Leave that for now," Marion said, coughing into her hand. "Is the house warm?"

"Kadow is lighting the fires as we speak, Your Excellency," Ursula replied, as matter of fact as ever.

"Good, how much wood is there?"

"Plenty, Your Excellency," she replied, busying herself with tidying Marion's wardrobe. "Alexander told me his self."

"And how is Sisi?"

"Well enough, Your Excellency," Ursula replied. "She's gone out."

"Already? The sun's barely up. Did she say where she was going?" Marion asked.

"No, she took Charlie, her pony."

She suspected Sisi had gone to see Caspar. Since the passing of Caspar's father, she had acquiesced to Sisi's importunate demands and allowed the boy to move into a cottage in the valley. It was good for Sisi to cheer her friend, as long as the liaison remained within the bounds of propriety, which she was sure it did. After all, society was ordered according to the Heerschilde, meaning it was God's will that Sisi marry a man of her own standing, an aristocrat's son, a von Seydlitz, or a von Lehndorff, but certainly not an invalid foot soldier from Barthen.

"At morning Mass, Sisi is to play the opening chorale on the harmonium," Marion said. "I hope she's back in time."

Ursula attacked the condensation on the windows with typical Ostpreussen vigour. She paused and stared out of the window, before asking, "What's that moving funnel in the sky – over there?" She pointed into the distance.

Marion took a look and replied, "Oh, it's a column of smoke. From the direction, I'd say it's a fire in Königsberg."

"Smoke on the horizon spells trouble," Ursula said, sucking her lips.

"I hope not," she murmured. During the years of occupation, they saw the occasional plume of smoke against the horizon over Königsberg way. The two enemies – Prussia and Russia – rarely skirmished in the city, preferring to confine their fighting to the larger battlefield set pieces.

Marion came down the spiral staircase, Ursula in tow. The blazing fire in the hearth sent out a breath of warmth against the chill of the day. Servants scuttled by, occasionally pausing to rub their hands in the afterglow. A dark figure sat in the shadows by the entrance porch, bent over and cradling a child in her arms.

"Sasha?"

Sasha grunted and stared fixedly at the ground.

"Sasha," Marion repeated. "Come near the fire, otherwise little Joachim will get a frightening cold – and so will you," she added, putting an arm around her shoulder.

Sasha shrugged her off and gave her a glance of withering contempt.

"What's the matter?" Marion asked.

"Nothing," Sasha said, in a raw Russian twang.

"Come on, tell me," she said, touching her hand. "Oh, you're so cold."

"Mein klein kind," Sasha muttered to herself, rocking the babe from side to side. Marion was worried by what she saw. Sasha's clothes hung from her like a scarecrow. Her rounded face and dark eyes wore a gaunt, hungry look.

"What's wrong?" Marion asked. "Let me see the baby, the klein kind."

Sasha stood up and turned her back on Marion. The baby started bawling.

"Your Excellency," Ursula whispered in her ear.

"What is it?" she snapped at Ursula.

"I've been meaning to tell you, the babe's not feeding proper and nor is the mother – poor dear, she's worried sick," Ursula confessed.

"Why wasn't I told?" she complained.

Ursula pulled a false grin. "You've been away in Königsberg, Your Excellency."

"And for good reason – Silberstein's wagons are coming this morning," Marion insisted. "In the meantime, Sasha and Joachim need nourishment. Sit her down by the fire in the kitchen and get her some warm milk and mush. Tell Cook I sent you."

"Yes, Your Excellency," Ursula said.

"I'm going to Mass," she said, heading for the little chapel adjoining the castle. For every morning service, she read a psalm or a chapter from one of the Gospels. This morning she'd chosen a piece by John, her favourite Evangelist. His totem, the eagle, was a popular protection above the lintel of many a house in the land.

As she stepped into the chapel, Sisi was at her place by the harmonium. Before she could ask her where she'd been, the staff arrived – Grenda, Christoph, then Klein the carpenter, Krebs the gardener and others.

"Guten Morgen," she greeted them.

"Guten Morgen, Your Excellency," they replied.

They bowed, not to her personally, but to her position, just as their mothers and fathers had done, and their mothers and fathers before them, and so on, back into the mists of history, to the era of the Northern Crusade and the Teutonic Order. Their service was as timeless as the dance of the mists on the waters. Nothing changed; not the service, nor the respect, not the words of the hymns, nor the joy of the singing – so that the land, and the angels that lived in the land, could hear and be warmed by their song of love. That was romance.

To her, their thanks was akin to receiving a precious gift, freely given. It was the same for the staff, each in their place, loving their work, guiding their hand to clean, to cut, to harvest, with the same care as their fathers and mothers. It was worship at the altar of life itself.

Leopold conducted the service, which was another kind of worship, worship to the greater Lord. To finish, they recited the Lord's Prayer with emotional solemnity, reserving particular emphasis for the phrase, "Give us this day our daily bread."

They filtered out of the little chapel and stood in the forecourt, chatting and expressing their feelings of enduring optimism.

After a while, Krebs walked slowly up the path alongside the lake. Everyone knew he was anxious for the expected arrival. He disturbed a red squirrel, which chased across his path and raced up a tree.

Marion waited by the chapel entrance, nervously fingering her amber crucifix.

By mid-morning, she was growing impatient. Grenda was less so; he was whistling to himself as he cleaned the trap and brushed down his mare.

After another long wait, she said, "Grenda, take a ride up the Königsberg road. If – no, when – you encounter Herr Silberstein's wagons, come back at full gallop and tell us he's on his way."

It wasn't long before they could hear his whistling again as he rode into the forecourt. "They're coming." He pointed back up the avenue of linden trees.

Marion heaved a huge sigh of relief.

Still they held their breath. The afternoon shadows were cast by the bare trees, the horse's hooves on the leaves, rustling, falling on the ground, empty shadows.

Four horsemen turned the corner of the lake and approached.

Something was missing. The wagons: they must be following behind.

There was a muted cheer as the horsemen entered the forecourt.

"It's them!" Ursula shouted.

Silberstein and the three others dismounted. Two of the men, a brother, and a son of Silberstein, stood either side of him. While the trio regarded her with grim, melancholic intent, that didn't deter her – Jews always seemed to appear like some terrible fate had befallen them. Their clothes appeared scorched and their boots were covered in a black sooty material.

"Welcome to Schloss Ludwigshain, Herr Silberstein," she said, as cheerily as she could. "You said you'd come and here you are."

"Yes, here I am." He was curt. That wasn't unusual.

"Where are the wagons?" she asked.

After a short pause, he said, "The wagons won't be coming."

"Why? What's the delay?"

"There was a fire in Königsberg."

"Yes, we saw the column of smoke. What of it?"

"I'm sorry to tell you that the fire swept through the Lastadie docks and burnt down my Sonne warehouses," he said.

It felt as if someone had kicked her in the belly. It hurt. It hurt badly.

"Oh. No. And my feed? My seed? My grain?" She was frantic.

"Gone up in flames."

"What? All of it? It can't be."

"I'm afraid so. I came here to tell you myself. If you want, return with me to Königsberg to see for yourself."

She paused for what seemed like an age. She was swamped by feelings of despair.

This can't be. She tried to digest the dreadful news. It gave her heartburn. She swallowed more bile. "That won't be necessary," she said.

"Thank you for trusting my word, not many would," Silberstein added with a heavy frown. "The heat of the Lastadie docks fire has scorched my financial affairs and I must return to deal with the growing crisis. I'm devastated this has happened, and to you of all people."

His sorrow was sincere and she answered, "Thank you for saying so, Herr Silberstein. Tell me, do you know what started the fire?"

"It was an act of God."

There was only one conclusion to draw – a black finale to a black escapade.

For God to punish her so severely, she must have strayed far from the path of righteousness.

CHAPTER 15

The Abandoned

The gods know nothing, they understand nothing.
They walk about in darkness.
All the foundations of the earth are shaken.
THE BOOK OF PSALMS 82:5

Her head ached. The crown of her head was as soft as a sponge and even the pillow was hurting her. The debilitating pain had got her out of bed in the middle of the night and she'd ended up sleeping, or rather trying to sleep, sat upright on the chair.

There's a terrible injunction on my people. If I cut the cords of the wicked, will they be freed from it? Will they be fed?

Like a circling vulture, this worry preyed on her mind. Dawn broke sluggishly, frozen in time like a block of ice. Ursula brought her tray.

"I'm tired of eating alone," Marion grumbled, pacing the floor. "Tomorrow we celebrate Christ Mass. Take it downstairs, I'll break my fast with my people."

"Yes, Your Excellency." Ursula was compliant today.

In the kitchens, Cecilia, Christoph and the rest of the staff were standing at a long table. Otto stifled a yawn – no doubt he had been awake all night, like her. Hans sat by a table to one side next to a place set for his sister, except there was no sign of her.

As Marion entered, Kadow asked her, "Will you say grace for us, Your Excellency?"

She did not feel any grace that morning, so replied, "No, you carry on."

Kadow stood stiffly, head held erect, his double chin adding to his sense of authority. Pressing his palms together, he said, "Thank you, Lord, for the earth beneath our feet. Thank you, Lord, for the water we drink. Thank you, Lord, for our daily bread."

They waited like statues while she took her place.

"Sit down, will you!" She swished a hand at them. "And break your fast. Today is the 23rd of December and we've plenty of work to do to prepare for tomorrow."

"Amen!" They agreed, sat and enjoyed their warm milk and mush.

They spoke about the wood to be chopped, the meat to be brought out of cold storage, vegetables and herbs to be prepared; and how the day's meagre portion of wheat had to be cooked.

"And don't forget the ale!" Kadow chimed.

"Because tomorrow is a special day," she said, "bring up some bottles of wine from the cellar!"

The staff gave a rousing cheer.

Normally, Sisi organised the decorations in the Green Room, where the Nativity play would be performed. In her absence, Hans volunteered.

"Can I help too?" Nicol piped up. Konstantin's eldest boy was keen.

"Of course you can," she said. "But you first need to bring everything down from the attic. You be careful up there on those beams."

"I know where everything is kept, Mama," Hans said, clearly anticipating an exciting expedition into the upper reaches of the castle.

She had to smile to herself. The times may change, but children didn't. They prevailed, they endured, and they enjoyed themselves whatever life threw at them.

The rest of her people were content in their lot, yet she knew they had put on a brave mask. Like Sasha, they wore this gaunt, harrowed look in their eye, and their skin was a pale shade of pink.

In her mind, a Rhadamanthine judge raised a clamour.

How can you allow your people to live in penury? Cut the cords of the wicked!

The judge's voice was loud and insistent. It took all her powers of concentration to shut it out and negotiate the meal without spilling any milk, which in the circumstances seemed like a pyrrhic victory. Pastor Leopold would give her the spiritual guidance she craved. When they finished, she went to the chapel. Opening the door, she found Fermor kneeling before the altar, praying aloud.

"Oh Lord, I am ignorant of Your purpose," he was saying. "Teach me to hear Your words. Show me how to recognise Your signs. Allow me to understand Your ways, so that Your purpose may become my purpose."

There was a humble man. Should she confide in him? He must have seen the troubled look in her eye, because he said, "Come, Your Excellency, the Confessional is always open."

His tone reassured her and she said, "While I can provide my people with a festive meal, I fear the days and weeks that follow. The seed burnt in the warehouse is an Act of God, a punishment for my failures."

He said nothing but appeared to be listening to every nuance in her words.

"I have abandoned my people," she said, fighting back the tears. "I feel that God has abandoned us."

"That will never be," he said firmly. "God is always with us. We have only to open our hearts to Him and He will flood us with His love. Does He not love us by showing us the light-giving rays of the sun every morning? Does He not persuade us to sleep by bringing the blanket of night, sending us into His arms for rest and repair? God is not far away. God is not even close to us. God is so entwined with everything we do that sometimes we fail to abide His omnipotent presence. Know that He is there, with every step, every breath and every heartbeat."

He smiled at her with radiant warmth.

"I shall dwell on your words," she said.

A short silence was broken when the latch on the chapel door clanked open. Konstantin walked in, son Egor in hand.

"Don't ever do that again!" the father was saying. Egor peered up at his father with the face of a guilty seraph.

"What's he done now?" she asked.

"You don't want to know, Your Excellency," Konstantin said. His breath smelled of vodka. "I-I must speak to Fermor," he stammered.

"Yes, go ahead," she said, tousling Egor's hair. "I'll look after him."

Konstantin staggered towards the altar. She sometimes wondered how he could continue to function having drunk enough to knock out a brown bear.

She led Egor to the back of the chapel and sat down in the end pew. Her headache returned and she closed her eyes, hoping it would clear. She opened them. It didn't.

Through the mists of pain, she heard Egor say to her, "I'm gonna be in the Native play."

She gathered her senses and corrected him. "Egor, it's called the Nativity play."

"That's what I said," Egor replied in all innocence.

Near the altar, Fermor and Konstantin were talking in hushed tones. The Russian plunged his face into his palms and wept, his rounded shoulders heaving with each sob.

Her heart went out to the big man.

"It's Joachim, the new born," Konstantin was saying. "Three months old and he's ill."

"What's the matter with him?" Fermor asked.

"It's his head."

Her interest piqued on hearing this word.

Egor let go of her hand and opened the chapel door, letting in a cold draught of air. From outside, Marion thought she heard Sasha's dulcet tones. Marion closed her eyes again as the pain seared through her scalp. When she opened them again, the chapel door was closed. She assumed Egor had gone outside to see his mother.

By the altar, Konstantin was drying his eyes with his sleeve.

"What's wrong with his head?" Fermor was asking.

"How do I know?" Konstantin threw his arms in the air. "The crown is soft and squishy, like a boiled egg. Sasha has bound his head in towelling and still the boy cries."

Fermor tried to comfort Konstantin and then the chapel door opened. That must be Egor. No – it was Sasha, cradling Joachim.

Sasha's instinct was as sharp as a needle. "Where's Egor?" she asked Konstantin.

"Egor?" The big man paused for a moment, like he was contemplating some deep philosophical question.

"He's… I thought he was with you, Your Excellency," he said.

"He went outside to be with you, Sasha," Marion said, acutely alert to the boy's absence. "Didn't you see him?"

"No, I didn't." Sasha's diamond dark eyes narrowed into an anxious frown.

"He must be there, I heard him speak to you!" Marion said. She looked in the porch. No one: only the cold east wind. They stood on the chapel steps, scanning the forecourt for signs of life.

"I've just arrived. I didn't see anyone. He's not here," Sasha remarked.

Those words insinuated themselves into the upper reaches of her conscience and hung there like a sword of Damocles.

"He can't be far," Marion said. Frantic, she ran across the forecourt towards the shore of the lake, shouting, "Egor! Egor!"

Egor didn't respond. But the staff did. Kadow rang the alarm bell and they raced out from the Schloss. Joachim started crying. Sasha's frown deepened into a trench. Marion's headache pounded against her temples.

Konstantin's vodka-soaked heart exploded in a volley of exasperation. "Where could he have gone? There are wolves in the forest. And he's six!"

Konstantin was right.

Egor was guileless and innocent.

Anguish tore at her throat.

The staff raised Egor's name to the heavens – in the Garden Room, the State Room, the attic, the Long Gallery and especially his favourite hiding place behind the butchery. They searched the tanner's yard and the wine cellar. Behind the woodshed. In the miller's barn, in the kitchens, inside empty barrels. In the cold store. In the old coach house. In the stables.

Egor had vanished.

Joachim was screaming. Sasha's eyes were wide in panic. "He's gone. My little boy's gone. The wolves have him. They've got him in their lair. No, I can't lose him."

Marion didn't know whether to comfort Sasha or continue the search. She did neither very well. In the end, she found herself with Sasha, Joachim and Ursula in the Green Room, where Hans and Nicol had neatly arranged the chairs for the Nativity play and laid out the Christ Mass games and masks they'd brought down from the attic. None of that mattered now. What a way to start Christ Mass!

Marion shook with anxiety. The knot in her stomach was now a ball of fire. She couldn't bear to look for Egor, yet she couldn't bear not to either. Her mind recoiled from the horror of what she had done. Memories of her past reared their ugly head. It was Dieter all over again. One moment's absent-mindedness was all it took. This time she was an adult.

How could I have let him wander off like that? I am ensnared by the cords of the wicked!

She searched under the chairs, beneath the stage, behind the curtains, anywhere, everywhere.

"EGOR."

Outside, she heard shouts and horses neighing.

Ursula called her over to the window. "Your Excellency."

"Have they found him?" Was it hope or fear that asked the question?

"I don't know, but come over here."

She peered at the forecourt. A coach had pulled up by the lake shore, its six horses panting heavily. The only six-horse train she knew that passed this way travelled the old Amber Road from Venice to Vienna, through the Moravian Gate and north to Königsberg. The coach door was wide open. A young man she didn't recognise stood by the shoreline, pointing to the middle of the frozen lake. He walked gingerly across the ice. Slowly, he slid over it, until it cracked. Before it gave way, he dived towards the centre of the lake in one last desperate lunge. There was a splash, a flurry of waves, and the frozen waters engulfed him.

"Oh, dear Lord!" Marion said. "He's going to drown!"

They rushed to the lake. Grenda, Kadow and Christoph were standing by the shore next to the coach driver.

Krebs was shouting, "It's not deep. You can touch the bottom." He was the head gardener, he should know.

All of a sudden, like some leviathan coming up for air, the ice cracked from beneath and a man arose out of the lake. With the water up to his midriff, he waded towards them. He reached the shore, soaking wet, freezing cold and steam coming off his body.

In his arms, he was carrying, or cradling, a wobbly sack.

It was no sack.

The sack was moving.

It was a little boy.

"Egor!" Konstantin raised his son's name to the heavens. The man put the boy down and there he was, returned from the depths. The ice prince, the boy found.

"Oh, you are my saviour! Thank you," Konstantin murmured, cupped both his hands around the man's, shook them with vigour and warmth – and not just any warmth, but Russian warmth.

"Egor," Konstantin cried, and buried his face in the boy's chest, weeping uncontrollably, mumbling the Lord's Prayer as a thanksgiving.

Egor's milk-white face was a typical mix of guilt and mischief.

The coach driver draped a winter cape around the saviour's shoulders. He shrugged it off, saying, "No, give it to the boy. He needs it. Get him dried off and into fresh clothes and a warm room. Be quick about it!"

"Oh, Father, can I still go skating tomorrow?" Egor exclaimed, clearly none the worse for his ordeal. "And there's the Native-ivity. I'm playing one of the three wisest men in the whole wide world."

"Mmm, don't think so," Konstantin said, wiping tears from his cheeks. "Wisest man indeed! You're not quite ready to play that part." Konstantin held him at arm's length and looked at him, saying, "Now, we must find your mother. She's worried sick about you."

As Konstantin lifted his son back to the Schloss, the coach driver was talking to the saviour. "I've taken a long detour to drop you here. I need to travel on to Königsberg. Here are your belongings," he said, as he deposited a large wooden chest and a medicine bag on the ground.

"And to whom should we give thanks for saving the little boy's life?" Marion asked.

"Doctor Joseph Skoda, at your service, ma'am. And you might be?"

"This is Marion Gräfin von Adler," Ursula said. "And you will address her as Your Excellency." She was a stickler for protocol.

"And I am your new physician, Your Excellency."

Despite his sodden appearance, she could see he was in his late twenties. He was tall and thin, with grey-blue eyes and his main distinguishing feature was the almost complete absence of a chin.

"I have a letter of introduction from none other than Doctor Gerard van Swieten of the University of Vienna. Would you like to see it, Your Excellency?"

"In good time," she replied. What a relief. Letters could wait. "What a day for you to arrive, today of all days! You are more than welcome here! And you're so young to be coming with such high recommendations. Kadow, please show the gentleman to his chambers."

Skoda nodded and said, "Thank you, Your Excellency."

Marion heaved a huge sigh of relief. Her headache had threatened the life of a little boy. The Lord had given her a salutary lesson and a miraculous reprieve. It wouldn't be the same next time. There couldn't be a next time. It was nearly time to cut the cords of the wicked.

CHAPTER 16

The Fourth Blessing

All Prussians understand themselves to be in service
to the land on behalf of God.
OSTPREUSSEN SAYING

The next morning was as clear a day as Marion could remember. There was not a cloud in the sky and a hoarfrost sparkled on blade, leaf and furrow. After Christ Mass, which as Lutherans they celebrated on 24th December, she asked Kadow to fetch Sasha and Doctor Skoda to meet her in the Long Gallery. The gallery afforded splendid views of the grand avenue approaches to the castle from the river. While she waited, Marion looked down on the staff and children, racing their sledges down the frozen valley slopes. Amidst whoops of joy and much laughter, the children threw snowballs at each other and competed to see who could slide the furthest.

Sasha arrived hand in hand with Egor.

"You know why I've asked you to come here?" Marion said to her.

"Yes, Your Excellency," Sasha said. "It's about what happened yesterday."

She nodded and asked Egor, "How are you today?"

"No ill effects," Sasha answered for him.

"I'm glad to hear that," Marion replied.

"But he's upset," Sasha said.

"Yeah, I wanna play with them," Egor said, pulling a frown and pointing to the children slipping and sliding on the snowy landscape.

"He's incorrigible," Marion replied.

"Mmm, I don't know what that means, Your Excellency," Sasha replied.

"It means he can't be corrected and never learns," she said. "Listen to me, Sasha, I say this from my heart. I want to apologise for my negligence. I never meant Egor any harm and I love him dearly as my own."

Sasha turned those deep, dark diamond eyes on her and said, "Your Excellency, Egor's a troublesome menace, we all know that. It's not the first time he's got himself into trouble and it won't be the last – just ask Caspar!"

Sasha burst into tears. Marion did too. They hugged, woman to woman, mother to mother. Egor clung to their hips and they wept together.

"Thank you, Sasha," she said and felt a huge weight lift from her shoulders.

From the Long Gallery, they looked down at Ursula and Amelia, busy constructing a snowman with the children. Ursula delved into her pinafore and produced two round, flat stones, a long stick, and a horseshoe. The children plunged these into the snowman's face, and everyone fell about laughing.

When Doctor Skoda arrived, he examined Egor and pronounced him fit and well. Marion took him to one side and asked him about his serendipitous arrival the day before.

"When the coach was driving along the avenue," she asked, "what alerted you to Egor's plight in the lake?"

"Out of the corner of my eye," he said, "I saw on the lake surface a flash of blue against a frozen sea of white. It stood out. That's how I knew something was wrong. I stopped the coach, rushed across to the shore, and saw a hand rising out from the middle of the lake, clutching forlornly at the air."

"It was a Christ Mass blessing," she murmured.

"Egor doesn't know how fortunate he is," he said, patting the boy on the back. "If I had been glancing the other way, he would not have lasted much longer in those freezing waters."

"I don't know how we can ever thank you enough," she said.

"Think nothing of it, Your Excellency," Skoda replied. "I am here to help."

"That reminds me," she replied, "when you can, please examine Joachim – that's Sasha's baby."

"Of course," he replied.

By midday, the wind gusted in from the east, battering every extremity. With the sun struggling to compete, everyone drifted inside to the warmth of the hearth fire in the ante-room to the Banqueting Hall. Kadow served the adults a glass of mulled wine, while Ursula and Amelia gave the children warm milk.

"To Schloss Ludwigshain," Christoph called for the toast.

Everyone cheered, except one.

It was Katharina, who stood alone, still wearing her mourning dress. She was sobbing quietly. Marion went to comfort her.

"Come, Katharina, let's celebrate the birth of Our Lord," she said.

Katharina said nothing: her lips were trembling like a leaf in the wind, and her eyes seemed to gaze out into emptiness, like someone had extinguished the light from her soul. Marion was worried about her and felt her struggle. For once, she couldn't find any consoling words. Gottfried would have known what to say. At times like this, she felt his prolonged absence most keenly. The King could have allowed him home for a couple of days' Christ Mass leave. It upset her to think he was sleeping on straw in a Silesian barn.

Herr Doctor would know how to help Katharina, so she went to look for him. To her surprise, she found him practising his blandishments on Sisi, pressing her to accompany him into the Banqueting Hall. Her daughter blushed red, but that was nothing compared to the heavy disappointment on Caspar's face when, albeit reluctantly, she took the doctor's arm.

Sasha arrived, cradling Joachim. She was trying to feed him, but it appeared the babe was again refusing milk and letting her know how upset he was about it.

Herr Doctor was so engrossed with Sisi that he sauntered by the nursing mother until Marion called him back, saying, "Doctor, can you examine Sasha's baby?"

"Err, yes," Skoda hesitated and quickly added, "What's troubling the little boy?"

"He cries a lot," Sasha said.

"Is he feeding?" Skoda asked.

"He does for a while, but then stops," Sasha replied.

Sasha offered him to Skoda, who reached for the child awkwardly and almost let him slip from his grasp. Marion decided the man lacked a bit of confidence, what with a new position in a strange land.

"You nearly dropped him." Sasha's black eyebrows bestowed on him her best black look. She was less forgiving and more volatile. She was Russian, after all.

Amelia peered over Skoda's shoulder and said, "I can see the problem. Can't you?"

"Errm," Skoda hesitated.

"It's obvious," Amelia added. "Even I know what it is."

"Yes, yes, I've got it!" Skoda said. "He's a newborn. The towelling's wrapped too tight around the crown of his head. Until one or two years old, the scalp is as soft as butter."

"Is that what it is?" Sasha exclaimed. "I didn't want him getting the rheum in the head, what with all that shitting and spitting." Sasha laid the child on its back and with deft movements, removed the towelling. Soon the child was beaming like the sun at dawn.

"That's better, isn't it?" Skoda remarked.

"Thank you, Doctor. Ah! It was so simple. Good at rescuing children and good at doctoring them? Who'd have thought it?" Such was Sasha's diagnosis.

When Marion finally found Katharina, she left her talking to Amelia.

Kadow ushered them into the banquet for Christ Mass lunch. Konstantin took regular swigs of his favourite tipple, Russian strawberry vodka he kept for special occasions. Even Sexton Fermor and Pastor Leopold partook of a beaker or two of fortified wine. It was, after all, a Communion of sorts.

While everyone enjoyed the excitement of the day, Marion couldn't stop thinking about the baby's soft head. When no one was looking, she reached under her silk headscarf and touched her own scalp. She pressed her finger into the crown of her head and buried it right up to the nail. Argh. It sent shooting pains through her head, so she stopped. That must be because of the cords of the wicked. They gave her the headache that made Egor slip through the net of her attention. She was wicked. The refrain whispered in her soul.

Cut the cords, cut the cords of the wicked.

Thankfully, her dreadful reverie was cut short by the blissful sound of children singing and crying as the staff served the first course of a hot, weak broth and a wedge of bread.

The Banqueting Hall was a magnificent setting: around the walls were huge colourful tapestries depicting the exploits of the knights of the Northern Crusade, bludgeoning their way across the land and performing heroic deeds in the name of Our Lord.

The rest of the meal consisted of stewed pork with potatoes and greens, and then boiled apples and pears and lashings of stollen. The plates were wiped clean. That was the best meal they had eaten in ages. No more grumbling stomachs, at least for a while, and Marion felt a little better about herself. Everyone hurried off to the Green Room for the Nativity play, Konstantin staggering along at the rear, enjoying another tipple with Alexander and Otto. How those three could drink.

One hundred of them were packed into the room. With the stage at one end, the staff sat on the floor. Marion sat at the front on the high-backed chair from the State Room. Ursula called it her throne.

Outside, the east wind tore through the bare trees, while inside they were warmed by a spirited performance of the timeless story of the birth of Jesus the Christ. Who else but Sasha and Joachim could play Mary and the baby Jesus? Konstantin played Joseph, a role he enjoyed immensely.

Accompanying Otto as the three wise men were Alexander and Christoph, wearing false white cotton beards and pointed hats.

By their local tradition, the three wise men had to name one blessing each that they thought the Lord had visited upon the estate during the year. It had been a difficult year, what with the deaths of Caspar's father and Doctor von Ottenhagen, and it had culminated in the tragic fire at the Lastadie docks. But there were blessings and the wise men had to find them.

Otto stepped forward with the first. "We're so pleased Sasha has given us a new babe in arms. May Joachim live long and prosper amongst us!"

Konstantin raised a huge roar of delight, and everyone shouted in agreement.

Alexander said his piece. "My blessin' be our Egor. Two times this year, his life 'bin saved, one time by young Caspar, t'other by Herr Doctor here, newly arrived, he be. Them be miracles for me, they do."

Christoph said, "This year, we were blessed with the arrival in our midst of Ian Fermor, our new sexton. That he walks amongst us is a true and living miracle."

The three blessings filled the room with gaiety and laughter.

She adored these moments: the ease of being with kind, the kindle of belonging, and the spiritual glow of communion.

The people stood and sang the song of old, the songs of the land, to the land. They toasted with their beer, their wine and their vodka, and sang their hearts out, because the earth can only hear songs of and from the heart.

For her, this was the fourth, and most important, blessing of all.

CHAPTER 17

The 'Kerchief

Through forests I'll follow and where the sea flows,
Through ice and through iron, through armies of foes,
Annie of Tharaw, my light and my sun,
The threads of our two lives are woven in one.
ANNIE OF THARAW

Ian Fermor enjoyed every lesson in the tiny schoolroom. Set as an annex to the chapel, it was always quiet, so he could concentrate on reading and writing German. He liked learning. It was good for the soul. There were three other desks: for Caspar, Nicol, and Bruno, the son of Klein. Konstantin, the teacher, even allowed Caspar to have his dog, Boris, by his side. Caspar was convinced Boris could learn to bark in German. Fermor was not so sure.

For natural light, the room boasted only one small window. So, with the pale sun burrowing into the horizon early during the January afternoons, Konstantin often sent Fermor into the chapel to raid the box of candle stubs.

Towards the end of one lesson, there was a knock at the door. Fermor was convinced it was Sisi. She always came to meet Caspar about that time. But it wasn't: instead, a tall, erect figure in a well-worn dark suit lowered his head under the lintel. Hat in hand, he brushed off a sprinkling of snow from his shoulders. The flames on the candles flickered to the great east wind, sending lithe shadows on the walls.

"Herr Kadow," Konstantin announced, more in surprise than anything else. For once Konstantin occupied the rarely-visited lands of sobriety, which meant he'd brought with him his full repertoire of passions. "What brings our esteemed butler to my little classroom?"

Kadow grinned and didn't seem to know if the remark was a rebuke or a compliment. Scratching his double chin, he held up a letter and replied, "This does, mein lieber freund. It's from Gustav. The first I've received since he left."

Kadow couldn't read. His younger brother, Gustav, had been a smallholder on the estate, when last July he had sailed to England to escape the latest round of conscription.

Konstantin turned to the class and asked, "Who would like to read Gustav's letter?"

"I would," Fermor volunteered.

Kadow's hand was shaking as he handed it to him. The single sheet of paper felt dry and crisp to Fermor's touch. The words were written large and bold, like a child's writing.

"It's dated September, 1761." Fermor cleared his throat and read:

"Dear Brother,

You know I cannot write. I've made friends with a Pole from Gdansk who kindly writes this on my behalf.

I left Ostpreussen with high hopes of growing rich in a new country. I sailed to the port of Liverpool. Living in a Protestant land with a German king, I knew England would be my saviour. It felt good to be away from the rigours of war.

I share a room with other Prussians, Poles and Lithuanians. So, fear not, I am not alone. My companions seek the same freedoms as I do. The factories and workhouses offer us all a bright possibility. The great machines in them will make our work easier to bear.

Soon we will earn plenty of silver guineas to send home.

I hope the Graf and Gräfin and the King prosper under the guidance of Our Lord.

I will write again as soon as there is more good news.

May the Almighty be with you and Sophia.

In good faith,

Gustav."

Kadow heaved a huge sigh of relief and said, "I'm glad he's safe."

Fermor handed him back the letter. Kadow folded it carefully and placed it in his inner pocket.

"Thank you," Kadow said to him. "I must get back to my work. The grandfather clocks won't wind themselves up." As the butler left, Sisi breezed over the threshold.

"There you are. Come in quick, junge Fräulein!" Konstantin said.

"It's only me." She always said that. Fermor thought it was disingenuous for a girl who would one day marry a count, or a colonel, or even a prince of the realm, and give birth to children who lived in castles and ruled over lands the like of which he could only dream. That made no difference to Boris. He nuzzled up against her as she stroked his hairy coat.

It was the penultimate day of January, 1762, not an especial day, except for Sisi von Adler, who had come into this world some seventeen years previously. Caspar knew that, as did the rest of the class, because he had been all of a tremor for the whole day. He could contain himself no longer.

"Happy birthday, Sisi," he blurted out as she came and sat next to him.

"Oh, you remembered," she said, feigning surprise.

"Yes and a happy birthday from us," Konstantin added, as the five of them broke out in a short, vigorous applause, to which Boris added a celebratory howl. "Now what was I saying, before I was so rudely interrupted?"

"You were saying that that was the end of today's lesson," Fermor suggested.

"Was I?" Konstantin said. "I don't remember that. The world's playing tricks on me again. Is Til Eulenspiegel in the room?"

"No, he's busy elsewhere," Fermor replied. "We know that when Mistress Sisi arrives, the end of the lesson is nigh."

"True enough," Konstantin admitted with a rueful smile. "There's no point fighting the rising tide."

As Fermor and the others packed away their writing, Caspar said to Sisi, "I-I've got something for you, junge Fräulein."

"Oh, really?" Sisi fluttered her eyelids. She must have been practising.

"Yes, I've not one, but two birthday gifts for you."

"Birthday gifts? For me? Oh, that's wonderful." Sisi's green eyes glowed with liquid fire.

From behind his back, Caspar produced a small bunch of flowers with bright green stems and heads that drooped like tiny white angels.

"Oh, snowdrops. How did you know they were my favourite?" Sisi exclaimed, admiring the delicate white petals. "I've not seen any so far this year. Where did you find them?"

"I-I searched everywhere," Caspar admitted, nodding his head like a snowdrop in the wind, "until I found a clump in the shade of a willow tree."

"Caspar, thank you," she said and tenderly brushed his hand with hers, a gesture within the bounds of propriety.

After an awkward silence, she asked, "Was there mention of a second gift?"

"Oh, yes," Caspar said. "This is a very special one."

"This is so exciting," Sisi exclaimed.

"I want you to see how much I have learnt and what a good teacher Sexton Konstantin is. He has helped me a lot."

"Yes, show me," she said, glancing at him affectionately.

He pulled out a piece of paper, on which was a scrawl of barely legible handwriting.

"Let me explain," Konstantin said. "Caspar was inspired by the classic poem, *Annie of Tharaw*. He's changed the names in it. You'll see what he's done."

"I love that poem," Sisi said, beaming from ear to ear.

Caspar read:

"Sisi of Barthen, my true love of old.
You are my life, my goods and my gold.
Sisi of Barthen, your heart once again,
To me has surrendered in joy and in pain.
Sisi of Barthen, my riches, my good.
Thou art my soul, my flesh, and my blood!"

"It's from the heart, that's what matters," she said, clutching her hand to her chest.

For a fleeting moment, Fermor thought she was going to declare her undying love for him, but instead, she patted his hand again.

"Here," she said. "Please accept this keepsake in return." She presented him with her pink 'kerchief. "See, on the four corners is a bunch of snowdrops, their white drooping petals shaped just like a bell. I embroidered them myself."

"Oh, I will treasure this as long as I live," Caspar said.

That day, everyone was happy in their work, even Boris.

CHAPTER 18

Candlemas

If Candlemas is mild and pure,
Winter will be long for sure.
If Candlemas brings wind and snow,
Then spring will very soon show.
POPULAR MEDIEVAL SAYING

Marion noted that it had been forty days and forty nights since the Christ Mass. The celebration of the Feast of Maria Lichtmess, the Purification of the Virgin Mary, or Candlemas as the pastor liked to call it, took place on 2nd February. The preceding days had been unremittingly cold, with heavy snow, sleet and rain keeping them inside for long periods. The adults passed the time cleaning and playing parlour games and preparing for the spring, which never seemed to get any closer. The children needed no encouragement to amuse themselves, running around the vast corridors of the Schloss, playing hide-and-seek and ending up in rooms they should never have gone into, especially Egor and his elder brothers, Gerhard and Nicol. At nearly fourteen, Nicol should have known better and should have been in school. Even Hans had joined the rapscallions, plundering precious family artefacts from boxes in the attic. Marion had grown tired of reprimanding them.

On that same early February day, Ursula handed her a letter from Gottfried.

January, 1762.

Dearest Marion,

Thank you for your missive and kind thoughts. They mean a lot at this difficult time.

Rumours emanate daily from the Russians' camp – which is nothing new. What is new is that the latest ones herald important change. Alas, neither the King nor his chief minister can be heard whispering a word of explanation. The King's inner circle resembles one of those newly-discovered vacuums – nothing gets in and, equally, nothing gets out.

Rest assured, as soon as I know more, I shall write to you, my dearest.

I miss you and I wish I was home with you.

Your faithful husband,

Major Gottfried Graf von Adler.

She ran her fingers over it to feel the paper that he had recently touched, before tucking the letter away in a casket along with the others.

Ursula helped her get ready before they joined the Candlemas procession in the vestibule. The men, women and children of the estate were there, a candle in gloved hands, wrapped in scarves, thick coats, mufflers and winter boots. Sisi and Hans nestled by her side.

Old Leopold hobbled along, clutching his back, leading the procession. Apart from Egor and Nicol, it was kept in immaculate order. While the rain clouds had cleared, they had deposited so much water that the muddy tracks were as slippery as walking on eels.

Marion threaded her way to the front of the procession, pausing to talk to her people as she went. In the depths of their souls, there was a nagging fear. Like all fears, it was erective – eventually, it would show itself.

Cecilia was first. A dour soak of a woman, she was nonetheless quite an artist when it came to weaving and sewing, skills which she had, with moderate success, passed on to Sisi.

"Sisi told me she is practising her embroidery," Marion said.

"She's developing, eh, how you say, slowly," Cecilia replied. Marion had to drag every last word out of her. "She managed a 'kerchief embroidered with snowdrops."

"That's good, isn't it?"

"Mais oui," Cecilia replied. "Her heart is elsewhere, as you can imagine."

"I can? How do you mean?"

"Oh, it's the boy. She's smitten with him. They walk, they talk and they ride together."

"I see," Marion said.

"You didn't know?" Cecilia said.

Was she scoffing at her? "I know she's fond of him. Is that having a detrimental effect on her learning?"

"C'est bien possible, Your Excellency," Cecilia replied with Gallic candour.

"Thank you for confiding in me." She was about to walk on, when the French governess issued another salvo of discontent.

"I would like to say something else, Your Excellency," Cecilia said, glancing round to see if anyone else was listening. They weren't. "We're cooped up inside. It's no good. The men have little to do. They moan, claiming they feel as useful as a plough in winter. And food – well, we're hungry, aren't we? For the thirteenth day, there's thin potato gruel. Ce n'est pas juste, Your Excellency. I thought you would want to know, you being a caring soul."

"Well, yes, of course I want to know," she said with sympathy. "I will see what I can do. We both know what it takes to survive an Ostpreussen winter."

Cecilia nodded and Marion walked on. While this was depressing news, it was nothing that she hadn't expected.

Next in line was Christoph, whom she hoped carried better tidings.

"With spring approaching," she asked, "how are our food stocks? Normally we should be about halfway through them."

"Yes, normally," Christoph said with a wistful air. His back seemed more hunched than before. His face was pale and pinched, his forehead drawn into deep furrows, like plough lines on the fields. "About this time of year, we'd prepare the ploughs, the yokes and the oxen. Chance would be a fine thing. In Candlemas' past, I've stepped out with the ploughs, the women leading them, the men behind them. By the end of the day, we've ploughed a dozen fields."

"Today is a fine day, so can't we make a start?"

"Yes, today is fine, but up to now the weather's been treacherous. It's too wet underfoot, Your Excellency. The oxen would never pull the ploughs. And with the little feed they've had, they're weak. It'll wear them out before it's time for the morning service."

Fear gripped her round the throat. She asked, "And the food stock levels?"

"Hah!" he scoffed. "This winter is bad. The stock we have today, we'd expect to hold in April. We're at the start of February. You need to know, Your Excellency," he whispered, "I've put Otto to guard the food stocks."

"They wouldn't, would they?"

"Not our people, though they're near the end of their tether," Christoph confided in her. "We're all a-hungering. Mind, there are thieves roaming the countryside who'd sooner run you through with a sabre than spit on the ground and look you in the eye."

"Thank you for telling me," she hissed. A guard on the food stocks was unprecedented.

She got to the front as the procession reached the pheasantry in Löwenhagen. Except for a few wisps in the undergrowth and in the churchyard, the early morning mist had cleared.

Konstantin was hovering at the church boundary to greet the procession. He had this cross-eyed look which betrayed to all and sundry his previous night's visit to the local inn.

"Greetings, Your Excellency," he slurred. "Welcome to Löwenhagen." He spoke about it like it was as far away from Ludwigshain as the suburbs of Berlin or St. Petersburg.

Amelia was with him. Pale and sickly, she looked like a wraith, poor thing. She still managed to greet her cordially, saying, "How are you this fine day, Your Excellency?"

"Yes, it is quite fine," Marion replied.

"You forgot the old wisdom?" Amelia asked with a glint in her eye.

"Oh, remind me, please." Old wives' tales were legion; she had difficulty keeping up with them all.

"*If Candlemas be mild and pure, winter will be long for sure.* 'Fraid it's about as pure and mild as you can get today, there's no denying that."

"No, indeed, there's not," she said ruefully. That was why people were grumpy. Hardship exaggerated by superstition made for a foul-tasting broth.

"Everyone's wondering," Amelia added, "how to stretch the morsels 'til spring, especially if we can't feed the livestock. The harvest of the first garden plants of spring seems a long way away."

There was nothing Marion could say. She walked up to the front of the church to take her seat, thrust her hands in her pockets and pulled out a strand of straw. It had probably been there since last year's harvest. If only she had the magic powers to conjure a harvest from the ground, or make the wheat grow from stubs into golden fields that swayed softly in the warm breeze.

Then came the ceremony of Candlemas, when the candles to be used during the following year were blessed. One at a time, each person approached the altar clutching a candle. There the pastor intoned some holy words and made the sign of the cross over it.

Everything proceeded pleasantly until Alexander stepped up. He didn't even wait for the blessing. Pointing his finger at Fermor, he said, "You're still eating our food! You're the Devil incarnate. Ever since you come, we lost our harvest, we seen an execution, and our seed 'bin burnt to a cinder!

If that's not bad luck, I don't know what is. I say you're the evil influence. I say you go and good riddance."

Fermor was shaking with the ferocity of the rebuke.

Marion stood up and said, "Alexander, as both huntsman and bonesetter, you're a valued member of our estate. Yet today you defile the holy church with ignorant talk. We're a Christian community. What's good for one is good for all. We allowed Fermor to cross our threshold. He works hard. He doesn't drink. He doesn't take the name of the Lord in vain. Sit down and let's finish this ceremony, for the good of the community."

Normally that would have been enough balm on the waters, but today was no normal day.

Alexander threw his lit candle onto the floor and trampled it into the flagstones.

Otto took up the gauntlet. "What Alexander's sayin' is for the good of us all! And you knows it! We should've let him die out there. Should never have made him sexton. He's suffocating us to death."

"Quiet, Otto!" she said. "You disrespect me; you wouldn't dare to do this if the Graf were here."

"The Graf would not let this ghost haunt us," Alexander snarled. "I've said my piece. We're off."

He and Otto stormed out of the church. Amelia trailed sheepishly after them. No one else followed.

Marion had a bitter taste in her mouth. A couple of dissenters and everyone felt dragged into the pits of hell. The service over, as they filed out of the church, she called Ursula back.

"Is it only Alexander and Otto? Are there others? How many? Tell me."

"You don't need me to answer that question," her chambermaid said, munching on thin air. "Like he says, we had the Russians. We lost the harvest. We had the fire. It's only natural folk try and explain such misfortune."

The silence weighed heavily on her shoulders. The only sound was their feet shuffling on the cold stone floor.

She had to admit Alexander and Otto were right: something was to blame for this continued misfortune. It had to be her. She had believed the harmony of the community was made of unbreakable cords. It wasn't. Strand by strand, they had unravelled and were replaced by the cords of the wicked.

She had anticipated a ceremony of purification; instead it had further polluted the community.

Now she faced a simmering revolt from within.

CHAPTER 19

A Servant of the Adler

He who sups with the Devil should have a long spoon.
MEDIEVAL SAYING

That night, Marion slept fitfully. Waves of pain rolled up on her shoreline. There was a tempest. Bolts of lightning speared across purple skies. She lay awake, feeling exhausted and drained. Then she'd fall asleep again and dream of thunder in the heavens.

There was a rap at the door and it squeaked open.

"Who is it?" she asked.

"It's me, Ursula."

"It's late. What are you doing here?" she groaned, sitting up.

Her chambermaid carried a wick lantern across the room. The flame sent shadows flickering onto the wall paintings and tapestries. The portrait of Albert I, the Grand Master of the Teutonic Knights, seemed to glower at her, as if she had wronged him in some ineffable way.

"I've come to see if you are well," Ursula said.

She glanced at the window. "Uh, I saw lightning. There's a storm."

"There's no storm, Your Excellency," Ursula said, standing by her bedside. "It's snowing buckets and it's settled in a dense white carpet."

Ursula wore a thick woollen nightgown, hat and gloves.

"It's the middle of the night. What are you doing in my room?"

"I was passing and I heard you moaning."

"Was I?"

"Yes, Your Excellency, you were."

"What was I saying?"

"You weren't saying anything. No words I could hear anyways. You were letting out these little yelps, one after another, like you were in pain or suffering bad."

"I don't remember."

"That's strange." Ursula held the lantern by her side and the light reflected up beneath her chin, lending her face a ghostly appearance.

"I'm well enough," she insisted. "Go back to your bed. Leave the night patrol to Otto."

"Otto has the night off. It's Alexander's turn tonight," Ursula said, before trudging out of the room.

Marion fell into a deep sleep.

There was another knock on her door. This time she got up to see who it was.

"That you again, Ursula?"

As she approached the door, it seemed to swing open of its own accord.

"Fermor? What do you want?"

Ian Fermor held a lantern low down, like Ursula had done. It lit his face, accentuating his curved, aquiline nose, high cheekbones and thin, pointed chin.

"Come with me," he said. It was odd, because without a second thought, she did exactly that. She also wondered why she didn't seem to have any choice in the matter. That was not what frightened her most though. She followed him out of the door, along the gallery corridor and down the spiral staircase. She noticed that her feet didn't seem to touch the ground. She glided like an eagle, like when they were hovering in the sky and had an eye for their prey. As she walked, she tried to hear the sound of her own footsteps. There was none. She was walking on thin air. That was what frightened her the most.

"What's happening? Where… are we going?"

"Are you hungry?"

"Yes, of course, we're all hungry, but—"

"Then follow me." Fermor's voice was hoarse; like he had a heavy cold or a sore throat. "I'll satisfy your hunger," he added, which to her sounded more like a threat than a promise. Again, she felt fearful of this man's ambiguous intent and his essential power over her will. She could do nothing to alter it and drifted along after him.

The lantern lit the way ahead; the tranche of light followed Fermor like it was coming from his face, like his face was the light.

He led her out of the north-facing door. Snow was falling from the sky like milk-white diamonds, sparkling in the palpable stillness of the night. They travelled – or floated, she wasn't quite sure what they were doing – along the front of the Schloss until they reached the two barns where the meagre supplies of wheat, seed and corn were stored.

Alexander was hunched in a corner of a doorway. Some guard he was; his snoring would have woken the dead, if there had been any around. None of that seemed to matter, because she noticed she was still wearing her nightgown and wondered why her feet and hands didn't feel the biting cold. Now she came to think about it, she didn't feel anything. No cold, no warmth, no sensations at all. It was even more curious that Fermor, leading the way, left no footprints in the snow.

He eased them towards a narrow alley that ran between the walls of the two barns. Despite the protection afforded it from the elements, the snowstorm had deposited a light dusting in the alleyway. It was secluded. She hesitated. What might he do to her?

"No, stop. I can't go any further," she said. "Tell me what this is about."

"I told you, I'll satisfy your hunger," he said, turning to speak to her. His face resembled a great bird, his hook-nose and large, staring eyes lending him the appearance of a hawk, no, it was more like an eagle.

"Why are you doing this?"

"You helped me, Your Excellency. I want to help you," he replied. "You are one of us."

"One of 'whom'?"

"A servant of the Adler, the eagle, the twin-headed eagle."

"I'm an Adler and the twin-headed eagle is on my husband's coat of arms. Is that what you mean?"

"If you believe that's all there is to it, go back to your warm bed," he said. "If you have an inkling of a greater purpose, follow me. Higher service is always freely given."

He glided on without waiting for an answer, leaving her alone and swathed in the night. She felt compelled to follow. Besides, the Adler had encouraged her at a moment of crisis when she was in the Columbine Inn.

Fermor held the lantern out in front of him; its light seemed to shine through him, like he was transparent or made of air. It was easy for her to see the way ahead. When they were about two-thirds of the way down the alley, he stopped and said, "I've brought you here so you can see it for yourself. You need to remember this place."

He pointed to the ground and added, "This is it, see here."

"See what?"

"This patch of grass."

"What of it?" she asked.

"It has no snow on it."

"I can see that. And?"

Before he could reply, the end of the alley from which they had come was filled with a swishing light and shouts of alarm. "Oi! Who's that? Is someone there? Show yourselves! Or I'm coming to get you!"

Alexander had woken up.

"Quick," Fermor said. "Follow me." And he floated up into the air, above the barns, and over the snowy landscape as if it were the most natural thing in the world to hover around in a body lighter than air.

She glided through the walls of the Schloss and was soon drifting into the safe confines of her bedroom. Somewhere along the way, Fermor must have slipped away into the night and she found herself back in her body and in her bed.

CHAPTER 20

The Black Horse

When the Lamb opened the third seal,
And there before me was a black horse!
Its rider was holding a pair of scales, saying,
'A quart of wheat or three quarts of barley for a day's wages.'
THE BOOK OF REVELATIONS 6:5-6

When Marion woke up, her legs ached. She felt like she had been walking in her sleep, yet she was still in bed. That was strange. Then came an Ursula knock on the door.

"Come in." She was groggy.

"Your Excellency, there's trouble brewing." Ursula sounded anxious.

"Where? What's happening?" she said, getting out of bed.

"Alexander and Otto, they're in the chapel – with Fermor."

"Don't tell me, I can guess the rest," she said, throwing on some clothes.

She flew down the spiral staircase. There was mayhem in the vestibule – swollen by incessant rain and all that snow, the front door wouldn't close. Klein was trying to shave some chippings from it. Grenda was bringing an armful of wet logs through the door when he should have been using the back entrance. Joachim was bawling in Sasha's arms. Egor was lying on his back on the ground with his arms and legs thrashing like an upturned beetle.

"Kadow," she said as she raced out the door, "use your authority here. Bring a semblance of order to our people."

Marion burst through the chapel door, Ursula in tow. Alexander had Fermor by the hands, Otto by his feet. Both were burly men so to them Fermor was like a will-o'-the-wisp. They were half-dragging, half-carrying the junior sexton down the aisle towards the entrance. Hans and Konstantin were barring their way. The other boys from the school,

Bruno, Caspar and Nicol, were alternately jeering and cheering at the comic scene. Boris joined in the cacophony with some annoyed and persistent barking.

Hands on haunches, Pastor Leopold arrived and yelled, "This is a House of God. Put down my junior sexton at once!"

Alexander and Otto dropped Fermor, who thumped onto the flagstones. Fermor stood up and brushed himself down. The schoolboys pulled faces like someone had given them a special treat and abruptly stolen it away.

Pastor Leopold wasn't finished. "Sexton Fermor is a man of God," he hissed. "And you treat him like a skinner. Well, what have you got to say for yourselves?"

"Don't care. He goes or I go." Alexander was singing that song again this morning.

"He stays." Marion was adamant.

"You haven't heard?" Alexander said in that snide way of his, like he knew something she didn't.

"Heard what?" she asked.

"Last night, I was guarding the food store in the freezing cold. He was there, Fermor, trying to steal it for himself! Hah. What do you think of that?" Alexander blurted out his accusation.

It prompted her memory of last night's escapade.

"The patch of grass!" she cried in triumph. They gawped at her like she'd spoken in Hungarian, until she added, "I'll show you. All of you; come with me."

"Where are you taking us? What's all this about?" Alexander was anxious to know.

"Trust me," she urged them.

She led them through the vestry and out of the back of the chapel to the barns and outhouses. Ursula and Fermor walked beside her. Konstantin and his pupils came too. Boris tracked their every move with excited barks.

"This is your doing," she murmured to Fermor.

"What do you mean, Your Excellency?" he replied.

"You came to my room last night," she said.

"No, it was I who came to your room last night," Ursula admitted. "You're confused."

"No, I'm not," she insisted. "You came after Ursula, didn't you?" Was she going mad? By now, Kadow, Klein, Christoph, Amelia and Sisi had joined them, trudging through the down of snow.

"I'll show you," she said. "A patch of grass. He – Fermor – led me to it last night. I'm certain."

"This is like chasing hunt after a wild boar," Alexander pointed out. He should know, he was the master.

Marion led them into the alley between the barns.

"Alexander," she said, stopping about halfway along it.

"Your Excellency, I saw him right here. How did you know?" Alexander's pox-ridden face glowed red with confusion.

"I told you," she said. "Look at these great clodhoppers. They're yours, aren't they?"

"S'pose so," he said with an air of reluctance.

"If you saw Fermor here last night, where are his footprints?" She plunged her hands on her hips to emphasise the question.

Alexander scratched his head. "Dunno."

"Oh, I think you do. You track wolves and bears. You once tracked a lynx. You're as canny as an old fox."

"Wouldn't know about that, Excellency."

"Don't play the innocent lamb with me, Alexander," she scoffed. "There's only one set of footprints, and they're yours. Admit it, you were mistaken."

"Looks that way to me," Otto piped up, waving his withered hand at Alexander like he'd been a naughty boy.

"Unless he walked on air, he wasn't here," Alexander admitted begrudgingly.

"Good, now that's cleared up, let's find this patch of grass," she said.

"What's this patch of grass, Your Excellency?" Fermor asked.

She edged down the alley, staring at the ground like she was stalking prey.

"Here it is," she said, with a sigh of relief.

Ursula was in her ear. "You've got half of Schloss Ludwigshain out here in the freezing cold. What's so important about a patch of green grass?"

"Yes, it's green! That's it. Don't you see? There's not even a sprinkling of snow on it."

"Yes, and…?" Ursula asked.

"… The rest of the path is covered in snow. Something's melting the snow on this patch."

"Mmm, now you come to mention it, that is odd." Ursula added a frown.

"Dig it out. Let's see what's underneath." Fermor perked up. "Someone fetch a spade."

"Got one here," Krebs said.

After a lot of effort, he broke the frozen earth and dug out a square of turf about knee-deep to reveal… a square piece of wood about the size of a chair seat.

"What's that?" she asked.

"It's got a latch. It's a trapdoor," Krebs said, taking off his cap and wiping his forehead. "I worked these lands for nigh on two score year and I never knew that was here."

"Open it!" she said.

Krebs was a huge man with thighs like tree trunks. After a lifetime of hard physical work, his hands were permanently scarred with so many cuts, bruises and scars. He quickly prized open the encrusted latch with the edge of the spade and knelt down to peer into a black void.

"It's too dark to see," she said. "Someone, bring a lantern!"

Egor ran off for one.

When he returned, Krebs shoved the lantern into the void, revealing the four sides of an open shaft, with a ladder.

"Where does it go?" Marion asked. This was getting interesting.

"We're going to find out, Your Excellency," Krebs replied. Lantern in hand, he climbed down the ladder.

He called up, "I'm at the bottom of the shaft. There's a tunnel!"

Krebs climbed back up the ladder. "It's old, at least fifty year or more, I'd say. Reckon it leads back under the Schloss. It's narrow though. Needs someone to squirrel their way along it."

"Who wants to go?" she asked.

"Father, I'm a red squirrel. Let me go," Egor shouted, hanging on his father's leg.

"Are you sure you want to let him go down there?" she asked.

"Only if he goes with Sexton Fermor," Konstantin replied. "He's a good man. I've seen him in the schoolroom. I trust him with my son."

"Whoopee!" Egor yelped.

"This isn't a game, Egor," Marion reprimanded him. "You can only go if you follow Sexton Fermor's instructions. Promise?"

"Promise," Egor said, pulling a serious face.

"Off you go," she said. Oh God, what if something should happen to him – again?

"I'll make sure he's safe," Fermor murmured, as if he'd heard her inner fears.

The two of them were gone for what seemed like an age.

A thousand thoughts and questions rebounded in her mind. What were they going to find down there: a hoard of silver thaler; a library of

Gnostic books; a secret burial vault of a long-forgotten Teutonic Knight? After a while, there were noises in the tunnel. They must have found something. What if they found nothing?

Egor came up first, his clothes smudged with mud, wearing a broad grin.

"What's there?" she asked.

Then Fermor emerged. Everyone gathered around in the narrow confines of the alley.

"There's a vault at the end of the tunnel," Fermor said, excited beyond belief. "Egor, show Her Excellency what you found in it."

Wearing a mischievous smile, he said, "Hold out your hand, Your 'cellency."

He held his fist over her palm and released it, letting out a trickle of something like seed into her hand.

"Oh, my Lord. Cereal grain."

"Yes!" Fermor said. "Egor found it in the vault. Tell her what else you saw in there."

"Big round bits of wood, taller than me," Egor said, holding his hand above his head to indicate the height.

"Barrels," Konstantin suggested.

"Yeah, them," Egor said. "Lots of them."

"And this grain was in them?" she asked, not quite believing what she was asking.

He nodded.

Out there in the snow, the cold, the frozen wastes of wintry Ostpreussen, like witnesses to a miracle, everyone knelt, unbidden, a gesture of surrender and thanksgiving. It was an unforgettable moment. As she prayed, she realised Fermor had kept his promise to her: 'I'll satisfy your hunger.'

Truly, the cords of the wicked had been cut.

They had been saved from the Black Horse.

CHAPTER 21

Twelve Stars

When daylight came, Jesus called his disciples to him
and chose twelve of them.
THE GOSPEL OF LUKE 6:13

The glad tidings swept through the Schloss like a clean brush. An ecstatic crowd of staff knelt by the trapdoor, murmuring prayers like it was the entrance to the tomb of Jesus. Marion allowed time for their piety and gently moved them on, since they needed to bring tools to the shaft entrance. To shore up the tunnel, Krebs brought a wheelbarrow loaded with planks of wood.

Konstantin slapped Fermor on the back, saying, "Well, young fella, we'd better get cracking if we're going to clear the way to the vault."

"I agree," Fermor said. "I wonder what else is in it."

Fermor lowered himself through the trapdoor, clutching a handful of spades, trowels and rakes. In the tunnel, the men erected lantern cradles at intervals along the walls. Fermor and Konstantin took turns to excavate and make safe the tunnel, while Otto and Alexander shifted the earth into one of the wheelbarrows Krebs had managed to persuade down there. When full, it was exchanged for an empty one and wheeled along to the tunnel, an activity that involved running the gauntlet of the women keeping the lanterns alight.

"What you got there?" Amelia asked Otto as he passed them by.

"A wheelbarrow, full of God's earth," Krebs replied. What he lacked in imagination, he made up for in horticultural prowess.

"You are pushing it," Amelia jibed, which set the women cackling like a flock of geese.

Marion guarded the trapdoor. While Christoph supervised the safe disposal of the earth, she asked him, "Why didn't we know about this tunnel before?"

"I don't know, Your Excellency," he replied. "There are cellars beneath the Schloss. But these two barns are some distance from the main castle building."

"Do we have a ground plan?"

"If there is one, Your Excellency, it'll be in the Graf's study," he replied.

"Show me."

On the way, it was a delight to hear the staff singing songs and making rhymes and enjoying the dignity of working together. It was a long time since she'd heard any spontaneous laughter.

In the Graf's study, Christoph unrolled an old ground map of the castle.

"Look here," he said. "The map shows there was once a gatehouse in the spot where you found the trapdoor."

"There was no gate though, not then, not now," she observed.

"The gatehouse was built on top of the tunnel," he said.

"What happened to it?"

"Oh, I remember, when I was a lad, there was a bad storm," Christoph said. "The roof of the gatehouse fell in. The building became derelict. I suppose the trapdoor and the tunnel were forgotten about. Before you married the Graf, the gatehouse was knocked down to make way for the two barns. It's God's will that they weren't built on top of the trapdoor."

By the time they returned to the shaft, Fermor and Konstantin had widened the tunnel and supported its walls with planks of wood. It was clear for entry.

"Good, well done," she said.

"There are about twenty steps from the tunnel down into the vault," Fermor told her.

Tentatively, she descended into the vault. She felt both tremors of terror and excitement. It was like she was walking down the aisle to get married. Otto, Konstantin, Fermor, and Christoph followed behind, their lanterns spilling light into the dark crevices of the tunnel.

A row of cradled lanterns lit the vault. It was like a cellar, but its ceiling was domed. The atmosphere was still and quiescent. She wondered who, before them, had last breathed its air. Whoever it was, she thanked them profusely for leaving behind several dozen barrels of cereal grain.

She ran the grain through her hand.

"Not a trace of mould!" she murmured to herself.

This was a gift from God, to compensate her for the loss of her seed in the warehouse fire. She could keep her promise to her people. She could satisfy their hunger. Fermor had helped her to do that, in no uncertain way.

She called the men and they joined her in the vault.

"We need to bring the barrels up here," Fermor said.

"They're too heavy," Konstantin said. "We'll never lift them up the shaft."

They made a chain of men, women and children to transfer the grain into small sacks and haul them into the daylight, where they were placed in the storage barns. When they finished, the wings of dusk were drawing in.

Alone in the vault, she was deliriously happy. It was a miracle and she paused to thank the Lord. She ran her palm over the top of the now-empty barrels and hummed a little childhood tune. She stopped at the end barrel and by chance peered behind it. Holding up the lantern, she noticed a glint of light on metal. On the ground, behind the end barrel, was a wooden chest, about a forearm in length. Although it was tucked into the corner of the vault, it was odd that no one had noticed it.

She placed the oak chest on top of the barrel and discovered that the metal was a handle, not a lock. She wiped away the top coating of dust and coughed as it billowed into her face. The sound of her cough seemed to echo through the vault, louder than she would have imagined.

On the lid of the chest was an etching of Our Lady with stars around her head. As she contemplated the carving, the atmosphere in the cavern seemed to thicken. The image of Our Lady seemed to glow with an uncanny brightness. And Marion had the unerring impression that this iconic image was for her eyes only.

What was in the chest: a treasure, a map, a letter?

She opened it.

Inside was a silk cloth and underneath it, a book, the Holy Bible. Towards the end of it was a silk bookmark. She was being led to a passage. She opened the page to the Book of Revelations where a verse was underlined:

A great sign appeared in heaven: a woman clothed with the sun, with the moon under her feet and a crown of twelve stars on her head.

She wondered what it meant, and who put it there, open at that particular page. There was a noise in the stairway. She expected to see Fermor or Konstantin. There was no one – just her, the oak chest, the book and the empty barrels.

"Who's there?" she called. A remote echo gave her back her question. That scared her. The bishop had warned of false prophets. Her mind was spinning with images of Gothic demons with angels' wings.

“Show yourself,” she cried. The echo came back at her, stronger, clearer.

“Fermor, Konstantin, come out.”

Nothing.

“Egor, stop playing around.”

No one.

This was eerie. Her pulse was racing. Her hands, wet. Her throat, dry. She stumbled towards the exit. Tripping on the uneven steps, she fell and hit her head.

She lay there; half-aware of what was happening, her head throbbing like it was going to burst. In her mind’s eye, the stitches of her scalp unravelled themselves. She could not believe it. Her head was so painful. She wasn’t sure if it was really happening. One by one, the thread-like sutures in her scalp snapped open with a crack. Her head expanded, her brain matter pushing out from her skull, extending the scalp beyond its normal shape into that of a balloon. Like Lubbert Das. What in heaven’s name was happening to her?

It was incredible. The top of her head split down the seams. Her brain matter spilled out over the sides, squirming like the tentacles of an octopus, like a wig. It wasn’t an octopus, or a wig, it was – another head, the head of a bird and it was emerging from inside her brain!

It was coated in birth goo.

It was an eagle’s head. No, it had not one, but two heads.

She – her head – was giving birth to a twin-headed eagle!

Seeing stars, she fainted.

CHAPTER 22

Good Tidings

Good news always comes from far away.
YIDDISH PROVERB

Marion woke up. She reached up to feel a bandage bound tightly around her head. How had that got there? At least she was in her own bed. It was nearly dark outside. A pale tranche of light intruded through the gap in the curtains. The Teutonic Knights on the wall hangings brandished their swords at her. Thankfully, she wasn't one of the heathens they conquered during the Northern Crusade.

There was a knock at the door. It was more of an Ursula rap.

"Come!"

Her chambermaid brought in a tray of hot milk and some bread.

"I'm late. I must get ready for the service."

"No, Your Excellency, it's not the morning. It's time for vespers."

"Then why are you bringing me food to break my fast?"

"Your Excellency, you've slept through the night and most of the day."

"I have? Oh, now I remember. The vault. The barrels. The grain."

"Yes, and try the bread. It's just out of the oven. Cook made it from the flour from the vault grain."

Marion ate a mouthful. "Ah, it's delicious. Make sure everyone gets some."

"Already done, Your Excellency," Ursula said with an immense air of satisfaction. "How are you feeling after your fall? Doctor Skoda bandaged the cut on your forehead."

"Mmm, it hurts. It's pressing against the crown of my head," she murmured, as she unwrapped its folds. "That feels better."

"These are good tidings, Your Excellency, you finding the grain in the vault. We're saved, and you saved us. All day, the weather was balmy. What with the snow melting and that, Christoph reckons we'll soon be hitching up the ploughs. The Horn of Plenty finally worked!"

"The Lord is caring for us," she purred.

"Here's your tray, Your Excellency. There's something for you on it."

Her eyes lit up. "Another letter! So soon after the last!" She opened it and read:

January, 1762.

Dearest Marion,

Know that I am well.

I only have a few moments before I must attend the king – we senior officers are summoned to a council of war. Today I write with the most significant news: the Russian Empress Elizabeth Petrovna has died.

Her demise may prove decisive to our collective fortunes because Peter III is the new Emperor, and his wife, Catherine, is Prussian-born. The king is cautiously optimistic that Peter will reverse Russian foreign policy. We hope this is the beginning of the end of this dreadful war, at least with the Russians. If so, that would leave us fighting only one empress and the Austrians we can defeat.

Pray for God, the King, and for Ostpreussen!

I miss you so much!

Your faithful husband,

Major Gottfried Graf von Adler.

"The Graf," she gasped, "writes that the Russian Empress is dead and that Peter, her successor, may adopt a more peaceful stance."

"Oh, my. More splendid news!"

"Yes, ring the bell. I'll tell the staff."

Ursula bounded out of the room like a five-year-old.

Gottfried's letter heralded a sea change in the political situation. With Peter III's succession, they'd surely be embraced by the arms of peace, which in turn would usher more prosperity and good harvests. It would speed the delivery of the new Amber Room, yielding both profit and prestige to her brother. With new spring shoots, this year was the beginning of a new era for the Bernstein and Adler families, Schloss Ludwigshain and Ostpreussen.

As she dressed, she cast her mind back to the events in the vault. It was strange that the hidden Bible had been open at that passage from the Book of Revelations, like it had been waiting for her and her alone. The verse spoke of a woman with twelve stars on her head. After that, she'd had the dream vision where a double-headed eagle had emerged out of her head. She had to find out what those twelve stars meant. Fermor would know. He knew more about the Adler eagle than he revealed.

CHAPTER 23

The Riddle of the Sphinx

I call on the Lord in my distress and He answers me.
THE BOOK OF PSALMS 120:1-2

During the service the next morning, Marion joined the smallholders and staff in joyous celebration, their voices filled with the warm tenor of hope. Ably assisted by Sextons Fermor and Konstantin, Pastor Leopold led the paean of thanksgiving to her, while reserving special praise for the Lord, who had answered their prayers and banished their distress.

At the end of the service, they waited patiently in line, fingering caps and bonnets, and took it in turns to show her their gratitude.

"Your Excellency, bless thee," Amelia said, adding a brief curtsy.

From a safe distance, Manfred doffed his cap.

Grenda was next, whistling his tunes as ever. Somehow, they seemed more jaunty than before. "So happy, Your Excellency. My son's in Silesia fighting for King and country. Now he's got something to come home to."

Christoph preferred Biblical rhetoric, "We'll not see the Black Horse here again."

Despite, or was it because of, their benevolent wishes, she couldn't help but feel slight pangs of guilt; she wasn't totally responsible for finding the grain in the vault – she shared that with Fermor. In her dream, he had led her to the patch of grass.

Amidst the simple thanks, there were heartfelt tears and sobs of joy. By the end, her chest was heaving with emotion and Ursula pushed a 'kerchief in her hand for her to quench the tears.

Alone in the chapel, she was filled by a profound sense of relief. She fiddled with the carved amber crucifix that hung around her neck, a treasured gift from her grandmother. It evoked memories of her childhood in Fischhausen – of playing on the amber beach, of the beauty and stillness of the Frisches Lagoon, of watching the sailing boats glide serenely along the sea canal to the Lastadie docks in Königsberg.

There was a noise coming from the vestry. She hoped it was Fermor putting away the church paraphernalia. She rapped on the door.

Footsteps echoed on the vestry flagstones. The door opened.

"Gräfin," Fermor said.

"Sexton," she said. "I would speak with you."

"Come in, how can I help?"

The room was full of surplices, gowns, scapulars and other church garments, like ghosts of the past hanging on the wall.

"Two nights ago," she began, "you appeared to me in a dream and led me to that patch of grass."

"I-I don't remember that," he stammered. "But it's comforting to know I played a part in it."

"I wanted you to know," she admitted. "There's something else. Behind one of the barrels in the vault, I found a Bible open at this page. Please, read the verse that's underlined."

She gave him the book and he read:

"A great sign appeared in heaven: a woman clothed with the sun, with the moon under her feet and a crown of twelve stars on her head."

"I thought you might know what it meant," she suggested.

"It's to do with the Adler," he said with an air of certainty.

"Why do you say that?"

"Because the crown of twelve stars is *on her head*," he said. He seemed impassioned about this Adler. "The eagle is the King of the birds, just like the head is the ruler of the body. And on the statue of Our Lady von Adler, the eagle has its claws in the Virgin Mary's *head*."

"To me, the connection to the Adler is a coincidence," she said, then took a different tack. "Answer me this: that patch of grass led us to the vault and the barrels of cereal grain. No one had been in those tunnels for years and none of my staff was even aware of their existence. So, how did you know the grain was in the vault?"

"Your Excellency, I didn't know. It's as much a mystery to me as it is to you," he hissed, like she had asked him to solve the Riddle of the Sphinx.

"Then there was the way you appeared in my dream," she went on, "your presence, your spirit was full of power, majesty and grace. Just like an eagle."

"The eagle again," he stated.

"You don't sound surprised."

"No, I'm not, Your Excellency," he said. "After Captain Gurieli stabbed me and I was hovering on the edge of death, I had a vision of an eagle. It wasn't a carnal bird, no, it was numinous, ethereal. It emerged from the bowels of the earth. Its wingspan was as wide as the Baltic Sea. It told me it was the eagle of Northern Europe, the Adler."

"Incredible, but that was only a dream."

"You say you were led to a patch of grass in a dream. Dreams are signposts. Mine was a dream vision, a revelation."

She puffed out her cheeks and let out a long, slow breath, trying to absorb what he was claiming. "Are you saying a giant eagle – an Adler – guided you to that patch of grass and subsequently the vault?"

"It could be, Your Excellency," he said.

"Then why did you appear to me in the dream in the guise of an eagle? Surely that means something?"

"Yes, I think it does," he said. "Be thankful. It means the Adler is helping others like me to find what they are looking for. You needed cereal grain. It led you to it. The Adler is all-powerful. I am its servant."

"Then answer me this," she said. "The bishop warned of false prophets and devils with wings. I refuse to believe I was led to the vault because you are a servant of the Adler or whatever demon you say you worship."

Fermor folded his arms and stared at her. "The Adler is no demon," he said.

She shook her head. "How do you know that?"

"I was born and raised in a stone croft in Scotland. I fought wars alongside my uncle against you Prussians. Now I've surrendered to a greater good. I joined the church to dedicate my life to the Adler and its divine purpose."

"No! The Adler has no divine purpose," she scoffed.

"Oh, but it does," he rebuffed her again. "The Adler brought me back to the land of the living. Only God has the power of life and death. That's how I know it's divine. And it's saved people from starving to death. That's a miracle, isn't it?"

She had to nod her head.

He continued, and asked, "Why would the Adler show you that page in the Bible? Are you also one of its servants?"

"I'm not!" she snapped. "That's what you called me in the dream – a servant of the Adler. And the Adler didn't show me the page in the Bible." The moment she spoke, doubts gathered like vultures around her. Was she a servant of the Adler? After all, the vision she had experienced of the

Adler in the Columbine Inn had filled her with the defiance to stand up to Captain Gurieli. And what was this huge mysterious bird? Despite her misgivings, the sexton seemed convinced of his mission.

He seemed to be choosing his next words, and said, "Your Excellency, be careful that your doubts don't extinguish the fire of your passion."

For a moment, her tongue was tied. Before she could answer, he got up and left.

While she was none the wiser about how he knew of the vault, at least her people had their daily bread.

Of one thing she was sure, she was no servant of the Adler.

From now on, she'd be wary of Sexton Ian Fermor.

CHAPTER 24

The Pine Tree

Be merry, Shrovetide, for to-morrow thou wilt be ashes.
MEDIEVAL PROVERB

Nearly three weeks had passed since his conversation with the Gräfin, but Fermor remained perplexed. He was a servant of the Adler and he was sure that she was one too. Why did she refuse to believe him?

He pushed these anxious thoughts to the back of his mind, because the old pastor had asked to see him. Leopold was struggling with his health; his hands were shaking like a tree branch in a howling gale. The continued rain and cold did nothing for the poor man's chest.

As Fermor arrived in the vestibule of Löwenhagen Church, Alexander's wolfhound jumped up on him and nearly knocked him over.

"Get him off me," Fermor said.

"Yes, Sexton Fermor, right away," Alexander muttered, grabbing the hound by the scruff of the neck.

The pastor said, "Today is Shrovetide so we start preparations for Eastertide. Herr Klein will build us a real cross of pine, with wood drawn from a special tree in the surrounding forests. Alas, my bones creak more than an old church gate. That's an expedition I'm going to miss. I ask you, Sexton Fermor, to go in my place to find and bless the tree."

"I'd be honoured." He was excited at the prospect.

"Good," the pastor replied. "Take these three strapping lads with you," and he gestured to Hans, Caspar and Bruno. "It'll be good experience for them. Now all of you listen to the huntsman."

Alexander doffed his cap to the pastor and said, "We're going into the Horst to search for this holy tree. There's an eyrie in that part of the forest so we'll likely see eagles."

He paused to adjust his cloth cap, and then continued, "And other wild creatures, including big brown bears and wolves and hogs. Mind you tread careful. This time o' year, near winter's end, animals are starving for a morsel. The famine lights a fire in their belly and fills their hearts with courage. They'd soon as attack and eat a man as anything else. So, heed my warning. And you three boys, you must do whatever I says, with no hesitation."

The boys nodded.

Fermor glanced at the scar that ran beneath Alexander's eye, the trophy he'd acquired from a bear fight. The bear wasn't around to tell the story. Alexander was.

Klein and his son, Bruno, shared the lead donkey. Hans was old enough to have his own. Alexander insisted on walking, his wolfhound by his side. Caspar's limp consigned him to the wagon alongside his trusty Boris. Fermor sat next to them. Rattling inside the open wagon was a variety of axes and saws.

They set off in a line as straight as the roads built by the Prussian military engineers.

Fermor asked, "Caspar, you been on one of these expeditions before?"

Caspar either didn't hear him or simply ignored him and chomped on a piece of grass. The young man always seemed wrapped tight like a noose. Fermor didn't know if it was growing pains, battlefield trauma, or youthful infatuation for Sisi.

The morning was dry and cloudy, the paths still sodden. The thick mud made for hard going. Snow lay in isolated patches. Occasionally the sunlight glittered on a clump in the upper branches of the trees.

They broached the forest path around mid-morn. It was bitter in the shade. The cold hung like tiny daggers from his ears and the tip of his nose. He pulled the lapels of his winter coat around his chest.

Fermor was curious. "Out of all the pine trees, how do you know which is the right one?"

"Can't say for sure," Klein replied. His voice was like gnarled bark. "It's wondrous, it is. Presents itself, out of the blue. You know when a cow's ready for milkin', her udder swells with the milk and she tells you. It's the same with the trees. When you see it, you know. It's obvious. You just have to look for the signs."

Alexander tapped Fermor on the shoulder. When Alexander wanted him banished, Fermor would have twitched. Not now. Not since he had helped dig out the tunnels and find the seed. Alexander was his friend and he was pointing skywards.

In the high clouds, an eagle was circling lazily, effortlessly, seemingly gazing at them, gazing at it. Its wings were as broad as an angel's. What command of the elements! Fermor had seen birds of prey at home in the Scottish Highlands, but this one was truly majestic.

Through the trees, two elk were grazing on the edge of a meadow, snouts buried in the snow trying to find grass. They raised their antlers, sniffed them with nonchalant power, and wandered off into the dark, hidden depths of the forest.

They moved on, no one saying a word, the birds gliding in circles above the treeline. The branches budded with leaves, tiny fronds of growth, the summer's future in a gloved hand. In the distance was another lake, its waters softly rippling to the tune of a gentle breeze. The eagle drifted serenely down to just above the crown of the trees and flew low over the waters of a lake, its wings barely moving. They paused to admire its grace. It was awe in motion.

Fermor was half-expecting Klein to say, 'Here it is!' at any moment, but he was laconic to say the least.

Where the undergrowth was dense, they stopped, dismounted and beat their way through it.

They entered a clearing, an open meadow. There was a squeal and a rustle in the bushes. An animal – a boar – raced across the meadow in front of them with barely a sideways glance.

There wasn't much that frightened a wild boar, even Fermor knew that.

Klein did too. "Boys, get behind me," he snapped.

Alexander crouched on his haunches, listening, watching, senses pitching. The dogs were sniffing the air.

A flock of starlings flew off in alarm. The predator was near.

"Back up," Alexander whispered. They moved under the cover of the trees.

Caspar saw it first. He pointed to a large pine tree on the edge of the clearing some fifty steps from where they stood.

"Wolf!" he whispered. The whole forest heard the word, even the trees. The birds ended their singing. Fermor felt a knot in the pit of his stomach. The lone animal sauntered into the clearing and stood in front of the pine.

Their backs arched, their snouts on the ground, the two dogs made a low growling noise from the back of their throats.

Poised like a gladiator, a grizzled old she-wolf glared at them, ready for their next move. Fermor felt his palms moisten.

"Wait for my signal!" Alexander barked at Caspar.

Both their dogs strained at the leash, rising up on their hind legs, howling at the she-wolf. Unconcerned, the she-wolf stared back with cold, empty eyes.

"Now!" Alexander yelled.

The dogs raced across the open meadow.

Despite having two opponents, the old warrior arched her back, every muscle tensed for the attack.

Alexander's dog arrived first and leapt at the wolf like a lion. The she-wolf caught the dog in her powerful claws, halting its leap. Dog and wolf scratched and tore at each other's throats. Boris pawed at the wolf, biting and barking and growling. The old she-wolf was stronger, sharper, wiser, and threw off Alexander's dog and attacked Boris, mauling him with fang and claw.

From the air, came a screech.

The bird flew over their heads and straight for the wolf. It was the eagle they'd seen earlier. It swooped onto the she-wolf, burying its talons into her back. It tried to lift the wolf off the ground, but she was too heavy – and too canny. Twisting and turning, she wriggled out of the eagle's clutches. Wincing with pain, she licked her wounds and scurried off into the penumbra.

The eagle flew off into the morning haze.

The sheer power of nature was a sight to behold. It happened so quickly. By the time Fermor got there, Alexander and Caspar were tending to their dogs. The wolf had wounded them both; their eyes were pale and empty, like they had already passed to the other side. The white snow around the base of the pine tree was dotted with clumps of fur and smeared with splashes and spots of red. The dogs' coats were matted in saliva and streaked in blood. Both bled profusely from deep scratches and vicious bites. Boris was worse. He lay on his side, trying in vain to lift his head. He peered up at his master with yearning, pitiful eyes. His throat was ripped open and his breathing was more like a horrible gurgle.

Alexander took one look at him, shook his head and said to Caspar, "You know what to do."

Alexander offered him his hunting knife.

"I's seen too much blood," Caspar said with a shake of his head. "Will you?"

Alexander nodded without hesitation.

"Fare thee well, old friend," Caspar whispered and stroked Boris for one last time.

Alexander leant the tip of the blade against the dog's heart and then plunged it up to the hilt. Boris' body shook violently then slumped into motionless silence.

Caspar knelt over him and for a moment Fermor thought the boy was going to weep openly, but all he did was close the dog's eyes.

"Sorry, lad," Alexander said.

"It's the will of the Lord," Caspar replied.

"How is yours?" Fermor asked Alexander, whose dog was limping but could walk.

"Tough as ol' boots," Alexander said. Tough as his owner, more like.

"Let's move on and find this pine tree," Fermor said.

"Why?" Klein said. "We found one. It's right here."

"Oh, yes. So it is," he said, slow to catch on.

"A wolf and an eagle aren't clear enough signs for you?" Klein said with a chuckle.

"Of course, I-I wasn't thinking," Fermor stammered.

Klein and Alexander shovelled away as much of the blood from the base of the tree as they could. Caspar cradled Boris' corpse and covered it in a muslin wrap on the wagon. He was going to take it home to bury.

Hats off, heads bowed, the three men and three boys stood in a respectful line. Fermor sprinkled holy water on the tree. After repeating verses from the Psalms, he said, "I bless this tree in the name of the Father, Son and Holy Ghost."

When he finished, Klein and Alexander wielded their axes. By the time the tree fell like some ancient Titan, the men were sweating profusely. They sawed it into manageable pieces and loaded them onto the wagon.

On the way back, Fermor reflected on the grace and savagery of nature. During his years as a sapper in the Russian Army, scouting the terrain ahead of the vanguard, he'd seen how easily a pack of wolves could down a grown man. Wolves were a constant menace and dangerous predator. Yet he'd never seen one overcome by an eagle! It was sumptuous, poetry in motion.

An eagle had pointed the way and saved their lives – again.

CHAPTER 25

The Scarlet Robe

They stripped Him and put a scarlet robe on Him.
THE GOSPEL OF MATTHEW 27:28

There was an Ursula rap at the door.

"Come in," Marion said wearily.

It wasn't Ursula, it was Hans. What a pleasant surprise. Her son lit up the room like a handsome Greek Adonis.

He smiled with those piercing blue eyes and sat down opposite her.

"Mama, I heard you weren't well," he said.

Touched by his concern, she replied, "Thank you for asking. That's the best thing that could have happened to me today. You're such a good boy. Your father and I have high hopes for you."

"I know," he said bashfully.

"One day, I'll hear the great organ resound across the aisles of Königsberg Cathedral and watch you marry a high aristocrat, after which you'll serve your country like your father and your grandfather before you."

"One day, Mama, I've not turned sixteen yet," Hans replied.

"Ah, but it's soon, isn't it?"

"Yes, in nine days, on 10th March," he said, his lower lip quivering with emotion.

She was proud to have seen him grow up into such a fine, upstanding young man. "And what are you doing to assist the estate today?"

"I'm going to Steinbeck village to Herr Klein's workshop. I'm helping to build the cross and the throne for Eastertide," he said.

"It's a long walk, so you'd better hurry up and in this rain…" She kissed her son warmly and he left.

There followed another rap on the door. This was definitely Ursula.

"How are the headaches?" Ursula wanted to know.

"They are tolerable," she said. In truth, the headaches were more severe, brought on by bright sunlight, so much so that she was growing anxious about the ambient light of summer days. For the moment though, she didn't want the whole estate knowing about it. They had enough to deal with without her burdening them with her own problems.

She changed the subject. "How are the preparations for Eastertide?"

"Going well," Ursula replied. It was like a game of cat and mouse talking with Ursula, who she knew connived to hide the more unpleasant aspects of the truth from her and this reply sounded ominously like one of those.

"I'll see for myself," Marion said. "I'll start with Cecilia," and headed out of the room.

"She's sewing the Roman soldiers' robes in the Green Room," Ursula informed her.

"I trust along the way that she's improving my daughter's skills in the gentle craft of embroidery," Marion said.

As she opened the door of the Green Room, she saw a man with his back to her, leaning over the back of a high chair. Jumping out of the chair was Sisi, who whipped around to face the man with a scowl as fierce as a wild boar. Hearing the door open behind him, the man twisted round. It was Herr Doctor Skoda, wearing a look of guilty surprise.

"What on earth is happening here?" she demanded.

"Nothing, Your Excellency, nothing at all," Skoda replied, with craven haste.

"It doesn't look like nothing to me. Sisi, are you well?" she asked, taking her daughter's hand. It was cold. Something had frightened her.

"Yes, I am fine, Mama," Sisi replied.

Her first impression was that he had been flirting with Sisi. Whatever had happened, he had made her daughter feel uncomfortable. Either way, it couldn't, it wouldn't happen again.

"Herr Skoda," she said, "it's quite inappropriate for you to be alone with my daughter."

"Yes, I-I…" he stammered, prickly about the reprimand.

"I'll give you the benefit of the doubt this time, but I never want to find you in such a compromising position again. Is that understood?"

"Y-yes, Your Excellency. Cecilia was just here, she'll be back…" Skoda replied, glancing expectantly at the door.

Cecilia's heavy footsteps conveniently filled the room. Sensing the air of dispute, she asked, "Who? Oh, it's you, Your Excellency…"

"Cecilia," Marion said, "tell me, was Doctor Skoda here when you left the room?"

"Mais oui, he was admiring our embroidery," she replied.

"I suspect that wasn't all he was admiring," Marion said. "You should not have left him alone with my daughter. She is of that vulnerable age that requires a chaperone at all times with male visitors, even an accomplished physician."

"I understand, Your Excellency, I'm sorry. I only left for a moment. It won't happen again," Cecilia replied.

"Apology accepted," Marion said and in a lighter tone, she added, "Now, this embroidery. I'm keen to see the fruits of your labours."

Cecilia motioned her towards a trestle table, on which was spread a long piece of scarlet material. "This is my work." Cecilia pointed to her exquisite embroidery of a Maltese cross on the hem of the cloak.

Marion peered at Sisi, who was standing with her back to her mother in front of the fireplace, rubbing and warming her hands.

"Sisi, dearest, come over here and show me what you've done," she said.

Sisi ignored her.

"Sisi," she repeated. "Let me see your developing embroidery skills."

Sisi turned in a huff, strode over to the trestle table and picked up a piece of the scarlet material. "Here it is, Mother."

Marion was pleasantly surprised. The embroidery was fine and neat, intricate, and clearly the product of strong and enduring powers of concentration. "My, this is good. And an improvement on the snowdrops you did on the 'kerchief."

"Do you think so?" Sisi said, ingenuous to the last.

"I do," Marion replied. "Let me see it so I can compare."

"I-I don't have it with me, Mother."

"Well, fetch it for me."

"I-I think I might have mislaid it," Sisi stammered.

"Mislaid? Are you sure? You are normally very careful with your things."

In a matter of moments, Sisi's face changed from her normal calm, relaxed countenance, to a visage of unadulterated fury. Her daughter burst into tears and raged, "If you must know, I gave it to Caspar as a keepsake. Is that what you wanted to hear?"

"I won't be disrespected by you, young lady. Go to your chambers, please."

Tears streaming down her face, Sisi stormed out of the room and slammed the door behind her for good measure.

Marion glanced at Cecilia, as if asking for an explanation for her daughter's errant behaviour. She received one too.

"Your Excellency, Caspar is maudlin over the brutal death of his Boris," Cecilia said. "Sisi is helping him mourn. La mort, comme ç'est dur pour les enfants."

"I see," Marion replied, as Cecilia went to attend to her charge. "I wish someone had told me."

There was only so much mollycoddling she could do. Her daughter would have to grow up and accept that life and death were equal parts of an unforgiving world.

CHAPTER 26

The Bonesetter

Kindness breaks no bones.
GERMAN PROVERB

Since early morning Mass, Fermor had been digging out the blocked ditches around the little cemetery by the chapel. The spade squelched in the sodden earth as he plunged it into mud. The rain was falling vertically out of a late March sky. He heaved another shovel out of the ditch, which finally cleared the blockage. A dribble flowed through the newly-formed gap. He cleared away more twigs, leaves and other debris snagging the ditch.

As he returned to the chapel, Doctor Skoda was leaving.

"How is the pastor?" Fermor asked.

"He's struggling with a fever," Skoda replied and hastened by him.

Fermor had seen a few barber surgeons and physicians hacking men's limbs in battlefield tents of the Russian Army. He wasn't impressed with them and he wasn't impressed with Skoda. The doctor had visited old Leopold thrice in as many days and despite his recipe of cold baths and bleeding with leeches, the fever persisted.

The pastor came into the vestibule. Hands on thighs, he burst into a prolonged bout of coughing and spat a gob of rheum into his 'kerchief.

"Here, allow me," Fermor said and gently ushered him into the warmth of the vestry. In the five months living and working in the chapel, he had grown attached to the pastor in a filial kind of way and was taking on more of the old man's duties. As well as the search for the holy pine tree, he had conducted today's Mass for the Feast of the Annunciation.

Pastor Leopold wiped his nose with his 'kerchief and said, "Eastertide is near. Find some Christ thorn to bind into a crown. Oh, and let me know how Herr Klein is getting on."

"I will, Pastor," he replied. Grabbing his hat and walking stick, he headed out of the chapel. Leaving the Schloss through the main entrance was young Herr Hans von Adler, also on his way to Steinbeck. Fermor liked the boy. In him, he saw a mirror of his own naive exuberance for life at that age. He walked in silence, listening to the soft thrum of the rain falling on the lake and the sound of their feet sloshing through the puddles.

He noticed the top of the pine trees and said to Hans, "Let me show you the wonder of nature. See the tips of those pine trees, the yellow shoots?"

"Yes, they are just like yellow crosses," the boy replied, his eyes wide in admiration.

"They're new growth," he replied. "As Easter approaches, the tallest shoots branch off and form those immaculate pine-tree crosses."

They admired the scores of crosses on the tips of the pine tree, until Hans declared, "I'm going to fetch one for Mama."

"No, wait," he cried. "They're too high up."

Despite the damp wood, impetuous young Hans scaled the lower part of the tree like a monkey.

Fermor stared into the hanging mist, trying to see how far the lad had climbed.

About halfway up, Hans dangled from a branch with one hand and cried excitedly, "Sexton, I can see them. I'm nearly there."

"Come back down," Fermor shouted to him.

Too late. As Hans turned towards the trunk, he lost his footing on the slippery branch. He fell and immediately grabbed a hold of a lower branch. He hung there, one hand clutching the bough, the other flailing in the mists. He lost his grip and fell. Plummeting to the ground through the haze of swirling rain, his body thudded into the sodden earth.

Stunned and confused, the boy came round. Thank the Lord he was alive.

"Can you get up?"

"Err, I-I think so," Hans said, groggy. With the aid of his walking stick, he propped the boy up in a standing position. As soon as Hans put weight on his foot, he screamed and collapsed on the ground in a heap.

"My ankle," he moaned, his face wrought tight in agony.

"I'm going for help," Fermor said, laying his coat over the boy. He ran to the chapel. Frantically, he rang the alarm bell. Hands on haunches, he waited. Folks gathered in the forecourt. The Gräfin arrived first. How did she always manage to do that?

Umbrella in hand, Ursula was saying to her, "Put on something warm. You'll catch your death."

"You sound like my mother," she snapped back. "Sexton, what is it?"

"It's Hans! He fell from a tree!" he shouted between breaths.

"Where?" she asked.

"Over there. By the big pine!"

Amelia, Alexander and the other staff rushed over to Hans, who was clutching his right ankle as if his foot was about to detach itself from his leg.

"Mama, it hurts like hell!" he cried.

"Oh, my poor Hans," the Gräfin said.

She turned to Fermor. With fury in her voice, she muttered, "Why in heaven's name did you let him climb a tree in such treacherous weather?"

"I… I was showing him the pine crosses and…"

"All this for… pine crosses?" she interrupted him. "I know I'm not perfect, but I think you should have tried harder to stop him."

"It was an unfortunate accident," he conceded.

"I accept your apology but you have severely disappointed me," she said.

"I am so sorry, Your Excellency." He was as craven as he could be. Oh, what had he done! The Gräfin, the one person with whom he wanted to keep good relations, had publicly condemned him. The guilt weighed heavily on his soul.

"He can't walk, so fetch the horse and trap," the Gräfin said.

Sloshing through the mud, Grenda brought the trap. The men hauled the boy onto it like a sack of potatoes and took him to the main entrance.

By the time Hans was in his room and dried off, Sisi arrived by his bedside and was showering her younger brother with prayers and sympathy. With no sign of Skoda, Alexander examined the boy's ankle, twisting it roughly this way and that, making a cracking, grinding noise. The boy was yelling and crying tears of pain.

"It's gone," Alexander announced. Well, he should know, he was the bonesetter.

"And…?" the Gräfin asked.

In walked Doctor Skoda, all knees and elbows.

"What's happened here?" he asked in that impertinent way of his.

"His ankle, Doctor," Alexander was saying. "It's swollen as big as a carrion crow's egg and just as black."

"I can see that for myself," Skoda said, pushed Alexander out of the way and grabbed the boy's ankle.

"Ow! That hurts!" Hans screamed.

"That's a clean break," Skoda pronounced.

"Nah. It's not broken." Alexander shook his head.

"Are you…?" Skoda stared at him, purple with indignation that someone should contradict him.

"Aye, Doctor, I'll show you," Alexander said, manipulating the boy's ankle, eliciting screams that lifted the roof. "Look. See, there's no movement in them bones."

"Stop that!" the Gräfin said. "You're causing him great pain!"

"Sorry, Your 'cellency!" Alexander said. "Sprain or break, he needs one of them splints. I got me some wood in the shed," and he headed off to fetch it. Amelia found some linen bandages in her medicine pouch with which to attach it to his leg.

The Gräfin had a suggestion. "Please, Herr Doctor, give him laudanum for the pain."

"Ah. There's a thing. I-I lost my supplies on the journey from Vienna," he said apologetically.

"No laudanum!" She shook her head. "What kind of doctor are you?"

"One that came in a hurry to serve Your Excellency," he replied.

"Yes, I suppose you did and you saved Egor's life," she reflected. "Well, find Grenda. He'll take you to the apothecary in Königsberg. Make haste. I don't want my child enduring this agony any longer than necessary."

"Yes, Your Excellency," Skoda said and scuttled out of the door.

What was the matter with these men? First Fermor had let her down – again – and now Skoda. How could the doctor have no laudanum?

The irony of it all was that the man who had excelled himself was the most awkward cuss of them all, Alexander the bonesetter.

CHAPTER 27

The King of the Jews

And twisting together a crown of thorns,
They placed it on His head and put a reed in His right hand.
Kneeling before Him, they mocked Him, saying,
'Hail, King of the Jews!'
THE GOSPEL OF MATTHEW 27:28

Filaments of mist snaked out of the ground. The air was damp and cool. Fermor liked the fragrant odours of the earth. He wondered if that was the smell that Adam and Eve encountered on leaving the Garden of Eden.

Accustomed to arriving in the fields early, the villagers gathered in the chapel at Ludwigshain in the dawn shadows of that April Good Friday morn. Fermor heard snippets of their conversation. With a mixture of joy and relief, many spoke about the planting and the seeding they'd done in the last few days, although most of the staff seemed keen to find out who Pastor Leopold would choose to carry the cross of Our Lord in the re-enactment of the Passion of Jesus. It was a highly prestigious role.

Outside the chapel, Alexander was crowing about examining Her Excellency's son. As his wife approached, Alexander turned away, spat with prodigious energy, and trod the spittle into the earth.

Amelia rolled her eyes and said, "Watering God's earth, are we now?"

Alexander must have had the skin of one of those thick hides Fermor had seen in the tannery, because Alexander ignored her jibes and busied himself with more last-minute preparations.

When the Gräfin approached, they went quiet. Her air was full of dignity, her eagle's gaze overseeing everything.

From the lake path came a woman in black. It was Katharina. She'd not changed that mourning dress for over two moons. She stumbled along like a drunkard. But she hadn't been drinking; the grief had taken hold and was squeezing the life out of her, drop by precious drop. Oblivious to their presence on the forecourt, she was speaking to herself, or to some invisible personage. It turned out she was regaling the ghost of her dead husband.

"Why did you have to die? Why did you have to leave me alone?" she was saying, and then broke down in tears, pressing her hands in prayer, and apologising profusely.

Doctor Skoda went to her, but she shrugged him off viciously, shouting, "Don't touch me!"

Marion whispered to him, "Help her, she's unwell."

Despite her protestations, Katharina allowed him to take her inside the Schloss.

Pastor Leopold, still recovering from the rheum, shuffled out of the church wearing the black robes befitting the anniversary of the crucifixion of Our Lord. Everyone had assembled in a large crescent around the entrance.

After another heavy bout of coughing, he said, "You want to know who I've chosen. It's someone who has journeyed close to death and lived to tell the tale. It's someone who meets our goodly notions of piety and who works relentlessly for Our Lord. That's why the person who is to play the part of Jesus the Christ in our Eastertide celebrations is Sexton Fermor."

Fermor gave his ears a rub. He glanced around. The people were applauding, smiling. It was true. He wasn't imagining it. Despite the many loyal servants of the estate around him, it was he, Fermor, who was chosen. His heart was bursting out of his chest he felt so proud. Even the birds were singing a sweet chorale.

Amelia placed the embroidered scarlet robe around his shoulders.

"This is how the Roman soldiers clothed our gracious Lord," the pastor said. "And taunted him, calling him 'King'."

Fermor knelt and kissed the cross. The wood was cold and damp on his lips. He put his shoulder beneath the burden of the cross. My, it felt so light, like he was lifting air. He dragged the cross the first few tentative steps.

The path to follow was the Via Dolorosa, the Way of Sorrow. Alexander walked in front of him, clearing the way. Folks congregated along the circular route he was to take – once around the outside of the church and back to where he started. Others formed a procession behind him, encouraging his labours and enhancing his passion with fervent prayers.

With each step, the cross became heavier. Beads of sweat rolled down his face. His shoulders ached; his breath was laboured. He dragged the cross around one side of the church, when a pain stabbed him in the side, from the wound – the one inflicted by Captain Gurieli. He fell on his knees and the cross thumped on the ground beside him.

"Here," a voice whispered in his ear. "Let me help."

He looked up. His vision was clouded. His head was spinning. Slowly, it came to a stop.

"Who are you?" he murmured.

"Alexander," the voice said. "That be my name."

Alexander lifted him up.

"Alexander, are you helping me?" he murmured.

"Of course, lad." Alexander hauled the cross up and over Fermor's shoulder.

As they reached the next turn, Fermor stopped for breath, exhausted physically and emotionally. The sins of the world were a lead weight, impossibly heavy. He struggled to take another step. The villagers followed, chanting the praises of the Lord.

A woman stood in the crowd, wearing a veil and a pale blue cloak.

"Mother? Is that you?" he asked. He hadn't thought of his mother since the night of the stabbing.

"No." The voice was as soft as a rose petal. "It's me, Marion Gräfin von Adler."

He grunted. His knees were weak. His head was pounding. There was a ringing in his ears. The beads of sweat dripping over his eyes made it hard to see.

Another voice said, "Let me wipe your face."

"Who's that?" He peered into the gloom. His shirt was drenched in perspiration.

"Sisi." The voice was as gentle as a lamb.

On his face, the cloth rested, cool, easing his suffering. In his side, the pain throbbed. He stepped forward.

"This is the Way of Sorrow, this is the Way of Grief," Alexander announced. The crowd echoed his chant. The effort of carrying the weight of all those sins made Fermor's head spin and he stumbled and fell for a second time.

Alexander helped him. Together they struggled with the cross, a deep trough in the ground behind them testament to their slow, unwieldy progress. Eventually they arrived back at the front of the church. Fermor shrugged off the cross and slumped to his knees next to a wooden throne. The villagers gathered in a circle around him.

Pastor Leopold was waiting. After another bout of coughing, he said, "They mocked Our Lord, saying, 'Come! Be seated on your throne!'"

Fermor could hardly stand, let alone ascend the wooden throne. His stomach in spasms, he vomited. His side was burning a hole right through him. Alexander helped him stand. Every word the pastor spoke seemed to intensify Fermor's unremitting agony.

A flight of swifts flew above the crowd, ducking and diving. A sight to behold, they carried on their merry dance. As if in response to some unseen sigil, they moved off in a susurration in the direction of the valley.

"This is a sign," the pastor said. "We are one with Mother Nature."

Fermor felt a weight press down on his head like an invisible cloud, his scalp unravelling along the seams, the pain excruciating.

The pastor asked Fermor, "Are you ready to be the true King?"

At first, his mind was scrambled. The true King? Then he realised what it meant, and he replied, "Yes."

With that admission, there came a flash of realisation.

A true King neither rules over a kingdom, nor possesses a tract of land.
Royalty is not a place; it's a state of mind.
To be King means to be master of myself.
And responsible for my actions.
Then may I fashion myself in the furnace of enlightenment.
And act in full concord with God's design and purpose.

That instant was crystal clear. Not only the rays of light and the way they played through the buds on the trees, but also the way Egor and Nicol were juggling pine cones at the back of the crowd, blithely oblivious to the gravitas of the moment.

In that epiphany, he knew many things. He knew about the innocent but burgeoning affection between Sisi and Caspar. He knew which of the Gräfin's ancestors had built the vault and opened the Bible at that page. He knew these things with the ease of waking up from slumber.

Above all, he knew how to assist the Adler.

Pastor Leopold picked up something from the table, shuffled over and stood next to him. He also knew the pastor was not long for this world.

The pastor lifted his hand above Fermor's head and cried out, "Hail the King."

Fermor felt something sting his head. A blinding pain shot through it. Everything in him shrank. The thorns dug into the soft flesh of his scalp like a knife through dough. Darkness fell across his eyes and the light disappeared.

There was something sharp and pointed, like a score of jutting pins around the top of his head. "What have you put on my head?"

"A crown of thorns," the pastor said.

Moments before Fermor blacked out, the pastor said, "You are the King of the Jews and this is your coronation!"

CHAPTER 28

The Way of the Lord

We live for the State of Ostpreussen,
And the State lives for us.
With mutual benefit and advancement,
Everyone improves inside it.
MEDIEVAL TESTIMONY

Fermor felt a renewed vigour in his step. He knew what he had to do to serve the Adler: act in accordance with its purposes.

By Easter Sunday, he was sufficiently recovered to assist at Mass. With sore back and arms, he helped Leopold into his crisp white liturgical vestments and placed the gold scapular around the pastor's shoulders. While Fermor felt physically exhausted, he had not expected to feel so emotionally uplifted. The experience of the Way of Sorrow had elevated him into a state of religious ecstasy.

The service opened with the singing of a psalm. The Gräfin and her family in the front pew joined in with gusto, as did Christoph and Kadow. Cecilia sang out of tune, as usual.

With fire and brimstone, Leopold launched into his sermon, "We have to fight for what we believe in. That is the Way of the Lord. He was not sent to make life easy for us. Neither sycophant, nor follower, he was a man of faith and conviction, a God's man. During Passover, he drove the merchants from the Temple of Jerusalem. He berated the moneylenders and overturned their tables. Why do you think he did that?"

The pastor puffed out his cheeks. When no answer came, he wagged his finger like he was possessed by the spirit of the Holy Ghost.

"You've forgotten? I'll remind you," he thundered. "The temple was not, and is not, a house of commerce. It is His Father's house. God made this world and we are His children. God's house is not just the church.

You and everything around you belongs to Him. He is the Creator of the air you breathe, the fire that keeps you warm in the winter, the water you drink, and the earth which yields your food. Take what we need from the earth, but rape her not. Fight we must against the sin of greed and the iniquity of blind commercial gain."

An awkward silence descended. Folks shuffled uncomfortably on their seats. A dog began barking outside. Fermor noticed the pastor was shaking from head to foot.

"The purpose of our lives," the pastor went on, "is to find ways to give thanks for life's multitude of blessings. Pray, practise piety and improve yourself, that's the Way of the Lord."

The pastor slammed the Holy Book shut. All of a sudden, as if he was struck by lightning, his body twitched uncontrollably. His hand shot above his head and knocked off his biretta hat, which twisted in the air, before floating serenely to the ground. Leopold grabbed his head with both hands like he was trying to prevent it from unravelling. His eyes glared wildly as if he had seen an apparition of the Devil. A bubble of spittle crept out from the corner of his mouth. With a prolonged sigh, he collapsed onto the floor.

Fermor got to him first. "He's still breathing!"

With Konstantin's help, they moved him onto a table in the vestry. Doctor Skoda picked up the biretta and followed behind. As Skoda examined the old man, Marion entered the room.

"Please, retire to your chambers, Your Excellency," Skoda said to her. "These trying episodes can only cause you discomfort."

"That's kind of you to say, Herr Doctor," she replied. "For me, this is anything but a trying episode. Leopold has been the pastor here for nigh on sixty years. He has seen famines and fought robbers; he gave the last rites to my dear mother and father, blessed my marriage and baptised my children. He is part of the soul of the community and I care deeply for his welfare. Regardless of your opinion, I *will* stay to see how he is."

Skoda took a step back and said, "As you wish."

"You will address me as Your Excellency," she rebuked him.

"Your Excellency," he added, like a little boy caught with his fingers in the honey pot.

"Good, I'm glad that's understood," she said. "Now tell me, what's wrong with him? Will he recover?"

Skoda cleared his throat. "He has a bad case of rheum. I've prescribed him baths and herbs."

"And they didn't help," Fermor said.

"And he's just had a terrible spasm," she said. "I ask again, what is wrong with him?"

"And there's his head," Skoda said hastily, pointing to the pastor's balding scalp.

"What's wrong with his head?" Marion asked.

"His fontanelles are open," Skoda replied.

"Fontanelles? What are they?"

"You won't have heard of them. They've only just been medically identified," Skoda said.

He could be pompous when he wanted to be. "Enlighten us. What exactly is a fontanelle?" she asked.

"It's a hollow gap, a soft line between the bones of the skull," Skoda replied. "There are five of them, separating the six bones of the scalp. They run across the top of the head and there are other soft lines down the side of his scalp. Everyone's got them. At birth and in very young children, the gaps are noticeable."

"And after that?" she asked.

"The gaps close as we grow up," he said. "I learnt of them during my superior training at the University of Vienna. That's how I was able to advise Sasha to remove the towelling from Joachim's head."

"So you did," she said appreciatively.

Herr Doctor replied, "See here, the pastor's fontanelles are as wide open as a baby's."

"Why are they so open in an old man?"

"The spasm was caused by bad vapours trapped inside him. They are seeping out through the rheum and through the open fontanelles, but that's clearly not enough to release them all."

Fermor squirmed inside at what he was hearing. When he touched his own head, it was as soft as the pastor's. Was he, Fermor, going to have fits too? Was he suffering from bad vapours? He glanced at the Gräfin, who frantically made the sign of the cross. She seemed to fear that too.

The Gräfin asked the doctor the very question burning a hole in his head, "What treatment do you suggest?"

"He is entangled by the cords of the wicked," Skoda said, as arrogant as ever. "They must be cut asunder."

Fermor felt a shiver down his spine. This was not going to end well.

"Are you actually suggesting trepanning?" Marion stammered.

"Why yes," Skoda said. "What else is there? If I don't operate, he'll die."

"If you do operate," she said, "he'll die."

"Far from it. Many survive."

Marion frowned. "Yes, as blubbering idiots. I witnessed trepanning performed by the Potsdam Players."

"I am not a member of a circus," Skoda said stiffly. "Trepanning is an established medical practice accepted by the great physicians and barber surgeons of the day."

"That may be. Though in my opinion, it's primitive, cruel and barbaric," the Gräfin said.

Fermor could sense the open fontanelles in his own scalp. He had the feeling his head was held together by a mesh of twine. Moving his head quickly, or sneezing, or turning it sharply, struck the fear of God in him, lest the twine unravel and his head burst asunder.

The one relief was that Her Excellency shared his opinion of trepanning.

Finally, she said, "I will fight for what I believe in, that is the Way of the Lord."

CHAPTER 29

Te Deum

Yet only one woman dies and the nation revives;
Nay, is sustained by that power most eager to seek her destruction.
What dependence may be placed on human affairs
If the merest trifles can change the fate of empires?
Such are the spoils of Fortune who,
Laughing at the vain prudence of mortals,
Excites the hopes of some and pulls down
The high expectations of others.
KING FREDERICK THE GREAT

Marion was standing by the window, early May moonbeams dancing through the curtains. Out of the night came a terrifying squawk. An eagle, flying low over the treetops, was bearing down on her. It kept coming. Beak open, wings wide, it was heading straight for her. It was going to smash through the window and plunge its talons into her soft skull.

Relentless, it swooped down. She saw its eyes, gazing at hers, gazing at its.

No! Stop!

Then… at the last moment, the harrowing cry of a lone wolf unnerved the aerial beast, and it veered away and up and over the roof.

She awoke, panting, her body covered in sweat. Outside, the rain fell softly on the roof, making a constant thrumming.

The Adler was threatening her sanity. What could she do? Seek help from the bishop? He'd condemn her for hearing the voice of a false prophet. Confess to Fermor? He'd make her a servant of the Adler, the very beast that had just attacked her. Confide in Skoda? No, he'd remove parts of her scalp and trepan her. Heaven forbid!

A loud knocking at the main front door resonated through the Schloss.

A few moments later, there was a strident rap at her befroom door.

"Urgh, come in," she groaned. "Who is that at this early hour?"

Ursula brought news. "A messenger is asking for Your Excellency."

"Who sent him?"

"I don't know, Your Excellency," Ursula said. "I ain't seen him before. But he's wearin' leather, so serves someone posh."

"Tell him I'm coming," Marion said, throwing off the bedclothes.

As she came down the spiral staircase, she could hear strains of a lively conversation between Otto and the messenger outside the door. Moments later, they burst into laughter. What was funny?

When she arrived at the bottom of the stairs, Konstantin emerged out of the vestibule, pulling Egor and Nicol by the scruff of the neck, one scruff in each hand, both boys dripping wet from the rain.

"Remind me again what you said you were doing in the dark outside?" he was saying.

"Father, we were chasing owls." That was Egor. Who else?

"Chasing owls, eh?" Konstantin scoffed. "Did you chase any wolves while you were there?"

"No, Father, there were no wolves," Nicol replied, in all innocence.

"I need a drink," Konstantin said as he hauled them off to their rooms.

As Marion reached the front door, with Otto still chatting amiably to the messenger, a slight figure sneaked into the house. It was a girl in riding attire.

"Sisi!" Marion cried.

"Mother," Sisi replied, a guilty look on her face like a rash. "I – I've been out for an early morning ride. I got caught in the rain shower."

"So I see," she replied. "Well, will you join me to break the fast?"

Sisi shook her head and muttered something inaudible under her breath before scuttling off to her chambers.

The messenger stood outside the front door, a huge wooden structure as old as the Ark. The man's brown leather overcoat was splattered with mud and grime and his face was like the bark of a gnarled oak.

"Who's your master?" she asked him.

"Graf Finck von Finckenstein, Your Excellency," the messenger replied. The man sounded as prickly as a thistle and wore a wicked twinkle in his eye.

"Otto, you know you're keeping a messenger from the King's chief minister in the rain?" she scolded him playfully.

Otto smiled – for the night porter, a rare occurrence indeed.

The messenger stepped into the vestibule and said, "Here's a letter from him, Your Excellency."

She read it.

Immediately, she knelt on the ground. Lifting the letter to the heavens, she cried, "*Te Deum Laudamus*! Thee of God we praise! The celebratory hymn is to be sung today in Königsberg Cathedral and in all the churches of the land."

"Why? What's happened?" Ursula asked, her eyes sparkling with expectation.

Marion gripped the letter like it was a Communion wafer and said, "The Russians have sued for peace. They're preparing to return their conquered lands to us."

"Praise the Lord!" Ursula cried.

Even Otto bent the knee. He wasn't often religious, but he was today.

"Get ready, we're going to Königsberg," Marion said.

"It's only just dawn," Ursula was quick to point out.

"It's a midday service. Sisi must come – oh, and Sexton Fermor and Skoda. And… where is the Herr Doctor?"

"Here," Skoda said, walking down the stairs. "I've just removed your son's splint. He'll be able to walk again soon."

My, how the Lord's goodness was shining on them today.

When Marion arrived in Königsberg, the cathedral was swathed with victory banners, some torn by shellfire, others boasting the mud and glory of the battlefield. Draped high up along the nave, choir and transept, were rows of the Kingdom of Prussia flags, the gold-crowned black eagle, wings spread, claws grasping at sword and sceptre. Every pew full, the congregation spilled into the aisles.

They passed two distinguished gentlemen surrounded by an excited entourage of young dilettantes. Marion introduced one of them to Doctor Skoda.

"Herr Doctor," she said, "may I introduce the Professor Immanuel Kant of the University of Königsberg?"

"A great honour, sir," Skoda said, with a curt bow.

"Pleased to make your acquaintance," Kant said. "You are the Gräfin's new physician?"

"I am, sir, and you must be the renowned philosopher?" he asked.

"You flatter me," Kant said, in that crisp way he had of speaking. "And this is Doctor Daniel Rolander," and he introduced a bearded, Scandinavian gentleman with bright, clear blue eyes.

"My pleasure," Rolander said with a courteous bow.

"Doctor Rolander," Kant went on, "has recently returned from a voyage to Surinam in South America where he was collecting specimens. He is a keen apostle of the work of Professor Carl Linnaeus. Tomorrow he's giving a lecture at the Prussian Academy which I'm sure you'll find of enormous interest."

"Thank you for the invitation," Marion said. "We shall certainly attend." They took their seats next to Dieter and Aunt Charlotte.

The singing of the opening psalm was glorious, spurred on by the huge organ and a groundswell of relief and joy.

The bishop began his sermon. "Brethren, on this unique day in the history of Ostpreussen, I speak to you on the theme of human genius," he said, his voice echoing high amongst the rafters. "Human purpose is to mirror God's purpose. That is achieved by improving and enhancing Creation. Humanity moves closer to God by fulfilling His purposes!"

Marion was enraptured by the vision of the bishop, who followed the fledgling but exciting Lutheran movement of Pietism. The bishop continued in the same vein, "And what do we call a person whose creations are the image or mirror of divine wisdom and spiritual purpose? A genius. And do not think that being a genius is only for our own Immanuel Kant, we can all be our own geniuses."

A flutter of applause swept around the cathedral.

"In the natural world," the bishop went on, "harmony can be produced by God. God has sown the seeds. The task of the human race is to nourish those seeds and bring them to fruition. That is how we can drive the living world upwards towards ever greater perfection, in which we, the human race, are the most important and highest part."

With these profound words ringing in her ears, the chorister orchestrated the singing. It was so beautiful it sent shivers up her spine.

"Lord God, thy praise we sing,
Lord God, our thanks we bring.
Father in eternity:
All the world worships thee."

The singing of the *Te Deum* had a healing effect on those present. All those years of war, dissolved in a paean of peace. All those war-dead, remembered. All those victories, celebrated. The defeats, forgotten. Now the glory, for God.

"Let shine on us, O God, thy face:
Our only hope is in thy grace.
Our trust, O Lord, is all in thee:
O let us ne'er confounded be."

When the last note dissipated into the cathedral heights, a pall of silence descended on the congregation. It was as if everyone held their breath, waiting, wanting, and expecting a divine presence to reveal itself. It marked the end of a long, bitter road. Now the light of peace beaconed ahead and the brotherhood of man could once again take pride of place amidst the ruins of nearly seven years of war.

For the first time in a long while, Marion experienced that elusive feeling of quiet settlement, when the vicissitudes of life dropped away. It left her with a sense of belonging, when the spirit filled her life and her life filled the spirit. It was accompanied by a profound sense of homecoming.

"Fiat pax! Let there be peace!" the bishop cried. Everyone turned to their neighbour, looked them in the eye and shared a sign of peace.

Along the way to Dieter's house in Junkerstrasse, they passed the Columbine Inn. Hundreds of revellers were gathered outside, drunk on the intoxication of the moment, and prodigious quantities of vodka and beer. French Andre was leading the secular communion service.

Back at the town house, Eleonore served drinks. They raised their glasses to toast the peace.

Philip interrupted their celebrations, saying, "There's that man at the door again, sir."

"Which man?" Dieter wanted to know.

The butler handed him the man's card.

"Ah! Von Lehndorff," Dieter said, jumping up. "Show him in."

Heinrich Graf von Lehndorff strode in and kissed the ladies' hands and then said, "Herr von Bernstein, now that the Russians have sued for peace, the King wishes to commence the construction of the Amber Room with immediate effect."

"More wonderful news," Marion said. Sisi clapped her hands in joy.

Dieter stood up and paced the floor excitedly and spoke of practical considerations. "First, I require funds to buy the spare parts to repair the pumps. When can the King release them?"

"Very soon," von Lehndorff replied with delightful ambiguity.

"Excellent," Dieter replied. "The King's decision is timely. Because Captain Lester from whom I can order the parts, is on board his ship, which is docked at this precise moment in the Lastadie docks."

"Send for him!" von Lehndorff said with an air of triumph.

"I will," Dieter replied and made the arrangements.

"Now I must take your leave. I am to the front line. The King is already planning the next offensive," von Lehndorff said, standing up and adjusting his monocle.

"Offensive? I thought we had made peace," Dieter asked.

"With Russia, but not with the Habsburgs," von Lehndorff said.

His ominous remark laid a pall of silence over them.

Later, Philip interrupted their discussions to announce the arrival of Captain Donald Lester.

"Show him in," Dieter said.

Marion wanted to meet this man of the sea.

A barrel of a man of about forty years rolled into the room, wearing a frayed navy blue uniform with a captain's shoulder lapels. Bringing the freshness of the sea with him, he shook Dieter's hand with a firm sailor's grip and introduced himself. When he got to Fermor, Lester raised an eyebrow and asked, "Fermor? Ian Fermor? I know you, don't I?"

"Yes, you most certainly do," Fermor said, shaking Lester's hand. "You are part of the story that brought me here. You hired me as an engineering apprentice on *The Lion Rampant*. You knew my uncle and when we docked in St. Petersburg, you introduced me to him."

"General Wilhelm von Fermor! Yes, how could I forget him?" Lester said, with a beaming smile. "I see from your cloth that you now pursue a different course."

"I'm now sexton at Schloss Ludwigshain," Fermor replied.

"I wish you well in your new vocation," he replied. Then Lester turned to Dieter and said, "This is a meeting of old friends, Herr von Bernstein. We have also met before; some years ago, I delivered Newcomen engines to your amber mine. How can I be of service today?"

"I require valves, pistons and spare parts for those same two Newcomen engines," Dieter explained. "I'm proud to say that the commission for the work comes from the King himself."

"The King, eh? That should grease the wheels of progress," Lester said.

"And the cost?" Dieter asked.

"Give me the full list of the parts you require and I'll produce a bill of sale," Lester said.

"What are your terms of payment?"

"I can source the parts in Glasgow from my own funds," Lester said with a cheerful tone. "When I return here with them, I'll need half the funds. The other half you'll pay me when the parts are installed and commissioned."

"Agreed," Dieter said. "The King wishes to proceed expeditiously, so when can you make this happen?"

Dieter rubbed his hands. "Your God looks kindly on Ostpreussen today, because I set sail for Scotland on tomorrow's dawn tide."

"Excellent," Dieter said. "Oh, and there's one other matter. The spare parts and the machines require specialist instrumentation knowledge. Can you bring an engineer back from Glasgow with you?"

"I could," Lester said. "But you have an engineer right here."

"Who do you mean?" Dieter asked.

"Fermor, Ian Fermor," Lester declared. "He's a trained instrumentalist and engineer. Ask him. He's as qualified as anyone I know to do that for you."

"Much as I'd like to help," Fermor said, "I'm sorry, my first duty is to my new parish."

"Then I'll bring a fitter back with me," Lester said. "I could ask James Watt. Remember him?"

"How could I forget him? He and I were on the same instrumentation course in London," Fermor added.

"I saw him a month or so ago, he was trying to refine the inner workings of the Newcomen engine," Lester replied. "He'd be a perfect candidate."

"Yes, he would," Fermor replied. "I look forward to meeting him again and sharing a wee dram or two."

They sealed the agreement and made one last toast, "*Te Deum Laudamus*!"

CHAPTER 30

The Prussian Academy

Because love grows by works of love,
Man thereby becomes better.
MARTIN LUTHER

The Prussian Academy of Arts and Sciences was a large building with a brushed stone facade in the Egyptian style situated in the middle of the old city of Altstadt. Such was the interest Rolander's lecture had stirred up, Fermor, Marion and Skoda struggled to get near it.

Outside the academy, she read the pamphlet:

> *The highly regarded Doctor Daniel Rolander of the University of Uppsala, Sweden, and honoured Member of the Prussian Academy of Sciences, will speculate on the matter of the advancement of mankind through history and into the future.*

Greeting old friends as they entered, they passed down a corridor, along which were hung portraits of the noble families of Prussia, the von Finckensteins, the von Seydlitzs and the von Lehndorffs, amongst others. It lifted her spirits to be surrounded by such an extraordinary group of like-minded human beings, aiming to serve the land on behalf of God. On days like this, the passion for her country coursed through her veins more than ever.

The main auditorium was a high-ceiled rococo gallery, adorned with a life-size painting of King Frederick I on one side of the chamber, alongside tapestries depicting his great victories of Mollwitz and Hohenfridberg during the war of Austrian succession earlier in the century. On the other side was a marble statue of King Frederick the Great and tapestries celebrating his more recent victories of Leuthen and Zorndorf.

Immanuel Kant introduced Doctor Rolander. After acknowledging the applause, Rolander began:

"Lords, ladies and gentlemen, thank you for coming. I am going to reveal the visionary fruit of my long years of labour in taxonomy and classification and much more. The basis for this was inspired by the work of the naturalist, Carl Linnaeus, who has given us a coherent taxonomical system by which to understand all species and see God's Hand in their formation.

"I am going to expand on his ideas specifically in relation to mankind. Once, men lived in caves and wore animal skins. Today, we build bridges, read and write books and live in cities. These are the marks of progress, the evidence of development.

"We are of the genus Homo, meaning man. The first human species were archaic. They were an embryonic human race, primitive cave-dwellers. I call them Homo Sapiens. Sapiens means wise. If the genus Homo is likened to a plant, then Homo Sapiens can be compared to the roots, hidden, in the dark, drawing its food entirely from its planetary domicile but laying the foundations for what's to come.

"After Homo Sapiens, came Homo Sapiens Sapiens, twice-wise man. In the analogy of the plant, Homo Sapiens Sapiens is the stem, the connection between root and flower. We humans who live today are Homo Sapiens Sapiens. The stem breathes air and now draws its food from the light of the sun as well as the planet. The stem too is a nexus from the roots to the flower."

This was fascinating. Then he spoke about the next advance.

"Amongst all creatures, humans alone are incomplete. Fish cannot be anything other than fish. Neither can bees nor elephants. The only unfinished symphony on Earth is the human. It is my informed opinion that the Great Architect has a plan for how mankind will attain this third and final state of completion.

"I believe God seeded His Universe with pods of advancement called angels. Their purpose was and is to activate latent faculties, skills and abilities in us and thereby bring the human symphony to its right and proper crescendo.

"I can't say what these faculties or capabilities are, or what they will do, because we haven't used them yet – they're dormant. But I can say that the development of the third state began with the Enlightenment. If all goes well, soon Homo Sapiens Sapiens Sapiens, thrice-wise man, Homo Tri-sapiens, will walk on Earth."

Rolander paused for breath. Everyone did. This material was radical, unprecedented and spiritual. Marion was trying her damnedest to keep up with it.

"There is a grave warning," Rolander continued. "His angels seek to elevate the human race into Homo Tri-sapiens. There is a danger that their divine work will be wasted. Humans have free will, so they have choice. They can either choose to follow God's purposes or, alternatively, they can pervert these angelic influences into a degenerate, surrogate development. If that happens, instead of advancing according to the grand plan, society will go round in ever-decreasing circles, like in Dante's *Inferno*. Instead of divine progress, there will be secular change – instead of evolution, revolution.

"By the analogy of the plant, this third stage is the flowering. The flower is different in character to both root and stem. It has beauty and yet it is functional, attracting insect life for pollination, just as the angels are attracted to those who make a home for them.

"There is only one part of the human body that is unfinished and where that development can occur."

Marion was flabbergasted. She knew what Rolander was going to say next. Even so, when he said it, it was still a shock.

"The brain in the head!"

The room swirled before her, spinning round and round.

"Gräfin!" a voice said. After that, everything went black.

She awoke lying on a chaise longue. With a frown, she pushed away the smelling salts Aunt Charlotte was wafting under her nose.

"Where am I? I must get back to—"

"The lecture, my dear, has finished," Aunt Charlotte said in that blithe way of hers.

"You're still in the academy building and you mustn't go anywhere, not in your state," Skoda insisted, his face a picture of distress.

"What happened?" she asked.

"You fainted from the heat and the excitement, I suspect," Skoda said. "How are you feeling?"

"Much better," she grumbled. In truth, she felt like someone had clubbed her on the head. "I must get back to the Schloss."

"Dearest Marion, hear what the Herr Doctor advises, I beg you," Aunt Charlotte said.

"I-I must go. Now!" She was adamant.

"Why? What's happened?" Fermor asked.

"I-I don't know exactly. I just know I have to leave."

Summoning all her will, she staggered across the room. "Grenda, where's Grenda? We're going. Get the horse and trap ready."

“I insist on accompanying you,” Skoda said.

Moments later, they were in the trap on the way home and Grenda was whistling to the old nags and spurring them on.

CHAPTER 31

The Blue of Prussia

There is no Prussian who does not worship God.
There is no Prussian who does not love his king and his country.
There is no Prussian who is not loyal to the land and its heritage.
OLD OSTPREUSSEN SAYING

In the warmth of the spring day, Grenda raced the mares until sweat was pouring off them. They clattered over the cobblestones and were soon kicking up a trail of dust along the dry country roads.

Something was wrong at home. Marion knew it in her bones, in the very soul of her being. It wasn't good. She girded herself for the worst.

Amidst these plumes of worry came flashes of Rolander's lecture. The head – that was where the next development of the human race would occur. The head was going to… going to what? The brain was encased in a bony skull. The skull kept the brain matter enclosed, contained, confined. Nothing would change that. She wondered if it mattered that the crown of her head was soft as butter. Fermor and Pastor Leopold's heads were the same. Babies too. It didn't mean anything. The vision of the eagle emerging from an egg-like skull was… a coincidence. It had to be. It simply had to be.

The alternative was unthinkable.

Following the course of the Pregel valley, they veered inland towards Steinbeck and edged into the village square.

There they were. A troop of about forty Hussars had halted by the well to water their horses. For a moment, she feared they were Russians. Then she spotted their blue uniforms adorned with silver braid. They were Prussian. Marion breathed a huge sigh of relief. False alarm. They were friends.

Grenda persuaded her to let him water the horses.

"Make it brief, then," she urged him.

Sections of the cavalry were guarding five covered wagons at the back of the column. She assumed it was a valuable cargo. The presence of home cavalry units attracted villagers who loitered on their thresholds, waving their caps.

While she waited, she went to greet the officer in charge.

A clutch of cavalry officers shared a copper cup of drinking water that was chained to the well. One of them turned to her as she and Skoda approached.

"Oh, Colonel von Marwitz, it's you," she said.

"At your service, Your Excellency!" von Marwitz said. His reply was conspicuous for the absence of the warmth he had shown her at the ceremony of the Order of the Black Eagle.

"Where are your men doing?" she asked.

"The Hussars are carrying out an important mission," von Marwitz claimed, "so please leave the vicinity of the village as soon as possible."

"I will, when you've answered my question," she replied. The troops in squads of six were stationed outside each house. She wondered why.

The colonel gave the signal to one of the squads, who thumped on the door of a nearby cottage.

"That's Klein's cottage," she said.

"Open up in the name of the King!" The officer brandished a parchment in his hand. "I have a requisition order."

It must be for more food – which they didn't have.

The door opened. Old man Klein's face peeled from behind it.

The conversation quickly grew heated. Shouts echoed across the village square.

"Get out of my house!" Klein shook his fist and tried to slam the door.

The officer kept it ajar with his foot. Brushing Klein aside, the soldiers burst into the cottage, asking, "Where is he?"

From inside, came the sounds of angry dispute.

"Colonel, this intrusion is intolerable," she complained.

Two soldiers emerged from the house. They were dragging a man behind them like a sack of potatoes. A man? No, it was a young boy. It was Bruno.

The brutality of her country's own soldiers was a shock to her. Trembling, she asked, "What's Klein's son done wrong?"

"Nothing. He's being recruited," the colonel said, adjusting his arm in the sling.

Then, she remembered. At the Order of the Black Eagle, the colonel had told her he was assigned to recruitment.

"Is this what you call it?" she snapped. "I'd call it abduction."

"Young, old, I don't look at their age," von Marwitz said, glaring at her through steely eyes. "Please, Your Excellency. I ask you again to remove yourself from the vicinity."

"This is my land and I'll leave when I'm good and ready. I want to know, why are you doing this?"

"I'm following orders."

Where had she heard that refrain before? This was madness: her own Prussian Army conscripting the youth of Ostpreussen. They were worse than the Russians. The cavalry officer and his henchmen dragged poor Bruno, kicking and yelling, across the village square towards the wagons.

Klein chased after them, screaming, "Stop! He's only twelve. You can't take him to fight."

Klein noticed her presence. "Your Excellency," his voice was beseeching, "please, do something."

"I'm trying," she said through gritted teeth. With his good hand, the colonel adjusted his monocle as he scrutinised the column of names on a sheet of paper held up by his adjutant.

Colonel von Marwitz asked, "How many is that?"

"Forty-nine," the adjutant answered.

"Anyone missing?"

"Only one – Herr Caspar von Barthen."

Von Marwitz turned to her and said, "We can't find Caspar. Do you know where he is?"

"At this precise moment, no, I don't. I've been in Königsberg for the *Te Deum*."

"Indeed," the colonel said. He seemed unimpressed by her patriotic excuse.

"Caspar's mind is undone," she said. "It's been blown apart by cannon fire and the sight of severed limbs on the battlefield. He was rendered unfit for duty. He can't fight his way out of a haystack."

"Irrelevant," the colonel snarled. "I lost a limb in battle. I wanted to return to the front and I was forbidden. I serve my king and country. I follow orders. He's a man of Ostpreussen, he should do the same. If, or rather when, you find him, it is your duty to inform me of his whereabouts!"

"I know that," she snapped. The whole edifice of war seemed to be an instrument solely designed to both crush the human spirit and rupture the human soul.

"And what about the boys you've conscripted? Bruno is barely out of his swaddling clothes. They'll be less use than cannon fodder on the front line. And why are you recruiting when we're no longer at war with the Russians?"

"The Russian Army remains in the field, though they have ceased fighting against us," Marwitz explained. "Our sole enemy is the Habsburgs. Our brave soldiers have been at war for six years. The ones that are still alive and fit to fight are few. They are exhausted. To defeat the enemy, the army craves fresh blood, new troops. These boys may be young but they are brave. They will fight to the death for God, for Frederick and for Ostpreussen."

"Can't you see these boys are the future fathers of our nation?" she wailed. "You are stripping our land of its tomorrows."

"I disagree, Gräfin. Should we lose, be under no illusions, we'd suffer another invasion. And that, Gräfin, would cripple our country. The Austrians won't treat Königsberg Cathedral or your precious Schloss with the near reverence that the Russians have. The Austrian Empress Maria Theresa is a cunning vixen, who will protect her glorious empire in any way she can. This conscription is securing our future. These boys should be volunteering to help us defeat the Austrian Medusa. For the last time, please be on your way," the colonel said, as he trooped to the back of the column of wagons.

She followed him. The soldiers threw Bruno into the penultimate wagon.

She walked over to look inside it. Before she got there, the colonel grabbed her arm, saying, "Stop there!"

She glared at him. Ignoring his demand, she strode to the back of the wagon. The faces of a dozen frightened boys stared back at her.

"Nicol?" she said. "Is that you?"

"Yes, Your Excellency," the boy said, his face a picture to be pitied.

Konstantin's young son – this was worse than she originally thought. Who else had they recruited? She strode to the last wagon and peered inside. It was shrouded in shadows. One of the boys at the very back of the wagon looked vaguely familiar.

The boy reached out a hand and cried, "Mother!"

"Hans? It can't be. That's my son. They've conscripted my son! He's a mere boy. He can barely walk, let alone fight! Colonel! This is madness!"

As she cried to the heavens, the column of wagons rolled by, the young boys staring out of the back of them, confused and terrified.

Her own son, snatched, abducted. She was utterly distraught.

This was the ugly, personal side of war. She'd seen her own staff suffer the same over the years, young boys, young men, ripped from the bosom of their families and hauled off to the battlefields of Silesia. Now it was her turn. And it hurt.

She knelt down and prayed.

"Lord, let my son return to his family safely.

Lord God, let his father come back in one piece.

Lord of Hosts, give me the strength to keep the home fires burning on the estate."

CHAPTER 32

The May Dew

The maid who rises on May morn,
And washes in dew from the old oak tree,
Will forever after handsome be.
MEDIEVAL FOLK SAYING

As was his habit, Fermor was up before dawn. Yesterday had been a sad occasion, marked by the burial of Pastor Leopold. The poor man had finally succumbed five days before on 15th May. Tragically, it was the same day as the Gräfin's birthday.

It was a shock, because he had to share all the pastor's extensive responsibilities with Konstantin, at least until another pastor could be found. But it shook him to the quick in another way, because he wondered whether Leopold had died as a result of those head pains. If so, was the Adler in any way responsible for the pastor's demise? Had the Adler taken a man's life in pursuit of its divine purposes? Surely not. There had to be some other reason for his death, and he resolved to find out what it was.

Today, though, was a glorious May morn when he opened the door of the little chapel next to the Schloss, inviting in the ceaseless chirping of fledglings and the vibrant smell of spring in the air. Over by the lake, he noticed a shadowy movement under a tree. It was a person but, in the half-light, he couldn't see who it was. He or she crouched by the shallows under an oak tree and stood up. By her silhouette, he could tell it was a young woman. With her back to him, she appeared to be rubbing her face. He walked over the forecourt towards her.

"Sisi!" he exclaimed. "What *are* you doing?"

"Sexton," she said, turning and wiping her face with a cloth. Wearing a guilty look, she hastily tucked something in her apron and said, "You're not from these parts, are you?"

"Originally from Scotland, me," he replied.

"Around here, it's a May tradition," she said, gifting him a winsome smile. "Here, I'll tell you the rhyme:

The maid who rises on May morn,
And washes in dew from the old oak tree,
Will forever after handsome be."

Truly, her face was glowing.

There was a scuffling in the bushes behind the oak.

"Who's that?" he cried.

"Oh, it must be a rabbit or a squirrel."

She moved to block his view. He edged to one side to take a closer look. Branches were swaying. But there was no wind. Someone had recently brushed passed them.

"Who's there?" he asked.

"No one," she said. "Come, let's go back into the house." She set off apace.

His suspicions aroused, he ignored her, walked towards the oak and called out, "Whoever you are, come out and show yourself."

A young man stumbled out of the bushes, a peaked hat shadowing his face. His rough-hewn clothes were stained in mud and covered in pollen and bits of grass.

"Caspar!" Fermor exclaimed.

"Sexton," Caspar said, blushing with shame.

"You were supposed to have been conscripted. Where've you been hiding these last two weeks?" Fermor asked.

"I-I…" Caspar stammered.

Sisi came back to defend him. "He's not going back to war. He's staying here with me."

Caspar sucked on a loose thread in his collar, giving him the appearance of a scared little boy.

"Don't worry about the sexton," she said to Caspar. "He won't tell on you, will you?"

Fermor shook his head. "I'm a man of God, not of war. My first priority is to Him."

"See, I told you he'd listen," Sisi said with an air of reassurance. She plucked a package from her apron and gave it to Caspar, saying, "Here's some bread."

Caspar grabbed it from her and stuffed his face. He must have been ravenous.

"You listen to me," she said to him, like a big sister to an errant younger brother. "Meet me in the usual place, same time, tomorrow morning. Go. And don't let them catch you!"

He scuttled off into the morning shadows and was soon swallowed by the undergrowth.

"Thank you for promising not to say anything," Sisi said to him, as they walked back across the forecourt.

May dew or no May dew, he had an unerring feeling that it wouldn't end well for Caspar or for Sisi.

CHAPTER 33

The Glasgow School of Revolution

Glasgow people, Greenock folk and Paisley bodies.
POPULAR SCOTS RHYME

Donald Lester disliked the even keel of the land. He much preferred the roll of the ship beneath his feet. As he predicted, the voyage from Königsberg had taken nearly two weeks. In the three hectic days he'd been back in Glasgow, he'd returned to the bosom of his family and met old acquaintances in the dockland inns. The River Clyde was bustling with schooners and sailing ships from round the world, so much so that the port had recently invested in a new dry dock.

International trade presented broad, new opportunities to a man of his impoverished upbringing. Through good fortune quickened by hard work and cunning, he'd glided through the ranks from ordinary seaman. He met Thomas Sorensen, a Danish émigré, who owned *The Lion Rampant*, a Scottish ship that ploughed the Baltic, calling at Copenhagen, St. Petersburg, and Königsberg. Soon, he attained the captaincy.

This was his time. Lester felt it in his bones – a time to make his fortune and show those in his village what a great man and sailor he truly was. As he made his way to his friend James Watt's little backyard, he could smell the sweet odour of success in the air.

"James," he said, giving his old friend a strong handshake. "You look well."

"And you too, Donald," James Watt replied.

"Are you keeping busy?" he asked.

"I am indeed!" James sniffed at the air. Watt had this way about him of a man in a hurry. "I recently worked with the Glasgow port authority. I designed the pump that drew the water from the new dry dock, the first of its kind in Scotland."

"That was your design, eh? Still using the old horse-drawn method?"

"I'm afraid so, it's very inefficient. I am working diligently on the design of a mechanical method," James said, drawing his attention to a sprawling worktop full of pistons, valves and cylinders, as well as an assortment of wrenches and hammers.

"This is where you work with the engines?" Lester asked, admiring the array of machines. Most were in bits, except one, a small engine on a table on its own. "What's this one?"

"A model of the Newcomen engine," Watt said. "The original design is nearly fifty years old. It's riddled with inefficiencies and I can't see how to overcome them. Once I do, you watch, my design will transform the world."

"That's quite a promise, even for an ambitious young man like you," Lester replied, taking a pinch of snuff.

"You have no idea," James said, fiddling with the settings on one of the instruments. "It'll be a sea change, a revolution like that of Copernicus. You've heard of him?"

"Of course," Lester replied, and then sneezed loudly into his 'kerchief. "Dear Nicolaus, he brought about a revolution in our view of our true place in the solar system."

"Exactly," James Watt said. "What he achieved in the realms of astronomy, I shall attain in the realms of instrumentation and engineering."

"I believe you," Lester said.

Watt paused for a moment and seemed inspired by a vision of the future. "My new design will release slaves from bondage and free serfs from the yoke of the land. It will make ordinary landowners and the moneyed gentry rich beyond measure."

"I share that dream," Lester said.

"Well," James said, adjusting his tatty wig. "You didn't come here to pass the time of day. How can I be of assistance?"

"I've gained a new foreign contract," he began, pacing the workshop. "It's to procure, transport and install spare parts for two Newcomen engines in the Anna Amber Mine in the Kingdom of Prussia, a commission that bears on King Frederick himself."

"Great news! You deserve it."

"I'll need an engineer to fit the parts. You'd be working on real live Newcomen engines," he added.

"I am sorely tempted, but I shall reluctantly decline," Watt said. "My work here's too important. I must find a way to improve the Newcomen engine."

"Care to recommend someone?"

"Yes, Charles Robison, John's brother," Watt replied. "He's a young Scottish engineer."

"Thank you, James," Lester said and took his leave.

He peered back at James Watt, wiping the grease from his hands with an oily rag and studiously leafing through a mighty tome on his desk.

On his way out, Lester read the sign above the lintel, 'The Glasgow School of Revolution.'

CHAPTER 34

Family or Nation

The King is the first servant of the State.
KING FREDERICK THE GREAT

To distract herself from the pain of Hans' conscription, Marion had thrown herself into the work of the estate. The month of May was always busy, what with ploughing and seeding and the associated festivals. The herds had to be renewed. The byways cleared. Everything needed replenishing except, it seemed, her family. Despite her profound sense of patriotism, she was embittered. How could they recruit a lad, a mere boy, her son? And on the day after he'd had his splint removed. What was he going to do, hobble into battle? He didn't even have any boyish stubble. It wasn't recruitment, it was abduction!

She had written to Gottfried in the hope that he would wield his growing influence to safeguard their son. So far, she had not received a return letter. His silence spoke volumes. He would expect her to do her duty promptly and with fulsome pride. In his world, there was no room for personal advantage and especially not the abuse of power for one's own benefit. The best she could hope for was that he shielded Hans from greater danger.

And Leopold had passed on, and on her birthday too! Nothing seemed sacred any more.

Her head was aching and her vision deteriorating. She kept seeing colours flash before her eyes, like bolts of lightning. In the past, she'd been frightened by visions of eagles. Now, they terrified her.

Who could she tell about the dream visions and the severe headaches? Not Skoda, that was certain. The man was a capable physician with some ailments, yet incompetent with others. It rankled with her that he had arrived without laudanum, or, for that matter, any herbs at all. Nor did she like his inappropriate behaviour towards Sisi.

What about Fermor? In her dream, he had helped her find the vault and resolve their food crisis. But he had sown threads of mistrust in her by the way he had neglected her son and by his zealous fascination with the numinous Adler. He probably believed it was one of the angels of which Daniel Rolander spoke. She could give him one last chance.

After a full day, she slumped into a chair in the Green Room to watch the glory of the dying embers of the evening sun. Ursula brought her a refreshing drink of ginger and loitered in the doorway. Ursula loitered for one reason only: when she was plucking up courage to tell her unpleasant news.

"What is it?" she grumbled.

"I-I…" Ursula said.

"Oh, woman," she snapped. "Spit it out. Whatever it is can't be as bad as losing my Hans."

"You know the cook keeps a wary eye on supplies."

"Yes, and…"

"Well, morsels of food are tiptoeing out of the kitchens," Ursula said.

"What food?"

"Mostly loaves of bread and some bits of cheese, Your Excellency."

"How long has this been going on?"

"About three weeks."

"And the cook's got no idea who could be taking it?"

"No, Your Excellency. They disappear overnight. Ask Otto. Other than the castle ghost, he's not seen a living soul in the kitchens."

"Thank you for telling me," she said. "Please ask Sexton Fermor to come and see me."

"Yes, Your Excellency."

Soon after, Fermor entered the room. Before she could say a word, he sat down in front of her and shovelled a hand through his red hair, saying, "Your Excellency, you asked to see me. I know what it's about. I confess. It's been preying on my mind."

"What is it, Sexton?" This was unexpected. Now she was the confessor.

"Sisi," he said.

"Yes, what about her?" Her interest was aroused.

"She's been meeting Caspar in secret to give him food," he blurted out.

This didn't surprise her. She replied, "This isn't a rumour?"

"No, it's true, I saw them together."

"When?"

"About a week ago."

Sisi was the kitchen mouse! She should have known. Her own daughter, thieving food for a runaway conscript! The shame of it: she composed herself and said, "Tell me what happened."

"Early one morning, I found them out by the lake. She gave him bread."

"Why wait so long to tell me?"

"I-I, she made me promise not to."

"You're a fool." She gripped her hand into a fist. She couldn't confide in a man like that.

"I'm so sorry, Your Excellency. I should have come to you straight away."

"Yes, you should," she said. "And you call yourself a man of God, a servant of the Adler!" she exclaimed. She was furious – with Fermor and Sisi. "Leave. Ask Ursula to bring Sisi to me. On second thoughts, I don't trust you to do that. I'll ask her myself."

After a while, Ursula came back with Sisi.

"Take your hands off me," Sisi complained, shrugging herself from Ursula's grasp.

"Thank you, Ursula," Marion said. "Please wait outside the door."

Ursula did just that.

"Child," Marion began. "You've been stealing food from the kitchens and helping a conscript to avoid justice. What has got into you? Your father and I did not bring you up to be a thief nor aid a convict. It's a betrayal and it's unforgivable."

"I'm not a child," she moaned, "and yes, that's what I've been doing and I'm proud of it. He needs help and understanding, not conscription."

"That's not for you to decide. Where is he?"

"He's hiding between the two barns, near the trapdoor."

Marion asked Ursula to fetch him.

When Caspar limped into the room, he doffed his cap and said to her, "Beggin' your pardon, Your Excellency."

"Oh, Caspar," Sisi said, affectionately touching his hand.

"I can't stay 'ere long," he said, peering around the room as if he expected someone to jump out from behind the screen or emerge from one of the tapestries. "I'm on that there list, I know, Sisi told me. It's an awful, hauntin' thing to be on a list. Me don't like it. I don't want to be on no list."

"I know, Caspar," Marion said. "That's the conscription list of Colonel von Marwitz. You must give yourself up to him. He'll see you're properly placed."

"No, not him, I'm not going back to the army, not now, not ever," Caspar said, shrivelling up like a dried leaf at the mention of the colonel's name. "He don't like me, he's the one who's chasing after me."

"In that case, I'll tell him myself," Marion said. "I'll put in a good word for you. But I doubt it will do any good. The simple fact is you are a deserter."

"*In that case*, Mother," Sisi sneered, "I'll leave. I'll run away with Caspar."

"What?"

"Yes, together, we'll run away from the stifling confines of Ludwigshain," Sisi said.

Marion ignored the stinging rebuke. "Listen to me. Do not get swayed by youthful passions. Eloping is a dream. Besides, you've nowhere to go."

"Don't be so sure about that, Mother," Sisi growled. "We'll get passage to England or America. They have factories there. We'll get work and start a new life."

"Think again, young lady! You have responsibilities to me and to the estate. You are going nowhere. And you will never work in a factory," she said.

"I don't rightly know what a factory is," Caspar said. "It must be good because Gustav went there. He sent a letter. We read it in class. He's clever is Gustav."

"I strongly disapprove of them," Marion said. "Factory work is servile and the conditions destructive to human dignity. There's more honesty in the independence of the family farmer. Together we live well, serve the land, and in so doing, give thanks to our God. A factory has machines. Machines can't give thanks to God. Only humans can do that. Machines can't forgive. Machines don't have courage, care or compassion. Only humans have those great qualities. God doesn't recognise machines, they have no spirit. God recognises humans because they have spirit, a spoonful of God. God doesn't want improved machines. God wants improved humans."

"I don't rightly understand all that, Excellency," Caspar murmured and then gave a little beckoning wave of his hand to Sisi and limped towards the door.

Sisi turned to follow him saying, "Mother, if you inform the colonel, I *will* run away with Caspar."

What a choice – family or nation? Her husband and son had been taken from her and she couldn't bear to see her daughter walk out on her. It would break her heart. In a moment of weakness, she muttered, "Wait."

"I'm listening," Sisi replied and folded her arms.

"I'll not inform the colonel."
"Do you mean it, Mother?"
"Yes, but only if you stay."
"I agree," Sisi said and ran off after Caspar.

CHAPTER 35

The Lastadie Docks

To be without learning is to be without eyes.
LITHUANIAN PROVERB

Donald Lester speared *The Lion Rampant* down the narrow channel, through the Hollander Baum and into the Altstadt. In the five weeks since he'd left, the Lastadie docks hadn't changed much. The burnt-out warehouses from last November's fire remained derelict. The wharf was lined with schooners and brigs, their rigging flapping in the morning's stiff Baltic breeze. Flocks of gulls shadowed the fishing vessels, trying to catch a late breakfast. Sailors and passengers, stevedores and merchants, jostled each other along the quay.

"Send word to Herr von Bernstein that we have arrived," he said.

"Yes, Captain," the first mate replied. "Shall we load the equipment onto the quay?"

"Och, no," he replied, taking a pinch of snuff. "Bring it onto the deck – so it's ready for unloading. Don't you dare move it off this ship until I say so, understood?"

"Captain, sir!" The first mate sauntered off along the deck.

Lester refused to release the equipment to Dieter, King Frederick the Great, or the Holy Roman Emperor for that matter, until the first half of the payment had been settled in full. That was the deal and he was sticking to it.

In Scotland, he'd borrowed every available guinea he could to raise finance. The Jewish moneylenders had driven hard but fair deals.

Hanging onto the ladder leading to the hold, Lester admonished the crew if they even so much as scratched a cylinder or grazed a valve. Each piece of equipment was placed on the main deck like a crown jewel and secured with a tarpaulin. He rubbed the scruff from his hands, pleased with a job well done.

Dieter von Bernstein arrived with his entourage. The man was lame and, however much his elegant clothes and perfect coiffure said otherwise, this was his tragic but defining feature.

That didn't stop Dieter grabbing Lester's hand with breezy enthusiasm, and saying, "I brought my wagons." He pointed to several open carriages drawn up on the quay. "And my men to unload the equipment. I can't wait to get going."

"Nor can I, Herr Dieter," he replied, laconically.

As Dieter's men strode up the gangplank, Lester ordered the first mate, "Do not let them aboard."

The mate and his knot of burly helpers made a phalanx at the top of the gangplank.

"What's going on here, Captain?" Dieter scowled.

"I think you know," Lester hissed. "We had a contract. I delivered my part. I'm waiting for you to deliver yours."

"I see, so you want to be paid," Dieter said.

"Half now, half after installation and commissioning, that was the agreement. Or is the word of a Prussian not his bond anymore?"

"What with their tolls and taxes, the Russians have sucked us dry," Dieter replied. "And my amber mine is flooded because the pumps don't work. I've earned less than a skinner in six months. I need this deal as much as you do."

"What about von Lehndorff?" he replied. "He's had five weeks to give you a down payment. Where is it?"

"I wish I knew," Dieter said, rolling his eyes.

"So until it comes…" he growled.

"I'll send urgent word to him," Dieter said anxiously.

"Do that. I'll not wait until kingdom come!" he added, chewing on his disgust. "I'll unload my other cargo of slate and whisky. Once I've loaded my return cargo, I'll be ready to embark. You've two days."

"What? Where are you going?"

"Just you get me the money." Lester was fed up with it all.

"What about von Lehndorff? When will we get the equipment?" Dieter wanted to know.

"Von Lehndorff holds the keys to the King's coffers, which are locked tighter than a Scotsman's purse. It might take weeks to get so much as a pfennig out of him. By then, I'll be back here ready to do business."

As they talked, the first mate reported to Lester, "Charles Robison's taken ill, Capt'n. The man's face is whiter than Highland snow. Not fit for nothin', if you ask me."

“Not like his brother then. Navigate round the world, could John. How bad is our Charles?” Lester replied. That was bad tidings. Since they embarked from Glasgow, Charles Robison had vomited almost every meal, leaving him weak in mind and body. Lester was relying on him to commission the equipment.

“Serious enough to warrant a hospital bed,” the first mate said, spitting a globule of tobacco onto the deck.

“The hospital will care for him. I know the one at Löbenicht. He’ll be well again soon. Send for a horse and cart,” Lester replied.

“Yes, Captain,” the first mate said.

“That equipment,” Dieter said, pointing at the tarpaulin, “is useless until it’s installed. What happens if Robison doesn’t get better?”

“It’s a concern,” Lester said. “Do you have any ideas?”

“Yes, as a matter of fact I do.” Dieter could be condescending when he wanted to be. “Let’s try and get him well again as soon as possible. Listen, my sister has a new physician, a Doctor Skoda. I’ll ask her to send him to attend to Robison.”

“Good, do that,” Lester said. “He’ll find Charles in Löbenicht Hospital.”

CHAPTER 36

The State Room

The greatest and noblest pleasure we have in this world
Is to discover new truths,
And the next is to shake off old prejudices.
KING FREDERICK THE GREAT

Marion was dimly aware of the subtle, pre-dawn light playing on her outer eyelids. She heard a banging on the front door. Who was it this time?

"Open up!" A man was shouting outside the front door.

"Wait!" came Otto's stock reply.

The raucous sound of their voices made her sit up in bed. There was a brusque Ursula knock on her door followed by the woman herself, hair tied in a bun, and neat and prim in her chambermaid's uniform.

"Is it Gottfried?" Marion asked, more in hope than expectation.

There was another thunderous knock at the front door. Marion nearly jumped out of her skin. The lake geese rose into the air as one, flapping and squawking in complaint.

"What was that?"

"Come and see, Your Excellency," Ursula said, peering at the forecourt through a gap in the curtains.

Marion joined her. "Troops! I might have known."

"Ours?"

"Yes, they're Hussars." She recognised their commanding officer; his arm in a sling, a flash of sunlight on his medal, the monocle, the indomitable bearing – Colonel von Marwitz.

"They've surrounded the Schloss, Your Excellency," Ursula said, a tinge of anxiety in her normally dulcet tones.

"And I know why," she said. "Tell the colonel I'll see him in the State Room."

Ursula must have also guessed the colonel's motive and asked, "Shall I call Sisi, Your Excellency?"

"I'm sure she'll come and find us on her own," she replied.

Marion sat on the throne in the State Room. The tapestries of Teutonic Knights fighting the heathens filled her with the courage to face insurmountable obstacles. Despite that, her head pounded like it was going to burst open at the seams, a major inconvenience. Sisi joined her as Kadow showed the colonel into the room.

The colonel was in no mood for civilities. "Your Excellency, when I saw you in Steinbeck just over a month ago, I told you I would return to find Caspar von Barthen. Here I am. Please, I hate nothing more than time wasting, so tell me where he is."

She shrugged her shoulders. They'd taken her precious son and now they were coming back for Caspar.

"Where is he?" von Marwitz asked, his ice-blue eyes peering into her soul. "If you know, you must tell me, it's your duty!"

"I don't know where he is." Well, that was the truth: she didn't know exactly where he was at that moment.

"How did you know he was here?" Sisi asked, staring at the colonel.

"I received information to that effect," von Marwitz replied.

"Who told you?" Sisi asked, glancing at Marion with growing suspicion.

"I am not at liberty to reveal my sources," came the officious reply.

"*You* told the colonel! How could you do that, Mother?"

"I didn't." She was indignant. "It was someone else."

Sisi folded her arms in a huff.

The colonel turned to Sisi and asked, "Fräulein, you know where he is."

Sisi glared back at him and yelled, "You brute! I'm not telling you anything!"

Marion gripped the armrests of her chair. "Sisi, how dare you! Apologise this instant to the colonel."

Sisi stormed across the room, slamming the door behind her.

"Colonel, I apologise profusely for my daughter's insolent behaviour."

"I don't have time for these antics, Your Excellency," the colonel said stiffly. "My men will find him. If you won't tell me, I'll ask Doctor Skoda. He's a reliable soul. As is that sexton of yours, what's his name – Fermor?"

"I'm afraid neither is here – we've suffered a terrible tragedy," she explained. "Skoda escorted our doctor's widow, Katharina von Ottenhagen, to the insane asylum in Königsberg. Sexton Fermor went with them yesterday."

"I'm sorry to hear about that," the colonel said. "In the meantime, please advise your staff that until we find the deserter, no one will be allowed to leave the Schloss."

An adjutant and a soldier burst through the door, half-walking, half-stumbling into the room, each one holding one of Sisi's arms.

"You're hurting me!" Sisi complained.

"How dare you manhandle my daughter! Put her down this instant!"

"Do as she asks," von Marwitz said calmly.

Sisi rubbed her arms and gave the soldiers her best frown.

"She was trying to sneak out of the back door," the adjutant explained.

Marion tried to comfort Sisi but her daughter turned away in disgust.

"Adjutant, stop searching the rooms," the colonel said immediately. "Fräulein was leaving the Schloss, which means the deserter is somewhere in the grounds."

As he passed Marion, he added, "Your daughter knows where Caspar is and, despite my reasonable requests, she refuses to help. I advise you to convince her to tell us his whereabouts, because I will not tolerate this unconscionable rudeness for much longer. Do I make myself clear, Gräfin?"

He strutted past her with a nonchalant air and left the room.

Sisi stood in the corner, nursing her arms and her grievances, then ranted, "He's not a deserter. Caspar's like a sapling with broken branches. He needs to be healed, not frog-marched into battle! And you gave me your word!"

Sisi walked slowly out of the room with a strange sense of finality.

Marion paced the State Room. In her husband's absence, she was the proprietor of the estate. How could she maintain standards in the face of what was unfolding around her – war, famine and death, and now the Adler and the softness in the head? She had the feeling she was walking through one of those huge swamps in the Masurian Lakes, unsure of her footing and liable to sink into the marsh at any moment.

Absorbed in these thoughts, come late afternoon, she barely noticed Kadow appear at the doorway wearing a beguiling look.

"They found him," he said.

"Where?" she asked. At that moment, in a flash of insight, she had seen him crouching behind wooden barrels. "Oh, don't tell me. In the vault!"

"Yes, how did you know?"

"A good guess." But it felt more like a new prophetic ability.

There were noises of an altercation in the vestibule.

"What's that?" She came to see what was happening.

The colonel was in the forecourt outside the entrance. About to mount his horse, he turned to her and said, quite matter of fact, "The prisoner is being escorted to Königsberg."

"Where are you taking him?" Marion asked.

"To the magistrates' court, Your Excellency. He is to be tried for desertion," the colonel replied.

CHAPTER 37

Löbenicht Hospital

Listen, my children, I am so glad that
the land can hear these songs again.
OSTPREUSSEN SAYING

It was early morning as Fermor accompanied Doctor Skoda from Junkerstrasse to the insane asylum. The streets were crowded with bewigged lords and their ladies, uniformed soldiers and sailors, as well as drunks, pedlars and cutpurses. To avoid any potential upset to Katharina von Ottenhagen, they veered off into the back alleys and eventually deposited her at the asylum, a most excoriating experience if ever there was one. When they left her, they both said goodbye, but Katharina did not seem to have any awareness of where she was, let alone who she was. Dressed still in her black mourning attire, she cut a pathetic figure, devoid of sense and sensibility.

They quickly made their way to Löbenicht Hospital. Its facade reflected traditional Ostpreussen values – sturdy and solid, a functional building bare of outward decoration. The lawns were as smooth as glass, the flowers in their beds in straight lines like Prussian soldiers on parade, their yellow and red flower heads bobbing obediently in the gentle breeze.

At the entrance, a man sat eating a leg of meat. He wore a dirty white smock covered with bloodstains. This failed to put him off his meal, because he sliced a chunk of meat with his hunting knife and shoved it into a bearded mouth. When he finished chewing, he threw away the bone, attracting a pair of hungry magpies.

"I'm Rudolf, the hospital attendant," he said, wiping his hands on his filthy apron. "Who are you? What do you want?"

"Doctor Skoda. I'm here to attend to a Scotsman by the name of Robison," he said with unconcealed irritation.

"Oh, him, came in yesterday?" Rudolf asked.

"That would be him," Skoda said.

"Follow me." Rudolf led them through a labyrinth of doors and corridors until they reached a sumptuous cloister, decorated with stone mullions and Gothic friezes.

Fermor observed, "This is just like a monastery."

"In former days, it was a Catholic Benedictine convent," Rudolf explained.

"I thought as much," Fermor replied and paused to admire a sculpture in a grotto. It was a weathered life-size sandstone statue of the Blessed Virgin Mary. Her hands were by her side, her palms open, her posture supplicant and her visage beseeching. What caught his attention was what was on her head: a halo out of which protruded twelve rods or arms, each one ending in a five-pointed star. The ravages of time had dissolved the colours and the surface of the stone was flaking.

None of that diminished the startling impression the statue made on him. Twelve stars emerging from her halo; with a small stretch of the imagination, it tallied with the twelve stars above the head of the woman in the Book of Revelations – the passage Marion had found in the vault. It appeared to be a physical depiction of the same verse. The twelve stars intrigued him. The subtle purpose of his life flushed through him. The statue was a clue to how he could better serve the Adler.

"Come on, will you? We've no time to dawdle," Rudolf said.

Tearing himself away, Fermor followed Skoda and Rudolf into the ward. It was like walking into a battlefield. The smell of rotting flesh was pungent. The men had heavy wounds, deep scarring and amputated limbs. Here, life sat on the edge of a knife. Some suffered in silence, writhing in their beds, others moaned and cried out loud for mercy.

Charles Robison's bed was at the far end of the ward, next to a window overlooking the cloister. Robison was in his late twenties, about the same age as Doctor Skoda. Robison had a strong chin, sallow eyes and red hair, and wore a white over-garment that was the same pallor as his face. Fermor wasn't sure if that was the colour of the disease or the colour of fear.

Doctor Skoda took Robison's pulse at his wrist and felt his forehead. The young man was perspiring like a waterfall and shivering at the same time.

"How are you feeling?" Skoda asked him.

"Weak and cold," Robison replied, his voice barely audible against the groans and mutterings from the other patients.

"What d'you think?" Rudolf asked.

"The lad's feverish," Skoda replied. "Bleed him and be quick about it."

"I've been busy cutting limbs off all day. And I've not finished yet. And we've no leeches. If you're in such a hurry, you bleed him!" Rudolf said.

"Me? No," Skoda was indignant. "I'll not do the work of a cutter."

"By the grace of God, I'll do it when I can," Rudolf admitted with a heavy sigh.

Skoda held Robison by the wrist and laid a palm on his forehead. "He's boiling up. With such heat in the body's vapours, he needs a cold bath. That'll bring down the fever."

Rudolf replied, "Yes, Doctor. We'll see to it."

"Good," Skoda said. He turned to Robison and said in a cheery voice, "We'll have you up and out of here in no time."

Fermor had his doubts about that.

CHAPTER 38

On the Horns of a Dilemma

History is the School of Princes.
KING FREDERICK THE GREAT

When Fermor and Skoda arrived back at Junkerstrasse, Dieter was just leaving his house.

"Come with me," Dieter said. "I have an appointment with von Lehndorff."

As they mounted the trap, Dieter asked after Charles Robison.

Skoda grunted. "He's feverish. His humours are unbalanced. Under my treatment, he'll recover."

"That's a relief," Dieter said.

The sun was setting by the time they entered von Lehndorff's offices. Fermor was astounded by their opulence: golden statues of buxom women, busts of laurel-leafed Roman emperors and numerous martial portraits, mostly of King Frederick and his father.

Von Lehndorff sat behind a huge mahogany desk, its dark wood brimming with Prussian steadfastness.

His usher showed them to a seat near his office door, while they waited for von Lehndorff to finish an interview with a gentleman dressed in the English style, à la George. From the Englishman's accent, Fermor gathered that he was a senior representative of the British Government. As the King's Kammerherr, von Lehndorff had connections in high places.

"Et bien, merci, Comte von Lehndorff, toujours mon plaisir," the Englishman said in broken French. "When I return to England, I will pass on your king's message. After this dreadful war has ended, we hope that we can remain close allies in our shared Protestant beliefs."

The man bowed and left with his small entourage of bewigged gentlemen. After scribbling a note, von Lehndorff peered through his monocle, saw them sitting there, sniffed, and in a brusque hand movement, ushered them over to the chairs by his desk.

"Yes, yes, what is it?" he said, taking a pinch of snuff. "I'm a busy man."

"The Amber Room?" Dieter said hesitantly, expecting that would be enough to jog von Lehndorff's memory. It was.

"Ah, yes, the King's pièce de résistance! I'm glad you're here, because there are movements afoot. I am not at liberty to tell you exactly what they are, state secrets and all that," he added with a knowing guffaw. "Well. How is the mining going?"

"That is why we are here, Your Excellency, the mining hasn't started," Dieter said.

"Why on earth not?"

"Captain Lester has docked and his ship carries the pumping equipment," Dieter explained, "but he refuses to release it until he receives the initial instalment."

"I'm afraid I can't help you with that," von Lehndorff said, adjusting his wig.

"I thought the King was going to supply us with some funds," Dieter said with mild complaint.

"The King's reach is sometimes more than his grasp," von Lehndorff explained. "The state coffers are empty, swallowed by the war effort. You heard me talking to our English friends. William Pitt was a staunch ally to us in London. Alas, he's lost his post, and now the English will no longer support us financially. That's a severe setback."

"What do you suggest we do?" Dieter said.

Von Lehndorff leant over his desk, looked Dieter squarely in the eyes, and said, "Let me put it to you as delicately as I can. The King has asked you to provide material for an Amber Room, a request that is a great honour for you and your family. If I were you, I would do everything in my power to please the King. Only then will you fully reap the rewards of grace and favour. On the other hand, should you fail to provide it, the King may consider you careless, negligent and unpatriotic. You wouldn't want him to think that, would you?"

Dieter shook his head. "If I am able to finance a loan, the moneylender will need a repayment date. Can you at least advise me when I might receive monies from the King's coffers?"

"Herr von Bernstein, that is a question for a soothsayer, not for me," von Lehndorff said, holding up his hands. "However, the King does expect you to deliver the amber promptly."

Dieter resembled someone who'd been thumped in the belly. Finally, he mustered an air of defiance and said, "Without the funds, we cannot release the equipment or repair the pump. Without the pump, we cannot extract the amber. Without the amber, our reputations will lie in tatters! We are truly on the horns of a dilemma."

Like brushing away a fly, Graf von Lehndorff waved him and his objections aside.

Time to leave. Dieter heaved himself up from the chair and stumbled out of the room, Fermor and Skoda behind.

CHAPTER 39

Embarkation

Get wisdom. Cherish her, and she will exalt you.
Embrace her, and she will honour you.
She will give you a garland to grace your head,
And present you with a glorious crown.
THE BOOK OF PROVERBS 4:6-9

Dieter refused the horse and trap and trudged through the cobblestoned streets.

Fermor wasn't sure where they were going and he didn't really mind. He had tagged along because someone, he couldn't quite remember who, Marion he thought it was, had asked him. He couldn't remember why. He was pleasantly lost in the contemplation of divine matters. That covered most things, since God was in the aromatic rose petals in the garden he was just passing, in the flaky, rib-like clouds in the sky and even in the flying ants that landed on his bare forearm. God was everywhere and in everything.

He breathed in and he breathed out, God saw to that. He, Fermor, did not even have to remember to do it. It was like falling asleep and waking up. Such grace! Even the act of walking was imbued with God's laws. He wanted to live according to those laws, be their mirror image. He was desperate to improve on Creation and move closer to God by fulfilling His purposes. He recollected words from the bishop's recent address, 'A genius is someone whose creations are the image of divine wisdom and the mirror of spiritual purpose.'

Fermor wanted to be a genius and be participant in the unfolding of Creation. Well, who wouldn't? He wondered what would happen to Creation if there were no more human geniuses.

Dusk was falling. The sky glowed with a glorious pink hue, like the carnations blooming in the rectory garden. This eventide wore a silken quiescence. It was spiritual in nature and reminded him of how grateful he was for each communion. He'd witnessed the business about amber funds and wondered why he had once sought riches aplenty as a main life goal. Thankfully, the Lord, his Keeper, had showed him the error of his ways. Now, he dedicated himself to the glory of God and His representative angel, the Adler. Not for the first time, he watched the clouds in the Ostpreussen skies move and shift and coalesce. He saw wings, a bird's head, a beak and claws. It was an eagle, a giant eagle, drifting effortlessly across Ostpreussen skies. Strangely, no one else seemed to have noticed it.

Back on the cobblestones, the Lastadie docks loomed ahead. He guessed they must be going to see Captain Donald Lester. Fermor didn't like Lester. When they'd met some years before and Lester had hired him on the voyage from Port Glasgow to St. Petersburg, they'd been like two ducks on a pond. Since then, they had both changed. And Lester had changed for the worst. The man carried a rapacious greed, which Fermor decided he would have as little to do with as possible.

On the quay, a knot of Russian stevedores sat around a large oak table outside the Baltic Inn, singing haunting songs of yore, no doubt fuelled by a large intake of home-grown vodka. Along the quay, a single-mast schooner was being roped to the bollards, the waters of the Alter Pregel lapping against her bows.

They soon found *The Lion Rampant.*

Captain Lester was no time-waster. "Bring my funds?" to which he added an intimidating stare. "Hah! With those long-drawn faces, I see your pockets are as full as a Glasgow beggar's!"

"I'm afraid the King's coffers are empty," Dieter said.

"What do you propose to do now, Herr Dieter?"

"Will you accept a signed IOU from me?" Dieter replied.

"Nah!" Lester grimaced to emphasise his refusal. "Me, I've shook too many hands of unscrupulous folk, who've saddled me with more debts than I care to remember."

"I'm as scrupulous as Job," Dieter insisted, "but it's going to be difficult for me to convince you of that. Tell me, what will you accept?"

"Cash – Prussian thaler will do, English guineas will be even better."

"That's impossible, at least not for some time, until I can talk to the bankers and…"

"… I'll be taking my leave," Lester said, rubbing his hands. "The two days are up."

"What about your crew member, Robison?" Doctor Skoda piped up.

"What about him?" Lester replied.

"He's seriously ill in hospital, yet you don't even have the good grace to ask about him." Skoda was visibly upset.

"Charles Robison is young, Scots and as hardy as a thistle. I've seen weaker men than he survive the cutter and come out the other end all the stronger," Lester sniffed.

"Why do you have to leave?" Dieter interrupted.

"Profit, Herr von Bernstein, profit," Lester repeated his mantra. "My ship's only making a profit when transporting cargo. Besides, every day I'm here, the harbourmaster charges a docking fee."

"Where are you going then?"

"I'll run the winds up to St. Petersburg. By the time I get back, you'll have the funds and Robison will be fit and healthy."

"I see," Dieter said, with an obvious air of disappointment. "Are you taking the equipment with you?"

"Yes, I am."

"I'm sorry you don't trust us," Dieter said, shaking his head.

"I'm not," Lester scoffed. "Don't worry. I've not brought it halfway round the Baltic to let it rot in my hold. Have no fear, I'll be back. And with my hold bursting with high-class Russian vodka that'll swell my coffers with a few silver thaler."

"How long before you return?" Dieter wanted to know.

"I'll be back in a few weeks. Will you wait for me?" he taunted.

"Of course," Dieter said, his voice sounding like a wisp of smoke blown away by a powerful gust of wind. "And we'll have the funds for you, I promise. This deal is as important to me as it is for you."

"I don't doubt that," Lester said. "If you don't mind, Herren, I have a ship to prepare for embarkation."

CHAPTER 40

The Trial

Behind all of this is God as the source of all Creation
and therefore of Law.
THE SACHSENSPIEGEL (THE SAXON MIRROR)

Marion walked up the steps of the Altstadt Magistrates' Court, Sisi and Dieter on one side, Skoda and Fermor on the other. She had arrived the night before with her daughter to find Dieter's house in a swamp of despond. Dieter was anxious about Lester's sojourn to St. Petersburg.

"If Lester doesn't come back," he was moaning, "we'll be lost. Hell will freeze over before the King forgives us. He'll requisition the amber mine."

Marion tried to reassure him. "Lester's invested heavily in this enterprise. He's not going to find another buyer for the equipment, so he'll be back, you'll see, Brother dear."

In her turn, she was anxious about Sisi, who had more than tried her patience. Worse still, her daughter was still convinced that she, Marion, had betrayed Caspar's whereabouts to von Marwitz.

Besides, Marion's health was deteriorating – whenever the sun's glare became too bright, her head felt like someone was beating a drum inside it. Her vision became blurred and she felt dizzy.

Then there was Herr Doctor. When they'd arrived the night before, Skoda continued to take an uncommon interest in Sisi. It made Marion reflect on the episode with the scarlet robe in the Green Room. She was reluctant to fully accept Skoda into her community but at the same time her people needed a physician. She dismissed her concerns and decided to give him the benefit of the doubt.

Colonel von Marwitz stood at the entrance to the magistrates' court. With his arm still in a sling, he was discussing matters with his adjutant.

The court was held in a room with lime-plastered walls and a high ceiling. Behind where the magistrate sat was a huge, coloured fresco of the coat of arms of the Kingdom of Prussia, the black spread eagle, its claws clutching the orb and sceptre of state, a golden crown above its head.

The chief magistrate, suitably bewigged and robed, was Rudiger von Seydlitz. Like everyone in Ostpreussen, Marion knew the family name. Rudiger was the younger brother of Lieutenant-Colonel Friedrich von Seydlitz, whom she had met at the Order of the Black Eagle celebrations. Rudiger would fulfil the spirit, if not the letter, of the law. It did not bode well for a merciful outcome.

Caspar was led, or rather dragged, into the court. The poor boy! As well as slumped shoulders and a hang-dog expression, he wore a pair of heavy foot manacles.

The court usher read the charges, "Caspar von Barthen, you are charged with failing to present yourself for conscription and deliberately avoiding subsequent searches."

She knew how this legal wrangling was going to end. If only it were over quickly, and with the minimum of pain to her daughter, who sat, elbows on knees, chin cupped in her hands, glaring at the court officials.

Called to give evidence, Colonel von Marwitz confirmed both charges.

"Unforgivable!" von Seydlitz muttered, through the thick hair of his walrus moustache. "Does the accused have anything to say?"

Caspar made a keen examination of his ankle manacles.

After a pregnant pause, Sisi spoke on his behalf. "Your Honour, I am Elizabeth von Adler and I am here to plead for Caspar, who works on our estate. He's injured in mind and body, having already been conscripted once, and sent home through grave injury. This time, he ran away because he was afraid to go back. Please, release him from this second conscription."

"Thank you, young lady," von Seydlitz said stiffly. "I have a lot to do today, so if that concludes the case, we will move to the judgement."

The magistrate conferred with the colonel and declared, "In Ostpreussen, we are the King's loyal and obedient subjects. If we don't follow his statutes, we have no state. If we don't obey God's laws, we abandon our future.

"Caspar von Barthen, please stand. You have been found guilty of two grave and serious crimes. The laws of our state are a mirror of the laws of God, enshrined in the great law book, the Sachsenspiegel, or Saxon mirror. Our society is ordered according to the Heerschilde. The penal code is determined by which of its seven levels the person occupies. You occupy the lowest. By your wilful negligence, you have offended the highest level, the King, the supreme representative of the state. The degree of punishment is never arbitrary, it is an exact retribution designed to match the gravity of the offence."

He paused and added, "Caspar von Barthen, you are hereby sentenced to twenty years' hard labour."

"What! Twenty years!" Sisi was railing, pointing at the chief magistrate. "That's a death sentence! What sort of justice is that? Caspar couldn't fight a blade of grass! Release him, for pity's sake."

"Order in court!" the usher said.

When the hubbub subsided, the magistrate said, "Take the prisoner below."

As Caspar was led passed Sisi, he pulled a pink 'kerchief out of his pocket and pressed it to his heart. It had snowdrops in each corner. Marion remembered that her daughter had given it to him as a keepsake.

Sisi begged the magistrate, "Please, Your Honour, I beg you to reconsider. For him, this sentence is worse than being on the front line, where at least he would be in the company of his fellow villagers. If the colonel was injured in fighting and forbidden to return to the battle lines, why not Caspar?"

Von Seydlitz tugged on his moustache and said, "Young lady, you have spoken well. I have heard your pleas for mercy."

Marion could hardly believe her ears. Was he really contemplating compassion?

"My Lord, I have a suggestion." It was Skoda.

"Who are you?" von Seydlitz asked.

"Doctor Skoda, physician to the von Adlers, Your Honour," he replied. "Let me examine the boy and I will give you my professional opinion."

"This is most irregular, but I will allow it," von Seydlitz added. "Be quick about it, the law brooks no delay."

"Yes, thank you, Your Honour," Skoda said. Turning to Sisi, he said, "And I humbly beseech your ladyship's permission."

Before Sisi knew what he was doing, he planted a chivalrous kiss on the back of her hand. Sisi blushed from ear to ear.

"That's quite enough, Doctor Skoda," Marion said, separating him from her daughter.

Skoda went down to the cells and returned within the hour. When the court reconvened, von Seydlitz asked, "What is your recommendation? Is it imprisonment in a military jail or conscription to the front line?"

Skoda wrung his hands, saying, "This was a difficult, terrible choice. I find that the von Barthen boy is unsettled in the mind, though his constitution is strong. Imprisonment will stifle his young spirit. I recommend a role at his old regiment, where he may put his recent knowledge of writing and reading to good use, such as an assistant secretary to one of the junior officers."

Marion could not believe her ears. Sisi was ecstatic. This was a blissful compromise, if only von Seydlitz agreed.

The chief magistrate cleared his throat and said, "In the light of these mitigations, the sentence is commuted. Herr Caspar von Barthen is to join as an assistant secretary in his previous regiment, there to remain for the rest of the campaign. I believe the regiment in question is encamped in Silesia."

"The exact location is, of course, highly confidential," the colonel replied, "but yes, I believe the regiment is part of the van."

"Case closed," von Seydlitz said.

As Dieter congratulated Sisi, Marion had words for the doctor. "While I must reprimand you for taking liberties with my daughter, I must also thank you for helping to ease Caspar's plight."

"I appreciate your candour, Your Excellency," Skoda said, with a sycophantic smile. "I hope I have pleased the junge Fräulein."

Sisi was typically unimpressed. "No, you haven't. You kissed my hand! If that wasn't gross enough, Caspar's still being forcibly sent away. So, no, I don't think I'm going to thank you."

Marion took a deep breath. "My dear, think about what they said. The Austrians are trying to reconquer Silesia. Once they're defeated, Caspar will be released from his sentence and allowed to return home."

"How many years will that be? This war has already lasted six." Sisi was indignant.

"Despite your protests, I think this is a successful outcome," Marion said.

"No, it's not. You broke your promise. You informed the colonel of Caspar's whereabouts," came the voice of rebuke.

"I did not."

"Then prove it," Sisi replied.

"I will," she said. "Ask the colonel. He'll tell you."

But he had left the court, leaving her crestfallen that her daughter no longer trusted her word. Caspar wasn't the only one on trial.

CHAPTER 41

The Promissory Note

My rights, my quarrels, my person, and the entire State
Seem to me to be matters too slight to be
of importance to Providence.
The worthless and childish squabble of
humans does not merit its concern.
KING FREDERICK THE GREAT

Marion's journey from the magistrates' court back to Junkerstrasse was noisy and uncomfortable. The sound of the wheels on the cobblestones rattled inside her head, aggravating her all-too-customary headache.

Sisi was slumped in the corner of the carriage, arms folded, head bowed in frenzied concentration. Marion decided to leave her alone. At least von Seydlitz had demonstrated compassion. Justice was done and was seen to have been done. That was all she could ask.

Arriving at Dieter's, Philip opened the door and informed his master that a man was waiting to see him.

"Who is it?" Dieter asked.

"The gentleman wouldn't give a name," Philip replied. "He said you'd know him."

"Where is he?" Dieter asked.

"He's with Aunt Charlotte in the study."

Marion accompanied her brother. Opening the study door, Dieter burst out, "Well, Herr Silberstein, what can I do for you?"

"I think, Herr von Bernstein, it is more what I can do for you," Silberstein replied, with a gracious bow.

Marion glanced at her brother and nodded.

"He has a most interesting proposition, Dieter," Charlotte said, her perfume filling the room with the delightful fragrance of rose petals.

"Please, tell us more," Dieter said.

"I'm here as a family friend and business acquaintance," Silberstein began. His constant energetic movements reminded Marion of those of a wren. "Every day, I am wracked by guilt about the fire at my Sonne warehouse. We were both forsaken by God that dreadful day! Now it is my fervent wish to make amends to you and your family."

"Herr Silberstein," Marion said, fluttering her fan, "you've helped us with good, sound advice over the years. I hope today you can provide my family with more manna from heaven."

"I will try my best, Your Excellency," Silberstein said. "Through my connections in the Chamber of Commerce, I have come to learn of your predicament with the King."

"So, it's common knowledge." Dieter bit his lip.

"I'm afraid it is," Silberstein replied. "Let me cut to the quick. You require funds. I'd be pleased to lend you them."

"You would? That's wonderful. What would you take as collateral?" Dieter asked.

"A share of the Anna Amber Mine; one-tenth will do it."

"A tithe is a big share," Dieter said, pulling his earlobe.

"Sixty thousand thaler is a big loan," Silberstein replied. "If you agree, the promissory note is here on the table."

Dieter scrutinised the note. "It says you will also provide a promissory note for the second instalment of sixty thousand thaler if it's required."

"Correct," Silberstein said.

Marion was curious. "Why this renewed interest in amber, Herr Silberstein?"

"You are right to ask, Your Excellency," Silberstein replied. "When it happened, I knew the warehouse fire was His punishment. Now, following deep reflection, I believe it was His way of guiding me back to the amber business."

"Go on," Marion said.

"Before the war," he added, "I purchased amber from you to trade in Prague and other cities on the old Amber Road. I still have many of those contacts. When I heard about your financial difficulties, I saw this as an ideal opportunity to rekindle our business association."

"I see," Marion replied. This was indeed a blessing.

"This is a family business," Dieter said. "Ladies, tell me, shall I accept the offer?"

"I have attended many a bar mitzvah with Moshe," Aunt Charlotte chimed. "Despite past tragedies, I have no hesitation in advising you to accept his kind and timely offer."

"As do I," Marion said. "The King will have funds in his coffers sooner or later. Dieter, once you repay Herr Silberstein, the full ownership of the mine returns to you."

"This is a mortgage on the mine, so you are correct, Your Excellency," Silberstein said. "However, should you accept, I want generous rates when I come to trade in amber."

"Agreed," Dieter said, clasping Silberstein's hand. He signed the document and said, "What a relief. Now I need to get this to Lester before he sails."

Clutching the promissory note, he rushed out of the door.

CHAPTER 42

The Forces of Enlightenment

Man is born free and everywhere he is in chains.
Those who think themselves masters of others
are indeed greater slaves than they.
JEAN-JACQUES ROUSSEAU

Marion enjoyed the cool breeze in the shade of the avenue of linden trees. She could hear the cries of joy from the children playing by the lake shore. Konstantin's slurred but booming voice interrupted the summer sojourn.

"I told you once already," he said. "Don't paddle in the water!"

"But Daddy, the geese and the ducks are paddling in the water. Why can't I?" It had to be Egor.

Marion shared a blithe smile with the harangued father. "Yes, I know that," he replied. "The ducks and geese can swim. You can't."

That seemed to keep Egor quiet. For a while, at least.

Five days had passed since Caspar's trial and Marion was beginning to put it behind her. Her thoughts and hopes were tempered by unsettling night-time dreams of eagles plucking eggs from mountain-top eyries. Her fontanelles and scalp were like bread dough. It was terrifying. The other day, by accident, she'd prodded her finger into her scalp. Before it had swallowed the nail of her finger; now it buried up to the first knuckle. Her skull was soft and squishy and it was getting worse. Was it the cords of the wicked? She shook her head and wished away her nightmares.

Next to her was this idyllic domestic scene, Konstantin sipping vodka like it was holy water, guarding the little ones and failing. Sasha was nursing baby Joachim; the little fellow had a fulsome smile and mysterious deep blue eyes. What a bellow on his lungs when he wanted his mother's milk. Ten months, how time had flown!

Her gentle musing was interrupted by the sounds of a horse galloping down the lake path, stirring up the birds, alighting from their roosts with cries of alarm. The horseman pulled up in front of their lakeside group. It was Philip.

"Letter for you, Your Excellency," he said, handing her a missive.

Dieter had sent a rider, so it was important.

She read:

Tuesday, 15th June, 1762.

The Anna Amber Mine, Fischhausen.

Dear Sister,

I hope this letter finds you well.

With Silberstein's promissory note, I settled the first instalment with Captain Lester. Despite that, the man still embarked for St. Petersburg. I'm convinced he's blinded by the pursuit of pfennig and thaler. That was four days ago. Hopefully, by the time he returns, the King will have released the funds for me to settle the second instalment.

I now know every bump and crevice and hole on the Fischhausen road, because I've spent that time cajoling and persuading three pairs of oxen to haul my precious cargo of Newcomen engines to the mine head. And yesterday, we finally arrived and unloaded them. I can't tell you how good that feels to be able to continue father's heritage.

I was expecting Charles Robison to have arrived by today to install and commission the engines, but instead I received a letter from Doctor Skoda. He is attending Robison in Löbenicht Hospital and informs me that the poor boy's health is deteriorating. This is terrible news, because in Robison's absence, we must search elsewhere for an instrumentation specialist, which brings me to my request.

Sexton Fermor is trained in instrumentation and knows the Newcomen engines. All our hopes now rest on him. Ask him please to help us and travel to Fischhausen. Then we can pump out the water from the flooded mineshafts and excavate the material to service the King's requirements for a new Amber Room.

Help your family. Plead with Fermor to come. I know you will.

Your loving brother,

Dieter von Bernstein.

She put the letter down and said, "Kadow. Ask Sexton Fermor to come and see me."

"Yes, Your Excellency," her butler replied, and walked stiffly, head held as high as a swan, back to the Schloss.

Prayer book in hand, Fermor emerged from the chapel.

"You wanted to speak to me, Your Excellency?" he asked.

"Yes, I do, Sexton. I've received this letter from my brother. Here, you can read it."

Fermor sat on the grass verge and took his time. With each passing moment, his brow seemed to wrinkle a little deeper. He swished away a fly and said, "I feared this would happen, Your Excellency. I'm afraid I can't help you."

She had imagined he would readily agree, so this was more than a surprise. "Why not?" she asked. "Don't you have the expertise?"

"It's true what your brother says," Fermor admitted. Speaking as if he had a bitter taste in his mouth, he went on, "While I have been trained to service and operate the Newcomen engine, it was many years ago and I can barely remember it."

"If you set your mind to it," she said, "it would come back. I know you have more to do around the parish in the wake of Pastor Leopold's sad demise, but you would only be absent for a week or so. Konstantin could take up the reins."

"I'm aware of that, Your Excellency," he replied. "The truth is, I can do it, but I don't want to."

"Why not?"

"Getting grease on my hands, smelling the odours of hot metal and suffering steam burns – that was in a previous life. I nearly died as an engineer servicing these machines and look at me now – I'm reborn into a purposeful life, serving a greater good. I don't want to retreat back to my old life."

"I won't compel you. If you don't want to help us, you'll still be sexton here and I'll still respect you. This matter is of the utmost urgency to me and my family. I was born a von Bernstein, known in Ostpreussen as the Amber family. Since the beginning of the war, we have been deprived of this rich source of wealth. On the Samland Peninsula, there is more amber than anywhere else in the world. We need these machines to work. Only you can help us. Our reputation depends on it, as does our future prosperity."

"I understand, Your Excellency," Fermor said with a sigh. "I will explain myself. When I trained in London, I was a passionate advocate of progress and the liberating power of machines. I saw technology as a way to free the populace from the yoke of the land. Working and living here, on your estate, amongst your people, I have seen what an enlightened landowner can achieve. You are firm but kind, you rule your people with a strong hand, yet they adore you and work themselves to the bone for you and for each other. There is a true sense of community here, a communion with a greater purpose, in which your people don't serve you, they serve the land on behalf of God and you do the same. That way, everyone points in the same direction. It's like a piece of amber, you rub it and a piece of fluff or a feather will stick to it. That's what your estate provides, a sticking together of different people under a single movement.

"In a dream vision, I saw that there are huge forces at play in the Enlightenment. Doctor Daniel Rolander spoke of them too. They are epitomised by the Adler, which I believe to be an angel of the Lord. Because the lands of Northern Europe have ordered their society and their laws to be a mirror image of God's laws, the Adler has chosen them to benefit first from its new inciting influence.

"Once I was a supporter, but now I am sceptical of the forces of progress. I doubt these machines and inventions will bring the benefits that are claimed. There are dangers, the biggest of which is the huge propensity for misuse of this great influence."

"I see," she said, sniffing the summer air. She wasn't convinced. She had more to say. "You strive to hold yourself to high principles. In this case, doesn't charity begin at home? We gave you back your life, literally. Amelia nursed you daily. I helped her. The whole community prayed for you and eventually accepted you, even though you were an enemy soldier, albeit originally from a different country. Since then, you have repaid that kindness in full: you saved the community from starvation. I ask you one more time, on behalf of my brother, help install the Newcomen engines. Roll up your sleeves and get those hands full of grease, for me, Marion Gräfin von Adler."

"I hear you, Your Excellency. But, on this occasion, I cannot accede to your wishes."

"At least sleep on it," she hissed.

He nodded and said, "Yes, of course."

CHAPTER 43

Eaten by the Gods

God is the God who judges amongst the gods.
THE BOOK OF PSALMS 82:1

That night, Fermor got up and went for a walk. He seemed to float more than walk, which was unusual, because he didn't remember being able to float. A weightless Fermor, that must be a first, he thought whimsically to himself. Since his association with the Adler, he was growing accustomed to strange appearances and numinous apparitions.

Beneath him was a terrain of low, undulating sand dunes. A long, thin sandbank protruded from the dunes and reconnected further down the coast to the same land mass, forming a lagoon. Flying the flag of the black spread eagle, the ship plied its way through a small gap in the finger-like sandbank. In the distance, he spotted the single peaked spire of Königsberg Cathedral.

He was looking down from above on the coastline of Ostpreussen.

Wispy clouds swirled around his feet as he glided through the air. He imagined a bird or two would fly past him. None did. This new, ethereal, lighter-than-air self was thrilling, spectacular even. Flying high, he was a bird, though he couldn't see that he had any wings. He swooped down on an open mine, a quarry. And – this was surprising – he flew straight *through* the land. He imagined that he was going to bounce off the grassy knoll he had aimed at, but not at all, he flew into it and found himself travelling *through* the earth.

No light, no smell, no sound, just darkness. The earth was dense, compact and fertile. He didn't mind not being able to see what was ahead. That was nothing new – it described his life. He was mightily confused and more so by the increased softening in his head.

He was convinced that this new facility, this ability to fly and to hover outside his physical body, had appeared by virtue of his association with the Adler. It filled him with confidence that the Adler would trust him in this way. He was determined to follow its purposes, which he was sure would soon be made clear to him.

He arrived in an underground tunnel, shards of amber glistening in the half-light. The earth enclosed him in its embrace. It was warm, dark and moist, like a womb. He felt at home in this space, a peace like he'd never felt before. The darkness was palpable, primordial, within which everything was latent.

Ahead, a flicker of light. A candle flame, lighting the gloom. A filament, a tendril of brightness, of hope, of being. All that concentrated darkness couldn't put out that candlelight. It was pre-eminent. Light was life-giving, life-allowing, filling the void with majesty, order and meaning.

He was drawn towards it. He travelled down the long corridor, worms and slugs oozing out of the tunnel. Life burst out from the deepest caves and from the hallowed earth.

If the Earth wasn't there, then he wouldn't exist. Nor would any life. So, the Earth was sacred, because it was there. He was sacred too, because he was there – upheld, maintained, every moment, every breath, kept alive.

The tunnel twisted and turned, the light beckoning him. Ahead, the tunnel opened into a domed chamber, seams of yellow amber protruding here and there. He made out a vague form, as if the darkness moulded itself into a recognisable shape. He glided towards it.

A person sat with his back to him. The light around the person wore a yellowish, mustard tinge. A bird, a large bird, was sitting on the person's head. The bird squawked, its petulant cry filling the chamber, emptying the void of silence. The bird turned to him. Something was in its beak.

He realised what he was seeing.

Oh. My. God.

The crown of the person's scalp was open. Its claws buried deep into it; the bird pecked at the exposed brain matter.

No, surely not.

Yes, the person sat there willingly, as some sort of sacrificial act at the altar of enlightenment.

"Stop!" Fermor cried.

Frightened, the bird alighted and flew straight at him. The eagle flew right through him, like he – and it – were mere tendrils of smoke.

The person turned. It was…

… Marion.

In a haunting voice, she asked, "Do you know what it's like to be eaten alive by the gods?"

Which gods? was the thought on his mind when he awoke, sweat pouring off his body.

Then he knew: the Adler lived in the Anna Amber Mine.

The Adler was a servant of God. He wanted to be eaten by the gods. Care and compassion, magnanimity and mercy, honour and humility, they were the medicines of the gods. To be eaten alive meant to surrender to these medicines completely.

He had to go to the mine.

Tomorrow.

CHAPTER 44

The Twelve Pillars

Faith consists in believing when it is beyond
the power of reason to believe.
VOLTAIRE

On his way to Fischhausen the next day, Fermor broke the journey and stayed the night at Dieter von Bernstein's town house in Junkerstrasse.

When he came downstairs in the morning, Aunt Charlotte was waiting for him – or so it seemed.

"Who are you? What do you want, young man?" she mumbled, waving her walking stick at him, like he was a street urchin who'd thrown a potato skin at her.

"Dear Aunt Charlotte," he began in his best accent, which even after recently learning to speak German, wore a vestige of sing-songy lowland Scots.

"Do I know you, scoundrel that you are?" she said, prodding a disgusted finger at him.

"I-I wanted to speak to Doctor Skoda," he stammered. *Why doesn't she recognise me? What's the matter with her?*

"Well, he's not here," Aunt Charlotte said, in a way that made him feel as insignificant as a doormat. "You're fit and well. You don't need to consult a physician. Bah! The youth of today! My generation was made of iron," she added. With a desultory wave of her hand, she headed off towards the back garden.

Young Eleonore, the maid, was passing. Dressed in a pink apron, her hair was neatly arranged in a bun and tied up inside a white cap. One or two silky blonde strands protruded from it, lending her a delightfully extravagant air.

He noticed she carried a tray of letters, which he assumed were for Aunt Charlotte.

"My dear," he said. "May I take them to Her Ladyship?"

"Well, yes, Your Lordship, if you insist," she said. While Fermor felt a pang of guilt on being called Your Lordship, he decided not to correct her.

Eleonore curtsied and bestowed on him a deliciously wicked smile, which, coupled with a twinkle in her soft blue eyes, made him think of the time when he might have accepted her subtle invitation and followed her into her parlour. He was a man of God now and such matters of the flesh were behind him, hopefully. With an air of pious reluctance, he took the tray from her. As his hand brushed against hers, a youthful warmth and innocence coursed through his veins. So many mortal temptations, when only the night before last, he'd pledged himself to be eaten by the gods!

As he scurried off in search of Aunt Charlotte, he couldn't decide which of the two women confused him more, the old temptress or the young one.

The garden was blooming with subtle white roses, brilliant red tulips, interspersed with a well-tamed box hedge and a highly manicured grass verge. The bees were buzzing around the azaleas and he was caught by the delicate beauty of a foreign intruder – a Chinese chrysanthemum bathed in a golden yellow hue.

"Aunt Charlotte," he called. No answer. At the end of the garden was a small oak which had shed its spring blossom and dowsed the earth beneath it in a circular curtain of pretty silken white. From behind its trunk came none other than the old temptress.

"There you are." She gave him a quirky smile, as if that could compensate for whatever misdemeanour he'd unknowingly perpetrated.

"These came for you," he said, handing her the letters.

"They did? For me?" she barked. She glanced down that aquiline nose at him like he was one of those garden snails that thrived in dark, moist surroundings. "Where did you get these from? Oh, are you the new post boy?" she asked. Her eyes seemed to cloud over, as if she was no longer aware of her surroundings.

"No, I'm a house guest," he tried to explain.

"I don't know you," she complained, "who are you?"

"I'm Sexton Ian Fermor of Schloss Ludwigshain," he insisted.

"I'll give you a bash with my trowel, you insolent boy." She made an aggressive gesture with her garden implement. He backed away from her protestations until, thankfully, a heavenly angel on two legs arrived to extract him out of his earthly predicament.

"Now, now, Aunt Charlotte," a girl's voice said.

"Ah, sweet Eleonore," Aunt Charlotte replied. "Who is this man? What's he doing in my garden?"

"Come, come, Aunt C," Eleonore said, taking the old bird by the elbow. "Let us find ourselves a seat and see who has written you these letters."

"Yes, dear, let's do that," she agreed, all sweetness and light. On the way out, Aunt C cast him a Parthian glance of withering disdain.

"Don't worry, Your Lordship," Eleonore whispered to him. "She has these turns. She just needs a cup of tea."

"I'm going to Löbenicht Hospital," he said with his best winsome smile. "I want to see Charles Robison."

"Doctor Skoda left here earlier this morning to attend to him," Eleonore replied, patting Aunt Charlotte on the hand.

He smiled and beat a hasty retreat.

The city streets were bustling with vendors selling their wares, the ladies with their colourful feathers and summer finery, the gentlemen in their black top hats covering copious wigs and wearing full-length dress coats. Horses, carts and carriages trundled along the cobbled stones, as the waters of the Pregel River sparkled under the city's seven bridges. The day was filled with life and Fermor felt good to be part of it.

It was just as well, because he was in for a shock. When he arrived at Robison's hospital ward, his bed was empty.

He found Rudolf quaffing his thirst on a beaker of beer.

"Where's Robison? Has he been discharged?" he asked.

"Nothing of the kind," Rudolf replied. "He's downstairs."

"Oh, which ward is he on?"

"Ward? No, he's not on a ward. He's in the autopsy laboratory," Rudolf said, without a trace of emotion. "He's resting in the arms of Our Lord."

"Dead?" He stood there in disbelief. "How? What did he die of?"

"That's what Skoda and Sömmerring are trying to find out."

"Sömmerring? Who's he?"

"That's Doctor Johann Sömmerring. His son, Samuel, is with him. They're conducting an autopsy on Herr Robison. Go to the gallery and you can witness it for yourself."

"Err," he muttered, "I think I'll…"

"Squeamish, eh?" Rudolf observed. "I was too the first time I saw the innards of a human being. The blood leaks all over the place. Makes such a mess. And it's so slippery. Ach! And the smell. Nauseous." Rudolf added an obligatory pinch of the nose.

"Yes, thank you for the introduction," Fermor said. He was already feeling queasy.

"Listen," Rudolf said. "There's a seat outside the autopsy laboratory. Wait for them there."

"I'll do that," he said with a sigh of relief.

The way to the autopsy room led him past the grotto with the statue of the Virgin Mary. He paused to ponder the meaning of those twelve stars above her head. They were mentioned in the verse from the Book of Revelations too, but he seemed to be missing a piece of the puzzle.

Outside the autopsy laboratory, he found Skoda giving the registrar details of the death.

"Name of the deceased?" the registrar asked.

"Charles Robison," Skoda replied.

"Please confirm the date of the death."

"Earlier this morning, 17th June, 1762."

"His nationality and occupation?"

"Scottish," Skoda replied. "He was a crew member of *The Lion Rampant*, Captain Lester's ship."

"Ah, death is tragic and to die away from home is more so. Imagine, a lonely corpse at his own funeral," the registrar muttered with a rueful shake of his head. A man and a boy emerged from the autopsy room wearing blood-splattered aprons. They resembled butchers more than doctors.

Skoda introduced them. "These are the Sömmerrings, Johann and Samuel, father and son."

Johann was a gruff old fellow, with bushy eyebrows, deep-set eyes, a pointed chin and a character to match. Samuel, on the other hand, was a bright-eyed young protégé, as keen as a dog chasing a squirrel. He must have been born with a scalpel in his hand, because at no more than six or seven years old, he was already attending his father's autopsies.

"They helped me perform the autopsy," Skoda added.

"Well, that's not strictly true, Doctor Skoda," Doctor Johann Sömmerring said in a crisp rebuttal. "At the first incision into the carcass, you vomited the contents of your stomach over the autopsy room floor and disappeared."

"And I had to clear it up!" little Samuel complained.

"I-I'm sorry," Skoda stammered. "I think the quail's eggs unsettled my stomach this morning."

"So it would seem," Doctor Sömmerring said.

"What were your findings?" Skoda asked.

"The young man died of inflamed lungs," Sömmerring senior explained, rubbing his palms together like he was about to pray to the Almighty.

"It's tragic that a man should be cut down in the prime of his youth," Fermor said.

"During the autopsy, we made a significant and historic discovery about the cranial nerves," Doctor Sömmerring said.

"What are the cranial nerves?" Fermor asked.

"The nerves in the brain," Doctor Sömmerring replied. "They help the body move around and control the five senses. If the brain is the ruler of the body, the cranial nerves are the ruler's chief ministers. Up to now, it was thought that there were only nine."

"And…?" Fermor asked.

"Today we confirmed that there are twelve," Doctor Sömmerring said.

"Why is this important?" Fermor asked with a frown.

"The twelve cranial nerves are the ways we comprehend the world outside of us," Sömmerring senior replied. "The human is a temple. Spiritually, these cranial nerves are tantamount to the twelve pillars of that temple."

As he contemplated this new discovery, Fermor said, "It was nice to meet you, Doctor Sömmerring, and your son. But now I must take my leave." He turned to Skoda and added, "I'm heading to the Anna Amber Mine."

On his way there, he could hardly concentrate on the route, he was so excited. He kept thinking about the twelve stars above the head of the statue of the Virgin Mary, as there were in the verse in the Book of Revelations. Now there were twelve cranial nerves.

It all pointed to the head, the brain in the head, just like Rolander had said.

Sömmerring had said that the twelve cranial nerves were the twelve pillars of the human temple. What if God wanted to enhance that temple?

What did Rolander say? *We are Homo Sapiens Sapiens. God has left pods of advancement, called angels, to develop and promote human genius. When a Homo Sapiens Sapiens develops into a genius, that person becomes a Homo Tri-sapiens.*

He was convinced that the Adler was one of those angels, meaning it was the herald, the progenitor, of Homo Tri-sapiens.

Who or what was he going to meet in the bowels of the earth?

CHAPTER 45

The Bernstein Coast

Good fortune is often more fatal to a ruler than adversity.
During the former, they are intoxicated with presumption.
The latter renders them circumspect and modest.
KING FREDERICK THE GREAT

Fischhausen was a small natural harbour that overlooked Frisches Lagoon, a freshwater bay separated from the Baltic Sea by a long, thin sandbank with a gap large enough to allow shipping into and out of the port of Königsberg. Its other notable landmark was the renowned Anna Amber Mine.

Fermor had been there for seven days.

And on every one of them the oxen had moaned. First it was when they were pressed to haul the heavy and cumbersome cylinders all the way to the mine head. How they bellowed like the demons from hell. The men weren't much better. They needed all sorts of cajoling to lift the pistons into the midst of the engines.

Finally, they were ready. Today was the day. With a smattering of his engineering nous and a lot of sweat and toil, the first Newcomen pump was in place and ready to be fired. The fire was lit. The flames licked the round, smooth, shiny base of the cylinder. It wouldn't be long before the controlled marriage of these elements gave birth to that quixotic element, steam.

Ian Fermor was proud of his achievement. Thomas Newcomen would have been too, to see his atmospheric steam engines operating so far from his home in Dartmouth, England.

They could hear the creaks and groans of the cylinder as the water inside it slowly evaporated and condensed into steam. This drew down the piston and simultaneously worked the beam engine, in which a large wooden cross-beam rocked on a central fulcrum. On the other end of the beam was a long chain attached to a pump at the base of the mine. As the pressure built, the cylinder refilled with steam, preparing it for the next stroke of the piston. Water was drawn into the pump cylinder and expelled into a pipe to the surface by the weight of the machinery.

Next to him were Dieter von Bernstein and Philip. Dieter had scoured the Samland Peninsula for men. He'd extracted an assortment of ex-miners from the local inns. There were only a few of those. He'd hired young boys who had avoided the latest round of conscription. There weren't many of those either.

Under Fermor's instructions, the labourers threw logs onto the blazing fire beneath the cylinder. The water in the cylinder was fed by an exterior cold-water feed, topped up as and when necessary. They waited anxiously to see the fruits of their labours.

Slowly, the piston moved. The grinding noise was excruciating. But – it moved. The water was gurgling in the tank.

"She's alive!" Dieter yelled, more in relief than enthusiasm.

To his surprise, Fermor had enjoyed these past seven days immensely. He had thoroughly reacquainted himself with the inner workings of the Newcomen engine, the valves, the pump, and the heating mechanism. It had inspired his passion for instruments and especially for steam.

"Well, Fermor," Dieter said, slapping him on the back. "You've done it. There were a few anxious moments. The worst one was to get the two valves governing the cold-water feed and the cylinder feed to work in unison."

"Never doubt." He clasped his hands in prayer and kissed the crucifix hanging around his neck. "It's working! It's pumping water from the base of the mine."

The men broke out into spontaneous applause and threw their caps in the air, yelling and shouting.

"Marvellous! How long to pump it all out?" he asked, ever the pragmatist.

Dieter gave a high whistle. "The tunnels extend for leagues. There's a main shaft to the base from which the tunnel labyrinth fans out in every direction. We've two engines: we'll operate one and then use the other to give the first a rest."

"Are we looking at days or weeks?" Fermor asked.

"Mmm, I'd say days," Dieter replied, a satisfied grin on his face.

Fermor breathed a sigh of relief. "I've been married to a piston, a cylinder and a couple of valves for too long. I am going for a walk along the Bernstein Coast."

"In case they break down, don't go far," Dieter called out.

Fermor nodded. Walking off into the dunes, he glanced back at the machinery; the beam rocking back and forth like some demonic angel, the blazing fire beneath the cylinder, the piston moving up and down, the whole contraption clouded by a mass of hissing steam, it was so incongruous amidst the sand, the coastal grasses and the azure blue sea as a backdrop.

While he was relieved that he'd got the pumps working, he hadn't forgotten the Adler lived down in the amber tunnel labyrinth. Soon it would reveal to him his great purpose.

The afternoon was fine; the clouds were arranged like so many ribs across the sky and the sand was warm beneath his bare feet. Across the bay was Fischhausen. It was located at the southern end of the Samland promontory, the shape of which on the Mercator map bore an uncanny resemblance to the snub-nose of a sperm whale, making it all the more extraordinary because Samland meant Sperm Land. To Fermor, this was grist to the mill, because on the west-facing edge of Samland was the Bernstein or Amber Coast. That was where he was.

He strolled along the beach, the waves rolling in, as they had done under the rhythmic pulse of the moon ever since Adam and Eve emerged from the Garden of Eden.

There was a piece of amber. He washed his greasy hands in the cool Baltic Waters and stooped to pick it up. It was no bigger than a grain of sand. With that yellowish hue, it was definitely amber. There was another piece, washed up by the gentle waves, the magical, golden fruit of the sea.

Holding it between thumb and forefinger, it was like a speck of gold dust. There was a bigger piece about the size of a pebble. It was soft but firm, so he could mark it with his fingernail. This was a gift. Nature was extraordinary.

Dieter had told him that amber was a resin from the bark of the tree, formed a very long time ago. It was old, ancient. He examined the piece in his hand. My, there was something inside it. It had wings and a body, and tiny, multiple eyes… an insect.

A long time ago, a tiny insect was crawling around on a tree, and here it was in his hand, preserved for posterity, caught in the clutches of time.

Amber was a sealant, a preserver; he'd learnt that much already.

CHAPTER 46

Catherine Palace

Prussians don't shoot fast!
OSTPREUSSEN SAYING

During the seven days *The Lion Rampant* had been moored in St. Petersburg harbour, Donald Lester had conducted his business but remained desperate for a big commercial deal to justify his voyage from Königsberg.

On the day of his arrival, he'd visited the dockside Hussar's Inn, where he'd learnt by chance that the phlegmatic entrepreneur, Vladimir Kharkov, had returned to St. Petersburg from his livestock trading in Königsberg. Lester had vivid memories of the day last year he had encountered Kharkov in the Columbine Inn: on 10th November, his birthday.

The news that Kharkov was now involved in foreign trade filled him with renewed hope. During the last week, Lester had despatched messages and riders and even the occasional carrier pigeon, to every part of St. Petersburg and beyond. Despite his best efforts, his rewards were nil and the day of his scheduled departure loomed like a dark shadow. He had also failed to discover the whereabouts of his old friend, General von Fermor, who he had learnt had recently relinquished his position as Governor General of Königsberg.

While he waited for news, he'd noticed small but subtle hints of change in the ambiance of the great seaboard city. Two days ago, the quiet of night had been punctured by the sound of gunfire coming from the old city. Later, he'd learnt that it was a clash between competing factions in the Russian Imperial elite, fighting for control of the state. Lester wasn't a politician, but he knew well enough that politics dictated trade.

Emperor Peter III and his wife, Catherine, had acceded to the throne in January. The pungent smell of gun smoke in the air meant something was imminent and it wasn't peace.

When, that morning, a dozen Russian Cossacks galloped onto the quayside and pulled up alongside his ship, he could not suppress a broad smile.

"Captain Donald Lester!" the trooper called up to him on the bridge. The man's Russian accent was thicker than a Slav's forearm.

"That's me!" He stormed down the gangplank to meet them.

"Message for you!" the trooper said, making a curt and perfunctory bow.

With typical Russian brevity, it read, *Catherine Palace, today, midday. Kharkov.*

He almost punched the air in delight.

The ride from St. Petersburg to the provincial town of Tsarskoye Selo took several hours. That, he didn't mind; especially when his eyes set upon the stunning building. The grounds were immaculate and spacious, and the palace was an icon of Russian rococo architecture, renowned throughout Europe for its sumptuous elegance.

The royal palaces of Königsberg and Berlin were nothing compared to the lavish beauty and grand opulence of this glittering architectural jewel. This, he decided, was where he wanted to end up, and he wouldn't stop until he realised his dream. It was more possible than ever before. In these changing times, the previously indestructible lines of demarcation between the classes, between the aristocracy and everyone else, between the rich and the poor, between the secular and the sacred, had begun to melt in the religious fires of the Reformation and the secular heat of the Enlightenment, providing unrivalled opportunities for the likes of him, a mere bairn from a stone croft.

Soon, kings would marry commoners and princes would marry peasants. Change was seeded in the wind. There was revolution, social revolution, in the air.

Slowly, he rode through the palace gates into the spacious, perfectly-tended grounds. The tree-lined approach to the rococo palace followed a stately avenue. Ahead stood the Catherine Palace, its four central white columns offset against the gorgeous pale blue facade.

Standing on its steps to welcome him was Vladimir Kharkov. "Welcome to the palace," he said, with that wistful smile. With his droopy left eye and a deep scar etched beneath it, Lester realised that the man resembled nothing more than a shameless thug.

"Thank you, nice to see you again," he answered.

"Come with me, I've someone who wants to renew your acquaintance," Kharkov murmured. He led him by the hugely impressive spiral staircase, into the Golden Enfilade, passing in turn, the White State Dining Room, the Crimson Pilaster Room, and the Green Pilaster Room, each as lavish as the last. Lester had to consciously stop his mouth falling open in admiration. This was beauty of an order he'd never witnessed, let alone imagined. People lived in embroidered luxury which he thought had died with the pharaohs.

As they entered the Portrait Hall, the next room along in the Golden Enfilade, Lester had the wherewithal to ask, "Who's this mystery man?"

"Wait, you'll see," Kharkov said.

They approached the next room along, a blush of gold and yellow. Standing on the threshold, his eyes rested on the ornate mirrors and gilded craftwork. He was admiring the fantastic ceiling painting, replete with angels, when Kharkov said, "Please, Captain Lester, this way," and he ushered him to the centre of this incredible room. It felt still, a quiescence he'd felt in the holiest of churches. Sitting next to a beautifully-carved wooden table, was a man he recognised.

"General von Fermor!" he squealed. "How nice to see you again."

"Captain Lester," the general said. "I'm so glad you could come. How long has it been?"

"Five years, I think, yes, five years," Lester said. "Your nephew, Ian Fermor, was on board my ship and I introduced him to you."

"So you did, so you did," the general said, his smile as ample as his imposing presence. Dressed in his full military regalia, he wore a row of medals over his heart while shiny epaulettes adorned his shoulders.

"His conversion to the clergy was unusual, don't you think?" Lester remarked.

"Not really," the general quipped. "He's still a foot soldier fighting battles, only spiritual ones. I've seen many a man exchange the sword for the good book. I suspect it's to do with the proximity to death. Is he still sexton to the Adlers in Ludwigshain?"

"Yes, he is."

"What do you think of our palace?" the general asked.

"Breath-taking," he replied.

"And of this, our very own Amber Room?" the general said, lifting his hand, and with an open palm, inviting him to admire.

"So, this is the original Amber Room."

His words seemed to hang in the air, as if somehow it wasn't right for mere humans like him to converse in its gilded presence. The ochres, brownish-yellows and deep golds were like a deluge of colour washing over him.

"The very same; a gift nearly fifty years ago from King Frederick I of Prussia to Emperor Peter the Great of Russia. It concluded a grand alliance between the two nations."

"Is this what the commotion is about?" Lester said, still gazing around at the tapestries and ornate decorations with a mix of awe and wonder.

"What commotion is that?" the general asked.

"King Frederick the Great wants to build his own Amber Room."

"The man wants nothing more than to emulate his father," the general confirmed. "Before the war broke out, he had the audacity to request the return of the Amber Room. Of course, gifts are not returnable. Even though our present Emperor Peter III is a great admirer of your Frederick and sees him as a hero of our time."

"I may trade with them, my dear General, but please, I am not Ostpreussen. I'm a Scotsman, like your ancestors and your nephew."

The general raised an eyebrow. His face had deep trenches marking the cheeks, a feature that made his skin appear like the coat on top of cold gravy.

"You didn't bring me here to glory in the mirrors, gilded woodcarvings and amber panelling, so why am I here?" It was about time he asked that question.

"You are an international trader," the general replied. "I need to discuss international trade. Besides, I received word that you wanted to see me."

"Yes, I most certainly did. Would you like to hear my plans?"

"By all means," the general said, adjusting the flowing locks of his wig.

"There's a grand fortune to be earned in these times," Lester began. "I have a ship, I have ambition. I have ideas. All I lack are the funds."

"I have the funds, you have the connections," the general suggested with a wry smile.

"Good, then I envisage setting up a trading cycle," he murmured. "I buy Scots whisky in Glasgow and sell it in St. Petersburg. Then I buy vodka and sell it in Königsberg. Then I buy pine and amber and sell it in Glasgow. And the cycle starts again."

"That chimes perfectly with my own plans. I can fill your hold with first-class Russian vodka. How can you pay me for it?"

"I have a promissory note," he replied, patting the note in his wallet.

"Show me… oh dear, it's one of Silberstein's. I can't accept much of that. One-third at best."

"One-third?" He was grimacing.

"I can give you only one-third of its face value. That's twenty thousand thaler."

"Why?"

"Let me put it like this, Herr Moshe Silberstein has a reputation."

"What kind?" Lester shook his head. The man was talking in riddles.

"That Acts of God follow him like bees around a honey pot."

"Oh, you mean the warehouse fire. That was deliberate?"

"Most certainly," the general said, leaning back in his chair. "The seed was emptied from the warehouse the night before. Once the fire had run its course, the traders on the Bourse assumed there was a grain shortage, which put the price up. Silberstein made a killing on the open market."

"Who did he sell it to? The Prussians?"

"Oh, you are naive, Captain Lester," the general said. "I understand he sold half to the Habsburgs and half to the Bourbons. Meanwhile the Prussian Army starved on strict rations."

"Austrians and French, that's hardly patriotic," Lester said, as his mind churned with this information and wondered how best he could make use of it. "How do we proceed?"

"Providence shines on you today," the general said, indicating the sheer magnificence of the room. "I'll sell you vodka to the amount of one-third of Silberstein's note. If that's agreeable, and I see you are nodding, then I'll arrange for it to be loaded on your ship prior to your departure."

"That's in three days, God willing," he replied.

"We can do business. Herr Kharkov is my assistant. He will draw up the paperwork for you to sign. Hand him the promissory note. Goodbye, Captain Lester. May the winds blow fair and fresh for you."

They shook hands and Kharkov led him out of the palace and into an enlightened future.

CHAPTER 47

The Disappearance

In the beginning was the Word,
And the Word was with God,
And the Word was God.
THE GOSPEL OF JOHN 1:1

On that Saturday evening, the golden sun was sluggish in its descent, as it always was at this time of year when the nights were short. Marion was in the State Room, on her throne, waiting for Herr Silberstein to come and see her to discuss the promissory note. He could only do so when the Sabbath had finished after sunset.

As she studied the terms of the note, Sisi opened the door and loitered at the entrance, dressed in riding gear. She appeared to be reading a letter, but then quickly shoved it in an envelope, which she hastily put in her pocket.

"What's that?" Marion asked her.

"Oh, it's nothing, Mother," she replied.

She seemed distracted, so Marion asked, "Are you well?"

"Of course, I've been out riding. You can see that, can't you?"

Sisi had worn this cloak of antagonism since Caspar's arrest, some three weeks before.

Marion rubbed her eyes. She was tired; the work of the land and the estate was relentless and unforgiving.

Her daughter's soft blonde hair was normally tied into a neat ponytail. This evening, strands flew this way and that, and it resembled an autumnal haystack. Sisi wore this pinched look, like she was walking on quicksand and at any moment expected to be sucked into the mire.

"Yes, dear, I can. Are you going to bed?" Marion asked her.

"No, not yet." Sisi hesitated by the door – she knew she was not supposed to be in the State Room in riding gear.

Marion reminded her anyway. "You can't come in here dressed like that."

"Is that so?" Sisi said with undisguised malice. "The rules of the house, aren't they?"

"Yes, and rightfully so," she replied. "We're Prussians. We uphold decency, integrity, and honour. They're our standards."

"You got rid of Caspar," Sisi railed. "Was that the decent, honourable thing to do?"

"Dear Sisi," she said, taking a deep breath. "Don't be silly. You can't possibly believe that I 'got rid' of Caspar?"

"Colonel von Marwitz had a good idea where to find him, so I'm convinced it was you. You're that kind of woman!"

"I'm not any *kind of woman*, Elizabeth, I'm your mother." She reverted to her daughter's full Christian name when annoyed with her.

"You put loyalty to the state above your family. You call that honour: absolute loyalty to the King and everything he stands for. That's the code, le code aristocratique."

"For the last time, I did not tell Colonel von Marwitz," she said, trying to diffuse an acrimonious conversation. "I kept my promise to you. It disappoints me that you persist in believing otherwise."

"It was you!"

"Sisi," she said softly. "You're not listening. Calm down. Caspar will be home sooner than you think."

"I miss him, every day," Sisi said, emotion welling up in her pretty little face. "And despite his quirky nature, he's my soul brother."

Marion needed to convince her that she was innocent. Too late, because Sisi turned on her and said, "I hate you!" and stormed out of the room.

Marion felt a spear through her heart. Her own daughter, how could she say that, when she had tried her best to bring her up as a decent, caring woman, a true von Adler? She shook her head and tried to read the last page of the promissory note. The words on the page seemed jumbled. She couldn't concentrate. She was relieved when there was a knock at the door.

"Come in, Sisi," she said, hoping her daughter had returned to apologise.

"It's me, Your Excellency," Kadow said.

"Where did she go?" she asked.

"To her chambers, Your Excellency."

"Then tell Cecilia to take extra care of her in the morning," she said.

"Yes, Your Excellency."

An hour or two later, with the State Room bathed in dusk shadows, Moshe Silberstein joined her. Kadow lit a couple of lanterns and brought them a pot of coffee, her one indulgence in these frugal times. She was fond of the silver coffee pot in which it was served. She traced her index finger over its subtle, swirling engraving. A safe homecoming present from her mother to her father on his return from the first Silesian Wars, it prompted gentle memories of her parents.

A cooling breeze gusted through the open window, making the curtain dance to its tune.

Silberstein sat opposite her in his long black suit, the crown of his head covered by a black skull cap. Once they'd dealt with the promissory note, Silberstein stroked his shaggy beard and took a sip of his coffee. His face wore a particular weary melancholia amidst a sea of wrinkles. She'd seen that visage on him before – usually it was a preface to a philosophical discussion.

He put down his cup and asked, "Which is more useful, a machine or a human being?"

His obscure questions were as common as potatoes. She'd learnt over time that he often didn't expect an answer; he just wanted to seed the air with it. This one intrigued her though and she answered, "Well, it depends."

"Let me explain," he said. "We are in the midst of a social revolution, a transformation wrought by factories and particularly by machines. They are going to change the face of the world and already we see people leaving the land and the creation of cities of teeming millions. Many may disagree, but I believe these machines will bring a great benefit to society, and in that way, be a blessing to the Almighty."

"Well, that's quite a statement. But you haven't answered the question."

"Neither have you, Your Excellency," he pointed out.

"Then I will try," she said. "I don't agree with your statement. And yes, wait, I'll tell you why. I believe that the first purpose of a human being is to pay back for the gift of life by being true to themselves and fulfilling every aspect of their God-given design. The greatest humans are the ones who have done just that. We call them geniuses."

"Very interesting," Silberstein replied. "But consider this; a machine will only do what it was designed to do. Humans, on the other hand, have free will. From the lessons of history, we can see that they are prone to turn away from the purposes they were designed to follow. In that sense, a machine is more reliable and therefore more useful."

"Your comments on history are correct but your conclusion is awry," she said, standing up and pacing the room. "I believe that a human is more useful than a machine and always will be."

"Why?"

"Machines make no return to God. Only humans can do that."

"That's controversial," he admitted. "You think that usefulness should be measured against usefulness to God?"

"Don't you?" she said.

He answered with another question, "What do you mean by a 'return to God'?"

"I'll give you some examples," she said. "Machines can't forgive. Machines don't have courage, care or compassion. Only humans have those qualities. Machines are not alive. Human are. Machines are coarse instruments with no spirit. Humans are fine instruments filled with divine spirit."

"Yet machines can improve the lot of mankind, by removing toil and hardship."

"Yes, on Earth," she said. "But not where the Almighty is concerned. You are a business man. You can understand that God has made a huge investment in the universe and in organic life in which the human is the pinnacle. Naturally, He wants a return on His investment. The best return He can get is an enhanced one and only geniuses can make an enhanced return."

"What do you mean by an enhanced return?"

"I'll give you three examples: the building, St. Peter's Basilica in Rome; the painting, the *Mona Lisa*; and the musical composition, the *Missa Brevis*."

"Are only artists preferred by God?"

"No, not at all," she replied. "There is such beauty and order in the universe. Carl Linnaeus discovered the order within organic life. Nicolaus Copernicus has revealed the secrets of the solar system. These are towering achievements that elevate our understanding of the universe and its Creator. They also make a sublime return to God."

"Mmm," he murmured softly through the folds of his salt-and-pepper beard.

She was surprised. He seemed to have been swayed by her impassioned arguments, but he wouldn't admit to it. They sat in mutual silence, musing on the vicissitudes of life and living.

After a while, Silberstein yawned and took his leave.

Moments later, she climbed the stairs and was soon in her bed, dowsed in the deep sleep of Siloam.

The next morning, Marion dressed for Sunday Mass. When she got downstairs, Otto was in the vestibule whispering to Kadow.

"Herren, is something amiss?" she asked.

"Sisi, Your Excellency," Kadow said. "She went out riding on her mare, Charlie."

"Crack of dawn, it was," chimed Otto, "and still not back."

The morning air was bright and warm. By the avenue of linden trees, the lake appeared placid and majestic, a pool of life. "I see, well, it's a beautiful day. She's been out early before, I'm sure she'll be back soon."

Marion waited patiently for her daughter at the Löwenhagen church, as Sisi liked to play the harmonium for the opening chorale. When she failed to show for the entire service, Marion felt a knot in her stomach.

When Marion returned to the Schloss and by midday Sisi still hadn't returned, the knot tightened.

"Something terrible has happened to her!" Marion said.

Ursula tried to calm her fears. "No, Your Excellency, she's safe. She knows how to take care of herself. She'll be back. She's just gone for a long ride."

"Bring me Cecilia. Her governess must know something."

Cecilia bustled into the State Room.

"Do you know where my daughter is?" she demanded. "She's taken off on Charlie and hasn't been seen since before dawn."

"Je ne sais rien, Votre Excellence," Cecilia said. The woman seemed to sneer at all things Ostpreussen. The French always thought that God only resided in France, lending them this infuriating hubris. On such occasions, Marion regretted following the prevailing fashion of hiring a French governess.

"You are confidante to my daughter and accompany her for long periods. Tell me, what has she been like since the trial?"

"She misses Caspar. They were comme les deux petits anges. Losing her brother, Hans, at the same time, and little Nicol, all three conscripted à la même fois. C'était terrible pour elle. She said God was punishing her."

Marion felt annoyed that she hadn't been informed. "Well, she can't just disappear off the face of His earth."

Cecilia shrugged her shoulders.

"I've just remembered something," Marion said. "When she came back from riding yesterday evening, she was holding an envelope. When I asked her about it, she was prickly and hid it away before changing the subject. Do you know who wrote to her?"

"Non, je ne sais pas."

"Well, please go and look for the letter in her room. Oh, and let me know if any of her clothes or belongings are missing."

"I will do that, Gräfin, anything to help," Cecilia said and scuttled off to Sisi's room.

She called her trusted staff, Grenda, Ursula, Kadow and Christoph.

Holding back her tears, she said, "Sisi has not returned from her ride. She could be anywhere. Christoph and Ursula, look in the castle and the grounds. Kadow, send riders to the local villages. Ask the Bürgermeisters there if they have seen her. She's been gone five hours. She could be in Königsberg by now. Grenda, send riders there, to Dieter's, and to our family friends: the von Helldorffs and the others. Charlie could be lame, or has thrown her, so check the bridle paths she uses. Please be careful. There are bears and wolves out there. I'm missing a daughter. I don't want anyone else to go missing. Find her and bring her home to the bosom of her family. Please, I beg you."

CHAPTER 48

The Bonnie Banks of Loch Lomond

'Twas there that we parted in yon shady glen,
On the steep, steep side o' Ben Lomon',
Where in purple hue the Hieland hills we view,
An' the moon comin' out in the gloaming.
THE BONNIE BANKS OF LOCH LOMOND

The night had been even stranger than the previous one. In the eastern sky, the first slivers of dawn sent long shadows across the deck. Lester paced up and down, waiting for a few stragglers of his crew to return. It was their last night in St. Petersburg and he was regretting letting them go into the old city. They would weigh anchor on the morning tide. While midsummer nights were short enough, Lester had watched anxiously as fires and explosions illuminated the ebullient night sky. Ominously, they emanated from the direction of the Winter Palace.

General Wilhelm von Fermor had been true to his word. In amongst the Newcomen engine equipment, the hold of *The Lion Rampant* was rammed with crates of vodka. The profit from their sale in Königsberg would easily fund Lester's next venture. To realise his dream of a stately home, even with his idea of a three-way cycle of voyages, he'd have to do a lot of sailing back and forth to the ports of Europe. He needed a way to expedite it.

Out of nowhere, the quay was awash with troops, their marching boots echoing rhythmically along the harbour side. Scores of them were marshalled to perfection and in no time, they'd stationed units alongside the ships and boarded them. His ship was next to a Dutch trader, the last in line on the quay.

"Who they after, Captain?" his first mate asked. They were clearly searching for someone. Soon they were swarming over *The Lion Rampant* like flies over a rotting carcass.

"We're about to find out." He was feeling philosophical that morning.

"Captain," the Russian officer demanded. "Show me your passenger manifest."

Considering the large investment in troops, they were searching for an important personage. Lester tipped his head at the first mate and said, "Tell them."

"Och, laddie," the first mate explained, "we've no passenger manifest, cos we've no passengers."

"You lie," the officer said with a grimace. "I will search your ship." The officer ordered his troops to aft and stern and another unit below decks.

"Who are you looking for? I might be able to help," Lester said.

"None of your business! If he's on board, you will pay with your lives." The officer stood so close to Lester that the man's spittle sprayed on his face.

He wiped it off. "I'm a Scots trader. I've no interest in your escaped convicts."

"He's not a… Ah, you think you're clever, eh?" the officer replied.

As they spoke, Lester's missing crew members sauntered along the quay, lungs bursting with nostalgia, singing:

"You'll take the high road and I'll take the low road,
And I'll be in Scotland afore ye."

When the Russian troops blocked their drunken progress halfway up the gangplank, they stopped singing.

"Let them pass," Lester objected. "They're my crew. They've done nothing wrong."

"What's up, Captain? Them Ruskies giving us trouble?" one of the crew yelled back at the top of his voice.

"Keep them there until we've finished the search," the Russian officer ordered. One of the crew on the gangplank relieved himself into the sea, to the evident disgust of the Russians. What? Had they never seen a sailor piss in the sea before?

From the Dutch trader came shouted orders in Russian.

"What they sayin', Captain?" the first mate asked.

"Don't rightly know, but they're jumping around like swamp mosquitoes," he replied.

On *The Lion Rampant*, a soldier came up from below decks, brandishing a bottle of vodka, or bread wine as it was also known.

"See what I found!" he cried, giving it to the officer.

The Russian officer examined the image on the label. "This is special vodka. Where'd you steal it from, Scottie?"

The winds of fortune had changed direction and they were tacking into a stiff headwind.

"I-I'll get you the cargo manifest," he stammered.

"Show me," the officer snarled. "This is only for elite Russian Imperial officers."

"Is it?" he murmured innocently. He was about to drop the general's name when a huge shout came from the Dutch trader.

"Found him!" someone yelled.

A clutch of excited soldiers manhandled a bewigged gentleman dressed in the elegant style of the day.

"Hah! There he is!" the officer yelled in triumph. "The snake had crept aboard the Dutchman." He shoved the vodka bottle in the direction of his adjutant and led his men down the gangplank onto the quay. Crowds of soldiers gathered around the captured personage, prodding their bayonets triumphantly into the air.

Amidst shouts of 'Glorious Russia!' and 'For Catherine!' the soldiers bundled him into a waiting carriage and whisked him off the quayside, the cavalry unit in hot pursuit. In a few minutes, the quay was emptied of bustle, noise and soldiers. All that could be heard was Lester's drunken crew continuing where they had left off:

"Where me and my true love will never meet again,
On the bonnie, bonnie banks of Loch Lomond."

"Who was he?" he asked.

"A count, by all accounts." The first mate couldn't resist, could he?

"Yeah, but which one? In these parts, they're as plentiful as daisies in a meadow," he observed wryly.

"Och, does the name Mikhail Vorontsov mean anything?" one of the drunkards asked.

"Nah, not much. Them Ruskie names sound the same to me," he said.

"Aye to that, Captain!" the drunk replied.

"The tide's full. The day's afoot. Haul that gangplank aboard. Raise the anchor," Lester cried at the top of his voice. "And get to it, you lazy louts!"

CHAPTER 49

The Search

Which of you, if you had one hundred sheep, and lost one of them,
Wouldn't leave the ninety-nine in the wilderness,
And go after the one that was lost, until he found it?
THE GOSPEL OF LUKE 15:4

Marion's bones felt like they were carved out of stone, her eyes stung and her head ached. On a cloudless day, the incessant glare of the sun blurred her vision, the light spinning fantastic webs before her eyes. When the sun was out, she normally retired to a shaded room. With a missing daughter, these were anything but normal times. To allow her to see where she was going and protect her eyes, she tied gauze made of transparent muslin around her head and over her eyes. It was better than nothing. She scurried around in the late afternoon, after the sun sought to kiss the horizon. Night was best, though there wasn't much of it.

It was Sunday – a whole week since Sisi's disappearance – and not one iota of news. This was the most traumatic period of her life; her husband was away, her son had been forcibly conscripted and now her daughter had disappeared. Was every member of her family to be taken from her?

She recalled the time when Cassie, her pet dog, had gone missing when she was a child. She had never stopped searching for her little dog and weeks later found her carcass under a thorn bush, her body ravaged by wolves. Her eyes had been pecked out by the crows. The awful image of her contorted, lifeless body haunted her to this day and even more so, now that her daughter was missing.

She had to cling to the notion that one day soon, Sisi would return unharmed. A little dishevelled, her hair in a mess, she'd walk in through the huge entrance doors and with a warm smile, bring sunshine back into their dark, tawdry lives.

Marion had written to Gottfried, apprising him of the situation as far as she was able. That was the hardest letter she had ever had to write: to tell a father that his precious daughter has gone away, disappeared.

The most bewildering question of all was this; why had she departed the sanctity of the family? She could be lost, but she was very familiar with the broad confines of the estate, so that was unlikely. Had she been attacked by robbers? Unlikely, since there had been no reports of them in the vicinity. Or taken down by wolves? That was possible, but Alexander had shown her their lairs.

The last possibility that impinged on her mind was this: Sisi had followed through on her threat and left home to chase a dream in the shape of a simple village boy. That was also unlikely, since she should have known there was no future in it. And besides, Caspar was far away in Silesia.

Oh, Sisi, come home, please.

With no news for seven days – seven whole days of torture – she began to doubt Sisi was still alive. She felt empty, bereft of feeling. The grief slowly, inexorably, scorched a hole through her soul. Loss was worse than grief, because at least with grief one knew where the person was – and there was the succour that their spirit had returned to the Almighty. With Sisi, there was only the not knowing and the fears that ate away at her sanity.

Sisi, where are you?

She'd followed up every passing comment and scoured the countryside, backwards and forwards, north and south, as far as Insterberg in the east and the Baltic Sea in the west.

Finally, late last night, Kadow had provided a smidgeon of news. Not about Sisi, but about Charlie, Sisi's mare. Gustav, Kadow's brother, had found her tied up near the Lastadie docks. The creature was starving and unkempt, but alive. If Charlie lived, then perhaps, just perhaps, Sisi did too. There was hope. That was all that was left at the bottom of the box.

With the transparent muslin scarf, she could at least venture into the midday sun. Her head still pounded, but it served to offset the worst of the pain. She, Kadow and Christoph trudged along the banks of the Neuer Pregel by the Lastadie docks. Rounding a corner, there she was, Sisi's mount.

"It's really Charlie," she chirped, stroking the horse's mane and giving her a carrot to chomp.

"Yes, and she knows you, Your Excellency," Christoph agreed, tapping his walking stick on the cobblestones.

"No sign of Sisi," Kadow added, with an air of malaise.

"No," she agreed. "Kadow, let me speak to your brother. He may know more of her whereabouts."

Kadow scurried off into the dockland crowds.

To find shade, Marion moved under the lip of the large Customs House and adjusted the muslin scarf. Passing sailors and stevedores made demeaning comments about her being as blind as a mole. She felt blinded by the sun and blinded by the events that had led Sisi to disappear, so blind that she couldn't see them if they leapt out in front of her.

While she waited, she recalled that Gustav once worked on her estate and had run off to avoid conscription.

"Gustav sailed to England a year ago," she said to Christoph. "So, why has he returned?"

"Like many other refugees, he wanted to pluck silver guineas from the trees in the new English industrial towns." Christoph was evidently unimpressed with their plight. "He had an accident on a machine. Injured and homesick, he boarded a ship bound for Königsberg."

"Mmm, I'm not surprised," she said. "Factory work is demeaning to the human spirit."

Kadow returned accompanied by a man on a crutch.

"Your Excellency, this is my brother, Gustav," he said.

"Honoured to meet you again, Your Excellency," he said, wearing a wicked smile, a black headscarf and a bronze earring in his left earlobe.

"What can you tell us about Charlie?"

"I saw the mare on the quay a couple of days ago. All lonesome she was, poor little nag. I brung her a carrot and I sees her name on the neck tag. And the picture of the big black eagle with two heads: only one place that could come from. So, I gets word to me brother here."

"You did well, Gustav, thank you," she said. "Have you seen a girl, my daughter?"

"A girl, Your Excellency?" he asked.

"Yes, the rider of the mare. She'd appear lost, forlorn, perhaps scavenging for food," Marion said.

"Can't say I have, Your Excellency." Gustav wiped his nose with his sleeve.

"Then… if you wanted to hide and sleep around here, where would you go?" she asked.

"Oh, you could start with that building over there," he replied. "Some of it is good and still in use. Other parts is all broken and derelict. Them would make a good hiding place."

"That looks familiar, what is it?" Marion asked.

"Löbenicht Hospital," Gustav replied.

CHAPTER 50

Insight into the Future

Each of the four had the face of a human being,
And on the right side each had the face of a lion,
And on the left the face of an ox;
Each also had the face of an eagle.
THE BOOK OF EZEKIEL 1:10

It was mid-morning and the pumps had been working for some days now, earning a much contented nod from Fermor. He and Dieter stood by the entrance to the main shaft, waiting for the winch to return one of Dieter's experienced hands to the surface.

"It's been some years since I've been down the mine," Dieter said, his voice tinged with nostalgia. "I've missed it like an old friend. My father and my father's father shored it up and extended it. Now it's my turn."

The winch creaked and moaned as the miner came into view. Wearing a broad smile, he was quick to allay Dieter's fears. "The shaft's still firm and good. I'd send my five-year-old grandchild down it, that's how safe it is."

"Excellent," Dieter said, and gathered the men round. "This day, 5th July, 1762, marks the beginning of a new chapter in the story of the Anna Amber Mine, because today we can hopefully recommence mining!"

Weary from their labours, the men still managed a hearty cheer.

Dieter turned to him and said, "Sexton Fermor, you've earned our undying thanks for commissioning the machinery. With your work here done, you may go back to your religious duties."

Fermor hadn't expected this and took a sharp in-breath. Besides, it wasn't an amber mine, it was a sacred place, a temple. The Adler – the great eagle of Europe – lived in it. He was its servant and he would have his encounter with it. He needed to find an excuse.

"Herr Dieter," he replied. "I can stay a little longer – the supply wagon taking me back to Schloss Ludwigshain isn't leaving until this afternoon. And I'm as curious as you are to see the inside of the mine. Do let me come with you."

"You are most welcome," Dieter said. Turning to the miners, he continued, "The network of tunnels extends under the sea, so if there's any sign of pooling water, or a miasmic smell, leave quickly and raise the alarm. Everyone, take a lantern. We'll split into six pairs. Fermor, you're with me."

He and Dieter paired off and were soon crouching in a low tunnel. Dieter was ahead of him, carrying a lantern, edging forward. Despite the enclosed space, Fermor felt blessed to be closer to the Adler. To enhance the communion, he paused to smell the pure, still, salt-laden air. A voice resonated in his soul…

This is the source.

When he snapped out of his reverie, Dieter was no longer in his line of sight. The light from Dieter's lantern seemed to be swallowed by the thick, tenebrous darkness.

"Herr Dieter," Fermor called.

The darkness didn't answer.

Strangely, instead of fear, he felt safe, insulated, protected. His lantern cast long shadows along the tunnel. He touched its walls and ceiling. This was a womb, an amber womb.

He edged forward through a webbed gloom until he reached a crossroads, marked by a domed chamber. The pressure on the crown of his head was huge and his temples were pounding. It felt like the time after Gurieli had stabbed him – when the Adler was near.

He squatted with his back against the tunnel wall. In the distance, at the end of one of the tunnels, a light moved towards him. No, it was two lights, pinpricks, like glowing eyes. The sound of wings flapping and a high-pitched bird-like scream filled the amber chamber.

Majestic, it was the Adler. He'd found it. At last. He was at home, at one, in communion with the high. The subtle form glided effortlessly towards him. Brilliant, numinous, sublime, it moved straight through him like a passing wraith.

His eyelids drooped. He felt drowsy, as his dream body squeezed out of every pore, like smoke escaping through a grill. His physical body remained leaning against the wall of the amber chamber.

Floating like a cloud, he drifted along the tunnel and followed the Adler up the central mineshaft into daylight. This was it. The Adler was leading him to a place of revelation, an altar, where all would be made clear.

As he floated into daylight, the Adler was nowhere to be seen. Instead, he saw Dieter's miners, swarming around the twin Newcomen engines, full of noise and power, hissing steam and overheated metal. Up and down the piston thrust, like a blacksmith's hammer on a forge. With increasing fascination, he watched the element of water transform into boiling hot steam.

In a flash, the epiphany came.

He saw it.

The improvement to the design.

The change was small, simple, but hugely significant. He saw the Adler drifting down the mineshaft. He followed. Soon, he was back at the crossroads in the domed chamber. His physical body jerked when he re-entered it.

Someone was shaking his shoulder.

"Fermor, wake up." It was Dieter.

"What happened?" he said. He felt groggy, intoxicated.

"Can you stand and walk? Yes, that's it, one step at a time." Dieter steadied his elbow.

"Thank you, Herr Dieter."

"You seem to lead a charmed life, Sexton Fermor. In future, keep close to the man in front," Dieter admonished him. "In the labyrinth down here, men have gone mad, prey to every kind of flight of the imagination."

"It was happening to me," he said.

"What do you mean?"

"I-I was flying. I had a vision…" Fermor stammered and immediately regretted it. It was too soon after the insight. He'd had no time to understand it.

"A vision? What did you see?" Dieter pressed him.

This was not the time to divulge it. "I-I'm not really sure," he said.

"Never mind, I'm glad you've recovered. Ah, here's the main shaft. Let's get you back to the surface."

From the shaft entrance, Fermor headed to his tent. Grabbing his notebook, he sketched out the diagrams to show how the placement of the new cylinder and valve would strengthen the operation of the pump and prevent it from frequent malfunction. He wrote down the expected improvement in the efficiency of the pump. The rest of the page he filled with more sketches showing how the steam could be employed to propel a wheel.

A spinning wheel.

He paced the tent, staring intently at his page on his writing desk.

The plan of an engine design was the last thing he'd expected from the Adler. But that was what it had shown him. Was this for the spiritual benefit and enlightenment of mankind? Was this to promote Homo Tri-Sapiens? And what on earth was he meant to do with it?

Questions, only questions.

Footsteps, someone was approaching. Before he could close the notebook, Dieter entered through the tent flap.

"I came to see how you are," Dieter said. Noticing the sketches, he asked, "Was that your vision?"

Fermor tore the page from his notebook, folded it neatly and slid it in his pocket.

"I like your plan of the Newcomen engine," Dieter said. "If I saw it right, it possesses some intriguing new features."

"You have the eyes of an eagle," he said. "And yes, you are right."

He never could tell lies.

CHAPTER 51

The Chambers of the Furious

Virtue against Fury
Shall take up arms,
And the fight be short.
PETRARCH

The sun was high in the sky when Marion approached the entrance to Löbenicht Hospital, where she encountered the enigmatic Doctor Skoda.

"How nice to see you, Your Excellency," he greeted her. He could be so ingratiating.

"You haven't been back to the Schloss for some time," she said. "What detains you in the city?"

"I-I was attending to Charles Robison," he stammered. "I did what I could to save him. The hospital has very few doctors, they're all at the front. I am helping where I can."

As he spoke, he wiped beads of perspiration from his forehead. It was a warm day, but not that warm. He looked unsteady on his feet.

"You're sweating. Here, sit down; is it the vapours, Doctor?" she asked.

"I am well enough," he answered. He mopped his forehead with a tattered 'kerchief and added, "It's my patients who are ill."

Two porters scurried into the hospital carrying a young woman on a stretcher. It couldn't be, could it? Marion had to look, if only to be certain. With a mix of fear and hope, she lifted her muslin scarf and glanced at the pale face of the sick girl.

Thank the Lord, it's not Sisi.

The stretcher-bearers hurried down the hospital corridor.

Recovering her composure, she asked Skoda, "Have you heard any news about Sisi?"

"Only that she has gone missing," he said. "I'm s-sorry, Your Excellency, you must be so worried. I pray she is safe and well. If I learn of her whereabouts, I will of course immediately inform you."

"Thank you, Doctor," she said. "I expect you to return to Schloss Ludwigshain in the near future; my people need you there."

"Yes, Your Excellency." He glanced at his pocket watch and pulled a frown.

"Is everything well, Doctor?" she wanted to know.

"Yes, yes, of course, I must attend to the girl they just brought in," he said. He rushed off as if he were late for an appointment, but in the opposite direction to the stretcher-bearers.

"What's the matter with him?" she muttered, shaking her head. "Why's he heading the way we just came – towards the docks? Oh, never mind. Kadow, your brother said the hospital has a derelict wing. Where's the entrance to it?"

Kadow pointed and said, "Over here, Your Excellency."

The old hospital still showed its origins as a Benedictine convent. First they found a long corridor of nuns' cells, each as tiny as a hermitage. Somehow, they squeezed their pious lives into one of those. The ramshackle furniture was coated in a thick layer of dust, its cornices sprinkled with an array of cobwebs. When she sneezed, she disturbed some of the local rodent population which Christoph shooed away with his walking stick.

In one part, the roof had caved in, revealing the pale blue sky overhead. Rocks and stones were strewn along the corridor, halting their progress. They stumbled into what appeared to be the convent's refectory, with overturned tables and upturned chairs. The area was strewn with papers, one of them a pamphlet for Daniel Rolander's recent talk, which looked like it had been used for other, less salubrious purposes. Above a podium, traced out in soot and dust, was the image of a crucifix. There was the distinctive smell of a wood fire and Christoph pointed to a pile of charcoal in the corner.

"Someone's living here," he murmured, prodding his walking stick into the embers.

By the fire were some ragged clothes, a plate and a cup.

"Is it Sisi?" she whispered.

"No, Your Excellency," Christoph answered, picking up some old clothes from the ground. "These belong to a man. From the agricultural pong, they've been here for a week or more."

From behind them, came footsteps and an angry voice boomed, "What you doin'? Leave my things alone!"

A heavy-set man loped across the refectory floor, one arm raised in front of him, the hand clenched into an angry fist. In a few long strides, he was pushing them away from his precious possessions.

"Get away, I said!" the man yelled.

Christoph said, "Manfred! What are you doing here?"

"Who are ya? What ya want?" he snarled.

"Manfred, it's me, Marion Gräfin von Adler, this is Christoph and Kadow. We mean you no harm." She held up open palms.

Manfred didn't seem to recognise them. Instead, he greeted them with his best scowl, while continuing to eye them with rampant suspicion.

"Manfred, you remember my daughter, don't you? Have you seen her in the last week?"

Manfred stared at them like she was speaking a foreign language.

"Seen… who?" Manfred asked. His eyes glazed over and he seemed to be listening to voices that Marion couldn't hear. He plonked down on one of two wooden boxes laid up next to the ashes of the fire and said, "I seen all them living things. I seen her. I seen them together. I seen battlefields and hospitals; matrons and doctors; men's limbs and mass graves. I seen bees and hornets. Eagles and lions, bears and wolves, I seen them all, I has," and he continued mumbling incoherently.

"Come away, Your Excellency," Christoph said, touching her shoulder.

"But… he said he'd seen them together. I'm sure he means Sisi. I'll ask him. Manfred, you saw my Sisi. Who was she with? When did you see her? Was she well? Where is she? Tell me, please, I'm her mother and…"

Manfred was chuntering in the direction of the other wooden box, where she assumed, he saw an imaginary person.

"… I know, Your Excellency," Christoph said. "He doesn't know what he's saying. We need to go. He could do us violence."

A wailing cry broke over them that seemed to rise up out of the bowels of the earth.

"My God, what's that?" She trembled, like someone had trampled on her soul.

While they were distracted, Manfred had scuttled out of the refectory.

"Follow him, he knows where she is," she shrieked. This was the closest she had got to finding her. She was not going to lose this chance.

They chased Manfred down a long corridor, along the east wing of the old convent until they reached a cloister.

"Which way did he go?" She was panting for breath.

There were more screams and raised voices in the distance.

Kadow pointed in that direction. "That there's the madhouse. That's where he's heading."

The cloister was full of dust and broken dreams. She imagined the ghosts of old nuns peering down at them, wondering who disturbed the peace of their divine office. Normally, there was no noise, only perpetual peace. Not today.

At the far end of the cloister, they entered a deserted forecourt. Beyond that was a semi-circular building. It appeared that at one time it had housed a series of convent cells, because above each one was a small, high window-opening.

"This is the asylum," Kadow observed. "It's for chronic lunatics."

Across the forecourt was a black gate, the back entrance to the asylum.

As they made their way towards it, shouts and cries punctured the air.

"Stop hurting me!" one man screamed.

"They're attacking! Help me!" a woman yelled.

"Save me!" another cried out in alarm.

The black gate was pitted with deep gashes, like someone had been throwing knives at it. In the middle of it was a small white door, no bigger than for a ten-year-old child.

A scream issued into the fractious air, conjuring the devils from their lairs. Someone banged an object against a wall. Others bashed metal objects together, until the drumming was incessant and deafening. The banging was deliberate and measured. Marion could hear it in her head, thumping, in time, monotonous. It spoke to her…

Si-si.

Si-si.

Are you there?

Si-si…

Her temples were pounding. She kept seeing images of Sisi gagged, lashed to a chair, her head drooped like a pale white snowdrop.

If Sisi was in there, would she even recognise her mother? That picture in her head was too awful to contemplate.

Christoph wore a look of utter bewilderment. His hunchback seemed more accentuated than ever. He asked, "What is this place?"

She read the sign on the lintel above the white door:

"The Chambers for the Furious.
Abandon All Hope Ye Who Enter Here."

"I'd no idea they were like this," Christoph said.

"They're possessed by evil spirits," Kadow murmured. "I don't know if I can face these demons."

"Listen, you must; if Sisi is in there, we must get her out. If not, then Manfred must tell us what he knows." She was not going to turn back.

Neither Christoph nor Kadow made a move.

"Then I'll go in there," she snapped.

The white door creaked as she opened it. She ducked under the lintel. As she stepped into the Löbenicht Lunatic Asylum, she was struck by a blinding light. She pulled the muslin scarf further down over her eyes. No difference! All she could see were black spots, pulsing in and out, like she had accidentally looked directly into the sun and been blinded by its piercing incandescence.

"Help me," she mumbled. "I can't see." She felt vulnerable and just when Sisi needed her most.

"Your Excellency, let's go back to the main hospital," Christoph suggested.

"No, we carry on," she insisted. "We find Sisi. We must. Christoph, take my hand, yes, that's it. Tell me everything you see."

"Yes, Your Excellency," he said. "We're standing in the middle of a long, curved corridor, which gives way to about twenty cells on each side. Thank the Lord, the cell doors are locked."

"Can we see inside the cells?" she asked.

"We can, they have viewing slits," Christoph told her.

"Good," she said. "Check every one."

She heard a slit pulled across. She assumed Christoph was looking inside a cell.

"Was she in there?" she asked.

"No, she wasn't in that one." His voice was tremulous.

What a relief. Or was it? "Are there no staff?" she asked.

"I'll see if I can find one," Kadow said.

"And look for Manfred at the same time," she called after him.

"I will do that, Your Excellency," Kadow replied and she heard the sound of his footsteps recede into the distance.

This temporary blindness was hugely frustrating. "Christoph, you are my eyes, speak to me."

"The corridor is dark, gloomy. My, this is a godforsaken place." His voice was shot with trepidation.

"Manfred may not be here, but we are," she said. "I am going to find my daughter."

These words brought a subtle change to the unruly atmosphere. For a moment, she heard melodious birdsong, which was strange. Normally on a summer's day, the birdsong was glorious and unrelenting. Yet today, that was the first she'd heard.

The woman in a nearby cell hummed a lullaby as if to a babe in arms. The other inmates fell as quiet as night. Marion wondered if they were listening to the gentle humming.

From the cell doors came this slow, metallic creaking, for about a minute. Then silence.

"What just happened? Christoph?"

He spoke softly, like he couldn't believe what he was saying. "Without warning, the doors of the cells have sprung open. The… the inmates are…"

"Are what?"

"… coming out of their cells. They're staring at us, no… they're staring at you."

"Is Sisi there?"

There was no answer, except for the gentle rhythmic humming, rising and falling, like waves on a tropical seashore, as sublime as a whisper of the spirit of God.

Her head was bursting at the seams. This time she was sure it was going to explode.

"She's come, she's here," a woman's voice said with such passion, it sent a frisson of power up Marion's spine. She seemed to recognise the voice.

"Who said that?" Marion asked.

"The lullaby woman, it's remarkable!" Christoph murmured.

"What is?" she asked.

"… It's Katharina!" Christoph choked on his emotion.

"Katharina?"

"Yes, it's her," Christoph confirmed. "Wearing her black mourning dress, now tattered and torn. Her eyes are like twin sapphires, and… she's staring at you."

Marion could hear people shuffling all around her and even feel their breath on her cheek and neck. It was as calm as a sea of glass.

"Your Excellency, Katharina's knelt down in front of you."

"… What?" *I wish I could see what was happening.*

"And now so have the others. There are about forty of them, they've surrounded us."

"Oh, my God." The pain in her head was excruciating. She could barely concentrate.

"She's come." Katharina's voice was resonant with awe. "She's brought the passion."

"She's come," the forty repeated in this soft, luscious voice. "The passion, it's here."

"Their faces are aglow with spirit," Christoph said.

"Let us worship," Katharina said.

"Let us worship," the forty echoed.

Marion swooned and leaned on Christoph's arm.

"Who are they talking about?" Marion didn't have to wait long to find out.

"The great one is amongst us," Katharina said.

These were inmates in a lunatic asylum, who were normally erratic, uncontrollable, violent people; the Furious. Yet in her presence, they were as placid and malleable as dough.

"We are not mad," Katharina carried on, like a prophet reciting an ancient testament. "It's the world that is mad. The merchants turn the world into a marketplace, smother its beauty, buy and sell the human soul and take away our natural strength. They remove us from the sanctity of the land and her natural cycles. The merchants want us to work in factories and live in conditions unfit for pigs."

"Unfit for pigs!" The forty shouted the reply in unison.

"Merchants will ruin the world," Katharina continued. "They will make mothers abandon their children; despoil the innocence of childhood; force children to work. They will pollute the seas, rape the earth and poison the air. The Four Horsemen will bring pestilence, war, famine and death. The merchants will say scientific progress is a panacea for these ills and that the Horsemen will be banished. But they will not be banished. They will stalk us for evermore. The greed of the merchants and the engineers' rabid desire for progress will suffocate the human spirit."

"Katharina, why are you saying this? Where is this coming from?" Marion asked. She was nearly fainting with the pain, her temples throbbing, her head pulsing. It felt like she was about to give birth.

"We bend the knee and worship you," Katharina intoned. "Give us back our sanity that we may serve you. Only in thy presence may we be one with the purpose."

Katharina's words were a revelation. "Our journey on earth is to supplement His works. Is there anything nobler in this time of distress than to freely pay back for the gifts of life and spirit, and in doing so, by one's own works, magnify His Creation?"

Silence reigned on the waters of the asylum. The spirit moved across the face of Marion's life like a cool breeze moved across the face of the waters, leaving small ripples in its passing. Ripples that extended to the far reaches of her life, enriching them with purpose, making them glow with insight. The weight of the numinous eagle on top of her head was pressing down such that she could barely stand upright.

Katharina had more to say, "We see the great one. It sits on you, its claws buried deep into your head. Its wings are so wide we can't see its wing tips."

"They're worshipping you, Your Excellency," Christoph said.

"No, they're not," she murmured.

"Then who are they worshipping?" he asked.

"The Adler, they can see it hovering above my head."

CHAPTER 52

The King's Regulations

The difficult situation and the newness of my kingdom
Force me to do these things and guard my borders everywhere.
VIRGIL

Lester was relieved to return to the still waters of the Lastadie docks. Not only had the departure from St. Petersburg been fraught with danger, to make matters worse, they had encountered a ferocious Baltic summer storm. As the ropes thudded on the quay, he allowed himself to feel the thrill of overriding opportunity. It was in Königsberg where he would take the first steps towards fulfilling his ambitious, new dream.

"Bring that consignment of vodka on deck," Lester ordered.

"Someone ta' see ya, Captain," the first mate growled.

Dressed in top hat and tails, an official was striding up the gangplank. His lackey ran along behind him carrying reams of paper.

"Rudiger von Seydlitz, Königsberg Magistrate, at your service," the man introduced himself.

"And I am Captain Donald Lester," he replied.

At that moment, a loud explosion rocked the harbour. Instinctively, Lester ducked and covered his head with his hands. A huge plume of smoke rose into the dockside air.

Lester stood up. "What on earth was that?"

Von Seydlitz had not even flinched. "Oh, they're demolishing the warehouses destroyed in the recent fire."

"Phew," Lester said, straightening his uniform. "For a moment, I thought I was back in St. Petersburg."

"Why? What happened there?"

"Great explosions and flares lit the night sky over the Winter Palace."

"Mmm, these are the dog days when there's always fighting in the cities," von Seydlitz said. "Summer riots, winter snow – it's all part of the natural cycle."

"No, it was more than that," Lester murmured. "This was a battle royal between factions."

"It would appear that Emperor Peter has his opponents," the magistrate said, taking a pinch of snuff.

"As we were about to embark," Lester said, "soldiers arrested some important personage, hauled him off like a sack of potatoes."

"Do you know who it was?" the magistrate asked, tugging on his grey beard.

"Mikhail Vorontsov, I think that was his name."

"That's very interesting." Von Seydlitz nodded his head.

"Who is he?" Lester asked.

"The Emperor's chancellor. The soldiers – were they the Emperor's men or did they arrest the Emperor too?"

"We didn't hang around to find out."

"I can understand that," the magistrate replied.

"You didn't come on board to chat about the Imperial Russian Court," Lester said, "so, what can I do for you?"

"I bring sad news," von Seydlitz said, as his lackey handed Lester a document. "This is a death certificate for a member of your crew, Herr Charles Robison."

"No, no, no, there must be a mistake," Lester said, shaking his head.

"We're Prussian. We're thorough. We don't make mistakes," von Seydlitz replied in all sincerity.

"Damn. Charles was young, fit and active, with his whole life in front of him. It's so sudden. I'm… I'm devastated."

"I'm so sorry," the magistrate said.

Lester took a moment to digest the awful news. He'd promised John Robison he'd bring his brother home safely. What was he going to tell him?

Turning to practicalities, he asked, "Where was he buried?"

"That's why I'm here," von Seydlitz explained. This sounded ominous. "The city's finances are limited and preclude the burial of a foreigner."

"What do you mean? Oh, now I understand, he's not been buried?"

The magistrate gave a simple nod.

"That's despicable." Lester spat the words out, followed by some choice Scottish ire.

"There's no need for foul language," von Seydlitz said by way of reproach.

"What would you have me do?" Lester asked.

"Settle the burial account, a small matter of twelve silver thaler," von Seydlitz explained.

"I don't have twelve pfennig to rub together, let alone twelve thaler. Look, these are my sole assets." He pointed to the crates of vodka on the deck.

"In that case, I'm sure you can raise the fee promptly," von Seydlitz said.

"Once this lot is sold and I've refilled my hold, I'm sailing to bonnie Scotland," he said.

Von Seydlitz sniffed the air. "I'm here to enforce the King's regulations, which prohibit you from raising anchor until the fee is paid."

Lester shook his head and said, "Where's the poor boy's corpse now – in the morgue?"

"Ah, normally, yes," von Seydlitz added, adjusting his monocle. "Unfortunately, the mortuary at Löbenicht Hospital is full of dead soldiers from the front so we had to find an alternative resting place. His body is in a vault in Schloss Ludwigshain. You should thank Marion Gräfin von Adler who offered a burial space for him at the chapel cemetery there."

"This is most irregular," he said. "I will settle the fee as soon as I can. I want to pay my last respects to poor Charles."

"I am glad to hear that," von Seydlitz said. Lackey in tow, he marched down the gangplank.

After Lester had made arrangements to sell his vodka at the Bourse, he hired a horse and trap and headed for the Anna Amber Mine. He kept thinking about how, in St. Petersburg, he'd very likely witnessed the downfall of an emperor – or at least his chancellor.

He wondered if General von Fermor was involved in the coup. During their meeting in the Amber Room, the general had given no indication that he knew of the tumult unfolding in Russian state politics. How would he, Lester, know, anyway? These Russians were like great white bears, which could stand in the middle of a snowscape and remain invisible. What if the general knew of the coup d'état and kept the information from him? One thing was sure; never underestimate a Russian general.

Lester reached the outskirts of the mine. The clanging sound of the wheel rocking back and forth was music to his ears. An array of huts and tents had been erected at the head of the mineshaft. A knot of armed dragoons guarded one of the wooden huts where, presumably, the extracted amber was stored.

His face covered in mud and grime, Dieter emerged from the mineshaft, Ian Fermor right behind.

"Welcome back, Captain Lester," Dieter said. "Thanks to your equipment and Sexton Fermor, the mine is in full operation."

"Good. You owe me the final instalment."

"I don't have it, the King has still not delivered," Dieter said.

"What a surprise! What are you going to do?"

"I have another promissory note from Herr Silberstein."

"Sorry! I won't accept another of his notes."

"Why ever not?" Dieter asked.

"Because when I traded the first one you gave me, I received but one-third of its face value."

"A third?" Dieter tutted.

"Yes," Lester said. "As an act of good faith, I'm prepared to waive the other two-thirds, which amounts to forty thousand thaler, which in principle you still owe me. But only if you settle the final instalment immediately – that's sixty thousand thaler please! Otherwise I shall claim the full reparation, that's one hundred thousand thaler."

"Pah!" Dieter said. "In Ostpreussen, Silberstein's notes fetch their full face value. If you received less, you were tricked, mein lieber freund. Who did you sell it to – a Russian?"

"Well, actually, yes, I did."

"Who?"

"Your uncle," Lester said, pointing to Ian Fermor. "General Wilhelm von Fermor."

"The general must have been very convincing," Dieter replied. "As far as I am concerned, Silberstein is a reputable trader."

"The general claims otherwise," Lester scoffed. "He said Silberstein torched his own warehouse and then sold your sister's cereal to your enemies – the Austrian and French armies! I don't trust Jews. And nor should you."

Dieter was adamant. "Actually, I do trust him. Our family has dealt with him for years."

"Give me my money," Lester hissed.

"I'll pay you," Dieter promised.

"You had better," Lester said. "If you don't, I'll come to Fischhausen with my crew and wreck the machines."

"You wouldn't dare," Dieter said. "I'd be ruined."

"Try me." Lester spat the words out.

CHAPTER 53

Pangs of Conscience

Render to Caesar the things that are Caesar's;
And to God the things that are God's.
THE GOSPEL OF MATTHEW 22:21

All the way back from the Anna Amber Mine to Schloss Ludwigshain, Fermor had contemplated the Adler's plan. The more he thought about it, the more he realised it was a work of genius. No doubt about it. The Adler had granted him the vision to see the improvements to the Newcomen engine, but had omitted one thing – what to do with it.

Mankind was in a parlous and fragile state. Fermor knew that these times were both emergent with promise but also pitted with dangerous obstacles.

One simple line of thought was this: he should divulge the plan to whoever would best make use of it. Originally, the atmospheric engine was designed by a Devon man, Thomas Newcomen, an ironmonger and a Baptist lay preacher. With a foot in both camps, Fermor felt a strong affinity for a man who must have suffered the same pangs of conscience as he. Both suffered the dilemma of divided loyalties: which was more important, the secular or the spiritual, civic or sacred, earth or heaven?

The improved Newcomen engine would transform the practical world of mankind. It could make a steam engine that propelled the piston and spun the wheel. A spinning wheel, what an innovation! The mechanisation would provide better living conditions, greater prosperity and a magnificent future for the world, so long as it was shared equitably. Yet he could also see that, used wrongly or unjustly, it could do irreparable damage to mankind's spiritual quest.

God created humans for a purpose, to make a return to God of things that God could not experience for Himself, such as love, endearment, compassion and other higher feelings. God sent the Adler to develop humans so they could create finer art, compose greater music and conceive ever truer representations of the order and beauty inherent in Creation.

While Fermor's plan improved the operation of a machine, machines could not produce an ornate sculpture. They had no soul. They were inanimate and could not make any return recognisable to God. Machines could provide a revolution in living standards and social reform, yet they would never achieve the ultimate spiritual goal, that of spiritual progress through human development. The Adler heralded a significant development – of the brain, the twelve cranial nerves. The stars of the galaxy would shine through the genius of humanity and bring about a spiritual progress.

The plan was a gift from the Adler. Because it arose from the spiritual realms, it must be for the benefit of those realms alone. To divulge it would weaken mankind's spiritual quest. It would be like profiting from religion; such as the sale of indulgences whereby the rich paid for their passage to heaven, or the sale of priestly sinecures to those who had never even read the Bible, the offences Luther condemned.

He, Fermor, would not be party to such wanton spiritual destruction.

There was a loud bang on the chapel door. Clutching the page torn from his notebook, he got up and opened the door.

A man stinking like a field of rotten potatoes, sweat pouring from his face, stood there, with one hand on the reins of an equally sweaty horse. The other hand was outstretched towards him and he said, "Letter for Sexton Fermor."

"Thank you," Fermor said. Opening the letter, he read:

Dear Sexton Fermor,

You are hereby officially informed that Captain Donald Lester has settled the burial duties owed on behalf of Charles Robison, deceased.

You are instructed to commit his body to the ground, at the feet of Our Lord, as soon as is practically possible, preferably tomorrow morning, 8th July, 1762.

May his soul rest in peace.

Signed,

Magistrate Rudiger von Seydlitz.

He had work to do to prepare for the funeral.

CHAPTER 54

The Colour White

Cast not your pearls before swine,
Lest they turn and rend you.
THE GOSPEL OF MATTHEW 7:6

Marion had tried to return to Schloss Ludwigshain in the glare of the afternoon sun, but her eyes were too sensitive to the light. To wait for evening, she'd stayed in the gloom of the asylum basement, listening to Katharina and the inmates humming to the Adler. The serenade soothed her fevered brow, but it was no help finding her daughter.

While she waited, Kadow and Christoph had checked every cell – in vain. Reluctantly, they had given up the search. Then, in the cool of the night, they had made their way home.

That was Monday.

Today was Wednesday, 7th July. She was cocooned in her room, with the curtains drawn and a muslin scarf covering her eyes. Over by the lake, she could vaguely hear the birds singing. It was cooler; she assumed the soothing wings of dusk were beating evenly over the gentle lands of Ostpreussen.

She abhorred the sunlight, craved the night. Was she a vampire? Doctor Skoda had told her he had once investigated a vampire scare in the Carpathian Mountains. The villagers there were immersed by a tenebrous possession, a miasma which made them see evil and darkness where there was none. In the end, he'd concluded that they were mad, deluded.

She wondered if that was her lot, to be cast on the slough of deceit.

No. It was real enough. Otherwise, why was she confined to her room with her head wrapped in swaddling clothes?

The inside of her head felt squashed like a walnut and pushed up against the inner membranes of her scalp. Her brain was struggling to grow, to be free and to escape its confinement.

She'd just heard that Robison's funeral was early the next morning. In this parlous state, she couldn't attend. She'd make excuses. With a blindfold and blackouts in the room, she couldn't read a book and suffered terribly with the slightest movement. Even lightly touching the crown of her head, the pain was immense. When she realised that her pate was expanding, she went into cold shivers.

She heard a horse and trap rumble across the forecourt, scaring a flock of birds, which flew off making calls of distress. She knew the feeling. The trap pulled up outside the front entrance. From her room, she could hear Doctor Skoda's dulcet tones.

She tried to speak, yet the resonance of her voice despatched spasms of pain through her head. There followed a heavy Ursula rap on the door.

"What is it?" she murmured.

"Doctor Skoda's outside and is asking to see you."

"Show him in," she said.

"Greetings, Your Excellency," Doctor Skoda said. "How are you feeling?" His voice sounded as cold as a Siberian glacier.

"The pains in my head are excruciating."

He shuffled towards the bed and said, "Can I examine you, Your Excellency?"

She allowed Ursula to carefully unravel the towelling.

He touched her scalp and, without warning, prodded it with his finger. "My, it is soft," he said.

The pain was insufferable. She blacked out.

She was vaguely awake, half-asleep. She was hovering in the midst of the Via Lactea. The sight of those millions of pinpricks of light in the Milky Way filled her with awe for the Creator. She drifted amongst star clusters, amidst galaxies spinning in quiet revolution, like they had since time immemorial.

She was part of this universe and it was part of her. She was the universe and it was her. It was like listening to a chorus of the immortals, where each cadence is a paean to the glory of the fact of life, all life. Then she realised that the universe was there to support her and to support human life, the gild on the crown of Creation itself.

After a while, she didn't know how long, she awoke. To keep out any flicker of light, she kept her eyes tight shut, but her ears were working perfectly well.

Ursula was reprimanding Skoda. "What on earth did you think you were doing?"

"Examining her," Skoda replied. "Wasn't it obvious?"

"She fainted with the pain you caused. That's not an examination," Ursula snarled. "You're no doctor. You're a barber surgeon, good for pulling out teeth, that's all!"

"How dare you, you little upstart! What do you know anyway?" he scolded her.

Marion grunted and moaned.

"Your Excellency, are you well?" Ursula placed a comforting hand on hers.

Nodding, the muslin scarf fell from her eyes. She blinked, expecting a bolt of pain from the onrushing light. Thankfully, the room was dark. Still the pain seared through her head. Her brain matter was pushing, probing through the fontanelles, like grass shoots through gaps between the cobblestones.

Skoda picked up the scarf.

"No," she growled. "Ursula will do it. She knows how."

Ursula's deft fingers restored the blindfold and the waves of pain subsided.

"Sisi?" she whispered.

"No news, Your Excellency," Skoda replied.

Unconvinced by his reply, she asked, "Are you sure?"

"We're very worried about her," he said. He had taken the art of patronisation to new heights. "What do you think happened?"

"I don't know," she said. Each word was an effort to articulate. "Manfred knew something. He said he'd seen Sisi with another person."

"Pah! He wasn't involved," Skoda replied. "He's just an ignorant skinner."

"Is he?" she said. "On the day Sisi went missing, she went riding on Charlie. Before she returned, Grenda saw Manfred enter the stables."

"What do you think Manfred did?"

"I suspect he delivered a letter. Later, I saw Sisi with an envelope."

"No! Manfred can neither read nor write. What was he doing with a letter?" he snapped.

"That's what I thought," she murmured. "He must have delivered it on behalf of someone else. Was it you?"

"Me?" he guffawed. "That's preposterous. Why would I send your daughter a letter?"

She coughed heavily into her 'kerchief. "That's what I'd like to know."

"Your Excellency, you are unwell," Skoda said, turning on the sympathy. "I beg you, lie back and rest. Your daughter's disappearance is distressing you. You're suffering from the cords of the wicked."

She waited for the latest spasm of pain to subside.

"I heard what happened with Katharina in the asylum the other day," Skoda went on. "The inmates believe you are possessed. An odd claim, if I may say."

Before she could reply, he went on, "This matter has come up before, Your Excellency. When I arrived at Schloss Ludwigshain, you told me about your head pains and I recommended trepanning. Look at this room and how you live. It's the middle of the day and the curtains are drawn. You live in the shadowlands. The inmates were right, you are possessed. Disperse the evil spirits inside you. Let me cut the cords of the wicked. I have my instruments here."

She gasped. "No. Never. I won't be reduced to a blubbering idiot. Leave me be. I will endure the pain."

"Ursula, please fetch my medicine bag," Skoda ordered.

"It's here," Ursula said, pointing to it.

"I have another bag in my room. Fetch it. Don't argue with me!"

"Yes, Doctor," Ursula muttered under her breath. Marion heard the door close as her maid left the room.

Alone with Skoda, she felt weak. She drifted off into a restless slumber, the uncanny realm where shadows mingled with the ghosts of the ancien régime.

Like the time she followed Fermor's ghost in her dream, her dream body floated *through* the Schloss walls, down into the ground, until she eased into the vault where Charles Robison's coffin was ready for burial. A winged being hovered over the corpse.

The Adler.

Gliding towards her, it stopped at an arm's length from where she stood. It was glowing with the spirit of the Lord.

She understood from it that, like her, it was incomplete, and that to complete itself, it had to be purposefully employed according to the promise of its design. To do that, it needed adherents, not followers or worshippers, but servants whose creations were the image or mirror of divine wisdom – geniuses.

The Adler told her it would herald an era of human geniuses who would create art that captured the enigma and glory of life, make gardens that healed the sick, and develop clairvoyance to render obsolete the letter and the homing pigeon.

The Adler promised a new collective consciousness in which the Four Horsemen of the *modern* apocalypse – pestilence, war, famine and *crime* – would cease to exist. Heralding a return to the original state of innocence in which humans were designed to live. In it, God would reign as naturally as He reigned amongst children, whose sense of play and joyful discovery of life would bring passion, inspiration and revelation.

The Adler was like the snow that lay as a pure white blanket upon the great plains of Northern Europe. It was virginal and pristine. The danger was evident: if any rogue footprints intruded onto it, they would soil its purity forever.

The Adler had servants. When Fermor had pressed her to be one, she had refused because she didn't trust him. The bishop had warned her of false prophets. Yet now she had encountered the Adler herself, she understood that it was of divine origin and that its motives were genuine.

All this time, the Adler was *looking* at her, as if examining her inner motives, her core being. Now it moved slowly towards her and penetrated her, enveloping her entire being in its emanation. A concert of sympathies, the communion felt as natural as the ordering of the colours in a rainbow. It spoke to her:

> *'I am the Adler, the true spirit of the Lord. My purpose is your elevation and my elevation is your purpose. To mankind, I bring pearls of wisdom, jewels of perception, and the torch of enlightenment.*
>
> *Be warned, there are those who would belittle, circumscribe, and make null and void this great purpose. These people would misuse my power for personal success and commercial gain. This would dissipate the sacred power I bring and its dregs would appear as a lesser, surrogate purpose.*
>
> *Remember, the colour white must always be as white as snow.'*

As her dream body juddered back into her physical body, she awoke with a jerk.

She was sitting upright in a chair and felt something on top of her head. It wasn't the Adler.

Skoda had torn the muslin blindfold from her eyes and was manipulating something above her head.

"What are you doing?" she cried.

"Don't move!" he replied.

She tried to lift her hands to feel above her head, but… couldn't.

"You've tied my hands to the chair!"

"I am the agent of release." Skoda's voice sounded demented.

"What are you talking about?" she gasped.

She twisted her neck from side to side and felt four small metallic discs digging into her temples and forehead. Skoda had erected an instrument on the crown of her head.

"Stay still," he rasped as he twisted something above her head.

A drill.

No, it couldn't be.

"You're mad!" she yelled. "It's trepanning equipment."

"I'm going to cut the cords of the wicked. You will be healed. Now keep your head still," he snapped, grabbing her neck and forcing the drill down until it bit into her scalp. That tiny pressure was immensely painful.

"Sisi!" she cried.

"She's not here and won't be coming back," Skoda said with a knowing leer.

The metal drill breached the top of her scalp. She was about to scream again, when he shoved a 'kerchief in her mouth and wrapped a blindfold round her eyes.

The world went dark. The scream resonated in her inner being. She was at the end. She'd not survive a trepanning. Her clothes stuck to her body, glued there by a frozen sweat. Her hands twisted in the rope, burning her skin, burning her mind with angst. She could smell the repugnant odour of her own fear.

The door was flung open.

"Stop this, immediately!"

Dieter, thank God. Her saviour, again!

He pulled the 'kerchief from her mouth and untied her hands. Ursula and Amelia made a fuss of her.

"You're a monster." She was exhausted and the words fell wearily from her lips.

"You're dying. I'm trying to save you," Skoda complained.

Dieter lifted the trepanning equipment from the top of her head.

"Leave!" he snarled. Skoda slunk away leaving behind a numinous trail of slime.

"Let's get you back to bed, Your Excellency," Ursula said.

Amelia tucked her in, saying, "Her hands are as cold as ice."

"She's so pale," Dieter said, pushing away a loop of hair from her face.

"Oh, my, Skoda was right about one thing. She's going," Ursula whispered to Dieter.

"Going where?" he asked. "Oh, my God. Call the sexton!"

At that moment, Fermor walked into the room.

"How… did you know?" Dieter stammered.

"I know my people," Fermor said. "I will minister to her. It's her time."

My time? My time? What's he talking about? Wait… does he mean? He can't. He does. He thinks… I'm going… to die.

She swallowed hard. She felt her life ebbing away through her fontanelles.

While Fermor prepared to deliver the Commendation, the staff filled the room with a deep reverential silence.

"I forgive you, Sister." Dieter's voice was dripping with emotion. He didn't have to say for what, because she knew – his limp.

She managed a thin smile and gently clenched his hand.

She summoned every last morsel of strength, all those nodules of grit squeezed from decades of hard Ostpreussen living and said, "Pray for my living soul!"

"By the grace of God, I will," Fermor said. He leant down and whispered in her ear, "You saved my life and I will save yours."

As Fermor read her the Commendation, Marion drifted off into a place full of the colour white.

CHAPTER 55

Ashes to Ashes

In the sweat of thy face shalt thou eat bread,
Till thou return unto the ground;
For out of it wast thou taken:
For dust thou art and unto dust shalt thou return.
THE BOOK OF GENESIS 3:19

Donald Lester watched as the gravediggers allowed the leather coffin straps to run through their palms. Slowly, they lowered the coffin until it nestled in the base of the burial plot, his friend's final resting place. Overnight, a handful of snails had left a trail of slime on the mounds of earth piled high around the sides. Funerals reminded everyone of their own mortality, especially when the deceased was young.

"Twenty-two days," Lester muttered to himself. "The Prussians refused to bury him for twenty-two days. It would never have happened in Scotland."

"Thinking of home, Captain Lester?" Skoda asked, stepping alongside him.

"You could say that," he sneered. Lester disliked the doctor. Skoda was like one of those sad souls who sat alone at a table guarding a near-empty glass and glowering at the rest of the populace like they were vermin.

Sexton Fermor walked around the burial plot, sprinkling holy water onto the coffin.

The funeral was full of ghosts, the ghost of Charles Robison rising up to heaven, the ghosts of his absent relatives and Marion's ghost waiting to follow him up the celestial stairway.

Lester had arrived in Schloss Ludwigshain the previous night. On hearing the awful news about Marion, he'd promptly paid his last respects to her. Fearing the worst, Dieter and the castle staff had kept vigil by her bedside through the night.

This morning, her chambermaid had told him that she still clung to life by a slender thread. Not only that, she had even whispered in his ear that Marion's son had been conscripted and her daughter, a girl he'd never met, had run away from home. What a tragic family!

In his overnight luggage, Lester had brought his bagpipes. He'd left all the members of his crew behind: he'd instructed them to make a delivery to Andre. The maverick proprietor of the Columbine Inn had bought his vodka consignment at the Bourse, having paid a twelve thaler deposit, and was due to pay the remainder at midday. Come what may, Lester intended to receive it in person. That didn't leave him much time to attend the funeral and see Dieter about receiving the second instalment.

The bright early morning sunlight brought out a gleam on the waxen leaves of the evergreens. Sexton Fermor opened the Bible and murmured the immortal words from the Book of Genesis:

"In the sweat of thy face shalt thou eat bread,
till thou return unto the ground;
for out of it wast thou taken:
for dust thou art and unto dust shalt thou return."

Lester bowed his head and murmured a silent prayer for his friend.

He arranged his bagpipes and waited until the screeching was replaced by a powerful, sombre funeral march. Blowing those haunting notes, he summoned a piece of Scottish soul right into Ostpreussen. It was a last lament, a song of lore for home and for love and for the love of the home. It was always about one or t'other. When the last note dissipated into the little cemetery, there was a long silence and time for reflection on life and death.

Fermor ended the service, saying, "May his soul rest in peace. Amen."

"Amen," Lester echoed the sentiment.

The gravediggers shovelled earth into the grave, each spadeful biting loudly on the top of the coffin.

As Sexton Fermor made ready to leave, Lester waxed lyrical, "This is a tranquil spot for Robison to be buried. The trees are in leaf. There's lush green meadow, a field of yellow cowslips and the blue Pregel in the valley. It's so peaceful here. This will be some consolation to his family."

"I'm glad you think so," Fermor replied.

"I'm pleased the Gräfin fights on. She's a force for good in the world. I hope she makes a full recovery."

"I do too, more than you can possibly imagine," Fermor agreed.

Lester trudged off towards the castle to deal with the brother, an altogether more tricky character.

CHAPTER 56

Let God Decide

Pray, and let God worry.
MARTIN LUTHER

Fermor slumped in the chair in the vestry. After the Commendation, the night-long vigil, and the funeral, he felt numb and frozen all over like he'd been walking through a snowscape. The anxiety about the Gräfin's perilous condition pulled on the strings of his conscience. During the night, the life force had further drained from her. She was feeble and incapacitated. She lived on, the thread of life slender and thinning by the hour.

Watching her spirit seep out of her mortal coil, he felt helpless. He'd seen young men die on the battlefield, writhing in agony. War was criminal and insane. The Gräfin was too young to die. Her children needed a mother, and her husband needed a wife. More than that, it wasn't written in her destiny to depart this world so soon.

He had to alleviate her suffering, or better still, alter her destiny. As sexton, his primary task was to nourish the faith of the congregation, be a bulwark against apostasy, and, in cases like this, offer comfort and easement in times of spiritual crisis.

Reflecting on his life's journey, he wondered how he had reached this juncture. He was alive for one reason and one reason alone – the Adler had revived him. After that, he was grateful to the Gräfin, who had nursed his mortal wound and protected him from those in the community who doubted his integrity.

Outside, as the sun cast long shadows on the lake, he could hear Egor and the other children yelping with glee. For them, they were oblivious to life's travails unfolding in their midst. For him, for Fermor, it was a time for mourning for the dead, for Robison, and the dying, for the Gräfin.

He had defied death. He had been born again. He had been given a second chance at life. Why not the Gräfin?

He knew what to do.

It might work. It might just work.

He'd try anything, anything at all. She'd saved his life, now he was going to try and save hers. God would hear his prayer.

He'd find out the cost – sooner or later.

Mouthing a prayer, he entered the chapel, knelt down, and pulled the page of his notebook from his pocket. He carefully placed it in the middle of the altar.

As he walked into the vestry and glanced back at the plan for one last time, he thought,

Let God decide.

CHAPTER 57

Yellow Nuggets

I said, 'You are gods.
You are all sons of the Most High.'
But you will die like mere mortals.
THE BOOK OF PSALMS 82:6

After Robison's funeral, Lester waited for Dieter in the State Room. He wanted the second instalment. Yes, he was sorry Marion was dying, but there was business to transact and he needed to return to Königsberg. When Dieter failed to reappear, he searched the house and grounds for him.

In the forecourt outside the Schloss, the grooms were taking the horses for a ride and a maid was sweeping the front steps. Alexander's wolfhound was chasing a squirrel across the forecourt and was barking at it from the base of a linden tree.

"Where are your manners?" Alexander scolded the beast. "Don't you know the Gräfin is dying?"

Skoda appeared from behind a tree by the lake. As usual, Herr Doctor was acting as if he expected a masked robber to jump out from behind the bushes and assault him.

"I'm going to the chapel to pray for Marion," Skoda said. "You coming?"

"Nah," Lester said. "I've paid my respects to the forces of religion and they haven't delivered. Now I'll put my faith in the forces of commerce." Besides, if the doctor was resorting to prayer, what did that say about the man's healing skills?

"If you are looking for Dieter," Skoda said, "he's at his sister's bedside. Oh, no, there he is, coming out of the front door with Moshe Silberstein."

As Skoda entered the chapel, Dieter walked over towards Lester. Dieter's clothes were dishevelled; he had a night's stubble on his chin and black bags under his eyes. It seemed entirely appropriate that Silberstein was wearing black.

Lester asked, "How is your sister?"

"We're grateful to God she survived the night," Dieter said, drawing a long sigh.

"I'm glad to hear that," Lester added a note of sympathy, but only a touch. "I'm afraid I need to leave soon, so please indulge me. We must discuss our business transaction."

"Yes, of course," Dieter said wearily. "We'll retire to somewhere private."

"Does he have to come with us?" Lester asked, referring to Silberstein.

"Yes, he does." Dieter was defiant.

As they crossed the forecourt, Lester noticed a chill wind had got up and the atmosphere was thickening. With dark clouds on the horizon, his nose for a storm was twitching.

When they sat down in the State Room, Lester was brusque. "The machinery is working. As per our agreement, I require the second half of the instalment."

"And I am pleased with the installation," Dieter said. "The first shipment of amber is due to be delivered to the King's quartermaster later today."

"Excellent news," he said. "I have high hopes for this enterprise. How do you intend to pay me?"

"You still won't accept one of Silberstein's promissory notes?" Dieter asked.

"No, I told you two days ago that I won't," he replied, trying to keep his composure. Silberstein had scuppered him once. He wasn't going to let it happen again.

"Do you really think I'd sink so low to steal from a trusted family friend and set fire to my own warehouse? That's slander!" Silberstein said, his face going purple with rage.

"No, it's true!" Lester insisted.

"If you can believe an ogre like General von Fermor," Silberstein thundered. "His business dealings have got more bends than a shepherd's crook."

Lester got up and pushed Silberstein in the chest. Silberstein glared back at him.

Dieter stood between the two rutting bucks and said, "Herren, that's enough! This is neither the time nor the place. My sister's upstairs. Now, please, behave yourselves."

"I don't have time for this," Lester snapped. "Pay me now!"

"I have something else to offer," Dieter said.

"This had better be good."

"Look," Dieter said. Pulling a handful of yellow nuggets from his pockets, he placed them on the coffee table and added, "You know what these are?"

"Yes, they're pieces of amber, so what?" he replied.

"Here, take them."

He examined the nuggets, gleaming like pieces of yellow gold in the sunlight.

"You can trade in amber anywhere in Europe," Dieter said. "These are my future and they can be yours. If you won't accept a promissory note, I offer you a share of the mine."

"I'm interested, but it depends on what share."

"A tithe?" Dieter said.

"One-tenth, is that all?" he cackled. "I'll take a third and nothing less."

"That leaves me with very little profit," Dieter complained.

"That's not my concern, that's what I want," Lester insisted.

Dieter stood up and said to Lester, "One third is a large share. It's a difficult decision which I need to weigh in the balance."

"You must understand, I took a big loss on the promissory note on the first instalment," Lester said, laying on the malevolence. "If I don't receive the second instalment in full, I'm coming to the mine to reclaim my spare parts and Newcomen engines."

"I know, you said that before," Dieter said, a flash of fear in his eyes. "I need time to decide – in peace. I'll go to the chapel. Wait for me."

"I don't have all day," Lester replied.

Dieter scuttled off to the chapel.

Silberstein took off too. Lester was on his own until Skoda entered the State Room.

"Did He listen to your prayers?" Lester asked.

"Why, yes he did in one way," Skoda replied, glancing lovingly at a piece of paper.

"What's that, a letter from your secret lover?" Lester asked.

"No, it's not," Skoda said, with exaggerated alarm. "Why would you think that?" he added and quickly folded it in his pocket. He seemed to compose himself and asked, "can I return to Königsberg with you? I have patients to attend to in the hospital."

"If you insist," he said.

Lester hated delay. After waiting a while, he looked for Dieter in the chapel, only to find that it was empty. He searched the forecourt, the gardens and the vestibule before returning to the State Room, where he found Skoda on his own.

"Let's leave," he said. "Dieter's disappeared. It's clear he's not going to agree to give me a third share, so I'm heading for his mine. I'll show him what the vengeance of a Lester looks like."

He and Skoda climbed into the trap and set off for Königsberg.

CHAPTER 58

Fiat Lux

And God said 'Let there be light,'
And there was light.
THE BOOK OF GENESIS 1:3

Marion blinked. As if her life wasn't strange enough with head pains, now she'd acquired an acute sensitivity to sunlight. Sunlight of all things! She spent her days in a room with the curtains pulled in the company of a blindfold. Darkness at night and darkness in the day, this was her lot since the asylum. The inmates had called her a saviour. She wasn't one, though she had now admitted to being a servant of the Adler. She was an adherent, who listened and watched for everything, most of all the meaning of that enigmatic phrase – *the colour white must always be as white as snow*. Thus far, it had yielded nothing of significance.

This morning she was held in the palm of a glorious silence. She was listening to herself, because deep in the many and various chambers of her soul, something good stirred – something she'd waited for a long time in her life, but almost daren't believe to be true.

This morning, the pains in her head weren't quite so nauseatingly intense.

Perhaps today she wasn't quite so wicked; perhaps today the morning sun had evaporated some of her evil vapours; perhaps today something had actually changed and she was going to get better.

That was one thing, but she still daren't remove the blindfold from her eyes.

There was a knock at the door. Ursula went to open it. The door squeaked open.

"Come in," she heard Ursula say. "She asked after you."

Dieter asked, "How are you?"

"Better. Much better, thank you," Marion said. "Even the headache has eased considerably."

"It's a blessing," Dieter said, his voice dripping with emotion. He paused.

She sensed some bad news. "Tell me," she urged him.

"Captain Lester has set off back to the docks, angry that his pockets are empty."

"What happened?" she murmured.

He told her the story. "I asked him to wait while I prayed for advice. Christoph came into the chapel and told me about your miraculous improvement. I rushed up here to see you. On my way, I saw Lester's trap racing out of the Schloss. I suppose he couldn't wait any longer. Oh, and Skoda's with him. I hope that's the last we see of him."

"I too," she said. "What will we do about the second instalment?"

"I will settle everything we owe, don't worry about that. I'm more anxious about you," Dieter said.

"Thank you," she said, adjusting her muslin blindfold again. Her hand brushed against it and inadvertently lifted it, and her eyes were flooded with light. She winced, expecting to receive the equivalent of a hammer blow to her head and fend off huge pulses of pain.

None came. Not one.

Miracle of miracles – the light, she could see the light! With no pain.

She ripped off the blindfold, jumped in the air, and yelled, "Fiat Lux!"

CHAPTER 59

The Dockside Meeting

Let every person be in subjection to the governing authorities.
For there is no authority except from God
and those which exist are established by God.
EPISTLE TO THE ROMANS 13:1

The sun was hanging like a great lantern high in the sky when Lester's horse and trap rolled onto the Lastadie docks. On the way there, Skoda repeatedly urged the driver to speed the horses. He was keen to arrive before midday for some appointment or other.

The quay was swarming with muscle-bound stevedores, passengers hauling their luggage, as well as peddlers selling chunks of bread and flagons of warm beer. In the distance, *The Lion Rampant* nestled against the dockside. And who should he spot striding up the gangplank – none other than French Andre, there to pay for the consignment of Russian Imperial vodka. At least he, Lester, would have investment funds for his next venture. He was still going to reclaim his parts from the Newcomen engines. In effect, he was owed one hundred thousand Prussian thaler. That was piracy. And no one robbed Captain Donald Lester.

When he turned to speak to Skoda, the man was no longer in the trap. He spotted the good doctor pushing his way through the throng towards the Lastadie warehouses. Strange, the doctor had said he had patients to attend to in the hospital, but that was in the opposite direction. He was suspicious, so followed him.

For a while, he lost sight of the doctor amidst the bobbing heads and colourful melange of people, until he snared him in the shadows of the Customs House. Skoda was talking to a young girl wearing a hood and with her back to him. Staying out of sight, Lester edged closer until near enough to hear their conversation. With the loud ambient sounds on the quay, he only caught snippets of it.

"Where is he?" the girl was saying. "He said midday… any day… he's never here… for over a week… so worried about him."

The girl seemed to know Skoda and he her, but who was she? Lester didn't know any young girls in Königsberg. Who was she talking about? And why was Skoda even talking to her?

"He won't show himself, he can't come onto the quay," Skoda confessed.

"What do you mean?" the girl replied, a note of exasperation in her voice. "How do you know that?"

"I'm here to help you, you must believe me," he pleaded with her. He touched her forearm and she pulled it away, like a bird with an injured wing.

"He asked me to take you to him," Skoda said.

"He did?" the girl said. "You've seen him? He's nearby?"

Skoda nodded.

"That's wonderful! Here, I received this from him." She handed Skoda a letter. She removed her hood, turned around and glanced at the crowd, perhaps hoping to catch sight of her missing companion. Innocent as a cherub, she had the face of a fifteen-year-old.

"I know," Skoda said, fingering the letter. "He's on that ship, *The Lion Rampant*."

What? That's a lie! Lester's ears pricked up. There were no passengers on the manifest. Skoda was playing tricks on this sweet girl.

"Really?" the girl replied, gazing longingly at the ship.

"We need to get on board, it's sailing soon," Skoda said.

The girl hesitated. Part of her seemed to want to go with the doctor, while another part was wary of him.

"Where's it bound?" she asked.

"Port Glasgow, Scotland," Skoda replied.

"Before we… I mean, when did you see him? How can I trust you?" she said, adding a frown to her suspicions.

"Wait," Skoda said. "I've something here that'll convince you." He delved into his pocket and pulled out a pink 'kerchief with snowdrops embroidered in the corners.

"That's mine!" She snatched it from him and pressed it to her breast. "I gave it to him after he recited the poem *Annie of Tharaw* to me in the schoolroom. How did you get hold of it?"

"He escaped from the front line and made his way back here and gave it to me to show to you," Skoda explained. "Let's get on board and I'll take you to your Caspar."

Who is this Caspar fellow? Lester had heard enough. He revealed himself and said, "Young lady, I'm Donald Lester, the captain of that ship and I can tell you there's no one named Caspar on board."

"I'm Sisi von Adler," the girl declared.

"I thought you might be," Lester said.

"You can't both be right. One of you is lying. Which one is it?" Sisi asked.

Skoda seemed frozen by Lester's sudden intervention. For a moment, he stood statuesque and then took a single, fateful, hesitant step backwards.

That slight gesture of uncertainty seemed enough for Sisi to declare, "Captain Lester has no reason to lie to me. You, Herr Doctor, are the fraud. Oh, now I understand." Then, as the waves of realisation broke over her, she railed at him, "I remember now. At the end of Caspar's trial, you made an excuse to go to the cells to see him. That's when you must have stolen the pink 'kerchief from him! And I suspect this note wasn't written by Caspar at all. You must have forged it. You sewer rat! Now I see it all. You lured me away from my home; wrenched me from my family. Oh, my God. I've been chasing phantoms!"

Skoda said, "Sisi, don't say that, I-I… I would never hurt you; you must know that."

"Charlatan!" she screamed. Something snapped in her. She hit Skoda in the chest with her fists – gently at first, then with force, and then with violence. Skoda took the blows, one after another. Crying bitter tears of woe, Sisi battered him in the chest and the face until his eyes were blackened, his nose blood red and his cheeks a deeper shade of purple. A crowd formed around them, staring, pointing, laughing at the girl and mocking the man.

Because he refrained from defending himself, Lester assumed the man was guilty as charged.

An official and a constable rushed out of the Customs House to break up the melee.

Sisi sunk to the ground, head in her lap, sobbing loudly.

"You've arrived in the nick of time," Skoda said, a purple bruise blossoming on his cheek. "She's mad, like her mother. Lock her up in the Chambers of the Furious."

"I'll be the judge of that," the official said. "Herr Skoda, I recognise you from my courtroom."

"And you're Magistrate Rudiger von Seydlitz," Skoda replied.

"At your service," von Seydlitz said, who then turned to Sisi and declared, "Fräulein, I'm afraid I must arrest you for assault and disturbing the King's peace."

The magistrate and constable led her away before Lester could draw their attention to his suspicions about Skoda, who seemed to have slithered off into the blue yonder.

Moments later, Lester noticed another altercation on the other side of the quay. French Andre was storming down the gangplank of his ship, the first mate in hot pursuit.

Lester ran over to them and asked, "Wait. What's going on? Has he paid?"

"No, not a thaler," the first mate replied.

"What! Nothing? Why not?"

"Hah! Some cock n' bull story about water. I'll give 'im water!" the first mate scowled and with his hand in an open fist by his groin, made as if to sprinkle piss on the ground.

"Canard! Voici de l'eau!" Andre thundered, prodding a finger into Lester's chest. First the girl, now a Frenchman. It was one of those days.

"What are you talking about?" Lester asked.

"Water!" Andre shouted. "Every drop of it! Here, see for yourself." He opened a bottle of the Imperial Russian vodka and poured it liberally over Lester's head. He tasted it. It *was* water! Damnation. His heart dropped as fast as a ship's anchor.

What a fool! He'd been duped. He'd forfeited two-thirds the value of the promissory note and lost the other one-third on a useless consignment of water. Sixty thousand thaler, gone, vanished! He'd lost face in front of his crew and half the population of Königsberg. Much as he hated to admit it, Silberstein had been right about General Wilhelm von Fermor.

It was about to get worse, much worse.

"Here's a single silver thaler," Andre snapped, throwing it on the ground with disdain. "To pay for the glass of the five hundred bottles! And I'll have words with the local Chamber of Commerce. You'll never do business in Königsberg again!"

Andre stormed off along the quay.

Lester watched him go. Shoulders slouched, he lurched up the gangplank.

"Piss poor deal that was, eh?" the first mate chimed.

Lester growled. He had a silver thaler and a barrel full of empty promises. At least he'd paid Robison's burial fees with the deposit for the vodka.

"Right!" he snarled. "You lot. Load up! Bring hammers, jacks, crowbars, spades, oh, and as much rope as we can carry, and some kindling. Nothing like a summer blaze to fuel the fires of revenge!"

"Why?" the first mate asked. "Where we goin', Captain?"

"To the amber mine!" he yelled.

The first mate grinned malevolently. "Come on, lads! Ya heard the capt'n. We're off on a wrecking party!"

Lester lumbered down the gangplank, only to be confronted by another knot of dockland officials blocking his way onto the landing quay.

"Captain Donald Lester?" the one in the front asked.

Lester glared at this apparition of Prussian officialdom, even down to the perfectly coiffured wig. The crew backed up behind him on the gangplank, as he replied, "That's me. What do you want? I'm a very busy man!"

The official replied with a withering frown, unrolled a document and with immaculate pronunciation read:

"On this day, 8th July, 1762, the harbourmaster hereby demands a levy of twenty silver thaler from Captain Lester of *The Lion Rampant* in lieu of docking fees."

"Fie, foh, and fum, it's all about fees! First it was burial fees, now it's docking fees. You'll have your thaler – in an hour," he said. This was more a rash promise than a statement of fact, since he had no means of earning that amount in a day, let alone an hour.

"Good," the official said stiffly. "You will not, under any circumstances, be permitted to weigh anchor until the fee is settled in full."

"I said, in an hour," he repeated through gritted teeth.

"That's when I shall return," the official said and strode up the quayside.

"C'mon," the first mate yelled. "What you waiting for? Let's start the party! To Fischhausen!"

With a shake of his head, he quipped, "Stop. We're scuppered, lads. We're broke. It'll take longer than an hour to go to the mine and get back. By which time, that piece of Prussian manure will be waiting for us and we'll be marooned here. No, we're weighing anchor. Let's run for it!"

Reluctantly, the crew did an about-turn and trudged back on board. He was about to join them, when a contrite Skoda sidled over to him and said, "Captain Lester, please, a moment of your time. I-I need to ask you something."

"What is it? I'm in a hurry," he said. "I heard you talk to that girl, the Gräfin's daughter, Sisi. Why didn't you tell the poor lass that her absence is killing her mother? You're meant to heal people and show compassion – and you call yourself a doctor? You deserved that beating. And what was all that nonsense about Caspar?"

"It was nothing, he's no one." Skoda's face was swelling up like a purple plum.

"Well, not to Sisi he isn't. If you don't mind, I have to set sail. The dockside officials, they're going…"

"… Wait, please, I… I want passage on your ship," Skoda said.

"You're the Gräfin's physician, why do you want to leave?"

"I can't go back to Schloss Ludwigshain after what's happened. You see, I so wanted her to come with me to Scotland on your ship," Skoda replied. "Now that's impossible, I want passage for myself."

This was laughable. *Is he saying what I think he's saying?*

"You mean? You and her? Och, now I get it. You wanted to elope with her. You…" He paused again, widened his eyes and said, "You're infatuated with the girl, aren't you?"

Skoda's face and wig were streaked with blood, but he still blushed from ear to ear.

"It's true, but there's more to it than that," he murmured. "I forged Caspar's writing and gave the skinner the letter to deliver to her. It was a ruse to get her away from the Schloss. Otherwise she'd never have run away from home."

"You selfish, shameless fraud," he said. "You played on a young girl's innocent affection for a simple shepherd! Doctor, you're deluded by your passions. She's from the ancien régime, she's aristocracy. You're a mere physician. You're not even Ostpreussen. She'd never follow a man like you."

"She was coming with me, until you interfered," Skoda railed at him. "If she wanted Caspar – and he's as close to the aristocracy as we are to the sun – then why not me? I could offer her a better life by far than he could. She's my Eugenie."

"Eugenie? What are you talking about? She's Sisi."

"Yes, yes, of course she is," he stammered. "I still need to get away from this place."

"Why should I take you with me?"

Skoda lifted his head high and delving into his pocket, said, "I have something that will buy me more than a passage. I have something that will make us both extremely rich men."

"Show me," Lester said. *Is fortune finally going to smile on me?*

CHAPTER 60

The Edict

Thou shalt not misuse the name of the Lord your God;
For the Lord shall not forgive one who misuses His name.
THE BOOK OF EXODUS 20:7

Marion clung to Dieter's arm for support as she made her way down the spiral staircase. At the base, the staff clapped and cheered her. Out of the corner of her eye, she noticed the front door open and someone walk in, bathing the vestibule in mid-afternoon sunbeams.

Turning to the staff, she said in a weary voice, "You're so kind."

As usual, Ursula was their voice, relief dripping from every word. "We're thankful our prayers have been answered and that you've recovered. If you had succumbed, who would have run the estate?"

"I would," a voice boomed.

Everyone looked. A man in a Prussian blue soldier's uniform stood by the entrance, the light gleaming through the stained glass above the entrance door, casting him in hues of purples and greens.

She squinted… and gasped when she realised who it was.

"Gottfried!"

Her husband wrapped his tree trunk arms around her. She felt protected in his huge embrace. His tattered uniform smelled of burnt charcoal, sweat and a faint trace of gun powder.

"My dear, you look so pale. And what's this about running the estate? What's happened?" Gottfried asked.

"It's a long story. I'll tell you about it in due course," she said, trying to inject a sprightly air into her voice. "What about my handsome man? Talking of which, where is my Hans?"

"I thought…" Gottfried said, paused and cupped his ear, as if he was listening for a noise outside, "… he wasn't far behind me."

"Really!" she squealed. "Our family will be complete… well, nearly."

"There's one missing. Where is she?" Gottfried asked, picking up on her slip of the tongue. "Ah! I know. Sisi always loved hide-and-seek." He crouched down and craned his neck behind a chair, making out he was playing the game. "Come out, come out, wherever you are."

Gottfried searched behind the chaise longue and the harpsichord, then drew back the curtains, while she mustered the courage to tell him. When his play-acting grew too painful to watch, she blurted out, "She's not coming out."

"No? She must be riding." Gottfried's blue eyes gleamed in the sunlight. "Let's go and find her. Dieter, coming? I know her favourite haunts. It's a beautiful afternoon and I want to reacquaint myself with the lake and the gnarled oak and the gurgling river and the wild geese and all the other nooks and crannies of the estate." He was so excited. "Ah, I can feel the vital strength of the land surge through my aching limbs. I already feel replenished. This is my home. This is where I belong."

"You didn't get my letter?" Her question was like a sword thrust into the belly of his contemplation.

"What letter? I've had no word from you for weeks. Nothing has got through."

"She's not here, Sisi's not here," she said.

Gottfried's expression changed from exuberance to concern, like a solitary black cloud covering the sun in a clear sky. "Where is she? In Königsberg? Why such glum faces?"

"She …" Dieter mumbled.

"… No, Dieter," Marion interrupted, "I'll tell him. Gottfried, Sisi isn't here because she's missing and we don't know where she's gone."

"What? Missing? How long for?" Gottfried asked.

"Twelve days."

"Twelve… days. I-I, this is… terrible." Gottfried's legs gave way beneath him and he slumped into a chair. "Why? She's a child. She can't go *missing.* She must be injured on a trail or in a wood. The wolves, the bears, the hogs…"

"No, we've searched every track and blade of grass. She's nowhere to be found."

"I've killed men with my bare hands, but this is scaring me," Gottfried said, his brow furrowed like a freshly-ploughed field. "Is she… dead?"

Weak at the knees, she leaned on Dieter. Speaking about Sisi exhausted her. She'd survived a close call with death and now she had to endure her husband's pain. It was as if Sisi had gone missing all over again.

"We don't know," she said and then Dieter stepped in and told him everything.

"If she's left this world," Gottfried said, "at least let us pray we find her, so we can grieve for her and lay her to rest."

"Amen," she said wearily.

From outside came the sound of horses and a wagon trundling over the forecourt.

"Who's that?"

"Come," Gottfried said, taking her by the hand. "At least there's some good news."

"Why? Who's out there?" she asked.

"See for yourself," he said, his hand as warm and his grip as tight as ever.

She emerged into the sunlight day and had to shield her eyes. At least she could see and stand and breathe again and with no pains in the crown of her head.

An equerry helped Colonel von Marwitz dismount. Behind them was a covered wagon. The colonel bowed to her and greeted Gottfried with a brisk salute. The equerry opened the back of the wagon and who should jump out but…

"Hans!" she squealed with delight.

"Mama!" he said, embracing her. She didn't mind that he smelled of dried mud and stale sweat.

"Let me see you," she said and looked him up and down, to check he was in one piece. He was. "This is a most joyous day!"

"I'm so glad to see you," Hans said. His voice was young, raw, but firm, like a soldier's. Oh, how he'd grown in such a short time. He was his father's son.

Behind them, there were two more happy homecomings: Klein was locked in a deep embrace with his son, Bruno, and Konstantin with Nicol.

Last out of the wagon was a callow youth. A young man with an old soul limped towards them and lifted his head.

"Caspar!" Marion chimed. "Welcome home!"

"G-greetings, Your Excellency," he stammered.

"I'm sorry, Sisi isn't here to greet you," she said.

Caspar nodded shyly, as if he was too numb to bear another emotional wound.

"Thank the Lord that you're safely home from the front," she said, fingering the amber crucifix round her neck. "Isn't it wonderful they let you come on leave with the others?"

"No, Mama, we're not on leave." Hans was definite about that.

Everyone gathered outside with an air of excited anticipation. Even the trees and birds and the lake and the red squirrel wanted to hear the news. The men were home. Everyone craned their ears. It was so quiet you could have heard a pine cone fall to the ground.

The colonel unrolled a document. Speaking in a clear, strong voice, he said, "This is an edict from the Russian procurator in Königsberg. It's dated today, 8th July, 1762, and it reads:

> *This is to inform all Prussians that the confusions between My Imperial Highness and His Royal Highness the King of Prussia, which have caused a bloody war, have now been remedied and that a treaty, concluded between the two sovereign courts, has established an eternal peace."*

The cry of elation resounded on the forecourt of the Schloss.

"Peace! Formal peace with Russia! At last!" she yelled, slumped to her knees and made the sign of the cross. Everyone followed. She led the prayers, "May this peace be truly everlasting and bring upon us the mercy of the Almighty!"

Gottfried stood up and said, "This edict brings a timely end to six long years of sacrifice, bloodshed, famine and disease. We have our country back. Never again will we cede it to anyone else."

The colonel added, "The news is that Emperor Peter, who loved our own king like a true vassal, has been murdered – not by a rebel, but by his dearly beloved wife, Catherine."

That didn't stop them singing the hymn of Prussia with deep, unblemished joy.

The afternoon sun cast long shadows over the lake and Kadow called out, "Wait! More horses."

Trundling down the path, through the shadows of the linden trees, was an official's open trap pulled by two black steeds. Two uniformed hussars dressed in Prussian blue formed a guard of honour. She craned her neck to see who it was. Two people were seated in the trap: Magistrate von Seydlitz and next to him... a woman... no, a girl... wearing a hood.

"Can this be?" Marion exclaimed, stepping forward.

Little Egor emerged from the bushes, ran behind the trap and launched himself onto it, clinging for dear life to its leather upholstery.

"Egor!" Konstantin cried, waving an intoxicated fist at the boy. "Get down from there!"

As the trap pulled to a halt, the coachman dismounted, leaving Egor perched precariously on the back of it. The girl turned and tousled Egor's hair in a familiar gesture of recognition. The coachman opened the door and von Seydlitz got out first.

Gottfried greeted him with stiff Ostpreussen formality.

Marion stared at the hooded girl. After twelve long days, she was afraid and desperate at the same time. A tremulous whisper of anticipation ran through the staff.

As the girl stood up, Egor mischievously jerked her hood back over her head.

"Sisi!" Marion shouted.

Sisi raced towards them at the entrance, straight passed Caspar, and flung her arms around her. "Mother," she murmured.

Sisi held her for what seemed like an age, sobbing and whimpering.

"You're home now," she said, stroking her hair.

Sisi greeted her father, brother and Uncle Dieter, before walking into a wall of rapturous applause from the staff. Even Cecilia had tears in her eyes as she embraced her.

"We'll gather in the State Room," Gottfried suggested.

On the way there, Sisi shook Caspar's hand and said, "I'm glad and relieved you are home safe and sound."

"I-I could say the same thing, Sisi," he stammered.

"You can call me junge Fräulein," she said sweetly.

"Yes, junge Fräulein," he replied.

Sisi smiled at him and followed the others into the State Room.

As they sat down, Marion realised that Sexton Fermor was not with them. She sent Grenda to find him. Then she noticed her daughter's hands and asked, "Sisi, why are your hands bandaged?"

"Oh, I had an accident, they'll be fine," she said sweetly. "I'll tell you about it later."

Kadow and Ursula served tea in their best porcelain cups. A family reunited after so long should have had stories to tell, but the silence was underpinned by a sense of relief mixed with exhaustion. This time it was different; her husband had been away so long, he was a virtual stranger. Over the six years, her children had grown up and shed the cloak of innocence. Hans had experienced the horrors of the battlefield, if only for two months, while Sisi had… yes, what had happened to Sisi?

"Sisi," Gottfried said in an insistent voice. "You owe your mother and me an explanation."

Sisi took a deep breath, "Yes, I do. I have been terribly foolish. I am sorry for the pain and anguish I have caused you, Mother. I was stupid and reckless.

"On the Saturday evening before last, I took Charlie out for a ride. When I got back, Manfred was coming out of the stables. I thought it was odd, and then found an envelope addressed to me in the paddock. It contained a letter which appeared to have been written and signed by Caspar."

"What did it say?" Marion was beside herself with curiosity.

"He declared his undying love and said he wanted to elope with me. He wanted me to meet him on the Lastadie docks at midday – but it didn't specify which day."

"Why did you believe it?" Marion asked. "We saw Caspar sentenced to go to the front. How would he meet you at the docks when he was in Silesia?"

"I wanted to believe that my intrepid Caspar had escaped and found his way back to Königsberg," Sisi confessed. "That day – the day I found the letter – I was furious with you, Mama, infatuated with Caspar, and deeply confused. I know I shouldn't have done, but I ran away."

Marion shook her head and asked, "Why did you wait so long – so many days – on the docks for him?"

"I knew you'd search for me, so I wore a disguise and lived in the ruins behind the Löbenicht Hospital. On occasion, I'd see Manfred there. He must have run away from the schloss at the same time as me. At midday, every day, I'd go to the docks to wait for Caspar. I kept seeing Doctor Skoda there. I hid from him because I thought he was looking for me on your behalf. I was about to give up hope when he bumped into me today."

Sisi took a deep breath as if girding herself for the next painful confession. "Skoda deceived me by forging that letter. Today, the frustration of the waiting and hiding for days on end burst out of me like pus lanced by a knife. I beat him with my bare hands – hence the bandages. As well as that, I was angry with you, Mother, for telling the colonel that Caspar was in the grounds of the Schloss."

"It wasn't your mother," Colonel von Marwitz said. "Doctor Skoda informed me."

"Why would Skoda inform on Caspar?" Marion asked.

"Skoda wanted Caspar sent to the front because he saw him as a love rival," Sisi admitted.

"Love rival? Doctor Skoda? What *are* you talking about?" Gottfried frowned in bewilderment. "How could love bewitch a man of *his* age?"

"*His* age? What do you mean?" Sisi asked.

"Skoda is an old man," Gottfried stated flatly.

"No, no, that's not true." Marion shook her head. "Skoda was the underside of thirty, my dear. You should know, you suggested him."

Gottfried hissed, "I never met the man in person. Gerard van Swieten recommended him. He told me that Doctor Skoda was an experienced physician near the end of his career."

"The *end* of his career? Then our Doctor Skoda is an imposter," Marion announced with an air of triumph and disbelief.

"This rogue must be apprehended," Gottfried said. "Von Seydlitz, please send word to have him arrested."

"I will. I'll also start an enquiry for the real Doctor Skoda," von Seydlitz replied, before striding out of the room.

There was a stunned silence until Ursula piped up, "Your Excellency."

"What is it?" Marion asked.

"I thought you'd want to know, Your Excellency, that Doctor Skoda left some of his belongings behind in his room."

"Clever girl!" she said. "See what you can find out about him."

She'd never seen Ursula move so fast.

Sisi added something else. "Mother, Father, I want to show you that I've learned my lesson. Kadow, please ask Caspar to come in."

Before Caspar joined them, Grenda returned and spoke to Marion.

"I found Sexton Fermor," Grenda said. "He asked me to pass you a message."

"What is it?" she asked.

"He's waiting to speak to you. He said you'd know where to find him," Grenda replied.

"I see," she nodded. "Prepare a horse and trap. I'll need them shortly."

"Yes, Your Excellency." Grenda doffed his cap and left the room.

Caspar came in and mumbled a curt, embarrassed greeting.

"Caspar," Sisi said.

"Yes, junge Fräulein," he mumbled.

"This dreadful escapade has opened my eyes," she began. "I see now I must reserve my affections for the man who will one day make me a fitting husband. That way, I intend to serve the Adler family and fulfil its heritage. You have been like a second brother to me and I will always treasure our close and abiding childhood friendship. As a token of my affection, I want you to have this back."

She handed him a pink 'kerchief with snowdrops embroidered in each corner.

"Thank ye, junge Fräulein," Caspar said, his lip trembling.

Marion's chest heaved with emotion to see her daughter conduct herself with such care and kindness. Before she could congratulate her, the door swung open and Ursula bustled her way in, waving a letter.

"Here's something," her chambermaid said. "Read this!"

Gottfried obliged. "It's dated 30th November, 1761, about a month after Doctor von Ottenhagen passed on. It reads:

Dear Herr Pieter von Thurgau,

In the light of our interview yesterday, I can confirm that your wife, Eugenie, died of an overdose of laudanum.

You administered that fatal dosage; therefore, you must bear full responsibility for her premature demise.

You must cease your medical training with immediate effect and present yourself at my offices to answer charges concerning the tragic but unlawful death of your wife, Frau Eugenie von Thurgau.

Signed,

The Constable of Vienna."

This was extraordinary. Marion gasped, "May the Lord preserve us! We've been in the presence of a murderer."

"Pieter von Thurgau. Incredible," Gottfried said.

"There's more," Ursula chimed. "In the same envelope as the letter was this locket."

It was an oval memorial locket. Marion opened it and stared, open-mouthed, at the portrait inside. "Oh, my God. The likeness. It's uncanny."

"What is?" Gottfried asked.

"It's you," Marion gasped, glancing at her daughter.

"Me? That's impossible," Sisi replied.

"The portrait in the locket. Look. This lady could be your older sister."

Sisi looked at the locket and stammered, "Why, yes, she could. But… who is this person?"

"This is Eugenie, Pieter's wife, or rather, dead wife," she stated.

"And…? I-I don't understand," Sisi said.

"Pieter von Thurgau – aka Skoda – killed his wife, albeit accidentally," Marion said. "To escape prosecution, I suppose he ran from Vienna and headed for Königsberg. On the way here, he must have encountered the real Doctor Skoda, travelling to take up his new post. Somehow, Thurgau must have stepped into Skoda's shoes, hoping his partial medical training would be enough to convince us of his authenticity. Arriving here, and meeting you, Sisi, must have been like seeing his wife's ghost. Stricken with grief over his wife's death, and his terrible role in it, he became obsessed with you."

"Ach! I knew the man was infatuated with me, but now I know why." Sisi shook her head.

"You are innocent in the whole matter, my dear, and it will never, ever, happen again," Gottfried consoled her.

As they talked, Marion slipped out of the room and went to find Grenda.

She had one last appointment to fulfil.

CHAPTER 61

The Arc of Enlightenment

The crowning time has come on you,
O people of the land: the time has come, the day is near;
The day will not be slow in coming, it will not keep back.
THE BOOK OF EZEKIEL 7:7

Particles of dust danced in the motes of the late evening sunlight as Grenda halted the trap in front of the church at Löwenhagen. Marion took a deep breath. What did Fermor want with her in there?

Inside the church was a thrilling stillness. It didn't take long for her to realise its source. The curtain that concealed the Our Lady von Adler chapel had been pulled back and the mysterious statue was in plain view. Whenever she'd seen it before, Marion had been drawn to the brazen power of the eagle. This time, her gaze settled on Our Lady, her tranquil demeanour showing a resolute surrender to demands both temporal and eternal.

Fermor stood close to the statue with his back to her, tapping his walking stick on the flagstones.

"Is that you, Your Excellency?" he asked, while keeping his back to her.

"Yes, it's me."

"You knew where to find me," he said. His voice was soft, compliant, with an air of submission.

"How could I not know?" she murmured. "This chapel is where I first experienced head pains over nine months ago. They gradually worsened, until this morning when they stopped abruptly. I can't tell you what a relief that was. The crown of my head is still soft but now I can walk in the glare of sunlight. Truly, I feel blessed to be alive again."

"I am so glad to hear that," he said.

"Last night, I had a visitation from the Adler."

He said, "Tell me more."

"I had my doubts, but now I believe," she said with humility. "I understand that the Adler is an agent of change, one of God's pods of advancement. In the shape of a crescent, its territory stretches from Ostpreussen in the east, Ireland in the west and Denmark in the north. It's the Arc of Enlightenment."

He tapped his walking stick and continued to face the statue of Our Lady, the eagle cocooning the crown of her head with its great claws.

She continued, "I'm honoured to be a servant to the Adler and its purpose to cause the third flowering of mankind. Like a tulip unfolding, it's going to happen in the head. If not mine, then yours, or someone else's; it's for the whole of mankind."

"Not anymore," Fermor said, rubbing his eyes. "I had to save you."

"What do you mean?" she asked.

"I too had an encounter with the Adler – in the amber mine," he said. "It sent me a strange revelation – an improvement to the Newcomen engine. On its own, it doesn't sound much, but its ramifications are huge. It will change the world forever and usher in an Age of Machines. I drew a plan of it on a piece of paper."

"What did you do with it?" she asked.

"It came from a sacred place, so I left it in one – on the altar in the chapel in Schloss Ludwigshain."

"Where is it now?"

"Doctor Skoda took it."

"Doctor Skoda? You fool. Don't trust it with him. He's an imposter."

"What? How so?"

"He tried to elope with Sisi and attempted to trepan me!"

"The monster!"

"Why give it to Doctor Skoda?"

"I didn't give it to him," he complained. "I left it on the altar for someone to claim. It so happened to be him."

"Why didn't you burn the plan?"

"If I had done that, you would have died, so the only way to save you was to give the plan away," Fermor said. "It was a choice between you or it. I couldn't serve both. I decided to save you."

"What are you talking about?" she asked.

"When the Adler is connected to us, its effect is to actually cause the skull of its servants to melt. But it was too strong for you. It was killing you. It killed Pastor Leopold. That was wrong. It should do no harm, even in the name of mankind's spiritual renaissance. You had saved me. I returned the blessing and saved you."

"And what happens to the Adler now?" she demanded.

"As soon as Skoda or whatever his name was picked up the plan, you would have immediately started to get better," Fermor explained. "Once Skoda had got hold of it for his nefarious purposes, the Adler would back off."

"But you didn't need to do that." She felt ire rise in her. This man was a fool.

"What do you mean? I had the best intentions."

"You preach service to the Adler, yet you don't understand its ways!" she thundered. "It's more powerful than you can possibly imagine. The Adler knew that the softness in the crown of my head was becoming fatal. It does have compassion. It does have mercy. It's not a praying mantis; it would never kill its servants. That's why it wrapped me in a healing cocoon and put me to sleep."

"Pah!" Fermor spluttered. "Is that what you believe?"

"I would have lived even if you had destroyed the plan," she replied. "I would have woken after three days, fully healed and recovered. Like you did!"

"I don't believe you," he insisted. "Besides, many saviours have trodden the path of enlightenment but we know only a few of their names. More will willingly serve the Adler."

"I wish it were true, but the Adler was a once-and-for-all or never-again," she said. "In my vision, I saw a blanket of white snow on the ground – representing the pristine and innocent force of the Adler. It came with a warning, of which Rolander spoke. If the produce of the Adler was ever misused for lesser, wrongful purposes, that pure blanket of snow would be soiled, the spoilage from which there would be no recourse. White must always be white."

"What are you saying?" Fermor asked.

"You've betrayed the Adler," she replied.

Still facing away from her, he shook his head slowly. "I know and I paid a high price for that betrayal."

"What's that?"

Slowly, he turned around and faced her and she saw. There was no light in his eyes. He was blind.

"Oh, my God," she muttered.

They stood in silence until she said, "The Adler was intended to deliver the twelve jewels in the crown of human genius, mankind's third and final spiritual coronation. By giving away the plan, the high spiritual energies of the Adler will not be used, nor will ever be used, as intended, for the transformation of mankind. Instead they'll be perverted into revolution, industrial revolution. There will be no crowning, only a surrogate development in the form of machines. You cut the head from the flower of human evolution."

CHAPTER 62

Death Throes

Glasgow, Scotland.
6th May, 1763.

Lester knocked on his friend's door. Hearing no answer, he pushed it open and entered James Watt's workshop. Engine parts, rusty valves, newly-made shining pistons, were spread over tables. Strewn on the floor were a variety of pipes, tools and other instruments.

"James!" he called out.

"Over here!" came the reply, and his friend appeared from behind a table of spare parts, wiping greasy hands on an oily rag. "I heard you had returned from your Baltic adventure. How did the King's amber commission unfold?"

"Providence shined on me," he said with a wry grin.

"Good for you!" James said.

"Last month, I received a remittance for one hundred and twenty thousand Prussian thaler in full and final settlement of everything owed. And that was paid to me, Donald Lester, a mere bairn from a stone croft in bonnie Scotland!"

"And I hear you've moved into a grand new house," James chimed.

"Yes, and what about you? How is your work on the design of the Newcomen engine?"

"Pah! I still can't work out how to improve it!" James said, wiping his sleeve across his sweaty brow. "A large proportion of the thermal energy of the steam is consumed by heating the engine cylinder on every cycle."

"I might have the answer for you. Have a look at this."

He handed James the plan. It was scuffed but eminently readable.

Watt nodded and with a broad smile said, "This is incredible! This is the missing link! This design fixes the problem I've been struggling with. How on earth did you come by it?"

"Let's just say it was a gift from the gods," Lester murmured.

"Oh, I believe you," James Watt said with a guffaw.

"I'm serious," Lester replied.

"Give me two years. I'll find a manufacturer who'll build me a prototype steam engine," Watt predicted. "That will be the iconic beginning of a new social revolution. What do you want for it?"

"A tithe. One-tenth of all profits accruing from the manufacture and sale of the steam-borne engine."

"That's fair. It's yours. Come back tomorrow and I'll have the paperwork drawn up," Watt said with unconfined joy.

"I will," he said. As he was leaving, Lester glanced at a newspaper laid out on a table. The headline read:

Treaty of Hubertusberg signed on 15th February, 1763. Prussia signed a treaty with Saxony and Austria effectively ending seven years of conflict in Europe.

He smiled. With peace on the horizon, he'd soon be rich beyond imagining.

As he walked out of the Glasgow School of Revolution into the Scottish spring, he could have sworn in the distance he could hear the screeching death throes of an eagle.

ACKNOWLEDGEMENTS

Even a historical novel has a history. This one started in 2001 with a trip to Königsberg, or Kaliningrad which is what the Russian city is now called. Then my travelling companions were Joachim Deichert and Ole Andreas Laursen, and I count myself both fortunate and privileged to still be able to name them as friends.

As always, I owe a great debt of gratitude for her patience to my partner Irene and to friends James Harries and Nick Deputowski, who have put up with me for almost as long as I can remember.

I also want to say a whole-hearted thank-you to my beta readers for their varied and erudite comments. They were; Joachim Deichert, Beverlee Swazee, Susanna Rees, Timothy Denton, Dixie Carlton, Patty Sherbourne and Sarah Byard. Warm thanks go to members of the Bristol Writers Group, you know who you are.

Thanks are due to Jana Remy of the German Historical Institute London and Lisa Traynor of the Royal Armouries in Leeds for their specialist assistance and advice.

Much of the novel was written and edited in the peace and quiet of Buckfast Abbey, Devon in the company of the Benedictine Monks there.

And a last thanks to my parents, may they rest in peace, for instilling in me at an early age an enduring love of books, reading and literature.

Matador